Contents

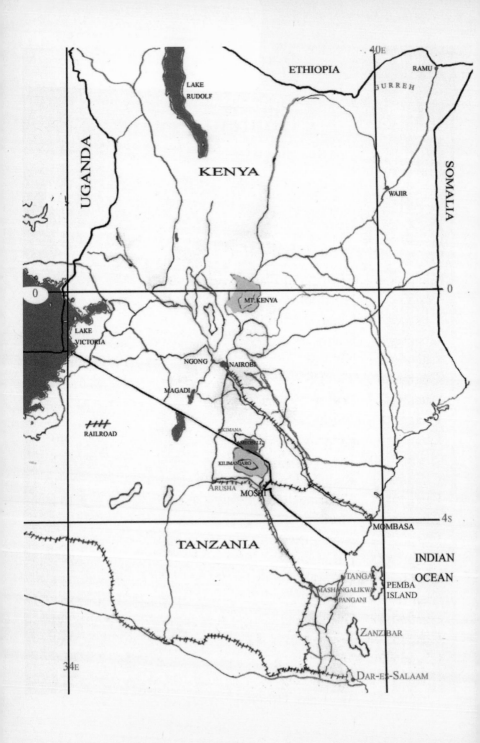

CHAPTER 1

The Ajuran Plateau

Kenya, 2002

Every adventure in the wild starts at the fringes of civilization. For a seasoned safari guide like Mbuno, the dirt-filled concrete island separating the car park from the main terminal of Nairobi Airport represented a no-man's land separating his escape back to the wild and the full-on Western chaos seen before him that he had no desire to cross into. His graying eyes carefully scanned the hustle and bustle of tourists hauling overstuffed hard-sided suitcases with uncertain wheels across the broken pavement as they exited into the equatorial sun from the smelly, packed, customs' hall. Even from there as he sat cross-legged atop an aging, dented, dark green, long-wheelbase, safari Land Rover, he could smell the baggage porters' sweat from too many Tusker beers the night before, thin wisps of tourists' perfume splashed on to disguise ten-hour flight odor, and the pungent smell of sandalwood oil used as polish throughout the airport, mixed odors now outgassing with the stampede of tourists eager to experience the "real Africa" the holiday brochures promised.

Patiently, like the Waliangulu expert tracker he was, his mind's eye had a fixed image of his prey; the faces, shapes, and baggage of the people he was there to collect. As the late morning sun beat at his back, there was not a breath of wind, not a cloud in the sky, but his eyes never blinked, his gaze never averted.

In the maelstrom before him, the airport swinging glass doors blinked reflected visions of milling people about to emerge. Once outside, the newcomers were descended upon by matatu drivers, unlicensed taxis, and hotel minivan drivers, ready to whisk the passengers away to the eagerly awaited sanctity of the urban reality to be found in Nairobi, the long lost white hunter Mecca of Hemingway, Holden, Roosevelt, and countless other African adventurer legends.

Mbuno had been through the airport customs' hall many times returning from safari in distant lands outside of Kenya. As he waited, seated on the ticking aluminum shell of the Land Rover's roof, ever intent on the flickering arrivals before him, he imagined, accurately, what the crew he awaited was facing inside.

Off conveyor belts in the sweltering baggage hall in Kenyatta International Airport, the man he was there to collect, Pero Baltazar was searching for his television production colleagues while keeping an eye out for the customs agent hired to help clear the pile of filming equipment, shipped as expensive checked overweight luggage instead of freight. In the button-down side pocket of his safari jacket, Pero no doubt had the bills of lading as well as copies of the original purchase/rental orders for all the equipment, the commercial insurance, the packing lists for each case and, of course, the certificates of origin. As the lone producer for this television shoot, all this paperwork, as well as the crew's safety, was his responsibility, Mbuno knew, just as he knew the customs officials hoped to

MURDER
ON
SAFARI

MURDER
ON
SAFARI

A THRILLER

PETER RIVA

YUCCA

Yucca Publishing books may be purchased in bulk at special
discounts for sales promotion, corporate gifts, fund-raising, or
educational purposes. Special editions can also be created to
specifications. For details, contact the Special Sales Department,
Yucca Publishing, 307 West 36th Street, 11th Floor, New York,
NY 10018 or yucca@skyhorsepublishing.com.

Yucca Publishing® is an imprint of Skyhorse Publishing, Inc.®,
a Delaware corporation.

Visit our website at www.yuccapub.com.

10 9 8 7 6 5 4 3 2 1

Library of Congress Cataloging-in-Publication Data is available
on file.

Cover design by Yucca Publishing

Print ISBN: 978-1-63158-041-3
Ebook ISBN: 978-1-63158-051-2

Printed in the United States of America

To my friends who are thinly disguised in this tale,
to my family who always have patience when I travel,
I say thank you. Enjoy.

catch a mzungu—a white man—without proper paperwork. Mbuno smiled, knowing Baltazar was surely prepared; he always had been before.

Mbuno also imagined Pero's partner Bill "Heep" Heeper, somewhere in the melee, one sloped shoulder from decades of video work, possibly secretly illegally filming the customs' hall chaos, catching the slight panic of some of the tourists at the "otherness" of the people all around them, the jumble of luggage spilling out and off conveyors, and the swagger of the customs officials. Pero would spot Heep and signal him over and, above all, get him to stop filming before someone confiscated the camera.

A tough but elegant and talented Dutchman, with sunbleached hair, Pero's partner Heep had been born in the shadow of Hitler, seen his relatives hauled off to concentration camps and, as soon as he could, learned a trade that matched his desire to "get to the land of the free." Once he had become indispensable to documentary filmmakers in Hollywood, he spent most of his time traveling the world as an award-winning cameraman and, lately, as an equally talented director of the partners' joint filming assignments. Mbuno liked him and importantly, trusted Heep's instincts in the wild. Of course, it would be Mbuno's job to keep the crew from getting injured or worse once they reached remote locations in the bush. Filming wildlife was always risky, but for over twenty years Mbuno had seen to it that his charges were protected.

Heep spoke four languages, Mbuno knew and was, always, under-spoken, professional, and determined. Over the years, Pero had found that Heep wasn't a man to cross. In the field, if kept supplied with whatever he needed, he stayed happy and efficient. If anyone on a shoot showed any accidental incompetence, he could blow a fuse. Mbuno had worked with them both and knew the score.

Coupled with the equatorial light dimly filtering in from overhead skylights, the fetid air in the crowded hall and the slightly heady 5,000 feet in altitude would give some people second thoughts about the safari of a lifetime. It always happened—Mbuno and the filmmakers had seen it all before. He watched a woman emerging uncertainly from the glass doors. She was set upon by taxi drivers plying their trade, grabbing her luggage and flight bag. Dressed in Florida pink shorts and pink T-shirt, dropping her oversized sunglasses on the ground, she began crying on the shoulder of her equally garish female companion: "I want to go home!"

Mbuno raised his voice, "Koma! Acha peke-ake!" (Stop! Leave her alone).

The taxi drivers looked towards the car park at the elder sitting on an official Land Rover. Mbuno's voice carried authority. One tourist was not worth trouble. They backed away from the women and turned towards the next gaggle coming through the doors, Japanese tourists with phrase books open and ready. The woman comforting the crying lady in pink waved and smiled at Mbuno who simply nodded and went back to his vigil.

Mbuno knew that Pero, unlike some of these first time visitors, would be happy to be back in Africa, especially East Africa and Kenya in particular. He loved the fringe of civilization. He always told Mbuno that it made him feel he was about to get off, get out, get away, at least for a while. Mbuno smiled at a memory of the expression both Heep and Pero used: "Stop the world, we're getting off."

Mbuno had read the advance material Pero had sent him via mail to Giraffe Manor where he now lived. Every TV or film crew Mbuno had taken charge of always used the same terms: "Filming, indeed even stepping into Africa, is forbidding and dangerous; the *Edge of the Wild* will take viewers beyond belief." The more danger they packed in the script, the more likely the sponsors would ante up the money needed to have the cable network agree to send them on filming adventures. Pero and Heep had explained on a time-lag phone line that they wanted to be out in the wilds of Kenya, away from the choking stench of the cities, making contact with native people, animals, and an especially dangerous seagoing crocodile—capturing the last vestiges of the Earth's wildlife on camera. Every year, "wild" was becoming harder to find. In truth, all three men were a little depressed that, all over the planet, zoos were springing up masquerading as National Parks and wildlife refuges. The whole of Africa was on the verge of "wild" extermination—the result of tourist dollars, industrial powers' exploitation, and locally rocketing populations.

What Pero's team were making was supposed to be "commercial wildlife genre" TV. In reality, it was repackaged, in-your-face, human stories in which the animals played only a supporting role. None of the team was fooled. They had cashed the checks and enjoyed the ride before and would do it again. Pero's personally stated justification was *a man has to eat, so he might as well enjoy the process.* The awards and Emmy nominations only stroked the ego—even if it was a bit hypocritical. Mbuno knew that as Pero was the creator and producer, he would—sometimes—become the general whipping boy for the cable network accountants fighting over expense billing, even down to the price of bottled water in foreign hotels. Somehow, Pero seemed to roll with the petty times to enjoy the richness of the last of the wild with his friend Mbuno and his colleague Heep.

From behind the Land Rover, an unfamiliar Indian voice cut through Mbuno's attention, "Mzee Mbuno?" Using the honorific term "elder" in Swahili made Mbuno smile and wave the man forward, so he could see both him and the crowds.

"I most sincerely apologize for keeping you waiting . . ." The Schenker badge on the Indian man's jacket identified him as the film crew's customs agent. The man was, as usual, clutching a folder stuffed with paperwork. "I have arranged for the transfer of the equipment as arranged to Wilson airport within three hours of clearance here. It took about fifteen minutes longer than expected because Mr. Pero and Mr. Heep had to explain all the equipment items to the Customs officials, a very serious waste of time, of course." Mbuno knew Pero had used this agent before and that all would be delivered, on time, to the private plane charter the crew was catching in three hours. As the agent waved goodbye and hurried off, clutching his folder, Mbuno caught first sight of Pero as the team emerged into the sun. The taxi jackals crowded in for the kill. Mbuno's sharp ears picked up Pero's barked "Basi, rufi!" (Enough, go away) and Mbuno smiled and stood up on the roof of the Land Rover, waving slowly.

Pero looked over the heads of the crowd and saw the small car park beyond that was full of the now-usual exotic mixture of European cars and off-road vehicles. Once this would have been the exclusive province of Land Rover, but now there were Toyotas, Nissans, BMWs, Mercedes, Isuzus, and Mitsubishi. The dark green beaten-up old Land Rover with Mbuno waving on top almost looked out of place, a sign of safaris past. To Pero, the seemingly ageless man had been waiting for them to arrive, he knew, his graying hair shining in the morning sun. To Pero, Mbuno was slowly becoming equally anachronistic in the sea of modern East Africa streaming from the Terminal eager to see wildlife from the safety of zebra-painted minivans, AC running, windows firmly closed against exposure to the land. Images, cameras, were everything, the real experience sanitized, safe.

"Mbuno, good to see you," Pero called and waved.

"And you too, Mr. Pero, and you, Mr. Heep, jambo!" Mbuno answered as he climbed down off the roof, his smile and extended hand showing true welcome. They shook hands, swapped grips to lock thumbs, then grasped forearms, then let go, laughed, and hugged. Clearly old friends, Pero and then Heep patted the aging Mbuno's back as Mbuno opened the passenger door.

A slim man of thirty-five emerged and said, "Simon Thomson, Kenya Parks Service," sticking out his hand. Simon was well known in wildlife circles as a crazy Kenyan who studied the flight patterns of birds of prey by soaring with them in a blue hang glider. The extremely long glider was strapped to the Land Rover's roof. Simon saw Pero and Heep studying it and commented, "Like a bat, with 'er wings folded."

Pero raised his eyebrows. In anticipation of the unasked question, Simon replied, "Mbuno here has reserved a four fouteeen," he meant a Cessna 414, which seated ten, "she'll fit up the aisle, no problem."

Nodding, Heep replied, "Well, you're both efficient, thanks Simon, glad to have you on board."

"Always wanted footage of me floating up there with the birds, you promised I could have a copy . . ." In accepting the shoot, he had faxed that he was going to use it to renew his research funding from Princeton University in New Jersey.

Pero nodded, "Yes, I promise. But I've gone one further. My father has a friend on the Board of Trustees at Princeton—he's going to screen it for the committee personally."

"Oh, that'll be fine, really fine, I very much appreciate it."

"And you'll get your full fee as well. They play fair, Simon."

He smiled, "So I've heard, word gets around. Mbuno here chooses his friends carefully." Mbuno nodded. "Now, who are these chaps?"

Heep explained that one crewmember was a South African originally from Madagascar, Ruis Selby, the other a friend of Heep's from Holland, Priit Vesilind. Everyone shook hands and repeated jambos. Mbuno had difficulty with Priit's name, pronouncing it, "Mr. Preet."

Priit thought that was fine. "What tribe are you from, Mr. Mbuno?"

In his singsong voice, Mbuno explained, "I am Liangulu, but we are not wanted as a tribe anymore. Our village is now part of national park land." He said it in a sad way, so the men knew that Liangulu tribal life was probably irrevocably changed, perhaps not for the better. These wildlife crewmen had seen the demise of tribes all over the world, knew the score. Priit, impressed with Mbuno's command of English and what was clearly Pero and Heep's regard for this small elder tribesman, had to ask, "How'd you fellows all hook up?"

On the way into Nairobi, Pero explained some of the jobs to Priit that he'd been on with Mbuno. He focused on the ex-elephant hunter story about Mbuno, now turned expert safari and film guide. He focused on Mbuno's cadre of clients, the high and wealthy, all of whom put their complete trust in the little Liangulu ex-elephant hunter. All true, but it wasn't the whole truth. Mbuno stayed silent.

Simon, of course, knew Mbuno's off-the-record story, being a Kenyan. The one where Mbuno saved a herd of elephants from slaughter and his tribe from banishment. That sort of gossip traveled fast, especially when a native managed to out-fox corruption at the highest government level. Simon was sure Mbuno was formidable as a friend or enemy.

As for Ruis, he and Pero had been in-country together with Mbuno years ago. Ruis knew bits of Mbuno's other story too. After all, he had seen Mbuno talk to elephants, calming them, for a better film shot. Ruis was in no doubt; there was more to the man than Pero was explaining to Priit. Ruis, like Heep and Pero before him, knew he could depend on Mbuno's bush skills, his Liangulu expertise, and his ages-old native knowledge.

Mbuno's tribe was called Waliangulu, which means "people of the Liangulu." Waliangulu were traditional elephant hunters, had been for tens of thousands of years. Mbuno could still track, on foot, and hunt rogue elephant with a bow and arrow. This mere man with generational elephant understanding and skills, when stood up against a five-ton African elephant, was more than a fair match.

Before civilization replaced nature's way of controlling wildlife, Africa was in balance with nature. If a tribesman needed meat, he went out and hunted. The most tender prey is always a young animal. However, a traditional hunter cannot get near to the young, protected by the herd, try as they might, so they settle on what they can approach. When armed with bow and arrow, or spear, on foot, hunters were always faced down by the old male or female protector of the herd. A test of wills and skills took place and, most of the time, the hunter usually prevailed, a tribute to the ingenuity of man. The old antelope or buffalo or elephant was consumed, every bit used, not a scrap left. The ivory was to trade for cloth or grain, the rest consumed or made into tools, hides or jerky. The old hunted elephant was probably sterile. The younger male or female that replaced it as herd leader bred the herd up, not down. Primordial wildlife in Africa once thrived because nature used to be in balance, a contest of skills.

Modern East Africa has different ideas. To preserve tourism, one by one governments had declared all hunting illegal, additionally wiping out the only traditional source of income and a way of life for tribes like Mbuno's.

That didn't mean the Waliangulu hunters lost their skills. The greatest of them became trophy taletellers at the

National Park campsites and hotels. Some were easy recruiting targets for the poaching gangs using AK-47s to slaughter whole herds. A few of them, like Mbuno, found other employment for their skills, taking people out on safari who wanted to be away from civilization, even if only for a few weeks at a time, on the fringes of the old hunting grounds, where civilization had not quite arrived, yet. He had taken out royalty, billionaires, actors, writers, tourists from Japan and, for many years, Pero's film crews. Mbuno had outlived all the older Waliangulu traditional hunters. He was now considered legendary. Pero and Heep considered him vital to any filming in Africa. They had been through this type of shooting safari before and knew they could trust him, with their lives if necessary.

Simon drove the long-wheelbase Land Rover with all the vents closed and the heating roaring, until Pero turned it off. It was morning and, being a Kenyan, Simon was feeling the cold. Pero was in the middle and Mbuno on the left. Pero and Mbuno exchanged news. Pero learned of his wife, Niamba, doing well at Giraffe Manor and Mbuno talked about the pending drought. Mbuno learned that Pero had been filming the Great White shark off Durban, which sounded very frightening. Mbuno likes the seaside, sometimes took his wife there, but not enough to deal with such *hatari papa* (dangerous sharks). Seeing Mbuno's grimace at the mention of sharks, Pero changed the subject to explain his plans for filming up north and then perhaps a quick stop at Alec Wildenstein's ranch Ol Jogi, which was not in the script, so far.

Meanwhile, the three on the back seat, Priit, Heep, and Ruis were complaining about the mess in the Customs and immigration halls at Nairobi Airport.

"It is just like always, no?" Priit's singsong voice always made Pero smile.

Ruis finished Priit's comment, "And they should film that damn mess one day, Heep, no one believes the chaos there when I tell them."

Pero answered for Heep, "The Kenyan authorities would arrest you. If tourists saw this on TV, they would never come here. Bad for business. Me? I prefer it this way. If it was efficient and easy, most of the people would come back, then there would be nothing wild left anywhere. Anyway, Ruis, you're a fine one to talk. Madagascar is worse, much worse."

"Okay, I'll grant you that, but they rebuilt this place for millions of dollars. . . . Couldn't they have made this work a little better?"

Pero knew what was really bothering him and chuckled, "You get hit with the twenty-dollar fine for a wrong visa again?" Not having American passports, they had no doubt needed to buy the "special visa" on landing, essentially a bribe.

Ruis smiled, shrugged his shoulders and looked sheepish, "Yeah, every damn time. They hate us southerners." And, being old hands at Africa filming, they all laughed.

Heep turned the conversation back to business, "Ol Jogi? You want to film Rudi again?" Rudi was a behemoth of a black rhino who loved sugarcane. The last time they had filmed there, for a car commercial, Rudi had tried to get in the car to steal the sugar cane on the back seat. As the car was doing over twenty miles per hour at the time, driving became more than difficult. A two-ton car is no match for a two-ton determined rhino with a three-foot horn trying to squeeze through an open window. The damage was extensive.

Laughing, Pero said, "No, my friend, we'll leave Rudi alone. But remember that cheetah pair they imported from South Africa? I thought we might be able to put cameras in the den and watch her give birth. They are due sometime in the next weeks I heard."

Simon chimed in, "The Park's team is up there studying them. They say they are perfectly tame, used to being near people. They can't be touched, run a mile if you try, but you could film them pretty easily."

The Land Rover had reached the turnoff for Nairobi National Park and Simon turned in. The guards at the gate saluted as the Land Rover approached. There was no need for permits or fees, not while they were in an officially recognized safari vehicle with Park permits on the windscreen. Inside the gate, they stopped for a moment to dole out sandwiches, bottled water, and soda that Mbuno had provided. As Simon drove on again, they started lunch. Simon was on his home ground here, "We're getting more and more big raptors in the park again. We've got three pair of golden eagles breeding now; see there's one pair over that Baobab." He paused so they could watch them swooping in a mating ritual. As they drove off again, down the dirt road, they passed a carcass being torn apart, probably a lion kill carcass. "The Egyptian storks are becoming a problem. They have taken to frightening off the hooded vultures even if they get to a carcass late. Very bold and brazen they are." He honked the horn to demonstrate. The birds didn't even pause their feeding.

They drove past a pair of giraffe, enjoying a morning feed on the high up leaves of Acacia trees. Just out of their reach on the very top, the five black waiting hooded vultures, backs to the sun, scanned the sky for signs of circling cousins. A warthog mother and six new babies started to scurry across the road.

Mbuno asked Simon to slow, so they coasted slowly forward. After the troop had crossed, Mbuno counted, "Now I count to three—one, two and three . . ." And then came the male warthog, big tusks and all, following them up, scanning side to side as he ran, seemingly on tiptoes. "The male, he never leads, it is his job to protect the family. She in front, he in the back. It is a good sized litter, very big."

For two hours they drove on, having a private safari guide tour, down the dip of the Athi River valley and up the other side, eventually to the Langata gate. As they came out onto the main road, they turned right, back towards Nairobi. The Park shortcut had avoided the traffic of town and acted as a ring road—an exotic ring road to be sure. After another ten minutes, passing through Langata District, they turned into Wilson Airport, Nairobi's second airport, on the southwest of town, mostly used for charter flights and tourists hopping to exotic destinations.

Wilson Airport is famous. It is the home of the Flying Doctor service and most of the commercial charter airline companies. There are an equal number of foreign and local pilots here. Every day flights depart to the most remote locations in what once were the real wildernesses or safari jumping off airstrips: Malindi, Mogadishu, Arusha, Magadi, Marsabit, Kisumu, Musoma, Lamu, Maasai Mara, Narok, Nakur, Lake Rudolf, and, of course, Tsavo.

Hemingway, Bogart, Hepburn, Peck, Beard, Gardner, Wilde, Adamson, Douglas, Wayne, Naipul, Leakey—the names of the famous who plied their claim to adventure alighting from Wilson still continued to grow with names like Spielberg, Hanks, Linney, Streep, Redford, Iman, Attenborough, Gates, van Munster, and others.

They pulled up at Mara Airways and saw a sign proclaiming Flamingo Filming Ltd. being held up by a Flamingo travel agent next to a gleaming Cessna 414. Flamingo Filming was really only a desk in the Flamingo Travel Agency manned by a secretary they could rely on, called Sheila Ndelle, sister of the UN security police chief. Being inside a large tourist travel agency, Flamingo had access to all the computer booking services. The agent handed Pero the tickets and vouchers for the camp where they were heading. Pero signed the receipt, locally called a chit, and Sheila quickly said goodbye.

The Kenyatta Airport Schenker customs agent was also already there, supervising loading. "All twenty-seven cases accounted for and complete, Mr. Pero Baltazar, Sir." Smiling, Pero thanked him and handed him an unsealed envelope he had prepared the day before. It contained one crisp $100 bill. The agent peered inside and beamed. "Thank you, Sir, very, very much, Sir." He paused and reached down for a small flight bag, "Oh, and this is your private bag, Sir." He handed it to Pero saying simply "It arrived yesterday, Sir."

"Thanks for the good work. Regards to Schenker." Pero extended his hand.

The agent shook it, nodded, and walked off, then turned and waved and disappeared around the corner.

"New man, Pero?" Heep asked.

Pero nodded, "But same company we always use. I was advised this was a new man, seems very reliable. So far things are going well." Pero glanced at the paperwork, "He managed to get the batteries in without duty, so he's pretty good." Kenyan customs were famous for charging duty on all camera batteries. Seems they cannot distinguish between special rechargeable Sony batteries for the Betacam and the ones bought at a drugstore. Or perhaps they chose not to see the difference in order to pocket the duty.

Meanwhile, Mbuno and Simon had gotten the glider loaded down the plane's aisle. There was no reason for delay. Pero signed the charter register that the pilot handed him who then handed it to a ground crew member, and everyone boarded. As the pilot went through the pre-flight visual check around the aircraft, Pero took his seat—right seat, behind the controls. As the boss, it was his prerogative. As a safety precaution, it was sensible. The Australian pilot squeezed into his left seat, nodded to Pero, and twanged, "You okay to give me a hand, mate?"

Two pairs of hands, sometimes, are better than one. Traveling to remote locations around the world meant that Pero was more than familiar with most small aircraft. When he was fully seated, lap belt on and tight, Pero found the small cubby hole near his right knee, took out and started to read the preflight checklist out loud.

As the pilot started the left and then right engines to full throttle, pulled back the blades' feather control to allow the engines to warm up, he said, "Thanks for the assist." Pero nodded, checked the altimeter, saw the horizon even out as it spooled up, and tapped the fuel gauges to make sure they were fully accurate. The pilot nodded, "The right and left tanks are topped up—checked 'em myself. That right gauge is faulty, it's on my list for the mechanics."

Pero nodded again—he knew it was not unusual for there to be small maintenance items. He reached for the second radio, "And the frequency?"

"One oh three point two after takeoff, thanks."

Pero turned the dials until the second radio was locked in, ready to use after takeoff when ground control would hand off to Kenya air traffic control. Then he settled back, folded his arms, and retracted his feet from the floor pedals. Pero was making sure the pilot knew he would not interfere with any controls, unless asked. The pilot looked over at him, smiled, and pushed transmit to ground control, "Mara flight eighty-two, bound for Ramu . . ."

The takeoff was smooth, uneventful, and as brusque as ever. At this altitude, full speed was needed on the ground before rotating the wings for lift-off. Once the speed indicator showed one hundred ten knots, the plane leapt off the ground, the wheels came up fast to help gain airspeed, and they gained altitude quickly. Heavily loaded with equipment and six people, the pilot had wisely kept the throttles and prop pitch set to full power.

Pero looked back and saw the crew settling in to sleep, with Mbuno in the tail, eyes closed, relaxed, probably dozing. They all knew it would be a bumpy ride; it always was that time of year, in the heat. The film crew was tired. An eight-hour red-eye flight is always tiring, even if they tried to sleep. Fatigue was creeping up on Pero as well, so he asked the pilot if he would be needing help for a while and he responded, "Nah, go on mate, get some shuteye."

Pero awoke with a start some time later—his nerves re-transmitting memory that there had been a sharp bump in the flight. Pero tried to calm wakened nerves. He turned in the seat and checked the crew. Everyone was dozing, only Mbuno was awake—who smiled reassurance and gestured forward. Pero looked to his left, the pilot was calm, nothing was wrong. But out the front window, he could see, in the distance, the filming target for the next few days. Mbuno knew where they were going.

The Ajuran Plateau is a mesa rising out of the desert nothingness that is Kenya's northeastern frontier. Looking like a small Rock of Gibraltar with a sharply sloping top (down to level on the north side), it glints red in the morning sun, appears dark and foreboding by afternoon. As a climber's test, the cliff face is formidable, especially if you put a hand anywhere near the vulture nests. As a film location, it is majestic and definitely "not in America, Toto," as the cable TV execs had demanded.

The pilot interrupted Pero's thoughts. "We're coming into Ramu, check your belts please." Pero turned to check everyone was complying and then read the pre-landing checklist for the Australian.

They overflew the Ramu airstrip, a dirt track about 600 yards long with a few buildings off to the east. There were no animals to scare off and no trees to avoid, so the plane made a tight turn and came around again, landing towards the north. On touchdown full reverse props were applied and the plane slowed dramatically. Pero pointed forward, and the pilot taxied up to two Land Rovers and one driver, sporting a Flamingo Tours baseball cap, standing in the baking sun and dust near the end of the strip.

Mbuno was the first off the plane following the pilot who dropped the door and steps. The pilot greeted the Flamingo Tours driver with "Jambo," but the man seemed to be in a hurry to address Pero. Somewhat breathless, he quickly proclaimed, "My name is Joshua. I am your driver, I did not know . . ." Before Pero could shake his hand, from behind him, a man had stepped out of one of the Land Rovers and elbowed Joshua aside. He was wearing a tie, the mark of an official.

"Please to call me Stephen, my name is Stephen Mbdele, I am from the Ministry of Culture and Tourism. I am your official guide and have responsibility."

In his most formal manner Pero turned only to the driver and replied, "How do you do Joshua, good to meet you." Pero shook his hand. For a moment Pero ignored the other man. Government people, so-called guides, were required of all filming crews in Kenya. They got $100 a day (US currency, of course), were political appointees, and had no merit nor benefit to filming whatsoever. "Joshua, have you received the District Officer's filming permit?" He handed it to Pero. The $500 fee was marked "paid in full." With that authority, from the local boss of bosses, Pero could pretty much do what Pero liked.

Pero turned to address the stooge, "How do you do, Sir, glad to have you along, *on my shoot*. Always glad to cooperate with authorities. Our office arranged your fee okay, did they?"

The man nodded, "Yes, but . . ."

Before he could add anything Pero interrupted, "Good, that's settled then, come along for the ride, stay out of our way, and we'll get along fine. There may even be a bonus for you when we are done." To soften the tone Pero shook the minder's hand. Pero refused to use his name on perverse principle. As the man started to reply with the usual official greeting and who's boss speech, Pero said, "Ah, yes, excuse me, will you, urgent matters to attend to, glad to have you along." Pero took Mbuno and Heep by the arm and walked out of earshot.

Pero really had no secrets, but it was always better to keep these stooges in the dark and on the defensive. Pero had seen them stop production just to demonstrate power. Like most petty dictators, if you kept them guessing, they became quite tame, happy to tag along.

"Heep, what say you, Mbuno, and I take one Land Rover and check out the plateau while Joshua and the rest of the crew set up camp and check equipment?"

Heep asked, "Who's he to go with?" motioning to the stooge.

"I'll deal with that. You get the plane unloaded and stowed, most in the second Land Rover, okay?" Pero walked back to the government agent and asked if he would like to be in charge of supervising the building of the campsite. He said he very much would like that, yes. Matter settled. Pero pointed him to the Land Rover being heavily loaded with Joshua's help.

Two hours later, the dust settling in eyes, throats, nostrils, and every nook and cranny of the Land Rover, Pero, Heep, and Mbuno were up north at the base of the Ajuran Plateau. Having reached the far side of the Plateau, the track up the slope was in front of them. They paused, as much to get their bearings as to screw up courage. Thankfully, Mbuno was driving and in low four-wheel drive they inched their way around fallen rocks the size of houses, through ruts that caused the doorsills to grate on the dirt and pebbles, and canted over at alarming angles as they traversed the hillside. It took forty-five minutes to drive to the top. The view was spectacular.

Already late afternoon, the sun was at an angle that didn't match what Heep wanted, the light behind them, not in their face. "It'll have to be an early morning shoot, Pero, I'll need the glider going down from here, see?" He swooped his hand into the void simulating the glider launch. "Then, we'll have to drive like hell to get down, or maybe have Simon launch a second launch from Simon here after we set up below. That drive down will be scary and dangerous. We need to catch Simon against the cliff face surrounded by vultures and we'll need the morning red glow of the cliff face to make that shot work." Pero agreed—they'd be up early tomorrow. It was time to get down off of there, back to camp in daylight.

Before they crested the slight ridge to start the drop down the steep backside, Pero asked Mbuno to hold up. Pero got out, climbed up on top of the Land Rover, and peered through binoculars towards the north towards the Kenyan border. Pero couldn't see anything unusual.

What Pero hadn't told anyone was that they had been contacted before the trip by an old Washington State Department contact who had asked him to look out for anything unusual in the border region and also ask around locally for any gossip about activity up north on the border.

Pero had, in years past, carried documents or sometimes smuggled tiny equipment marked as film stock *Not To Be Exposed* for the State Department. It was risky, but Pero felt their requests earned State Department support credits, credits he may need to cash in one day. Filming in over sixty-five countries involved risks beyond the physical. Sometimes you got on the wrong side of dictators and politicians. In that event State and therefore US Embassy help would be the only thing likely to save you. His contact, now a friend after all these years, at State made the same point every time he asked a favor. But this time, being asked to look out for something "unusual" puzzled Pero. He told his contact, "Hey, look, we're not a spy outfit, you need intelligence from the Gurreh region, arrange it yourself."

The man smiled, "Intelligence? Spy? What fancy words, Pero. Look, you're up there filming already, right? Save the taxpayers' money and if," he stressed the *if*, "if you see anything unusual or hear about armed insurgents or increased weapons trafficking, or, hell I don't know, the local chief's daughter has been defiled by Somali marauders, just let us know. Okay?"

Pero felt he could leave it at that. If he saw or heard anything, he could report it. If he didn't, he would still have done State a favor. "See something, hear something, I call you. Hear nothing, see nothing, I still did you a favor, right?"

"Right, thanks."

On the edge of the way down the plateau, scanning the border region through binoculars, seeing nothing, Pero decided he would ask the locals, maybe that night or the next day.

On the way down, the loose sand slid the tires sideways and they couldn't stop in time, crushing the front fender into the tire on a rock. Surveying the damage, Heep said, "Damn and blast!" So, while they tugged and pried the aluminum fender off the burst tire and changed to the spare for the next hour, it became their mantra: "Damn and blast . . . heave! Damn and blast . . . heave! Their muscles ached, their clothes were drenched in sweat, but eventually they started off again, tire changed and no more chafing of the bodywork. As they made the bottom of the slope safely, just as dusk fell, Heep said, "They'll have to take that descent a whole lot slower tomorrow."

Mbuno, who had said nothing to this point added, "Damn and blast slower." Smiles and chuckles helped lighten the mood.

Back at camp, Pero and Heep explained the videotaping plans for the next day. No sooner than Pero was through, the stooge spoke up. In no time at all, in his rhythmic East African accent, he was boring them all with a government lecture, probably page thirty-five of the official stooge-minder handbook. His mouth pursing, lower lip sticking out with every beat of the sentence, he intoned, "not to proceed beyond the track at the foot of the Ajuran Plateau. It is most dangerous! It is not safe! It is forbidden, it is not safe!" No one answered or even looked at him; their eyes were fixed on the flames licking dried, smoky, desert brushwood. Actually, his territorial imperative sounded okay to Pero, there were brigands known to be about, locally called *shufti*.

Pero had already warned the crew weeks before bringing them up here, that the Gurreh-Ajuran region also hosts a sometimes violent, always sparse, people of the Cushitic language tribes, eking out a hard living in harsh, arid conditions, up here near the border of Ethiopia, about fifty miles from Somalia. Pero had been here before a few times, sometimes with shufti danger just averted when they were filming and tracking the elusive scimitar Oryx. It was Mbuno who had made them stop filming and speed back to base. The shufti followed, but Mbuno's good sense got them into a defensible position. Pero feared a repeat of the armed attack—it all came so swiftly. Thankfully, on arrival, there was not a Gurreh to be seen, but Pero was sure they were aware of their presence—in this land, the local tribal knowledge is never to be underestimated. His hope was that as "muzungus" (white men), as they were called, seen working busily in the sun all day, they might be considered nuts and hardly worth the effort. Pero chuckled, watching the embers die down, seeing his dusty, scruffy crew, stamping cold feet. They certainly did not look like rich tourists, ripe for plunder, more used to sitting around a pool sipping iced drinks. And tourists never got up at the ungodly hour they were planning for tomorrow, especially not to go up an escarpment, and definitely not to leap off.

CHAPTER 2

North of Wajir

Long before the first rays of the sun inched their way across the middle of the desert and struck their tent flaps, deep in Gurreh territory, Pero's windup alarm clock rang its bell at four a.m. Habit taught Pero to swing out of bed—or in this case camp cot—then try and come awake. At least sitting with his feet on the cold floor Pero knew his bladder was about to kick in, forcing the mechanism to do something, maybe even actually return to feeling human. Pero thought of his body in the third person, somehow trying to will control over what was, as Pero got older, increasingly less reliable bits and pieces. His latest failure? Creaky knees in the morning and liniment before bed. Add that to failing eyesight now requiring reading glasses . . . Pero guessed he was just an ordinary middle-aged American whose faculties are falling apart, albeit thankfully slowly.

Mbuno, on the other hand, relished the morning, even when it was cold, because he knew his favorite meal was coming. *Chai* (tea) and *mkate* (bread) with lashings of Okiek *asali* (honey) he had bought for the safari. Although the desert morning was cold, only about forty degrees Fahrenheit, Pero and Mbuno knew Malka Mari National Park, where they were camped, would heat up nicely to 120° by lunchtime. From personal experience, learned the hard way, both men brought and wore warm clothing in the morning. It is easier to strip with the sun than shiver in the dark. And, at over six feet and a large frame, if Pero didn't bring it along, chances were he wouldn't be able borrow it from anyone else nor find it in some local *duka*, or shop. Mbuno, on the other hand, only ever seemed to have one threadbare green wool sweater over which he wrapped a *kikoi* (cotton skirt wrap), worn like a shawl.

Even though Pero always insisted crews wear stout desert boots, someone often forget to shake them out in the morning, only to feel that squirm and sting of a scorpion as the toes enter. That can cost a day's filming, which then becomes his problem. So, as part of a more boring routine, Pero woke each person in the dark of night, shook out their shoes, and dropped them on the sleeper to get things moving. Pero always thought it was a bizarre job being a producer, even if, at times, the filming location was exotic.

That morning there were no stingers, but Pero did leap back as a horned toad jumped over his socks. In the dim light, his imagination got the better of him for a split second. Out there, life is on borrowed time, it could have been a spitting cobra. Anyway, that's the image his sleepy mind left him with, adrenaline pumping

The night before, the conversation had fallen to past glories and recent triumphs. V*ideography*, as his partner Heep likes to call videotaping for TV, is a passion for them all. Get it right and the world is captured and carried to someone's living room. Their message is the medium and, as Pero was the producer, he was the ultimate messenger bringer. Whether their tales were thirty feet down off an Australian reef, or halfway up a mountain in the Urals, or freezing toes off on a windswept plateau in northeastern India, all had a common truth: the advent of dawn until dawn plus one hour is when wildlife openly exhibits itself.

So, when Pero ran a wildlife camera crew, he made sure everyone was up and active in the cold edge of night, to be ready. That morning the fire, stacked and lit by Mbuno and Joseph half an hour before even Pero's alarm went off, crackled and warmed. There was not much talk from the crew or the minder. All stood or sat, sipping hot *chai*. In Kenya chai consists of water, black tea leaves, sugar and milk all brought to the boil together in a battered kettle poured steaming hot into tin mugs clasped firmly in two hands, soaking up the warmth to ward off a pre-dawn chill. Only Mbuno ate bread and honey, somewhat shocked that Ruis and Priit refused their individual slices. They both smiled when Mbuno put the two together, took a handkerchief from his pocket and wrapped the sandwich for later.

As pre-dawn's early violet changed to rose, the desert owls caught their last meal before curfew, their cries like fingernails down a blackboard. The crew's steamy breaths reflecting the crackling fire, there were feet stamping and throaty coughs as sips were taken. They were all outfitted the same—green khaki extra-pocket trousers, rolled-down long sleeved canvas shirt (with double breast pockets), leather belts complete with holster for cell phones and walkie-talkies, socks, padded vests, and stout boots. Joshua, the rental Land Rover driver who they found most amiable, came over and said the cars were ready.

No matter where or when Pero was filming, as the crew left for location shooting, Pero would make a count of the boxes and bags going along. Like a schoolteacher and her charges on a day trip, Pero counted them into the bus and out of the bus. Into the Land Rover, out of the Land Rover. Into the plane, out of the plane. Every day, each location, over and over. That morning the loading of the Land Rovers took Pero and Joshua a full twenty minutes, working efficiently.

Heep was being patient, as always. After chai, he waited until the cameras were cleaned and checked by Ruis, he waited as the crew loaded last things into the Land Rovers, he waited as the sun peeked over the horizon, he waited as their cars inched their way across the rock and thorn bush-strewn desert, waited as the cars bumped, yard by yard, climbing the sloping backside of the plateau, waited as Simon's glider was being assembled and harnessed, waited as the vultures began their first heat-rising soaring off nests on the cliff face, and then he waited for Pero to tell him they were ready.

On Heep's command of "Action!" Simon ran the three steps to the edge, swooping down and away. The updraft of the first thermals of the day caught him, and he soared fifty feet above their heads. On their command into his earpiece, he dropped the nose, as planned, and swooped past the cliff edge to the right of Heep, out into the void.

The already soaring vultures gave him a wide berth. Those still on nests took fright and flight, rushing at him to defend their young against this larger predator bird. A few made contact with the hang glider but finding it not alive, simply became curious and flew alongside.

As usual, Heep was shooting this first day himself. He wanted the show's leadoff shot to be Emmy-worthy, to add to his collection. In a safety harness leaning over the cliff edge, he strained the climbing rope that Pero had attached to a tow-point of the lead Land Rover as an anchor. Making no sound, shooting both ambient sound and the flight mike, he held the over-the-shoulder Betacam steady with his right hand, suddenly gesturing to Pero with his left. He knew Pero was watching only him. It was how they worked. They'd been working as an effective team, off and on, for almost eighteen years. Without moving the camera or his eye on the viewfinder, he pointed with his left hand to a distant dust cloud approaching on the valley floor below. Pero looked down apprehensively. They had a visitor. A visitor who was going to break shot. Pero ran back from the edge, ducked behind the Land Rover, and used the walkie-talkie plugged into their soarer's ear. What Pero softly said wouldn't be caught on tape.

"Simon, don't answer, they're filming, you're doing great. Do us a favor and soar west a bit, will you?" Simon's response was a mike double-click, meaning "acknowledged."

Pero ran back to Heep's left side as he tracked the camera to his right following Simon's new flight path. Heep gave Pero the okay sign and continued filming. Pero's eyes focused on the approaching vehicle, still way too far off to identify. Pero calculated that it would intrude into their filming in under fifteen minutes at the speed it was doing, using a bad track that led straight back to Ethiopia and, Pero knew, eventually wound its way through gullies to finally reach Somalia, some fifty miles further on. Pero felt the tingle of danger creeping up his spine and resolved to order his crew to make a run for it, once they had collected Simon after he landed. Pero saw no point in heroics. Out here, heroes were jackal food, never to be seen again if the *shufti* caught you.

Heep lowered the camera, yelled "Cut," and called for tape and batteries as he walked quickly to the Land Rover. They didn't bother telling Simon out there in free-float they were leaving. He wasn't coming back up here anyway; he would ride the thermals, down eventually. There was a rendezvous spot they'd picked out on the valley floor directly below and they now had to rush to get there to complete the day's shooting, filming upwards against the blue sky. Seeing them rushing for the Land Rovers, Simon caught the thermal again and rose above the level of the plateau, joyriding with the vultures above the cliff face. Hanging around "up there," he gave them time to get down and into position. The thermals and updraft were "no problem" he radioed them, but they hurried anyway. The crews were already in the cabs by the time Pero took one last look, leaning over the cliff, at the approaching car, still coming, ten minutes to intrusion into shot, twenty-five minutes to arrival and possible danger. Pero ran and ordered the Land Rover to move before he even finished shutting the door

The drive down was more dangerous than the drive up. The two-foot ruts had been a slow inconvenience on the way up. On the way down, these could flip a Land Rover before the driver could correct the steering. They eased past the worst bits, especially the sharp bend, in and out and again back into the pitted ruts. They inched around what they had called the *Damn and Blast* rock, careful not to crack-up the Land Rovers. Finally, after only fifteen minutes of swift and nervous driving, they were off the plateau, on the flat again, so they gunned the engines, spun tires in the loose sand, and raced to catch filming continuity, matching the sun for Simon's landing.

On the valley floor about 200 yards short of the rendezvous point, Joshua's Land Rover bounced hard in a rut in front of them, swerved, misjudged the recovery, and gently toppled over in a cloud of dust. Heep wanted the shot. "On, keep going. No stopping."

Pero nodded to Mbuno, with his decades of experience, driving faster than any of them could have, they roared past the toppled Land Rover.

Suddenly Heep called, "Stop! This is fine, here." After the trailing dust had overtaken them, Heep leapt out and reached back in to get the camera off Pero's lap. Part of Pero's job was to keep vital equipment safe—an unwritten agreement between them. Heep turned, placed the heavy Betacam on his right shoulder, and aimed up to shoot Simon soaring with the vultures. No Simon.

They scanned the sky. No Simon.

The other Land Rover, plastered in dust, pulled slowly alongside looking none the worse for wear, windscreen not even cracked. Land Rovers are strong and it was a gentle tumble, easy to push upright. As they scanned the sky, no one said anything. They all knew not to. When Heep had his camera up, he could be filming, the camera's microphone active.

Heep lowered the camera and looked at Pero, frowning. The silence was palpable.

Pero climbed on top of the Land Rover and scanned the plain calling Simon on the walkie-talkie. Nothing. Pero could see no blue wing jutting up, no one waving in the distance. Pero could see the valley floor, bushes, and rocks, for ten miles, at least, in every direction except around the northeastern point of the Ajuran Plateau.

Now down on the valley floor Pero could not spot the mystery dust trail anymore.

Pero broke the silence. "Simon must be down, may be hurt." Pero looked at Priit, "Your Land Rover okay?"

Priit answered in his singsong accent; the clipped phrases almost Scandinavian: "The car is okay. A little dirty." Joshua nodded, "And some water spilled over the tapes. But I think they're okay. The generator" (for their batteries) "may be out of order. I'll need to fix it."

"Good enough. You, Ruis, and Joshua take the Land Rover and drive, slowly, towards the base of the cliffs over there." Pero pointed ahead of them. "Take it slow and keep a lookout, out the top." Like all safari cars the Land Rovers had observation roofs—a four-foot by three-foot hole cut to allow paying passengers to stand on the seats to better view the wildlife.

"Hey, and listen, watch for ravines. Maybe Simon fell into one of those." The valley floor was littered with flood-rain dry gulches.

Heep was already getting back into their Land Rover. Over his shoulder, one foot on the running board, Pero called back to Ruis: "One hour, no more, if the walkie-talkies don't work, we'll meet here. No one leaves without the other." Mbuno was waiting at the wheel.

Right now, Pero needed his expertise, again.

"Mbuno, go to the point there, see?" Pero pointed, Mbuno accelerated. "We need to go there and around, slowly, *tafadali*." Even after all these years with Mbuno, an order with a *please* showed respect. Respect is the cornerstone of civilization in tribal Africa.

"Yes, Mr. Pero, it is not easy, not very fast there. We go now." His English had improved over the years, but his unique word and verb placement rang in Pero's *western* ears for weeks after each shoot.

"*Asanti*, Mbuno." A *thank you* doesn't hurt either. "We need to find Mr. Simon, he may have crashed."

Heep, from the back seat, had a better idea, "Pero, Mbuno has better sight than both of us—let's put him up on top."

"Okay. Stop the car, Mbuno, I'll drive, you watch." Mbuno nodded. Soon they were off again, Mbuno sitting on the open hatch lip, swaying with the Land Rover's pitching and yawing, eyes fixed on the horizon.

The government minder had kept silent up until then, content to sit in the car and "earn" his $100 a day, sullenly. Now he spoke up. "No! You must not drive here. You are forbidden to drive off the track. There is a fine. This is a park. It is not permitted. This is a park, a park—it is not allowed." He pronounced park like *paak* and allowed as *allow-ed*. Both implied a command, not a warning. Pero didn't stop. Simon could be in need of medical attention. The minder became agitated. "You must stop. It is a park, it is forbidden."

"An extra fifty dollars for whoever sees Simon first," Pero countered. Pero shot the minder a stare, while wrenching the wheel to avoid a large rock behind a thorn bush.

The Nairobi man wasted no time, popped up next to Mbuno, and quickly said something in fast Swahili. It was clearly a command. Mbuno simply answered, "Ndiyo." If he spotted anything, he was to tell the minder, who would tell Pero so he could pocket the cash reward.

Pero smiled, his reward plan to work around these new Park rules had worked. Heep, knowingly, gave Pero a shake of the head and winked. It didn't take Mbuno's vision long to help their minder to make that fifty dollars. He pointed to his right. Pero quickly radioed the other Land Rover, "We have him, almost there, follow our tracks."

What Pero saw told him that Simon was dead. Pero didn't really have to double check. He turned off the engine and opened his door before the hand brake fully stopped the Land Rover, racing to get to the hang glider first, shielding Simon's body from view of the Land Rover. Ripping the duct tape, Pero pocketed their minicam off the main strut before the minder even got down and out of the Land Rover as he was purposefully delayed, having to squeeze past a suddenly unhelpful Heep who accidentally blocked the doorway, making apologies. Heep had guessed Pero would be retrieving the remote camera.

Moments later, the four were clustered around, walkie-talkie burbling questions from the other Land Rover. "Standby, fellows." Pero switched it off for a moment to think.

"What do you mean dead? It cannot be!" The stooge wanted to know, Pero knew he really wanted to know. The man prodded Simon's boots with his shoe toe as if to wake him. "Why is he dead? It is not permitted!" It was almost an accusation. He glared at Pero. Another look down and a tap to Simon's boot. Another glare at Pero.

What the hell did I have to do with it, Pero wondered. But he said nothing, since he knew this could not be an accident. As the blue nylon fluttered in the gentle ground breeze, the plastic made little crackling noises, setting his teeth on edge. Pero wanted to spin around and search the area about them, but he fought the impulse. If they were being watched, Pero wanted whomever it was out there who had murdered Simon to see them dealing with what looked like an accident, staring at the victim.

Mbuno squatted, said nothing, Heep standing next to him. Both men knew Pero had to take command here or matters could get worse very quickly. Kenya's government did not like people dying in National Parks—it was "very bad for business." Someone had to be blamed.

Simon's head, *poor bastard* thought Heep, was bent over at an impossible angle. The glider was intact, one stay loose, but nothing was even bent or broken. Despite being covered in thorns, the wing fabric was intact as well. It must have just brushed the thorny wait-a-minute bushes on landing. If the track in the dust was to be believed, Simon had landed, gliding in headfirst.

"Don't anybody touch this." Pero said in a sudden voice of authority. Pero was the boss, time to take command, to act the bully if needed. Pero had to get this under control and fast. He too knew there was sudden danger out here to his crew, real danger. A Kenyan was dead and the local police could hold them indefinitely while they investigated or extracted a bribe to let them go.

Heep walked a few yards off and radioed the other car, "Guys, bad news, poor Simon is dead, crash landed, broken neck." Their answer in Heep's earpiece made him answer, "We have no idea."

Pero turned to the minder "You go, now. Mbuno will drive. Go to the District Officer's office and ask for Chief Methenge, not the police officer, got that? If you come back with the police officer, I will make sure Nairobi fires you—and they will never pay your fee, ever. Get the Chief here with two or three of his soldiers. He can make the police report." The stooge wasn't happy, but the threat of losing his fee made him sullenly agree with a nod.

Chief Methenge was a Kikuyu/Luo tribesman elder as well as a political employee in this desolate region of almost no permanent tribes and certainly not his tribe, which was 600 miles to the south. The ex-President of Kenya, a Luo himself, Daniel Arap Moi had given hundreds of his tribal stooges familial favors of postings of prestige. Chief Methenge was lonely, idle, and keen to change office to something greener, preferably down south. It's not just the desirability of the vegetation down south; the tourist dollars are nice and green also—and much more plentiful in the big national parks.

To appeal to the Chief would make sense to Heep—and to the other crew members alighting from the other Land Rover now pulling up behind Pero—because they knew the Chief was into cash, whereas the local police, like all sub-Saharan civil servants, were into promotion by exercising power. Give them that power over the crew, falsehoods or not, and they'd all be there for weeks, maybe forever, on some trumped-up charges until the political folks in Nairobi got their pound of flesh from someone overseas in the form of dollars—and television production was seen as having very deep pockets. Besides, Pero was thinking, as justification to override his own fears, they had a schedule to keep, places to film, and nothing they could do here would make poor Simon any better.

Mbuno, on the other hand, knew this was a bad omen for what might be coming. Seasoned wildlife expert that he was, Mbuno recognized that this was no accidental death. And no one is killed without reason. The reason escaped him, for now. As the other Land Rover pulled up, Pero went over to talk with them, telling them to stay in the car.

Mbuno figured out that Pero would think that the Chief, not wanting to discourage future permit payers—this film permit had been $500 for three days shooting in his district—should want to deal with this "accident" quickly. Mbuno also knew Chief Methenge, Pero had worked with him before and Mbuno had been the guide then too. The chief no doubt still had the photo of himself, smiling in full war gear, on the cover of Nairobi's scandal sheet, the *Daily Nation*, which Pero had arranged: "Chief Saves Film Crew From Shufti Single-Handed!"

That time it wasn't a TV crew. Back then they had been filming a Peugeot car commercial and the attackers weren't shufti—they had been angry locals the chief hadn't shared his fee with so they tried to get some dollars from Pero directly, at gunpoint. The Chief's action wasn't single-handed—the police had stood behind him with rifles. Pero had to admit, he did save them though, and it could have been nasty. His timing had been impeccable. Maybe too good, but then all's well that ends well in Africa.

"Heep, why don't you go with them, with Mbuno, Ruis, and Priit?"

"Pero, that'll leave you alone here." Heep looked worried. Pero took him aside.

"Look, you need to get that tape in the Betacam safely tucked away, right? Swap it out fresh and pretend what's in the camera was the footage of Simon, okay? And I have this as well." Pero peeped into his safari jacket pocket at the minicam, out of sight. "Stay with Ruis and Priit, pack up, we may need to get the hell out of here, fast. But leave the tents up. Make it look normal. Have them drop you off on the way to the Chief's. And ask Mbuno to bring back the Land Rover— alone with none of you—and have my digital still camera in the glove box." Heep looked quizzically at Pero, then nodded, shouldered his Betacam, shot some footage of the dead, crashed Simon and then decidedly moved off. The minder followed him, black leather city shoes slipping in the sand.

At the door of the Land Rover, Pero asked, "Ruis, you remember Chief Methenge?" Ruis had been on the car commercial shoot. He nodded. "Good, go with Nairobi's fellow here and meet up with the Chief and explain that I, his friend, am guarding the body for him, only him, got that? I will not move from this spot until his Excellency shows up. Please be so kind as to remind him how *grateful* we were last time for his help." Ruis smiled, he knew what Pero meant; the Chief could smell money ten miles off.

Nairobi's fellow—the stooge—still hadn't caught on and was looking dangerously unhappy. Perhaps he was contemplating a call to his bosses. Pero wanted to avoid that until they were safely away. *Bribe number two coming up*, Pero thought, *here goes*, "And you," Pero said, turning to him, "I trust you will be willing to help here so we may thank you for your extra . . ." said again with emphasis and a rubbing of fingers "your *extra* help in this tragic accident?"

Suddenly, he got the message. He was not too bright, this boy, but he had a steel trap for a left hand—the one you take money with. He burst out energetically with, "Then we must hurry. It is most important to see Chief Methenge presently." He pointed at the crew, "They must be driving me there presently."

With a parting okay sign from Heep, they all finished piling into the one Land Rover and drove off in the ubiquitous cloud of dust, leaving Pero alone at Simon's accident site.

Time to find out what killed him, he thought.

Pero knew Simon hadn't died on impact. No one with Simon's paragliding experience stays in a prone harness, approaching landing. Headfirst, lying down, is hardly even safe on water. Here, there were boulders strewn around. Simon would have known better.

Apologizing out loud, "Sorry, friend," gingerly Pero made a closer inspection. Simon had never made it down alive. The broken neck had happened on landing. The bullet holes hadn't. There were two of them just visible on his left side below his shoulder. There was no pool of blood underneath him so Pero guessed he was killed by something small, something tidier than a usual bullet, perhaps a very small caliber weapon. Maybe it was a .22-250, high velocity stuff. Sniper armament. Very much against the law in Kenya, which tried (and failed) to adopt the British anti-gun laws. Out here on the Northern Frontier, the supply of guns from Somalis, Ethiopians, or crashed gunrunning planes was plentiful and, although clandestine, well known. Still, a sniper rifle hardly had value to the locals. Not big enough to stop something large, from a Cape buffalo to a rhino, and useless for poaching as it was so loud, a .22-250 bullet still had plenty of energy traveling at over 3,000 miles per hour. Nevertheless, hardly the weapon of choice for *shufti* either because those bullets could go straight through living flesh at close range, leaving only a small pencil hole as a token. Unless, of course, they hit bone, then the entry would be small and the exit the size of, well, a gaping hole.

Pero took a deep breath to steady his nerves—it was time to check Simon out. Pero continued his sadly lopsided conversation, "Excuse me, Simon," as Pero rolled the head straight, "There, that looks better. Now I'm just going to check you out. Don't wait for me—you carry on, straight to heaven. You can soar with angels there." Pero knew he was being overly talkative, prattling on, but, for him, almost holding his breath, shoulder turned away ready to flee, death created its own reality and needs. Talking to Simon made it all seem less revolting.

Pero unclipped the glider harness and tugged Simon out of the frame, ducking his helmet around the bar. The ultralight was easy to lift and move aside. Pero contemplated folding it up, getting those blue wings Mbuno had spotted out of sight. That rogue vehicle was out there. Connecting the dots wasn't hard. They had appeared—Simon had died. Pero's spine was still tingling, the very real threat still on his mind. But he hadn't seen a dust cloud for thirty minutes, so there was probably enough time. He hoped anyway. Or else they went back the way they had come. *Maybe our Land Rovers had scared them off.* Pero's ears did a scalp tugging, straining to hear any sound at all from behind. All was silent, normal, but his fear turned up the reception. Pero could still just hear their Land Rover to the south, maybe now three miles off.

It was unnerving handling a corpse, knowing the killers could be somewhere near, but Pero had to be sure. And Pero was also thinking of poor Simon—he had a family who needed this to be an accident for the production insurance to pay up. Pero had negotiated the million-dollar coverage himself. Any act of war or act of God was outside of the policy. Pero didn't know which one this was, but Pero was sure the insurance company would wiggle out of it if they could. He wasn't about to let that happen.

Pero rolled Simon over, unclipped the helmet, unbuckled the waist harness strap, pocketed Simon's walkie-talkie, and unzipped the anorak, careful to hold the flap sides upright. It had been a cold pre-dawn when Simon had put it on, grateful for the loan of a production orange Eddie Bauer anorak instead of his own thin Chinese black model. Even though he soared on the thermals, Simon, a wiry fellow, always wore an anorak. He was Kenyan born, thin-blooded, and used to heat. *Or had been* . . .

Pero traced the two holes through the open anorak to the butcher's slop of offal of Simon's insides—white bits of bone, ribs probably, floating in a red and purple mess. To keep it all in, Pero re-zipped the anorak and refastened the harness waist buckle. Without knowing which way he was flying when he was killed, Pero had no way of knowing exactly which direction the bullets had come from. One thing was clear—they had entered his front side chest and passed down and through his abdomen.

Pero needed nature to come to his assistance to protect Simon's family. Pero worked it out. It was at least a two-hour round-trip for the cavalry. Add another hour for the Chief to feel he had his act together. The total time calculated would suffice for Mother Nature to cover the crime. Pero unclipped the hang glider's stays and folded it into its "dormant bat" form as Simon had called it. It weighed less than fifty pounds, so Pero hefted it and placed it on the roof rack of the Land Rover. From inside the cab Pero extracted the ex-army blanket kept for cold misty mornings and draped it over the bundle, effectively camouflaging most of the nylon blue from view, and strapped it down. Twenty yards away Pero spotted a ravine, a dry lugger, a riverbed gulch ten feet deep, they had driven through. Pero backed the Land Rover back in and climbed on top. As Pero stood on top of the cab, he could scan the horizon from relative obscurity, his feet slightly above ground level.

The hooded vultures didn't take long. Their little pink wrinkled-skin faces and fluffy gray heads only served to accentuate the vicious razor-sharp jet-black beaks. Pero knew he had to wait until they were engrossed in their feeding frenzy, squabbling over the carcass, moving Simon's head, arms, and legs in little lifelike twitches. The birds were paying no attention to

Pero. Looking up, Pero saw they were marking this spot in their hundreds, along with incoming Egyptian Storks, soaring anti-clockwise here, just above the equator. The mysterious car would surely know where the corpse was now and if they still had some other motive, they could follow the vultures to discover where Pero was. It couldn't be helped.

Pero jumped down, reached into the back of the Land Rover, opened a tool lockbox, and took out an illegal revolver he had stashed there the night before. As he stuck it in his baggy pocket, Pero wondered: *If they came, could I at least ward them off for a while? For long enough? What was long enough?* Thinking that way, he knew he was frightened. Being frightened didn't worry him, controlling the fear did.

From the roof, Pero unclipped a section of the hang glider's tubing, about three feet in length, hid it behind his back, and approached the hopping birds. Vultures land with some grace on their huge outstretched wings, talons extended. On the ground, they sort of half-flap and hop towards their prey. It keeps them in a dominant position to land on top as well as keeps their wings free in case they need to make a getaway. Out here in daylight, with a fresh kill and no lion getting the first feed, they needed to beat the hyena and the storks to the feast. The hyena was already sniffing around, but being more wary of Pero, it kept snorting, circling, and raising the hairs on the back of his neck. The storks had no such fear. A pack of jackals, circling the whole scene, yapping, barking, some hundred yards off, wanted to get to the prime meat as well, before it was too late. Up here in the arid Northern Territory, a clean kill of meat, replete with liquid blood, is a meal from heaven. *Simon fell, just like an angel, to sustain them.* Pero thought that was what they might be thinking and was sure Simon wouldn't begrudge them. He had loved these raptors.

On the other hand, he wouldn't like this; Pero thought as he swung the pipe. He whacked one bird, then another. They died flapping about . . . Pero dragged them a few feet, between the car and the carcass, then sat on the roof of the car to wait. The ants and flies seemed the likely winners of the two dead vultures, too close to the car for the real scavengers to brave his presence.

Pero still saw no one else approaching. Try though he might, Pero could not spot any rising dust to the east. No mysterious car, so far. The sun was fully up now—it baked down, the desert floor simmered, the vultures kept squawking, pecking, and sucking.

Pero kept watch, turning to and fro, fingering the pistol for comfort, and listened to the silent walkie-talkie. He counted down the seconds, never mind the hour, till Mbuno would get back. The vultures and storks ripped their last flesh as the hyena moved in, snarling and excitedly whining over Simon's head. From time to time, as Pero added footage with the mini-cam, the hyena glanced over at Pero as if to say, "Stay there or you could be next."

It was a long wait for Mbuno. Pero wondered why only Mbuno's return was any comfort.

CHAPTER 3

Chief Methenge

On time, well, on time for Africa, the noise of three vehicles coming from the west warned Pero to stash the gun back in the lockbox. One of them was their Land Rover, Mbuno driving. One of them was the Chief's old black 1950s Humber luxury sedan, once more suitable to the streets of London. And one was a beat-up white and rusted flatbed Toyota with two bored-looking soldiers, one driving, one in the back holding two rifles. The Nairobi minder was stuck back there with him, looking miserable.

"Jambo, Mr. Pero, jambo!" Warm greetings from the Chief. They grasped forearms (never hands), showed no teeth (a sign of displeasure), smiled with lips closed, and exchanged pleasantries. But the chief got down to business quickly, more quickly than Pero expected. "What have we-a here? Where is-a this soaring thing?" Pero pointed to the roof rack. "Ah, you have-a saved it." It was a statement of fact, like the Chief had prior claim and now it was no longer up for salvage or personal confiscation. Pero suppressed a chuckle as he thought of the Chief soaring off the Ajuran Plateau in his "confiscated" hang glider. Not today, Chief.

"Is-a that him?" He pointed to the now exposed mass of clothing, dried blood in the sand and tough bits of bone scattered over twenty square yards.

Pero nodded.

"His-a neck broken?"

Pero nodded again.

"Most wrong. Most irregular. Very big fine."

"What? To die in an accident? The man had nothing. We paid him his first extra wage in five years. He works, worked, for the National Park people, Leakey's lot, in Nairobi as a bird of prey expert. You know, eagles and vultures?"

The Chief nodded. "Did you-a move him?"

"No Chief, I tried to protect him, see I killed those two other scavengers, over there, but there are still too many to attack with just a pipe, and half have already left with full stomachs. And the hyenas finally tore the corpse apart."

"The very big fine . . . the fine is not for him. He can not pay."

"Chief, you have always been a great warrior, protecting our crew," Pero lumped this and the past crew into one, after all they no doubt all looked the same to the Chief, "I am sure your protection will be most valuable today again." Pero walked over to the Land Rover Mbuno had driven back. Pero reached into the left side, flipped open the glove box and—good job, Heep—took out the small digital still camera. "May I ask if they can have your picture—again? The great Chief at the scene of this terrible accident?" Without hesitating, Pero handed the camera to Mbuno and said, "Look through here, and push the button again and again until I say stop, *tafadali*." Pero staged the Chief a little to the left, made the soldiers drop to one knee beneath him, rifles on knee, with the corpse and remaining vultures (ever intent on their meal now that the hyenas had been momentarily frightened off) over his left shoulder. Pero placed the minder a little further away on the Chief's left—a traditional place for a woman and, as such, subservient to the Chief—to frame the gruesome scene. Then Pero added, "Chief, if I may, may I stand to your right, like this?" Pero squatted, taller than the soldiers, but below the Chief.

"It will do nicely." Chief Methenge said, puffing out his chest. "Just fine. Take tha' picture." Mbuno had been clicking away. Digital cameras were useful, they made no sound, and he had already more than twenty pictures of this farce. Pero watched as Mbuno clicked one more. Pero walked over to him, quickly backing-up the viewer to the best image. A hyena could be seen clearly dragging a part of the rib cage away in a tug-of-war with a large Egyptian stork. Pero showed the glowing image to the Chief who was impressed, "That is-a very good. Where and when will I see it in there?" He meant the Daily Nation newspaper, of course, and soon.

"If I leave tomorrow to Nairobi, I can take it to them right away, Chief."

"Very good, you will do this." It was an order, not a question. Pero nodded.

"Good, now we will discuss the fine." He made to leave.

Pero stayed still.

Normally, they should drive off in his ancient limo to his "office." There Pero would sit in his official mud building that still had no windows and only a tin roof, with little whitewashed stones marking out the parking lot—a post-colonial car park in the middle of flat nothingness. They'd wrangle and Pero would have to sip one of his wives' Luo version of tea, blowing the curdled milk and beeswax—not to mention dead bees—away on the foamy top of the *chai*. But now Pero had a different priority. The killers were still out there and Pero needed to make sure, where and, maybe, who. The Chief might not know. The Gurreh tribe's people confided in him, but only when strangers were not about.

Watching his soldiers scavenge through dead Simon's clothing—totally in the open, without a care in the world—taking hold of the now crusty shinbones to pull the pink feet from re-usable boots, the Chief and Pero talked things out for a moment or two. He was puzzled at Pero's refusal to walk to his car and leave with him. Tea and important matters were being offered, did Pero not understand? "Chief, I left some valuable equipment behind when we were searching for poor Mr. Simon . . ." Pero gestured to the killing ground, the soldiers looked up, questioning if Pero was trying to exert authority over Simon's remains . . . "If you will allow me, I will have Mbuno drive our old Land Rover back to camp, with me following, after we back-track to there," Pero pointed vaguely back, a ways away, into the distance south of the Ajuran Plateau "to pick up my equipment, and then I promise I will come straight to your office, your Excellency, and you can explain your needs completely and fully. I am sure you will find me most happy to collaborate, as I did before," and then he added with emphasis, "exactly as before."

The Chief stroked his chin, made up his mind, and said, imperiously, "Yes, it is ordered." He looked at the minder who visibly shrank out of his path as they started walking back to the truck and Humber. "I-a trust you Mr. Pero, you are *mzee* of your people." Well, well, was Pero a chief then? It was a great compliment.

"Chief, Sir, this small mzee will not let you, ah, *down*. I will be there before tea time, to *down* my cuppa." Said with a smile.

The Chief frowned, and then got his play on words and opened his mouth and barked, literally barked, a laugh. All six teeth were deeply decayed. He turned to the men and said, "We go now." In Swahili, he ordered Simon's body parts to be thrown into the Toyota and he strode away. The soldiers started collecting the bits, like firewood, and dumped them over the white flap-down back gate. They made a hollow sound as they hit. There was no head anyone could find. Hyenas quite often take the head away for a nighttime snack, they all knew it. It could be miles away by now.

Silently, full of guilt, Pero offered an apology, *Sorry Simon, I could have prevented this but I needed your corpse to look this way, bones all chewed up, to cover your real cause of death.*

Pero noticed that the Chief's driver, who opened the door to his Humber, only had one sock on. When you are poor and only have one sock, wear it with pride was Pero's guess.

As he watched them drive away his morbid thoughts rambled to an African Foreign Minister, Pero met once, who didn't even have the one sock . . . Years before, late 1986 it was.

Pero was in the Nairobi shop of a man who was a friend to the Maasai, himself a blood brother. Macpherson Knot had a series of little tattoos on his forehead at the hairline, two blue ones Pero remembered, the mark of a rank of chief. Three and you are a chief among chiefs. Having spent years with the Maasai on his "walkabouts" since retiring from the British Army, Macpherson was a bit of a mystery to the Maasai. Over the years they found him trustworthy, deeply interested in their stories and, always, ready to come to their defense. Locally, the word spread and his little native artifacts' shop became known as a place where a "good British" would pay fair prices for crafts, advise on western ways and, above all, help when help was needed.

Macpherson (never Mac, "only rude Americans call me that, once, and once only") and Pero were sitting in his little office when the shop lady assistant came in to say there was a strange gentleman to see him. Macpherson told her to send him in while he reached under the desk for his Army Special

Forces' knife. The man who walked in was about forty. His hair and skin were freshly clean—his shirt was clean but not pressed. He had a tie on that was poorly knotted and the suit had definitely seen better days. He had come to ask for help. He had shoes, but no laces and no socks.

Mr. Mturbai had hitchhiked from Addis Ababa, the capital of Ethiopia. As the Ethiopian Foreign Minister, he was to attend a UN conference in Nairobi to determine why the food aid raised by happy singers in America had been left on the docks and had been, subsequently, sold off to line officials' pockets. He had come to be chastised. He knew it.

But Mr. Mturbai had come to tell the truth that no one wanted to hear. After decades of well-intentioned CARE and church aid, they had saved eighty percent of babies born, but no one had told them not to go on having a baby every year. Every woman of age always had done so for millennia, one child a year expecting eighty percent of them to die before maturity. So instead, the modern population steadily grew until there was famine. The UN stepped in and cut down the Commiphora forest and planted rice, because there was so much rain. Without the trees, the rain stopped. They received aid to plant wheat. The monsoon rains washed the root-less top soil into the Indian Ocean. Famine ensued. Geldof and pop singers recorded a happy unifying song. The West felt its conscience assuaged. Some camp people got rice and survived. Famine kills the very young or the very old. Any that survived were of breeding age. Still the missionaries and aid groups did not council family planning. In the starvation camps, women had malnourished babies. No one sang the song the next year, so babies died, along with the parents. Geldof got a Knighthood— he deserved it for his intentions, not for the end result.

Mr. Mturbai wasn't angry. He was African, used to Mother Nature taking her children and women "back to the soil." He wasn't emotional about that. He was emotional about being called a crook for profiteering off western rice aid. He stood there, impoverished, asking for bus fare so he could get to the last day of the conference and address people on fat salaries and tell them that next time you send rice, send trucks and gasoline to take it to the people. Oh, and while you are at it, if you really want to save these people, take them to your homes, your land, because the land they live on has gone, 300 feet down off the Kenya coast, red muck choking the coral there too, by the way.

Macpherson gave him the taxi fare and food for a meal and told him he could sleep in the shop if he wanted and gave him a set of keys. Mr. Mturbai wept. Not for himself, but for the irony of it all. Here was an ex-Colonial man with a little hole-in-the-wall shop helping when others wouldn't. The people he was going to be reprimanded by were living in white gin palaces, driving Mercedes, manicured lawns, getting fat UN and NGO salaries, and they, he knew, would not listen nor care.

Pero had his travel bag with him. Pero reached in and gave him a pair of socks, a pair of desert boots, and what cash he had in dollars, "for your trip home."

"Asanti, asanti sana, bwana." Thank you, Sir.

"Tell them the truth, even if they don't like it."

"I promise, I will." They shook hands.

The little man was assassinated two years later walking his kid to school. He still didn't own a car, let alone a Mercedes. Pero saw the photo in the paper. There he lay, feet splayed. Pero noticed he was wearing socks. Poor compensation.

Pero woke from his reverie as the Chief's Humber started first try with a backfire. With the one-sock chauffeur driving, the car did a nine-point turn to go back the way it had come, carefully avoiding the thorn bushes either side of the narrow clearing, a good precaution because of the bald tires. The

Toyota flatbed followed in the dust, their minder's face peering back at Pero, looking totally miserable because Simon's bones were bouncing at his feet.

"Mbuno, strap the glider down properly on that Land Rover while I get something out of this one." Pero opened the rear door of the long-wheelbase Land Rover and unlocked the toolbox again. Inside were his papers, private equipment, and revolver. It was only a small police .38. Pero took out binoculars and handed them to Mbuno. With his eyes, he could keep better watch than Pero. "We'll take this one. We'll come back for the other Land Rover later. I'll drive Mbuno—you sit up top and keep watch."

"So, am I watching for the other car, bwana?" That was so like Mbuno and somehow very comforting. Pero had used him now on over ten shoots in Kenya and Tanzania. He was old—must be over sixty-five—but was still the most trusted, experienced, white-hunter guide. Nothing happened in the bush that he didn't observe, nothing.

"Yes, Mbuno, I don't know where they went or who they were, but there is danger with them nearby."

Mbuno didn't reply, his face showed nothing, his eyes searched Pero's. If he knew about the *shufti* or guessed that Simon had not died accidentally, he could say, but old elephant hunters knew how to keep silent in the bush. Time would show Mbuno what he needed to know and do.

Pero drove off, engine revs low, stopping frequently, heading back towards the northeast of the Ajuran Plateau. Pero wanted to find the mystery tracks. Twice he thought he had spotted them, twice Mbuno told Pero they were their other Land Rover's tires. Pero couldn't find a trace of the mystery vehicle, nor could Mbuno. "Are they still here anywhere, do you think Mbuno?" They were proceeding slowly, carefully.

"No, Mr. Pero, they are gone. There is no foreign thing here now." He meant nothing un-natural, no animal disturbance to reveal the presence of a human. Suddenly: "Here," he pointed at what looked like nothing but flat soil, "Stop, you can see something was dragged, maybe a sack." So, they had covered their tracks. To catch these *shufti* who had killed Simon, Pero would need to find a way to smoke them out to spot them again. Or maybe they were best left alone. Pero privately voted for the latter, if only he knew where they came from, exactly who they were. They were clearly up to no good and spotting something unusual was exactly what his State Department contact had asked him to do, if possible. No one had said anything about a killing. The risks were perhaps too great.

They drove back to the other Land Rover and Mbuno climbed down, handed Pero the 'binos and took the wheel of the other car. An expert bush navigator, Mbuno knew to lead. So, Pero shut every door, roof trap, and window, locked his gear and gun away, and followed, heat mounting in the airless cabin, in Mbuno's dusty wake. They made their camp an hour later.

"Where's the body, Pero?" Heep and the team looked anxious. Heep would be. It was he who had convinced Simon to come up here with them. Simon normally only flew nearer the National Park in Nairobi. The Ajuran Plateau was more dangerous, had sudden air currents. Now Simon was dead and Heep would have to explain to Simon's three-year girlfriend, Margarie, a Princeton grad studying the movement of big raptors under Simon's tutelage. Her parting words had been on the phone to Heep—not to Pero, thank goodness—"Keep him safe Mr. Heeper, won't you?"

Pero was contrite, "Sorry Heep, the Chief's got the body, what's left of it. The hyenas and vultures did a pretty thorough job. Just too many of them. I'll ask the Chief later what he is going to do with it. Pretty gruesome."

"Damn." A pause, then, "Get footage of the vultures?" That was Heep, always the visualist, using work to mask his emotions. Pero knew he was hurting, Pero could see it in his eyes after so many years.

"Yeah, with the minicam. It's all yours." He handed it over "But somehow I can't see that bitch in LA wanting to view that tape." Heep knew what Pero meant. The "bitch" was one Nancy McEwen, appointed by the friendly boss of the television division. He made her their corporate liaison, the production coordinator, a corporate "minder" by any other title. He had no idea how useless she was.

Three weeks ago, her parting words of ignorance to Pero were "I've been to Africa, I know you don't need any cash, use your American Express to pay the locals and bill us." Yeah, give Chief Methenge an Amex card and he'd put it to good use all right. It made a handy scraper when he squatted in the bush. The thought of her looking at vultures and hyenas ripping a carcass to bits—especially a human one—conjured up images of a dead faint and accusations of abuse. She was a vindictive bitch to boot. Maybe Pero would be happy to pay her back a little, but later, if there was a later. Pero was still unnerved.

Heep was still all work, no outward emotion, "Pero, what are we going to do? Simon's footage, ours—I've reviewed it all—is great, especially the flight stuff and all. Can we use any of this? Should we use any of this?"

"Heep, let's leave that for later. Right now, I've got to get to the Chief's hut, negotiate another huge fine, see if I can prevent the minder from coming back here tonight with the police or, worse, calling Nairobi on the Chief's ham radio and yanking permits. Later, tonight, we can review the tapes and decide. My first guess is that Simon's accident is a great story. And we will, I promise, pay his family the insurance we got for him. You had better tell LA on the satellite phone while I'm away, and have them put in the claim. You know this will be in the papers by tomorrow. The Chief wants the publicity for helping us recover the tragic accident, which will be his spin. Tell LA they must avoid forceful negative discussions via the US Embassy with the police about insurance claims—at least until we're safely out of here—or else we may find ourselves in a long-distance problem." Heep knew what Pero meant. A few years before, when US aid was being withheld from Kenya's crooked President Moi, the Kenyan authorities "rescued" a crew shooting a big-budget Hollywood film and kept them incommunicado until the State Department negotiated their safe return. Of course, Moi got his Swiss bank account transfer before the star, Gina Maddox, even stepped on the plane to go home. Heep and Pero were way too small fish to merit such State Department support—Pero had no illusions, and he was sure Heep knew it too. *Add to that*, Pero thought, *if Nairobi gets any whiff that someone at State wanted us to scout for them up here . . .*

Later that night, with the Chief having been contented with another $500 of their production money, Heep and Pero were alone in his six-man, tan-colored tent, the thin nylon showing their shadows outside. On the satellite phone, Heep had put in the claim for Simon's accidental death. The bitch was none too happy. Neither man really cared about her. So, after they shut the satellite phone down, they squatted and viewed the footage, earphones in place, and nodded silently to each other, keeping the unasked questions and emotions at bay. Ruis and Priit had seen most of the footage earlier . . . but now Heep and Pero were viewing the secret minicam tape that Pero had shot. Heep looked worried. They took off their headsets as the footage went to blank.

Almost silently, he said, "You never tried to protect the body. You removed the glider, but didn't try and save him."

"He was dead, it didn't hurt him. I wanted to get his family the insurance, Heep."

"What do you mean?"

Pero put his hand in his pocket and extracted an unwashed flattened bullet, which Pero had found in the body, stuck to the inside of the pelvis. Pero showed it to him.

"Pero . . ." a quiet pause, "Pero, who did this?" Heep had covered war zones throughout his sixty years; he knew a flattened death bullet when he saw one.

Pero kept his voice low, "That car coming from the east, remember? I don't know who, why, or how. But it must have been them—no one else was around. If the claim or police report says he was shot, then there will be an inquiry for years and Simon's family would never see a dime. This way its accidental death, not an act of some imaginary war, and our production insurance will pay up, no problem."

"Okay, I understand. But it's time to leave, right now—this is not our battle up here. The Ethiopian *shufti* kill first and ask questions later." Heep knew *shufti* are usually army deserters, trained, but off the leash, dangerous, desperate. They are feared, with good reason: desperate men using violence as their only means of survival. Heep knew that the Sudan, Somalia, Ethiopia, and the Dafur were all riddled with them. "Anyway, the shot we have is useless without that backdrop of the cliff and Simon gliding."

"Okay, I agree and I'd already decided we'll break camp tomorrow morning and go, forget Ol Jogi, and go straight to Pangani to the croc farm, okay?" The end of their filming trip was planned for the seaside town of Pangani in Tanzania. Pero clearly wanted to move on, out of Kenya and the grasp of the local law, just in case.

Heep clearly understood the reason for a quick country departure as well, "You already in contact with the people there? How about the SeaSled I asked for?"

"Yes, I called Flamingo Travel and Schenkers from the Chief's on his ham radio phone. Everything is moved up, rescheduled." Pangani was opposite Pemba Island on the coast. It was remote, tropical, lush and boasted a great hotel. The croc farm there had huge crocs they could film, and it was definitely safer to be out of Kenya if things got hot.

"Is the change in schedule also okay with her?"

Pero knew whom he meant. Their on-camera expert could have been angry to have her schedule rearranged. "Well, she's made a few conditions . . . but she'll be okay, it's only a week, she'll still get back to Nairobi in time. The camp is thrilled to have us early, the tourists cut their numbers down, and there are four tents empty." To end the conversation and take responsibility away from his friend, Pero added an order, "And, Heep, it's done, over with, my responsibility. I've arranged for Simon's body to be sent down to Nairobi by the Chief—I paid the fare already. And the Cessna arrives tomorrow late morning. That's it, got it?"

Heep stood, pushing his hands on knees, looking tired: "Yes, okay, you're the boss, that's fine, well done Pero, as always. We'll leave first thing. Have you considered Mbuno?" Heep knew they could not leave at night and that gave Pero time to talk things over with Mbuno. Not taking Mbuno into their confidence was a bad idea, a really bad idea when Mbuno was the only one there with expertise dealing with bush danger. The way Heep saw it, and felt Pero should as well, their security was dependent on a would-be attacker seeing their two armed guards here in the National Park, even if they were barely armed. At night outside of the Park (with its Ranger patrols), they would be ambushed before they got onto the main road. Mbuno might be the only warning they would have, nobody could fool him in the wild, Heep was sure of that.

Daytime in the huge Park, as large as it was, they would have no problem with visibility over ten miles in every direction, but night was definitely not for travel. Their two armed escorts, left behind always at camp, could protect them here at night, standing by a roaring campfire, in plain view—providing Mbuno scouted the area for ambushes out of campfire light.

- After Nairobi, they wouldn't need guards anymore anyway.

Thinking of his unfinished special task for State, hating that their trip and Simon's death were all for nothing, Pero decided he needed to push their luck, just a little, but only in daylight and as safe as possible for the crew and then get the hell out. It was time to put a seed of a thought in Heep's head, see if Heep agreed. "Pity we didn't get the soaring shot from down below. It would have done Simon proud to have his last flight on network TV. As it is, you're right, the execs are sure to can the whole segment—without that shot."

Leaving Heep thinking, Pero went in search of Mbuno. Not finding him in the other tent or either Land Rover, he called out softly. The two guards, backs to the fire, pretending to be alert, were shocked into shouldering their rifles as Mbuno materialized just out of firelight. "*Mimi ni tu ni,*" (it is only me) he called out and they relaxed their arms.

Pero motioned Mbuno away from the men and sat on a boulder, "Okay if we talk, Mbuno?"

"*Ndiyo bwana*" (yes boss), Mbuno squatted next to the rock, eyes on the bush, not watching Pero. He took a sharp breath, "I know."

It was a statement of fact, not less than Pero expected, but Pero had to be sure just what Mbuno knew. "Know what?"

"Mr. Simon did not fall, he was killed."

Pero nodded and handed the bullet to Mbuno. "I had to cover it up."

"Ndiyo, big trouble if you had not. This Park is not safe. We should leave before troubles come back." Pero was not surprised Mbuno had put the pieces together. The clues were sparse and the odds were that *shufti* were the only explanation.

"We're going to Pangani tomorrow. The Cessna's coming late morning, in broad daylight, with the Chief's blessing."

Mbuno was silent, then turned to face Pero, "Then we only need to guard against the night, the very bad men who may still come. I have seen this before. The Troubles." And with that, he stood and walked into the darkness, picking up his pace to a trot, disappearing deep into the gloom. Pero sat for a while longer and wondered why Mbuno had called them "very bad men" and not *shufti*. Also, his mention of the Troubles, the time of the Mau Mau Revolt and carnage, really had Pero worried. Just what had they gotten into up here? A second thought popped into his head, exactly what was Mbuno's experience with the Troubles? One thing he was certain of, they were not going to miss that flight tomorrow.

Suddenly he regretted his hint to Heep. If Mbuno was this much on guard, matters might be worse than Pero had calculated. With a shiver, perhaps the desert night cold, he realized that, no matter what, he had to get the crew to safety.

CHAPTER 4

Ramu

The next morning they were up and packed, ready to go, especially early. Heep seemed anxious about something. He told Pero he needed one more shot and a big favor.

That's how Pero knew he would get to the top of the Ajuran Plateau one more time, as he himself had hinted and then regretted. Pero had dreamt that night that Simon's killers saw Simon soaring, so they must have thought Simon would have seen them. And now here Pero was, caught in his own subterfuge, having to agree with Heep, one more shot was called for not to waste Simon's life.

They drove in the first rays of daylight. At the base of the Ajuran Plateau, going in the opposite direction of "down to Nairobi" (as the minder had repeatedly insisted), Heep stopped the Land Rover and prepared the Betacam to record a descent of the glider. In the other Land Rover, Mbuno driving, Pero sat with the spare orange crew anorak on wondering how he had gotten himself into this mess. He knew he only had himself to blame. Still, it was daylight, surely the Chief had gotten out the word to any Gurreh bandits or *shufti* to leave the crew alone, everything should be all right. Pero carefully avoided thinking about the choice of weapon, a sniper's bullet, hardly the weapon for a poacher or ex-soldier.

Pero had done a few jumps off the side of a Swiss mountain, near Chateau d'Oex, in a similar hang glider. The height didn't worry Pero. The updrafts and distance to a safe landing did. Also, he knew that there was no way he could, or would, be able to fly as smoothly as Simon had. Surely, the footage couldn't match, would it? Was it pointless to risk his life for a video shot, for some messed-up concept of videographic integrity for a TV show?

But then again, there was the question of possibly identifying who had killed Simon. Pero thought if he could just spot something, anything unusual, round the backside of the Ajuran Plateau again, to see if there was a camp back there he had missed spotting or someone that had triggered that prompted the shooting of poor Simon . . . but why shoot? What purpose did it serve except to draw attention to the shooters? They couldn't know Pero had covered up their crime and why. Still, he also worried they might be prepared to kill again, so Pero asked himself the same question: *Why do this, Pero?* He knew why, it was his sense of fair play, of justice. Simon's death should not be a total waste. And besides, if he did spot something, and told State, maybe they could investigate or inform the proper Kenyan authorities and catch Simon's killer.

As they started the Land Rover up the rutted track up the side of the Ajuran Plateau, Pero left the driving to Mbuno and busied himself with the binoculars out the top hatch, looking north, scanning for any signs of a camp. The noise of their Land Rover would not carry far in this terrain. Sand and low scrub are natural sound-deadeners, so unless the *shufti* were close, which Pero doubted, they shouldn't hear them. Their dust trail was another matter. Anyway, yesterday their vehicle had showed up over an hour after they started the climb. So, Pero kept scanning assuming Mbuno and he'd have time before whoever was out there were aware of their presence. *Get up, get off, all done,* Pero thought to himself. That is, if there was really anybody out there.

And why would they have come looking, shooting at Simon? And why, if they were camped there to the north, just in Ethiopia, would they track and then shoot at Simon on the other side of the mountain inside Kenya? Pero had no answers, just worries.

A distant newspaper memory nagged its way into his thoughts. The problem was satellites at the equator. In orbit, they traveled in waves across the face of the Earth. They passed the equatorial regions between four and sixteen times a day, but passing over the equator, they could not be maneuvered nor have an angled look-down and therefore showed little oblique detail. Passing over nomadic camps, dug in the uni-color sand, you had to be extraordinarily lucky to ever spot an encampment at all. Last time the State Department thought they did, they told President Clinton and he bombed the desert in the Sudan, convinced the three nomads they had seen must be the al-Qaida camp they were looking for. Result? Four camels died. Cost? One Tomahawk missile and lots of red faces at State. On-site inspection was now demanded by the White House.

Oh, lord, thought Pero, *that's why they wanted me to look. They think something is there.*

Pero kept looking. Mbuno shot Pero a glance.

"Bwana, nothing there to see this morning, big game all gone west and the sun is in your eyes. I think too many hunters looking for nyama over there." He pointed east. "*Nyama* are not stupid." *Nyama* was the Swahili word for game—and meat. It is one and the same to the tribes' people . . . it's what makes the term "poaching" a Western concept.

"Mbuno, I'm looking for that car from yesterday. I wondered if they might be here again. If I could just spot them . . ."

"If they are here bwana, we must go. Shufti here very bad."

"Agreed. After you drop me on the top, you should leave immediately to make sure they don't have time to zero in on you."

"Zero, bwana?"

"Spot you."

"Oh, they have. They will be deciding if they want to come. This Land Rover is a thing to steal."

"They've seen us?"

"Oh yes, if they are there, they have seen us. I would see us." It was that simple.

Pero sat down, pensive. "Mbuno, if we get to the top and we see them or their car, you must decide if you want to risk driving down. We can radio for help."

In his calm way, Mbuno responded with authority, "Yes, bwana. We will have a look just now." And with that, they crested the top of the ridge. The flat plateau was, thankfully, empty. Pero had been half-ready to scoot back down ahead of the *shufti* if they rolled up on them up here. The two men got out of the Land Rover. Mbuno climbed on top of the Land Rover and used the binoculars.

Pero took down the glider, opened the triangles, and fastened the stays. Off the rear seat, Pero picked up the harness, Simon's spare one, clipped himself in, and looked up, "Mbuno, have you spotted anything?" Mbuno was still standing above the open hatch, looking around and around, like some sort of lighthouse keeper.

"Not clearly, Mr. Pero. Yes, there is something there . . ." he pointed. "Just there beyond the yellow earth." There was a patch of sulfur earth, in contrast to the red soil of the region. Volcanic residue, no doubt.

Pero took the proffered binoculars and peered. He could see nothing. Pero gave them back to Mbuno. "What do you see?"

He peered intently for a few moments. "They are maybe twenty moving, they have many cars, they have made mounds, there are no bushes on top. There is no car moving. It is confusing."

Although still early, an hour past first sunup, and the air was clear, Pero was still amazed at his vision. "Okay, Mbuno, take the Land Rover and get back down the track. When you get there, tell Mr. Heep to be ready to leave and roll fast. Tell our two guards to put their single bullet" (a .303, one bullet issued per guard, on police orders) "in the chamber and to be ready to protect the crew. I'll jump from here and get down as fast as possible."

"*Ndiyo bwana, tafadali*," (yes boss, thank you), "but not down too fast." He made a down swing with his hand, smiled and got in the driver's seat, started the motor and left. Pero watched him go, sadly. *Why sad? I don't know. Yes, I do, there is only one way out of here—off that damn edge.*

As soon as the Land Rover was off the mesa, Pero stepped into the triangle and clipped up. Pero had prepped Simon and watched him do this. "It's C of G neutral," Simon had told Pero. C of G is center of gravity to pilots. Too far forward and you cannot pull up. Too far back (aft) and you cannot control the aircraft. The only plane Pero had ever flown solo was a Cessna in California over the Sierra's near Edwards Air Force Base, through loads of thermals. Pero hoped that training would help here. Simon had leapt off the edge, gone down, but soon was rising again, way over their heads. He had had to fly the currents to get back into camera shot.

Today, it was a little earlier in the daytime. Pero needed to wait for the sun to match the light. It was cloudless here again, so that was okay. Pero had time to think, standing there on the cliff's edge holding the glider's rudder bar.

He keyed the walkie-talkie, "Heep, tell me when you think the light is right."

Heep's voice came back strained, "You sure about this buddy?"

Pero summoned what was left of his courage and firmly replied, "Land Rover on the way down, I'm set, ready. Out."

Twenty of them, eh? Twenty armed to the teeth shufti hell-bent on violence and pillage? Or twenty al-Qaida-affiliated terrorists out of Ethiopia, armed to the teeth and hell-bent on violence to keep their position secret? Either way, this wasn't his idea of an adventure anymore. Pero had gotten up here on the excuse of saving Simon's last moment of fame, with a side intention of spotting someone he could turn in for Simon's death—but now came the hard part: a leap into vulture history with a good landing (any landing you can walk away from is a good landing)—or a suicide plunge with no one the wiser, ever. *Ah well, to hell with it.*

Heep called ready on the walkie-talkie and then called "Action!"

It had seemed the thing to do in the circumstances after yesterday's disaster. He ran forward and was dumbfounded to be going up, not down. Now, prone as Pero was, there was only the ground beneath and he pulled the bar and dropped the nose of the hang glider down. His peripheral vision of soaring giants on each side, to guide the long descent, tracing the face of the cliff was breathtaking. The vultures above and to either side first told him he was in trouble—as well as the uncomfortable sensation of fear between his legs. Heights had that effect on Pero, especially as he was primordially unsure the flimsy blue wings of the hang glider would, or could, really fly. Added to which, as there were no vultures below, he felt sure they clearly expected him to plummet straight down any moment now. All this clicked through his brain in an instant, snap, snap, snap, reeling off reasons why this flight might still be really a bad idea.

Watching Simon yesterday morning from the safety of the cliff top, it all looked so calm, so serene. Now white-hot fear made every muscle in his body tight as wood and just as inflexible. Pero had had trouble lifting his legs into the pouch at the back, to fully swing into the prone position, just as another thermal caught the kite and lifted Pero like an express elevator. Pero could see way over the mesa now, and from the extra hundred feet altitude, the *shufti* encampment was plainly visible. Simon must have seen it, or they saw him high up, soaring and thought he had spied them. Pero knew right then that's what had triggered them. He was sure it would trigger them now as well. With the sun reflecting off the aluminum tubes and the blue of the wings, Pero was like a huge billboard proclaiming, "I see you!"

He keyed the mike, "Heep, get ready to leave, pack up and get set to go."

Heep sounded worried, "What's the matter?"

"I'm okay, but you'll only have one shot of this, I cannot stay up here, coming down now, get ready, one shot that's all you have, then straight to the airport. Copy?"

"Copy. Careful."

The lead vultures, sensing his amateur status, and maybe his nerves, really took a dislike to Pero and four or five banged on the wings and fabric hard enough to make him stupidly feint the bar away, which started a spiral down. When Pero got it leveled out, he was halfway down and, from where Heep was, Pero would be framed up against the cliff. Pero knew Heep needed the shot of the kite emerging from the cliff with the vultures in tandem, against the blue sky. The vultures camouflage simply made them disappear against the mottled rock face. So, Pero pushed the bar to the left and circled out, moving now towards the western cliff edge, where Simon had been flying. Pero took a straight line and the cliff disappeared off his right shoulder.

Soon, Heep called in his ear, the relief in his voice obvious: "Got it, come on down safely. Over." Pero also caught the excitement in his voice. It was always there, when the shot was just right. Pero smiled, feeling safer because he wasn't exposed over the top of the mesa now, so he angled the hang glider back towards Heep's position, east, and then Pero spotted them. There was one dust trail from a car being driven at speed, followed, a mile or two back, by a larger dust cloud, maybe two to four vehicles. One dust cloud looked very large, larger than a Land Rover, maybe a truck. A truck meant troops. In the sun's early heat shimmer, Pero could not be sure. Pero needed to warn Heep.

Holding the bar with one hand, Pero reached for the mike key on the walkie-talkie and blipped it twice. "Heep here, what's up? Over."

"Heep, danger, cars approaching. Load up, rev up, Mbuno's coming in fast. Possibly four *shufti*, repeat four *shufti* cars. Over."

"*Godverdomme!* Got it. Land in here close . . ." he cut out. Pero could see him place the Betacam in its gray case, slap the lid and hinges shut. He must have been yelling orders because everyone was running around to get things buttoned up. Soaring above them, Pero heard some of it, unintelligible, but authoritative. Pero resumed two-handed flying, heading for the Land Rover. Pero needed to slow this thing down. If Pero pushed too hard on the bar, the kite would soar up, not down, and then stall, dive and swoop. Like learning to drive a stick shift car, Pero thought, Pero had the hiccup thing going. So then, in desperation, Pero decided to simply make tight turns, to the right Pero thought, tight turns bleeding airspeed, causing the thing to go down.

It did. What Pero had not anticipated was that it went down fast. Pero struggled to get his feet out of the pouch just as he skimmed a few bushes, moved the bar the wrong way, stalled, pitched up, then down, and planted the nose. Aluminum tubing doesn't like a speed-planting even in soft sand. It bent up. Strapped in, Pero rolled over the top, felt the tube snap under his hands, felt the slice of his fingers, and prepared for impact, head first.

Wouldn't it be ironic if I broke my damn neck? he thought. *No bullets for Pero, simple stupidity will do.*

The helmet bounced off a fist-sized rock and Pero came to rest, tangled in a mess of straps with his backside sending severe agony signals to the brain. Pero unclipped the waist belt and the shoulder straps and fell clear, bottom down, into a thorn bush. Oh yes, it hurt. Two-inch African thorns make Mojave Desert cactus thorns feel like nothing.

"You okay, Pero?" It was Ruis.

"Yeah, get me out of here." Ruis gave Pero a hand up. Pero felt some of the thorns staying behind, sliding out of his skin.

"That's going to hurt." Ruis chuckled, the helpful bastard. "Come on, let's go."

They sprinted for the Land Rover, Ruis tugging Pero along. Pero could see Mbuno about 200 yards away and, way behind him, no match for his bush driving skills, a cloud of *shufti* followed. "Heep, you take the front Land Rover, I'll follow with the guards. Give me the satellite phone."

He handed it over, "No way, Pero—let them deal with it. Come with us."

The minder said out the Land Rover window, "We leave now. Right now!"

"Heep, you have the footage, we'll be right behind you." The professional in Heep listened, shrugged, and piled in the already revving Land Rover. As they started off, Mbuno slid to a halt. He started to get out, making his way towards the wrecked hang glider. "Mbuno, leave it, it's finished. Let's go. You drive." And to the soldiers, looking increasingly worried. "You two, stand up in the hatch and point your guns at them. Do not fire, you understand, do not fire. Got it?"

Like twins, they both said, "Yes, bwana."

Pero jumped in the back just as Mbuno started off and got his key out, reached into the locker for the pistol and binoculars. Holding the binoculars in his right hand, Pero peered back through the dusty glass of the rear door. He did not dare put his head up through the hatch next to the Chief's guards, not with a revolver in his hand.

Watching intently, his mind raced. Years before, his friend Tom Baylor at State had warned him: "Whatever you do, nothing we ask you to do will be important enough to let anyone know you are carrying it, collecting it or whatever. If you think you are being watched, simply stop and go back to your job. Never, ever, raise suspicions." Tom had gone to the same Swiss prep school, some years ahead of Pero, graduating when Pero was just thirteen. In the years since he'd started doing these favors for State, Pero had never needed to cash in the credits he felt he was earning, credits Tom Baylor always referred to as "patriotic duty." Pero was now hoping the support he always relied on would be forthcoming if needed. "Never, ever, raise suspicions," now rang in his memory. Had they raised suspicions merely by filming? Or running from whoever was chasing them?

Pero had a decision to make. Returning to his normal profession here meant running like hell from *shufti*. They were doing that, so far all was normal. The problem was, Pero now finally figured out that these killers must have guessed that Pero knew that they had killed Simon . . . and it was not normal to have that unreported. If they had, there would have been troops landing at Ramu airport to conduct a sweep. The head of National Parks, in Nairobi, would have insisted on it. His man was shot, after all. But there were no troops, no report, no ham radio intercept from the Chief to his office in Nairobi telling them of a killing. There was a death, that was all, a reported accidental death. Did the Chief report that scavengers had eaten the carcass before it could be examined? Probably not, because it would upset Nairobi officials that he had not guarded the corpse and the Chief would get the blame.

Whoever was chasing them, they had moved so fast and professionally, it meant they weren't normally listless, undisciplined *shufti*. They were trained, active, eager. They could have been watching Simon and then Pero fly high enough to spot their encampment. *Something big was happening here, or rather there*, Pero thought. *They would not take a chance. Otherwise, if Mbuno could see them, they certainly could see the blue glider break the skyline.*

Pero knew then they were al-Shabaab—nothing else fit. The papers were full of stories of the terrorist organization operating out of western Somalia. *Shufti* would have melted away in the landscape, not al-Shabaab. Even Kenya had sent troops up against their incursions.

Pero put the binoculars in the box and reached for the satellite phone. It was not a standard model and although it operated like one, normally, it was illegal. It had a second amplitude modulator. Press 411 and you got someone Tom Baylor said would always be listening, scrambled, direct. He said it had a perfect signal, always. They listened, you spoke, they clicked off—double click—when you stopped talking. It was how you knew they had heard you.

Pocketing the revolver, Pero held the phone out the sliding side window, put in his earpiece, lifted the side arm antenna and hit the buttons; 4-1-1. It rang clearly in some far away office. It answered with a click.

"Pero Baltazar here, north of Wajir in Gurreh-Ajuran territory near Ramu. Twenty, repeat twenty spotted al-Shabaab, I think, plus vehicles, one larger, suspect truck but fast. Dug in, mounded encampment spotted near or over Kenya border. We're running for the airstrip at Ramo, they are chasing. I suppose there is nothing you can do. Local police have rifles with one round only, so if they chase us that far, well . . . okay, that's all. Over." Pero heard the promised double click and the signal went dead, the phone automatically turned off. Pero tried to turn it back on. It was dead. He checked the battery indicator, full charge. Tried to cycle it, still dead. Tom Baylor hadn't explained that 4-1-1 was a one-time call, the phone thereafter dead. *Okay then, so what's left? Let's get the hell out of here*, was all Pero was thinking.

Driving fast in desolate terrain, even on so-called prepared roads is never safe. A sudden unseen, unheard, thunderstorm can wash away a road used the day before. After two miles, Mbuno had caught and was pressing the other Land Rover to drive faster by leaning on the horn. He looked genuinely determined. He also looked angrier than Pero had ever seen him. Driving this fast in the bush is unwise, very unwise. He needed to lead, not push. So Mbuno passed the other car.

More tourists end up in the hospital because of car crashes than any other injury in Kenya. At speed, suddenly you're motoring happily along a dusty trail, the next second you're trying to stop before you plant the nose ten feet down a ravine sliced though a dry wash. If you stop in time, you ease down and ease up the other side. If the gully comes on you too fast or is too small to spot soon enough, you crash if you're a novice. Mbuno wasn't a novice. Time and again, he wrenched the wheel, applied the gas, and fishtailed into, around, past or over gullies, large and small. The Land Rover following copied Mbuno's every move.

One gulley seemed to form between the wheels, getting larger and larger. As the gap became wider than the track of the Land Rover, they slid down to the bottom, disappearing from view, wheels spinning, Mbuno's will and skill urging them forward in the very loose sand at the same time luckily making a track for the car behind. When the road started to climb, he straddled the ruts, zoomed into the clear, and pressed on. Somehow, mile after mile, he maintained forward momentum and a more or less straight line for the airport.

Suddenly, one of the two guards shouted something down and Mbuno seemed to ease up a bit.

"He says they are dropping back, they may be stopping." Pero put his head up and the guards pointed to the receding cloud. They had come about fifteen miles, the assailants were another two or three miles back, but their dust cloud was growing smaller and, as Pero watched, seemed to "puff" out. They had stopped. As Mbuno drove on, still setting a fast pace, Pero saw the dust cloud reappear, smaller than before, getting further away. Pero guessed they had turned back, but at speed.

Although the danger seemed to have passed for their crew, to keep them out of trouble Pero needed to get down to Nairobi and out again, switching countries for this shoot, letting their trail go cold. Pero was now especially glad he had booked Tanzania. If these terrorists, madmen, al-Shabaab, whatever they were, were operating just inside Kenya, then Pero didn't want to be here. These assailants now knew their crew's whereabouts, Pero was sure of that—the question remained: would they follow?

"Mbuno, they are definitely stopping or already turned around."

"Very good, bwana, we will slow down a bit. Not very much, we need to leave and you need to get that Handy of yours out of here." Like many East Africans, Mbuno had adopted the German slang name for a cell phone, the Handy.

"It's just a satellite cell phone Mbuno, like Heep's. Only it is now broken." Speaking fast English, they both knew the guards, standing in the open roof space, wind in their ears, couldn't understand them.

"Mr. Pero, we have been in the bush many times, many years. You may not lie to me. I was a tracker in the Troubles, working with Mr. Bird finding the Mau Mau." Pero had met "Bird." He was a short man, an expert White Hunter, Mr. Thomas Wilson, now a gamekeeper on a private ranch. "Bird" was his code name, given by the British authorities during the Insurrection, the deadly uprising of the slaughtering Mau Mau—which brought Jomo Kenyatta to power on a sea of blood and the threat of more to come.

Mbuno continued, "It was our job to find and report the Mau Mau. Others then killed them. If they failed, we had to kill them, or be killed and have our families killed. These . . . they are not shufti, they are Arab Mau Mau. You are doing like Mr. Bird did. Now you tell."

"Mbuno, sorry I lied. I didn't plan deliberately to place anyone in danger, I was just asked to see if I saw anything unusual. It was Simon's glider that must have tipped them off. And I only made it worse this morning. I could see their camp from up there, clearly. It was stupid, I admit."

"I told you I could see them. I warned you."

"Yes, you did, but by then I had to jump off, if only to honor Simon's last flight, to look like him. Otherwise, I haven't been scouting around—I have no idea what they are really, where they came from, or what they want. We'll avoid them, leave here, and go film in Tanzania. Those people back there were dangerous, yes, and killers, probably . . ."

He interrupted, his voice scolding, "Simon was shot with a sniper rifle, you knew."

Pero was still puzzled, "How did you know so soon?"

"Blood has a smell from inside. A neck only broken does not bleed. I could smell it before you touched the body."

Pero nodded. He figured there was no fooling Mbuno who had probably seen too much blood killing in the bush. "Okay, but look, I only pretended an accident to avoid Chief Methenge keeping us all there, unprotected—you know he only has a few soldiers. If those Arab Mau Mau as you call them attacked, Chief Methenge wouldn't stand a chance, and nor would we."

Mbuno saw the sense in this and nodded.

Pero continued, "And we're running now, what else can we do?"

Mbuno was silent for a moment, as he negotiated a boulder and an Acacia tree before bumping onto the main dirt highway towards the airport at Ramu, "If they were watching the hill this morning, then they saw me too. So I stay with you and not go home, so if they follow us or do not leave us alone . . ." he left the threat to his family unsaid. "If they follow anywhere, there will be more trouble." It was a statement of fact.

Pero knew Mbuno's wife was living in Langata, a suburb of Nairobi on Giraffe Manor grounds. Giraffe Manor was a world-renowned sanctuary for Rothschild's Giraffes, a wonderful peaceful place. "And Niamba?"

"She will be safe there at Giraffe Manor. These Arab Mau Mau do not know my name, they may follow me as a man—but they do not know who I am. But Mr. Pero, I cannot lead these people to Giraffe Manor, they will kill." Mbuno was calculating everything as a wounded animal does, as if he was leaving a spoor. He clearly assessed that there was no need to risk leading the killers to home.

"Okay, Mbuno, you can come with us to Tanzania. That okay?"

"It will do, Mr. Pero, *asanti*. But, please," in that scolding tone, "get rid of those things in that box, they are a danger now to everyone." Pero knew he was right. Once spotted, anything incriminating would make the situation worse, even if only with the proper authorities. So they stopped the car, waived the other Land Rover on, and Pero dug a hole while Mbuno led the two guards off to settle some dust with their urine. Pero broke the radio up and ripped out the memory chip and cracked it in two. Pero placed the parts and the revolver in the shallow grave. The phone battery and shells Pero threw fifteen yards away. When Mbuno returned, Pero was settling some dust of his own against the thorn tree marking their grave.

Without a comment, they piled back in and drove off. Two hours later, in the full heat of the day, they arrived at the Ramu Airstrip.

The solitary policeman was waiting impatiently. "Inspection, everybody out. Stand over there." It was going to be a hot, sweaty morning.

CHAPTER 5

Nairobi

Ramu Airstrip is both a civilian small commercial airport as well as a remote, occasional, military airbase consisting of one dirt strip, a few whitewashed rocks, and a few corrugated iron huts. The inspection demand here, so close to the porous borders with Ethiopia and Somalia, was not surprising. If they had driven up here from Nairobi they would have had to go through inspection in Wajir, six hours hard driving to the south-southwest on a pitted, rutted "highway."

What was surprising was that the Land Rover rental agency—a concession of the National Park Service run by a woman on a local camel farm—was ordered to deliver the now-empty Land Rovers for inspection. The hard cases and their soft-sided bags sat, in a jumble, in the baking sun, awaiting their plane. The empty Land Rovers were driven into the inspector's hanger, a WWII relic Nizzen-hut with a chain mail garage overhead door looking like a rusty fishing net, sagging in the middle. After they were driven into the gloom, Mbuno and Joshua sprinted out into the sun as the jail door was lowered and then padlocked.

No one was in a hurry to inspect the Land Rovers. Pero suspected that this policeman would have to conduct the inspection himself later, at his leisure. There didn't seem to be too many people about to assist him, but that didn't dampen his air of authority.

Debbie Rose, a thirty-something, parchment dry-skinned woman, tough as nails, had her arms crossed, glaring at the inspector, while her huge Rhodesian Ridgeback dog, a lion hunter by breeding, wagged his tail against her thigh in a sort of reassuring "I'm here;" pat, pat, pat. Debbie ran the rental service. She was arguing in Swahili, vehemently, about getting access to her vehicles. The amiable Joshua was now glued to her side, trying to look more manly than she, but failing miserably.

Mbuno had walked back to rejoin the crew. They could hear Debbie pointing out the obvious—she needed the mileage and a physical inspection before she could close out their contracts, get her rental money. The shoot had put up a bond (so close to an easy illegal exportation across a porous border, often renters had to put up the value of the car as a good faith bond). Pero would have been, normally, very keen to get their deposit money back. Today, he just wanted to be away from there. There was no phone up there, just a patchy radio phone, a ham station really, with a post-WWII tube transmitter. Anyway, there was no authority in Nairobi they could "get on the blower" to straighten out this police inspector. They were stuck. Arguing would only make it worse.

On top of which, their Mara Airways twin-engined Cessna 414 was absent. They were not allowed to go to the flight center to inquire, on the VHF plane radio, the plane's whereabouts. "Until we have finished an inspection of your equipment, you are not free to leave." The officious man had been serious. His use of the pronoun "we" almost comical, his authority not comical at all. Even the government stooge had nothing to offer, being careful to stand a little apart from the film crew, just in case someone was about to get arrested.

Fifty yards off, he raised his voice to Debbie in Swahili again and she turned on her heels, pivoting in the dust, in their direction. The dog growled menacingly at the officer, then followed, looking happy as Debbie patted his head, "Good boy, nasty man." He wagged his tail more eagerly. Pero got the impression he would eat the policeman if Debbie asked him. It was clear the policeman had the same thought. He kept his hand on his revolver.

Debbie was not too pleased with them either. "You bloody idiots, what have you done to make him so damn mad? He says he'll keep my Land Rovers until an inspector comes up from Nairobi. I have a group of blue-haired ladies coming tomorrow and I need those damn vehicles."

Pero shook her hand and responded, quietly, "Look, we didn't do anything. A man died in a hang-gliding accident. Chief Methenge has it all sorted out, they're getting the body sent back to Nairobi."

"Who was it?"

"Simon, the raptor fellow from the Parks Service."

"Simon Thompson? Bloody Christ, how'd the bugger do that? And why do a bloody swan dive when he's using my damn vehicles?" Debbie was known to swear a lot, it suited her hard crust.

"Your sympathy is underwhelming. He died, that's enough of a problem for any of us—and for poor Simon. Why that causes this inspector to jack-boot all around is beyond me."

"Why? Why, you bloody wanker? Because Simon was a government man, you idiot. It should have been called in to the police, not bloody Chief Methenge."

The stooge spoke up, "It is what I wanted, what I ordered, they would not let me . . ."

Heep stepped forward, feeling Pero had a hard enough day, and stared Debbie and the stooge down, "Look, back off will you two? Chief Methenge called the police, as you can see. Pero made all necessary arrangements with the Chief for the return of the body to Nairobi. There is no police matter to investigate. End of story."

"Smooth, you and your Yank, bloody smooth. You think by going to the Chief you're going to go around this guy here?" She pointed. "Up here, he's god, if he wants to be, he can call in the military, the Chief can't. You better be prepared to wait a long time. And don't make the mistake of tipping him. Last couple who did that, after they were charged with getting out of their Land Rover with no permit to do so inside the Park, spent five days in his jail." She pointed down the airstrip to a mud hut with a soldier sitting under the roof overhang in the shade. As the roof was black metal, it would be, easily, one hundred and twenty degrees in there.

Pero patted Heep on the shoulder and took over addressing Debbie, "Thanks for the advice. Let's see if the Chief can sort this out."

"Oh, and how do you expect to contact him? There is no way he," she motioned to the inspector, "will allow that."

"I owe the Chief some money. He's coming here to collect it. Right about now . . ." Pero turned a little to his left to look past the dust airstrip. Debbie turned right to see what Pero was focused on. A distant cloud was coming closer from downwind, from back the way they had come.

"Oh Christ, this'll be bloody interesting." And with that, Debbie sat on her haunches, dog by her side and prepared to wait. In parts of Africa, squatting like this means you are out of the action, if there was to be any. It's a statement of neutrality, since it is hard to take an offensive posture squatting down. The inspector, ten yards away, noted her position and followed her line of sight. He crooked his finger and called Pero over. Not the government stooge, just Pero alone.

He started yelling when Pero got close enough for spit to drop on his boots.

The gist of his argument, and Pero must admit it was sound, was that he should have been appraised before the Chief was. Pero readily agreed. Pero plead previous experience with the Chief and none with him, which was a pity Pero assured him. Mollified, a bit, he asked all the standard questions: why were they here, what was their business, where were their papers (which he was holding already), where were they going, and so on. It was routine. He knew it and so did Pero, but Pero played along, pretending to be frightened. It wasn't that hard.

Then, knowing the local pecking order was about to be sorted out for real with the pending arrival of the Chief, he asked two more questions. Taking Pero's sleeve and turning him away from his crew, he asked: "Why did you go back up the Plateau after the man died?" Pero explained the need for the cut-away, continuity, shot from below. He nodded. "Why did you race away when you were through and where is the, what do you call it," he rifled through the sheaf of papers, their in-coming manifest, "hang glider—glider—a small plane, no?"

Pero decided to stick to the story they all knew. Pero had even told the Park guards to tell the Chief on the radio as they drove the last two miles, to make sure the word would leak out. All of East Africa is like a sieve for gossip when it comes to foreigners. "We saw cars approaching, very fast. They could have been *shufti* like before. I had crashed the hang glider on landing, it's wrecked, but insured, so we left it there, and, well look, I was frightened, so we drove straight here as fast as we could."

"Did you stop at all?" It was a loaded question, but Pero had experience here from years of traveling the world. These rural officials had little imagination, they were trained to ask simple questions to which they already had answers. Pero had seen it dozens of times over the years. Think you're smarter than they are and they'll trip you up, hold you for the slightest thing on the principle that if you would lie about something small, there's a bigger lie they can discover. *It's not bad logic, really*, Pero thought.

"We only stopped once. After the two guards reported the cars had stopped following, I had to relieve myself on a nearby bush." He looked down at his shoes, "I guess I was still frightened." The two guards, listening in, were nodding.

And that seemed to satisfy the policeman. He glanced first towards the dusty, ancient, luxury Humber, now visible at the end of the landing strip, then at the film crew and lastly at the fish-netted Land Rovers. The small mountain of equipment cases held his attention for a moment and finally he glanced at Debbie and her fierce, friendly, dog and came to a conclusion. "Mr. Baltazar, you and your men are free to go, with your cases. I will inspect the vehicles more fully tomorrow morning and Miss Debbie can have them then. They are safe for now. You must pay Miss Debbie. Agreed?"

"Yes, Sir."

"Good," Taking command, "Where is your aircraft?"

"It is coming, I was assured, I may need to radio Wilson Airport." The inspector waved Pero towards the tower and Pero walked off, feeling thankful. The Humber swept past Pero and made a bee-line for the inspector's back. Pero turned to watch. Mbuno called out, "Hatari!" Almost too late the brakes locked up, the wheels caused a dramatic in-line skid, dust flew everywhere. The Humber came to a stop inches from the inspector's heels.

To his credit, the policeman never flinched; both men were indulging in pecking order displays, two proud cocks in the eternal fight, up here in this arid, barren wasteland of the Northern Territory. Pero left them to their pageantry of power and verbal argument.

Meanwhile, a sudden engine buzz told Pero the plane was already inbound. It made a very low fly-by to secure the landing strip free of someone's goats (two at the end ran off bleating), banked, dropped down and made a perfect landing. Heep was the first on board, buckling in before they had half the gear stowed, quickly followed by the government stooge. The large Cessna twin-engined 414 was capable of holding ten, they were now only six and no glider. On the steps, Pero shook hands with Debbie, all smiles after Pero assured her they'd cover the fine the inspector was sure to levy tomorrow morning, and Pero gave her driver Joshua a handsome cash tip as well. The damage to the front fender and paint scratches from the gentle roll over were, Pero promised, their expense, at least for a new wing and a little paint. Pero knew there never would be a new fender, just another battered, hammered, skin on an ancient Land Rover with a lick of fresh paint. But the billing charges would be there and she'd pocket the difference. It was the way things were sometimes this far from civilization.

The Chief, having effectively dismissed the policeman, ambled over, all smiles, and Pero handed him an envelope, which he had the good grace not to open or count. "Your Excellency, I've added a little something extra for your help with shipping the body. Chief Methenge, *salaama sana*, and thank you."

"Salaama sana mzee Pero, do not-a forget to call to the-a paper people in Nairobi."

Pero promised it was his first priority, waved goodbye, and the cabin door was raised and locked. All of them exhaled when the wheels left the dirt strip. Pero looked back down the cabin and saw Heep shake his head and, folding his arms, lower his cap to cover his eyes. Only now that his work was done up here in this wasteland, Pero knew his friend would relive his emotions. Simon was dead and, at least in part, he had some responsibility. He would be also worried about the girlfriend. From past experience Pero knew Simon's death would hit Heep hard when he let go and dropped his guard.

Pero recalled that last year, Heep's daughter in Holland told Pero that Heep has just started crying, almost for no reason. It happened as he was talking to Kim, his grandson. After Kim wanted to know why his *grootvader* was crying, Heep had lied, "It was only a teddy bear I lost . . ." According to Heep's daughter, it was some time before Heep admitted that he had lost a cameraman to a rip tide off Argentina. It wasn't Heep's fault anymore than Simon's death was now. But that truth wouldn't lessen his sorrow.

Pero turned and shouted to make myself heard from the cockpit, "Hey Heep . . ." He raised his head, "Hey, not now Heep, we're still on the job in Kenya, you can call Kim later when we're clear, out of here, okay?" Pero saw in his eyes he was wondering what Pero meant. Then he got it and scowled. He raised a middle finger in response. Pero nodded, Heep shrugged and lowered his read to rest. Pero noticed his shoulders were still set squarely. He'd be all right.

Pero turned and looked out the cockpit window.

The flight to Wilson took over two hours, but was uneventful, if you can call the usual turbulence over the Northern Territory normal and uneventful. Being bounced around in this sky was becoming second nature for Pero and the crew.

The approach to Nairobi was over Thika, the place of the famous Flame Trees, then skirting the northern part of the urban sprawl, their route cut over Ongata Rongai and turned back east to land at Wilson Airport, elevation 5,528 feet. As they passed over Nairobi, the green was palpable compared to the Northern Province. Here there were trees, bougainvillea in better neighborhoods, grass on medians, and bush vegetation on every non-built-up plot. Just a few decades ago, there were giraffes walking down the main street, a century before that virtually nothing but the fresh water well Nairobi was named for.

Nairobi was once only a stop for the camel caravans and, later, for the steam trains needing water coming from Mombasa on their way to the green Mt. Kenya slopes (where the Kikuyu grew ninety percent of the crops for British Colonial Africa) or to the 1920s coffee and tea plantations of the Maasai Plain in Langata where the Blixens famously made their home.

Now, there were houses everywhere instead of open farmland. A country of under one million in 1925 expanded to twenty-five million in 1988. Once the population growth rate exceeded five percent per year, officials stopped guessing on the future. Where there had been giraffes in Nairobi now there was gridlock, belching car fumes and crowds—all packed in; beggars, peddlers, petty thieves, open air markets, open wall shops, exotic restaurants, light industry, car parks, chrome luxury stores and, ever a driving force, tourist hotels and shops. The architecture was small two-story remnants of the colonial "glory days" followed by towering skyscrapers—planned and financed by Scandinavians—looking totally out of place but for a smooth hue and coating to make them look "African"; namely brown pebbledash, hardly natural looking at all. And, never to be outdone for bad taste, German charities and conglomerates had poured concrete business office bunkers, many stories high, all angles, jutting gray blocks and, of course, glass, lots of glass to necessitate air-conditioning. The hotels were cookie-cutter modern structures except for three: the Stanley, which was Hemingway's and Holden's old haunt, now decidedly seedy but authentic; the InterContinental, which resembled something from the 1950s in Miami Beach; and the Norfolk with its low two-story almost-on-safari feel, set in gardens.

All this urban sprawl was waiting for them, every crew member knew, as their plane skimmed over rooftops, made a fast touchdown, and pulled up to the Mara Airways terminal, next to three other similar Cessnas, two Cessna Caravans, and three Beech Barons—all taking on or disgorging sun-burnt tourists and Samsonite luggage for their trip to or from the bush. The airport was busy. It usually was. Taxis, *matatus* (converted pickups or small buses loaded with passengers, up to three times the normal capacity by weight), dusty Land Rovers, shiny rich tourists' Range Rovers, or Toyota Land Cruisers, private station wagons (all white Peugeots, Toyotas, or Nissans), and the ubiquitous zebra-painted minivans that tourists thought gave them "an authentic African experience" as they peered, carsick, through the dusty glass at animals in tame National Parks. On a good day, a pair of lions in Amboseli National Park or the Maasai Mara Reserve would have as many as twenty of these tourist buses all lined up, everyone gawking, thrilled at the "wild" lions. The lions, meanwhile, were thoroughly used to mankind and would scavenge the Park dustbins at night for human food leftovers.

During the flight down from Ramu, Pero radioed the tower at Wilson and asked for a phone patch to the InterContinental Hotel. Mr. Janardan, the under-manager, who Pero had known for fifteen years, was more than willing to accommodate their needs of four rooms, all adjoining. Again, on the radio, the Mara Airways people learned that Pero wanted to retain the plane overnight, loaded as it was, ready for departure tomorrow in the early morning for Pangani on the coast in Tanzania. They had agreed, after a little wrangling over the "wait fee."

When they landed, Pero paid off the stooge. He was pleased to have been flown back instead of waiting for the weekly flight. Pero gave him his finder's bonuses as well as a handsome tip and, because they might need him sometime in the future, called him by name. Pero assured him they'd be writing a letter of praise to his superiors. Mbuno, shaking his head, listening to Pero being so nice to the stooge, went off to arrange transportation.

Pero told the crew to unpack and then pack only an essential overnight bag and turned the plane, under security, over to the charter people to pre-submit their forms and gear to customs. Paperwork and customs kept Pero, Ruis, and Priit busy, so Pero had asked Heep to use the use the Mara Airways office phone to talk to their travel agents about their visas and, if he wouldn't mind, to give a call to the office in LA.

When Heep was done with Flamingo Tours, he came back onto the tarmac where Pero was closing and sealing the last camera case with the inspector and took over the reloading of the aircraft while Pero went inside. Sheryl, the Mara Airways booking agent, and Pero arranged flight fees, transfer fees, stamp duty, billing, and loading/unloading. Sheryl was all bubbly, twiddling her gold cross, and cheeks flushed with excitement. By way of warming her up—because Pero had a flight change to arrange with the airline—he asked her what was so exciting, although Pero had already guessed.

"The reverend Jimmy Threte is coming very soon. He'll be addressing us in Elizabeth Park, just like the Pope, on Sunday at a *Meeting on the Hill*. He's my pastor from heaven," she said, using that catch phrase from Threte's TV show, aired in over sixty countries. Pero had heard him, often, on the radio of Nairobi taxis as they blared past, slowly, in traffic. "One Pastor for the World, One Pastor from Heaven," the slogans repeated, and repeated. It was mind-numbing. Sheryl, on the other hand, was really excited. Having one of the most powerful preachers on earth as your "personal pastor" was heady stuff. For Pero, it was perfect. It was how Pero was going to get Sheryl to agree to his special request. Pero had to bait the hook.

Pero congratulated Sheryl on her exciting week ahead and then explained there would be another thirty-five kilos of equipment going down with them—plus one passenger. The paperwork would come from Schenker this afternoon, Pero assured her. She knew the import agent Schenker. Everyone in East Africa did.

A Swiss German-origin company, they were, simply, the best. They were honest and very (how shall Pero put this?) reliably anal. Paperwork in Africa needs to be correct, in triplicate. The film companies always used them—or another at their peril. Tom Baylor said the State Department also used them, told Pero he could count on that. From Sheryl's desk phone, Pero called their Mr. Prinzle and complimented him on his new agent, the one who had met them at Nairobi Airport.

"Thank you, and your gift was most generous." Mr. Prinzle asked, "Was the private shipment in order?" Pero assured him it was. "Ah, that's interesting because the same shipper has sent a replacement shipment arriving tonight. Will you be needing it, or is it a mistake?"

"I did lose the last contents, filming was a bit rough up north, so I am glad they sent another. Can you have it here tomorrow at the airport? Mara Airways, early in the A.M.?"

"Yes, of course."

Pero then asked him if Schenkers had indeed received the equipment shipment from London they had discussed the day before. Mr. Prinzle confirmed, in his Swiss accent, that the special camera had already arrived and that the special batteries would arrive on the red-eye British Airways flight tomorrow morning. He assured Pero everything could be on one bill of lading, not two, and would be at Wilson in time for tomorrow's departure. He would clear customs personally and transfer the goods, under bond (he was licensed and bonded), to the plane, thereby avoiding the Kenya duty as they were bound for Tanzania. Pero didn't ask him how he knew that. Mara or perhaps Flamingo must have told him.

Pero signed off, handed the receiver to Sheryl, and leaned his elbows on the glass-topped counter and smiled. Doing business with the attractive Sheryl was easy. He went through the next day's loading schedule in detail until she looked a little bored. Although she was happy enough with those instructions, she was not happy with his final request. Pero wanted to change the flight plan with a stop in Arusha and then on to Pangani. Sheryl was not amused at all, "An extra stop would look suspicious to the Tanzanian customs' people." *Too damn right, it will,* he thought, *but I don't want to tip off anybody about where we are going, just in case.*

"Sheryl, please, I don't want you to file a flight plan for Arusha. The passenger we'll be taking all the way to Pangani has to make a quick stop to give testimony at the trials in Arusha in the late morning." Everyone local knew that the Crimes Against Humanity Trials were in their third go-round for Central Africa (Rwandan genocide), with a few of the Sudan Darfur remnants thrown in. The trials were dragging out, seemingly forever. "Sheryl, please look, I need this woman for our shoot in Pangani. It was the only way I could get her to come, when I moved up our schedule, if I agree to take her to Arusha first, to get her testimony over and done with. But if Arusha starts customs' problems . . . and you know how security is tight there . . . then we'll fall behind or she may be forced to stay there and she said that if she does, she'll cancel our shoot because she has to be back in Nairobi for Sunday, no matter what . . . Come on Sheryl, can you help, please?" Sheryl was shaking her head, "What can you do, can't you help? Oh, by the way, her name is Mary Lever." Sheryl's face snapped up, "Yes, Sheryl, that Mary Lever."

Everyone knew Mary Lever from the newspaper reports. The world's leading herpetologist and renowned "Dinosaur Lady," she was to reptiles, turtles, and snakes what Jane Goodall was to Chimpanzees. And Pero knew he had played the right card when Sheryl's head snapped up.

Sheryl's eyes lighted up and she giggled. "Maybe I can help, but can I get her autograph?" The thought of the autograph of the niece of the famous Jimmy Threte, her pastor, was already making her day.

Pero promised he would ask her, but what could Sheryl do to help Pero first? She thought fast, her eagerness driving her on, "I'll file you a flight plan to Pangani and then on to Arusha . . ." Pero started to interrupt, Sheryl held up her hand "But you'll divert to Arusha first if I give you the UN mail pouch to carry at the last moment. It takes priority. You can be angry that it is an inconvenience going to Arusha first. Don't unload any of your cargo, just let Miss Mary Lever off and give the mail pouch to the UN security guards."

Pero leaned over and gave her a kiss on the cheek. A perfect solution. Pangani's customs were a piece of cake. In Arusha, Pero might never have gotten that underwater camera on the manifest through customs. It was a secret cargo that Pero had yet to share with Heep.

Dusty and relatively unclean as true safari returnees always look, they all piled into the two taxis Mbuno had collared and sped off to the InterConti, as it is known locally. In the center of town, on City Hall Way (one of the few street names never de-colonialized), the InterConti is the only useful hotel for camera crews. They have *ascari*—guards—on every floor. When theft of equipment means loss of shooting schedules, an insurance claim has little meaning. Better to have a guard in place.

On the way into town, Heep explained that his call had confirmed the claim was in and good. Simon's people would get around five hundred thousand dollars for "accidental death whilst filming." Their production insurance premiums would shoot up, but that's life. Or death. Five hundred thousand dollars in Kenya had the buying power of two million in the States. Heep seemed genuinely happy at the insurance news. Pero knew it would help assuage Heep's sense of guilt for hiring Simon.

At the front desk, reception, Pero collected four keys and told the porters to bring the few bags they had selected, and the crew and Pero walked into the elevator. An officious desk manager, stuck his hand in the closing door, causing them to spring open, "One moment please, you have not registered properly. Which person is in which room, and is he" indicating Mbuno with disdain, "staying here"?

Pero peeled his fingers off the doorjamb and told him to go check with Mr. Janardan. The doors closed. On the fourth floor, overlooking the pool and the Pool Terrace restaurant, the rooms were all next to one another. Pero took the first one, with Heep next to Pero. Ruis and Priit in the end one and Mbuno sandwiched in-between. Mbuno seemed concerned. Pero guessed it was his first stay in a fancy hotel. Even on safari, in luxury accommodation, his place (and preference probably) would have been with the other drivers or scouts in simple accommodation with few modern amenities.

"You okay here Mbuno? Anything you need?"

"Is that TV like you have?"

"Yes. You want to see something?" He looked at Pero, puzzled. "I mean, is there a program you want to see, some type of program?" Pero turned it on. It was set to the hotel's information page, the penthouse restaurant, the Mistral, was being featured.

"*Asanti*. That looks nice. Where is it?"

"Upstairs, the roof restaurant. We could eat there if you want," and privately regretted it when he said it.

Safari scouts and drivers had one set of clothes, worn thin as a uniform. If it got dirty, they washed it at night and wore it damp the next morning if need be. One set of shoes, one pair of socks, one sweater, one shirt, one pair of long cotton trousers. After a week, they sometimes smelled pretty rank. It was the body ordor, from the beer. Mbuno never drank on duty, or anytime Pero had ever seen. He was an expert scout, preferring not to give away his presence to the wild game, the *nyama*, because of body odor. But Mbuno's clothes were filthy, dusty, scuffed. So were Pero's, but as Pero paid the bill, no one would dare complain to his face.

But Pero knew, right then, Mbuno had nothing else to wear and Pero didn't want him being made uncomfortable by another snooty hotel clerk. Pero went over to the phone, said good-morning, gave his name, and asked who he was speaking to. Jane was her name. Pero then asked Jane, please, to find and get him Mr. Ranjeet's, the clothing shop on Latema Road, off Kismathi Road, past the old Stanley Hotel, on the phone. "Of course," she replied.

"*Asanti*," and he hung up.

Pero showed Mbuno the window curtains' pull, the shower thermostat ("not two taps, just the one with a temperature control like the car heater knob") and the off button for the TV. Pero didn't bother to explain the remote control. Hell, it was even too complicated for Pero. It was all the new rage in Nairobi luxury: Internet, satellite, pay-per-view, thirty-seven channels, radio stations, and inter-room text messaging. Mbuno saw Pero staring at the damn thing and smiled "Asanti Mr. Pero, I will leave it showing the restaurant," (at that moment it changed to the pool) "or the swimming pool. I still cannot swim, but it is pretty." Most Kenyans cannot swim, Pero remembered.

The phone rang and Pero greeted Mr. Prabir Ranjeet, asked how he and Acira, his wife, were. "Everything is just fine Mr. Baltazar, just fine. Can I help you with any little thing?"

Looking at Mbuno, Pero guessed he was a medium T-shirt, a fourteen-collar shirt, a thirty-two-inch waistband and sandals, say size ten, or nine English. Pero passed all this information to Mr. Ranjeet, and asked for a safari kit, top to bottom. "Climate Mr. Baltazar?" Pero told him Pangani, coastal, and he replied "Ah, hot and humid, most fine. A hat as well?" Pero told him he'd never seen a Waliangulu with a hat, and he laughed. "Is all this for your usual driver?" Pero told him it was, Mbuno specifically. "Ah, Mr. Mbuno, he's very famous, very famous, been a guide for many, many years. I will do my very best, Mr. Baltazar, my very best. And I will, of course, add a sweater." All locals always had a sweater for morning or evening. They felt the chill at anything lower than eighty. "May I suggest that I get my cousin, Petam to send you over a pair of sandals?" Petam Bagotas were world-famous leather crossover sandals with tire re-tread for soles. All the rich and famous sported them if they came to Kenya. They were strong (until the glue gave out or the cotton threading rotted) but more importantly impervious to thorns. Pero looked at Mbuno and asked, "Petams for you Mbuno?"

Mbuno looked at his feet, clad in thin black dusty Chinese plimsoles, looked up and shrugged, but smiled. So Pero told Prabir to deliver a brown pair, not black (that was for city folk) along with the clothing, send the bills to the hotel, his charge, usual mark-up for fast service, fourth floor, room 422, to Mbuno personally and take no snobbery from the desk clerk.

Mr. Ranjeet was laughing, "You always make us foreigners here proud Mr. Baltazar. Mr. Mbuno shall have his items within an hour, maybe two."

"Thank you, old friend," and he range off.

Mbuno asked what the schedule was for the rest of the day. Pero told him he had the run of the hotel, but please, no visits home or outside. He could call home as he always does, "just use the phone there, push zero and ask Jane to get you the number. But I need to know where you are, always."

Mbuno said he would eat and then help Ruis and Priit with the batteries. They had taken the recharger off of the plane. Number one rule in filming: make sure the batteries are always fully charged. The hotel's current was steady and reliable. Pero asked if he was hungry and Mbuno asked if the crew was going to eat together. Pero told him yes and that he would be in about ten to fifteen minutes to pick everyone up, if that was okay. Mbuno nodded and commented, "I think I will try the car heater shower just now."

In his room, Pero dropped his soft case on the bed and went into the bathroom to splash cold water on his face. He stood at the basin, gripping the porcelain tight and dripping pink gray dust water off his nose. Simon's death and the remnants of adrenaline rush, twice today, the early start, and a restless night while he screwed up his courage to make that damn leap off the cliff face was beginning to take its toll. The sadness seems to grow within him, and he realized he looked tired. He splashed some more water on his face erasing the dirt streaks. *Ah, there you are Pero, now I can see you, now that this dirt and grime are off.* Pero looked, eye to eye, and told himself it would be fine, everything would be fine, remnants of his mother's intonation of comfort evident even to Pero. *Well, if I'm honest, I never really grew up, just got older.* The wrinkles on the brow and the graying of the temples stood as only a proof of time not a change of personality. Silently Pero said sorry to Simon once more.

Ten minutes later, Pero rounded up Mbuno with wet hair, Ruis, Priit, and Heep (as usual, he was showered and changed—always the first coming in from safari) and they headed down to the Pool Terrace. At the elevator, the floor guard, the *ascari*, pushed the down button and saluted. It was odd, but boyishly charming.

The waiter seated them in the corner as they were disreputable, except for Heep. Pero didn't mind, he wanted his back to a wall. He immediately explained the flight plans for tomorrow and everyone, except Heep, seemed okay. Heep wasn't happy they were going to Arusha. He said Mbuno and Pero should stay tight, close, with the crew if they went there. Pero understood. Heep and Pero had had a bad experience there about ten years ago. Heep was absentmindedly rubbing his left arm where it had been broken by a passing truck on the main through road in town.

"Look Heep, this will be a quick in and out, only for Mary Lever's testimony, so we'll stay put at the airport." Heep still looked miserable. He hated those tribunals.

To change the subject, they planned out the rest of the day. Ruis was going to stay in "and sit with those Brit Air girls over there," pointing to some really lovely flight attendants poolside, definitely not in uniform, in fact, not in much of anything. Heep said he was exhausted and would rest, getting ready for tomorrow. Pero knew he would run up a huge phone bill with LA and Amsterdam. He always did. He had a family to father, long distance. Besides, he wasn't made of stone, perhaps he needed a cry, it was what Pero was thinking, just over the edge of control.

Priit said he had video logs to fill in so they, naturally, covered the problem of how to label and log that morning's hang glider flight on the official location record. In the end, everyone agreed they owed it to poor Simon to log the footage as being of him, not of Pero. The shoot contract with the TV cable company called for so many dollars per second screen time for the "on screen talent." Heep had been careful not to put anything "in the can" that could be confused for Pero's image. "It was all distant, pinprick on the horizon shots. I zoomed in on the blue wing and vultures as you crossed off the cliff face, not even your legs were showing. It'll read as Simon."

Lunch was buffet style, it always was here. They all loaded their plates, none more than Mbuno. For a man over sixty-five, he could out-eat them all—mostly meat, slabs of it. They all ordered water or, in Heep's case Tusker Beer, it was his favorite, one at each end-of-day meal. "It makes Budweiser taste like piss water." Laughing, they agreed that was as good a company slogan, if ever they had heard one before. After the one beer, he drank tap water, only tap water, as usual.

Water for foreigners came from the bar in bottles for health reasons. The bar bill was always a serious, pencil-pusher problem at accounting time in LA, "We don't refund bar expenses." Pero always gave up in the end. It was a tossup, refuse their crew to buy bottled water, make them drink the local stuff and fall days behind schedule as they stay on the toilet, busting a gut. Heep, on the other hand, always drank the local water. After drinking most of the local water across the globe, he was immune.

After lunch, on the way to the elevator bank, Pero asked Heep if he was okay, he said he was, just hated the Arusha diversion. Pero told him that the past was the past; this would be okay, Pero was sure, "We're not leaving the plane, I promise."

"Yeah, right, you're the boss—just don't say I didn't warn you, I don't trust the tensions there. And now I have the other call to make. I don't want Simon's Margarie finding out from the police."

"Okay, Heep, but stay here at the hotel. No going out to console her. They may be watching Simon's by now. How many other hang gliders are there in Kenya? They can find out pretty fast, if and I say if, Heep, they have a mind to. We want to get out of the country without being spotted, okay?"

"Got you. Understood. But Pero, should I mention the half mil?"

"Well, they need to know if he had a will or stated benefi-
ciary. That's who will get the insurance. Don't raise her hopes
in case she's not it. On the other hand, give her money if you
think she's strapped. Wouldn't put it past the Park's people to
evict her from his house. They weren't married . . ."

"Bastards if they do. Okay, Pero I'll handle it."

"Good, thanks Heep, for all of us. Oh, and say hi to little
Kim but no crying."

He answered good-naturedly, "Oh, shut up you bastard."

They piled into the elevator and Pero shot a glance to the
desk manager, daring him to provoke a scene again. He glared
back, but stayed behind the wooden counter. Upstairs, Pero
walked Mbuno back to his room and gave him the electronic
key (with a demonstration, a few times). The ascari hovered
nearby and offered to help. Mbuno said he had decided to
stay put in the room, waiting. Pero knew he would, patience
was any tourist scout's stock in trade. Pero needed to get to
appointments in town and the ascari would keep him safe.

CHAPTER 6

The US Embassy

After a shower, Pero dressed in clean clothes and went down to the lobby to conduct hotel business with Mr. Janardan—to arrange payment vouchers to be presented, as usual, to Flamingo. Pero went past the front desk and ducked through the "Employees Only" entrance to the offices. Like most hotels, decor money was spent on the guests' presentation area. Back here, the peeling yellow paint and surplus government desks looked shabby and were. It reconfirmed the management's pecking order. Work in this room you are a servant to the hotel and the guests. Naturally, the manager, a taciturn Swiss gentleman, had plush, polished mahogany, offices in a separate wing. Back here, however, Mr. Jonathan had a broken glass-paned door, British-made Sellotape holding the crack in place. It seemed never to dampen his spirits.

"Mr. Baltazar, how very, very good to see you again." It was his standard effusive, Asian, singsong greeting, whether Pero had been away for just a few days or months, as was the case now.

Pero's reply was always the same, it was their ritual: "Keeping the whole hotel together, I see Mr. Janardan." He extended his hand, "I'm glad to be home."

They cleared away money business and Pero gave him what Pero thought would be his schedule and next hotel booking needs. Mr. Janardan apologized for the officious desk clerk ("A very snooty Kikuyu but he has relatives . . ."), but Pero told him not to worry. Mr. Janardan asked if Mr. Mbuno was being treated "properly now." Pero assured him he was. Mbuno knew the young ascari on their floor and the ascari now stood outside of the "mzee" Mbuno's door like it was his honor to protect him. They shared a laugh when Pero joked that even he would have to ask the ascari to disturb Mbuno from now on, "he is a now a very VIP guest!" Mbuno would love that one.

Pero handed him a USB memory stick that Heep had palmed to him before lunch and Mr. Janardan plugged it into the slot in his computer. It held only one image, the choice of the ones Mbuno had taken of Chief Methenge and guards with Simon's remains in the background. Pero explained the sad story, minus the bullet holes of course. "You want this in the Standard or the Nation, Mr. Baltazar?"

"Oh, let's spoil the chief and give poor Simon a good send off, so both."

"Very good, I will arrange for the Chief to be interviewed. Is he to be their guest, as last time?"

"Aw, come on! Not like last time, let's make it a quick stay." They both laughed. Chief Methenge had stretched his one interview out for a week at the InterConti at the company's expense. And there were some scandals when his wives came to stay, all six of them, frolicking by the pool.

"Three days then, one for each paper and a day for good will. You are still spoiling him. Word will get around. If they book a seat on a regular flight to Ramu, he will have to leave or face the drive back." It was a good carrot to hang before the Chief, regular flights left Ramu Friday and returned, with tourists, Monday. And maybe this time he would bring no wives.

"Thank you Mr. Janardan, efficient as always."

As he walked Pero out, making a point to bow a little while the "snooty Kikuyu" was looking on, the Swiss manager walked past. He stopped and bowed too and they shook hands. Pero had been a guest here for over twenty years and had referred hundreds of guests. Pero was the perfect client for the tidy, Swiss, Monsieur Cachet. He always paid his bill, on time or in advance, he left the rooms in order with the maids tipped (and happy), he never changed rooms after he was checked in (something hotels hate), tipped on the way in, never on the way out, and left appropriate, constructive, comments where needed to help the staff do better next time, thank you very much. Oh yes, M. Cachet and Pero had a perfect understanding. Pero couldn't stand him personally, but admired the way he ran the establishment. M. Cachet tolerated Pero better than most guests who are, all of them, an inconvenience to the perfect running of a hotel. An empty hotel was always perfect; it was guests that made his life untidy.

Out of the hotel, Pero waved away the offer of a taxi and turned left, heading for the US Embassy a few blocks away. When Schenker had given Pero information that another private package was arriving, it meant Pero's actions were being monitored by Tom and people at State, but Pero had no idea why he would be getting another special phone, if indeed one was arriving in the new special freight that night. It was all a little puzzling. They had left the north, so why was State assuming he'd need a special phone? There was only one safe place to gather such information safely in Nairobi. Pero set off for the Embassy.

It was a logical port of call even if anyone was watching him. Pero had made a point, on checking into the InterConti, of asking for his passport back after registration so he could get extra sheets glued into the back. Room for visa and entry stamps was getting "a bit thin," he had exclaimed. On the street, Pero tapped the passport openly on one hand, and then slipped it into his front pocket.

Idly he thought, *Why do people put things in their back pocket? If a pickpocket puts his hand in my front pocket, you can be damn sure I'd feel that!* His brain was doing its sideways thinking. Nerves always had that effect. He only had six blocks to walk, but checked window reflections and passing cars out the side of his eye. Nothing looked suspicious. Pero could spot no tail, yet. All US embassies are watched. But it was a risk Pero had to take. It was the only place Pero could now safely get a call through to Tom, and ask him, "What the hell?"

Pero knew that any information or instructions for the crew's safety must come from a mouth he can trust, anything else is a risk—either to who or where you are, or, worse still, it could make you a pawn of an unseen party, or perhaps the deadliest risk of all, a pawn in inter-agency politics. Pero had read too many stories of State Department agents like Valerie Plame being used that way. So, basic instinct told him that he should not ask nor accept instructions or information from anyone except Tom. If Tom said somebody else at the Embassy could help, then fine, but otherwise, Pero had decided to confide in no one outside of Mbuno, who seemed to know everything anyway. *Well, not everything,* he reminded himself.

Pero had no illusions. He wasn't a field agent or some action spy (*but you jumped off a cliff in a hang glider,* his inner voice reminded him)—he should be of no threat to anyone. Besides, Pero didn't really have the aptitude nor the desire for intrigue. That's why events in Gurreh territory that morning had upset him so much. It was the first time he had ever endangered people, especially friends and colleagues, and unknowingly at that.

Pero walked seemingly carelessly for the six blocks, coming to a halt before the concrete barriers now so common in front of any US embassy. The gates were guarded by cameras and a pair of Marines just inside "US soil" so they could carry their weapons, loaded and ready.

Every embassy is technically a bit of foreign soil to the country it is in. Nairobi, with the ramshackle building needed renovation, was no exception. On US soil again, Pero asked the Marine where he could get passport pages inserted and the Marine pointed at the main door and said, "Turn left on entering, past security." Pero made a point of looking up at the security camera as he approached the building.

Past security screening, Pero turned left and was stopped by a sweet young female Marine Sergeant. "What is your business, Sir?" Pero explained he was there to get pages put into his passport. "If you will take a seat, I'll take your passport and arrange for an appointment . . ."

"I really need to have it done now, if I can."

"Of course, the appointment will not be long. Can you wait?" And she gestured towards the wooden bench. Pero sat, dutifully. The sergeant turned and crisply walked off.

When she came back within ten minutes, Pero was impressed. She simply pointed at a door marked "Waiting" and handed him the passport. It felt thicker in Pero's hands, but he avoided checking.

No one else was inside the "Waiting" room, four chairs, and travel posters for Amtrak the only amusement. Pero sat and looked at the security camera again, open-faced. As the door shut behind him, Pero had heard the clack, locked. The sound happened again and then the door on the other side of the room, painted to match the wall, buzzed open. "Thanks, Charlie," a man said over his shoulder as he walked in. Pero knew the voice.

Mr. Phillips had been at the US embassy at the UN in New York for many years. Pero had met him several times in the post-Regan era, when they worked on a TV project Pero produced in the General Assembly. Arnold Phillips had been very helpful, intelligent and, above all, honest in everything he did, some of it against his superior's orders. His penalty for "disloyalty" against someone must have been severe to land him here in this backwater.

"Arnold, how good to see you." Pero stood and offered his hand.

Arnold didn't exactly refuse Pero's hand, but he did sit in a hurry after giving Pero's fingers a quick wiggle. "Pero, you look healthy, glad to see you as well." Arnold looked older, more worn-down, somehow less engaged. Without remarking on any surprise at seeing Pero here now, especially for this purpose, more than fifteen years after their last meeting, he launched into his task. "Look Pero, I have been briefed to tell you that you will have a special envoy arriving tomorrow on the 5:00 a.m. flight, KLM-Kenya Airways connecting through Amsterdam, one Tom Baylor from DC. He needs to debrief you in person. You must meet him at Wilson Airport, Hanger 16 beyond the Bluebird Charters' entrance ninety minutes after his plane lands. Only wait up to one hour in case he's late. Got it?"

"Okay, Arnold, I've got all that. But what the hell is going on? This sounds like spy stuff. I'm no damn spy, someone or somebody, maybe al-Shabaab were chasing us up north. We've ditched them, I'm pretty sure. Why the hell is Tom coming all the way here just to talk to me? Haven't you got a secure line in this place?"

Arnold's eyes gave him away. His head never moved, but his eyes shifted to the security camera. "No, no, Pero, it's just that . . ." he hesitated, "well, all this clandestine stuff is not my department—didn't know it was yours. I'm just a messenger, that's all, but, because I know you of old, I was the only one here who could be selected to speak to you," and his eyes refocused on his hands, clasped on the edge of the table.

Pero's blood froze and his voice dropped. "Arnold, how many people did they ask? Just how did they choose you?"

He answered in a whisper, "I wasn't the first choice."

Pero jumped up, the chair tipping over and smacking the concrete floor.

Arnold's head sank onto his chest, "Look Pero, I'm sorry, even I can see this is hardly a secure way to tell you something. You need to trust State, to meet this Tom Baylor. But everyone here was in a flap when the news came that al-Shabaab may be active back up north, so the Ambassador simply asked his secretary to ask if anyone here knew you. He didn't want us giving the message to the wrong guy."

Pero was furious, at both the State Department and the Ambassador—together they had provoked an open staff question and response at this embassy, an embassy full of local Kenyan employees. Pero was exposed, Arnold was telling Pero that other people were openly asked, there was a whip-around for Christ's sake, his name and past history were openly discussed and they finally choose someone who was perhaps not even secure, certainly not secret.

Pero knew, right then, East Africa was on fire, hot as could be. If you're exposed, you're blown, even if it's by your own people. Pero suddenly felt the need to get the hell out of there. He opened the passport and checked the added pages were glued in. "Thanks for this, Arnold." His face showed disgust.

"Look Pero, it's not my fault."

Pero managed a small smile, "Yeah, Arnold, I know, but answer me this, does anyone but you know what the message was?"

"Well, the Ambassador knew, it came in to him red-coded," Pero wondered what that meant, "all he asked his secretary was to find out if anyone in the Embassy knew you by sight."

"Okay, maybe it'll be all right. Do me a favor, will you?" Arnold was already nodding, "Gossip about this, that you met me, a TV producer, and you learned that we had an accidental death on a photo shoot and that the Embassy may have to intervene with the Parks Department here, got that?"

"Yes, is that what happened?"

"It is the truth. But make it sound like you suspect the TV crew were incompetent, okay?" Pero wanted the attention on the accident, how it could have happened, under whose care, not the death.

"Okay Pero, will do." Arnold stood, "No hard feelings?" Pero assured him there was none. *But what idiots*, he thought as he left the Embassy as quickly as possible.

It wasn't his job to figure all this out, just run. Pero was only a small cog in a bigger game, collecting information. As an *Outside Asset*, what Tom had referred to as a friend of State willing to help out now and then, if Pero used imagination to interpret what was going on, how it was useful, if it was safe or not, then the role Pero played might become too important, his minor usefulness might become too dangerous and the temptation to get involved could become too great. *Outside Assets* die that way.

Tom had summed it up last January as they sat having tea at Fortnum's in London after an accidental meeting walking down Regent's Street. Tom took the off the record meeting to catalogue Pero's need to stay away from getting involved. "Pero, the most dangerous thing about this job? Thinking. If you think it's important you will wait too long to dump it. If you think what it means, you will try and build on it, and expose yourself. And if you think you are indispensable, you are wrong, someone will use you, sometime. You're just an Outside Asset, that's all. A messenger boy. Helping color the map or helping someone who does the coloring. Let someone else do the watching, reading, and planning. Don't ever let yourself become more involved, stay away from thinking you're GI Joe out there. Don't ever get exposed. If you do, run."

So, here Pero was, exposed. Was he angry? *You bet. My own people have exposed me.* The embassy was not secure. Any embassy is loaded with local staff that is not, in any sense of the word, trustworthy with one's life. *The Ambassador should have known that. Tom should have known that. What's a red code anyway?*

Emerging from the embassy, Pero never looked back and strode off in the direction of the shops. He was determined not to over think. At least not consciously, so he got back to routine. If there were a tail now, routine would help his cover. Just another mzungu going about his business spending dollars. Time enough to run and hide tomorrow, after seeing Tom. That appointment he was determined to make, and enjoy yelling a little at Tom.

So the rest of the day was spent, as is so often for producers in the field, doing a hundred and one little tasks. Their crew had a shopping list of needs ("double A" batteries, shaving cream, insect cream, sun cream, anti-malaria prescriptions, drops against water in the ear (swimmer's ear), new desert boots, checking the weather and seeing Sheila at Flamingo. Lastly, he had the usual stop to see Mr. Ranjeet to order the cloth and kikois for relatives and friends.

Kikois, the traditional cloth sarongs and kilts worn by men and women in the heat of East Africa, are made in factories outside of Nairobi, the largest being in Thika that also has rampant malaria at a lower 3,500 feet. Malaria in Nairobi is rare because of the 5,000-foot altitude. Still, Thika is where the best kikois came from, malaria or not. It paid to wash the mosquito eggs out of them as soon as possible.

Mr. Ranjeet had first call on the Thika looms and he knew, if Pero were in town, he would sell a suitcase full and have it delivered to the InterConti for any planned departure. As they sat, they discussed the intricate weaving plaid patterns and Pero chose, no surprise here, the most traditional Kikuyu and Maasai heritage looks, always with the hand-tied fringe, sixty shillings extra. "Can I not interest you in the American kikoi?" It was a design of denim blue with a thin white line and a red stripe. Pero said no thanks and, having seen that his whole heart wasn't in the purchase, Mr. Ranjeet asked if his wife, Acira, could interest Pero in some chai, only he meant real tea, Indian tea.

"A cup of your wife's chai will do nicely Mr. Ranjeet, and if you have samosas, those sweet ones, I won't say no." A smiling Acira brought the tea tray with the samosas, whispered into his ear, and withdrew. Mr. Ranjeet and Pero sat there, on leather ottomans, in the middle of this cloth and clothing shop, customers all around, discussing the problems of the Asian community in modern Kenya, which continued to mount.

"There are just too many locals, Mr. Baltazar, who don't understand the problem with AIDS and breeding. Then, when they see that their community," (he meant the Asian community) "doesn't have the same AIDS problems, they get angry and accuse them of having money not to get sick. But we don't have their customs. I try and tell my friends, my Kikuyu friends, that it is dangerous to take your dead brother's wife to your bed even if it does secure her safety and future. Adopt her, that would be all right, marry her even, but no sex please, your brother died of AIDS. It is most tragic."

Pero agreed and prompted another conversation, aware that sex and AIDS were not conducive to a low profile in a shop.

For Prabir Ranjeet, his shop was his living room and he would damn well discuss anything he wanted. Pero's ticking brain, however, needed discretion. Pero lowered his voice, "After all these years, Mr. Ranjeet, could you not call me Pero?"

"Ah, Mr. Baltazar, in your custom, that is being familiar, is it not? An opening to friendship?" He knew it was. Pero nodded. "I prefer to treat you with respect, and think of you as a friend."

"And I you, Mr. Ranjeet."

"Then perhaps we can agree to the formality in name if only to keep up appearances?" Pero agreed. Mr. Ranjeet nodded vigorously. "Good, then, Mr. Baltazar, you must ask of me that which a friend would ask, not as a customer to merchant."

Pero blurted out, "I need to know who—if anyone—is following me." It was a simple request, if a bit blunt. If they had been in Istanbul or Cairo, Pero would have been asking the chief merchant in the Kasbah or Souk what was happening in his domain. Here, in Nairobi, Mr. Ranjeet was the equivalent.

"It is most strange. It is the first time you come here that you have been followed. Acira told me that our son, Amogh, back on holiday, remarked on it. Amogh is not quite a full man, yet, I have never given him, how would you say it, complete confidence? But he is growing up quickly now, since finishing university, becoming more . . . " and he smiled, "like *his old man* as you Americans say. In fact, he would like to know if you want the gentlemen apprehended. It is very brave of him." Gentle*men* struck a chord. Only a fish-out-of-water rival agency would use more than one for a tail. People on their home ground blend in, nor do they need the extra eyes. These were foreign "gentlemen."

Ranjeet's son, Amogh (meaning "always right"), was, Pero knew, indebted to him for a reference Pero gave him (and some secret financial help through a foundation) that enabled him to attend the London School of Economics (better known to students as LSE). Prabir Ranjeet had wanted his son to attend

Oxford and was initially only willing to pay for that. Amogh had wanted the LSE because it was, well, less racist in his opinion and could give him the degree necessary to become a banker. The Ranjeets were into money, and the movement of money, not always legally. Pero had cashed US dollar checks with him, often, and received a better rate of exchange than the official Kenyan one. Once Amogh was at LSE, Prabir Ranjeet, was, at first, resigned and then secretly pleased his son had warranted a scholarship.

"Please thank Amogh for me, but no. I just want to know who they are. How'd he do at LSE, get the degree he wanted?"

"Ah, yes, LSE has been excellent, you and Amogh were correct over Oxford. He is presently getting a master's degree there and has a position as a banker with HSBC starting just this July, it is most encouraging. We are very grateful to you."

"Not at all, friend, one day maybe he'll handle my meager savings and make us all a small fortune. He's a smart boy that one, you may be justifiably proud." Prabir sat up straight, proud of the praise and the trust Pero was offering. To look after another's wealth was the ultimate trust for Asian traders. Pero pressed home the question on the tail: "Any idea who the gentlemen are?"

"If you will wait a moment . . ." he went away into the bowels of the shop. A moment later, he was back, "Not good people, an Arab and an Afghani. The Arab is known to frequent the Pakistani shop next door. I could find out, very carefully, and call you. Would that be acceptable?" Pero thanked him and asked him, again, to thank Amogh for him. They sat drinking chai for a while longer, he coughed in the Asian way to break the conversation, so Pero rose, apologized for his need to press on with his errands, and they parted.

Pero had crossed the line. Pero was becoming involved, Pero was thinking, Pero was planning, Pero was not following Tom Baylor's advice: "Let someone else do the watching, reading, planning. Don't ever become involved. Don't ever get exposed." Some shufti up north had chased them and killed Simon—then someone on their side had exposed Pero. *It changed all the rules.* Pero thought, *Pero, you had better gather some information of your own and plan a safer escape than just hiding in plain sight, they know you are here.*

Three blocks over Pero stepped into the concrete doorway of Wessex House, walked up the three flights of stairs to the attic offices of Flamingo. No one was there. A notice was pinned to the glass door, which was firmly locked, saying "Envelope with the Doorman, show ID."

Pero walked back down to the entrance, showed his passport to the doorman wearing a threadbare jacket, sitting behind his particleboard desk, Daily Nation open on top, no telephone, no lamp, one chair and a Bic ballpoint. He took the passport, leafed through the pages, looked into Pero's eyes, and, having made his decisions, handed it back to Pero as he reached into his jacket pocket. He handed Pero an envelope. "Asanti," Pero said. The doorman made to wave an imaginary fly away and did not respond.

Back out on the street, Pero turned left and walked to the Stanley Hotel. The Stanley, especially the bar, is the old haunt of Hemingway, Holden and all the great white hunters as they came back from safari. Over the years, it has been refurbished repeatedly, sometimes will ill effect, but now looks a bit garish and out of step with its heritage. Pero still liked it though. The ground was the same as Roosevelt and the others had stood on. That was authentic enough for Pero. Besides, from the open-air bar, with its sidewalk tables and chairs, you can sit with your back to the wall and see the whole street. Anyone tailing Pero would, surely, stand out.

The carefully turned-out waiter shuffled over and Pero ordered a gin and tonic, no ice. Keeping an eye, or two, on the street, Pero opened the Flamingo envelope and read the contents. Everything was normal business, flight times, receipts, computer printouts of itinerary changes. No hint of Baylor's arrival, so maybe Flamingo didn't know, just the Embassy. So Pero sat back and watched the world go by.

Nairobi is a village. If you've been a few times, you know people who know people. Your face and theirs are recognizable, sometimes barely. "Oh, aren't you?" is a frequent opening. People sit at your table, you talk, reminisce, throw out names of old hands, newcomers, places that have changed, secret places that have not. All the while Pero was watching the street.

The man was pretty obvious really. Nairobi is not Mombasa or Malindi. There are few Arabs in Nairobi and the man with his dusty clothes pretending to have his shoes shined, twice, or carefully inspecting the rubber stamp maker's street stand for just the right design, well, he hardly looked the Nairobi type even though he was dressed as a westerner; gray slacks, baggy pale blue short-sleeved shirt, cream socks, black loafers, and a brown belt. He had no business purpose yet he was busy. He was not idle yet he was hardly an absorbed tourist. In short, he was Pero's man. What worried Pero was the red soil stain on his trouser legs below the knees. It could be from the Gurreh.

After an hour of chitchat with old acquaintances, refusing to stay longer, and reluctantly begging off dinner invitations, Pero made his leave from the table and wandered back to the hotel. Pero stopped at the pharmacy (Boots the Chemist) to buy malaria pills and batteries and watched out the window as the prescription was filled. The dusty man was met, briefly, by a stout man with an identical blue shirt under a gray suit, and sporting a yellow and blue tie. As Pero left the chemists, only the gray suit followed. Once back at the InterConti, Pero watched from the kiosk, buying a copy of the Herald Tribune. He did not enter the lobby. So, it was enough they knew where Pero was and from where he would depart, just perhaps not when.

Over an early dinner at 5:30, Pero handed out the crew's purchased items. The review of information on cargo, customs, planes, times, and details from Flamingo were accepted by the crew as normal business. Finally, as producer, Pero called for an early night. Pero told them Mbuno and he would depart at 6:00 a.m. and the rest needed to be out the door by 7:00 a.m. Wheels up—the time of lift-off—at Wilson Airport was scheduled for nine, so they had to be loaded and inspected by customs before 8:30. Mbuno would be up and ready, Pero was sure of that.

That night at 7:00 p.m., Pero awoke from an already deep sleep of ten minutes to listen, half-heartedly, to a spirited call from the bitch in LA telling Pero how inconvenient it was for her to have to wake up to get to the office to call Pero with the ten-hour difference. Pero avoided telling her not to be so cheap and to call from home. Although more calls would not make their relationship any easier. She carped on about Simon's death as if it was a personal affront to her and the company. Her rant reminded Pero of the government stooge toe-tapping Simon's boot asking why he was dead. Simon was being violated, again. Pero waited until she ran out of steam and she was forced to ask, "Are you still there?"

After a long pause, Pero simply gave her the shooting schedule and Mary Lever's name. Oh, that made her happy, yes siree. She forgot all about poor Simon. Mary Lever was ratings, baby, solid ratings.

The big networks had been trying to get Lever for a special ever since she rescued that child, in front of six tourist cameras no less, at Gator World. The kid had fallen into the pen with a huge alligator bearing down on her. Mary had leapt over the fence, grabbed the kid, and walked towards, and over, and down the back of the alligator to escape the gaping jaws. CNN ran, and re-ran, her interview for days, "You can't outrun a gator, it's a big dinosaur really. They can't jump and they can't turn as fast as a human, so you have to outwit them." Ever since she was called the Dinosaur Lady by the media.

"I will send you anything you need. Get her to become the regular presenter and we'll give you a bonus, say five thousand an episode."

Pero was still angry over Simon, "No, ten."

"Done. But don't negotiate her fee, leave that for us."

"Oh, good idea," Pero said being sarcastic, God Pero hated this woman, "I'll talk her into something that I can't tell her how much she'll be paid for?"

"Well, if you must, keep it below six figures."

"Per episode?" Christ, they wanted Lever really bad.

"Yeah, but that's your top authority. Got it?" It meant they might offer more. It also meant they had already discussed the show with the major networks or maybe foreign syndication. It meant there was a built-in need for a talking head (as a presenter is called). If they could get an on-screen presenter who was household famous, well, Pero could see their excitement. David Attenborough started it with his Life on Earth series (probably the best wildlife series ever made). If Pero could reel in Mary Lever, they could have a long, lucrative, run.

And the way things were looking on the vocational side, with State and all that, Pero might have to get serious about this job, instead of simply doing his day job better than most. *Out of the frying pan and into the fire*, Pero wondered what was worse, the world of backbiting, killer shufti or the world of Hollywood TV with backbiting, killer bitches waiting to bore you to death? *Tough call. In the one they kill you, in the other you die prematurely.*

They signed off the call with her demand—she always had to have the last command—that they "ship footage every day." Pero promised they would do the best they could. "See that you do." And she hung up. No point in explaining the vagaries of DHL or FedEx out here nor, for that matter, the magnetic risk to video footage by security screening. Heep knew they would be carrying all the footage by hand, all the way home.

Pero had just gotten back to deep sleep when Sheila called at 9:00 p.m., from Flamingo Tours, and told Pero the morning international arrival would be on time, offered no other details, and said good night. It meant Flamingo knew and that Tom Baylor would land at 5:00 a.m. and meet Pero as scheduled at 6:30. Pero checked that the clock radio alarm was set and rolled over.

It wasn't long before Pero was awakened again. Prabir apologized for calling so late but wanted Pero to know that, in gratitude for his custom at his shop, "My son Amogh, who is no stranger, would be happy to drive you to the airport tomorrow." Even in his sleepy daze, Pero figured out the real message. In his shop, Pero had told Prabir he was flying out of Wilson Airport for Tanzania. Yet Prabir had just told him might still be under surveillance by speaking nonsense, because Prabir knew that Pero knew that his son was called Amogh and, of course, what he looked like. There was no reason to say the name, other than to warn Pero about those Pero might not want to meet leaving the InterConti. So Pero told him that he would be ready at the door at six. Prabir said that would be fine, and rang off.

Pero rolled back to sleep. Like any training, sleep was a component of efficiency and could be forced. For Pero it was a mental return to happier times. Saying a mind-clearing mantra, closing his eyes, imagining what he wanted to think about, he drifted. Soon he was asleep.

The alarm seemed to go off almost immediately. Pero glanced over and saw it was already 5:00 a.m. The view out the window was that wonderful pre-dawn you only see this close to the equator. A pink-toned horizon ringed the blackness of space that, even in the lit streets of this city, shined through the gloom. The Southern Cross hung over the city feigning protection. Pero ate a banana and apple left in the complimentary fruit basket while watching the earth spin towards daylight. A moment of calm before what Pero suspected would be a very busy day. Pero was not looking forward to Arusha.

Standing in the hall next to the ascari who had just come on duty, Pero watched him knock respectfully on Mbuno's door, whispering, "Mzee? Tafadali?" (Chief, please?).

Mbuno responded, "Ndiyo" (yes).

The ascari opened the door, bowed, and said, for them both, "Jambo mzee, jambo sana."

Mbuno had emerged from the bathroom, hair still wet, in his new clothes, trousers rolled up inside to disguise the too-long pant legs. "Jambo, jambo sana. The clothes are just fine Mr. Pero, *asanti*." The Petam sandals on his feet looked shiny and new. A day in the dust of Kenya and they would begin to look worn and comfortable.

"You look great, Mbuno. Ready?"

He nodded and went back to the re-made bed for the parcel of his dirty clothes, the dirty shirt doubling as a wrapping, tied in a double knot. They walked together towards the elevator. The ascari sprinted in front of them, pushed the elevator button, and stood to attention. Mbuno stood there, without pride, but very still and erect, as they waited for the doors to open, giving the boy his reward for offering the older man the respect he, the ascari, could one day also deserve. It was bush tradition on perfect display. Pero wondered how many tourists were missing this authentic African experience on the fourth floor of the InterConti, only to be confined to their zebra vans for the rest of the day in the open-air zoo National parks.

For this fourth-floor display was the real Africa.

CHAPTER 7

Wilson Airport

Outside the InterConti in the damp dawn, with a light fog wisps, Amogh Ranjeet rested his forearms on the car roof, looking over at the revolving door of the entrance, awaiting his passenger. Smoothing his leather driving glove fingers, Amogh looked every inch the young stud that he was. His smile clearly showed that he enjoyed the self-image. The car he was leaning on reflected his youth and Asian-western influences perfectly. The year before, he had entered it in the East African Safari Rally, as the competition returned only to the local racing calendar since the World Rally Championship had dropped it for being too dangerous. Amogh, running as a private entry, funded by his family, had finished first in that category and third overall. Winning stickers on the doors, the vintage Porsche 911, twenty years old now, still looked aggressive, lamps jutting out over the droop nose. The car was tensed there, even with the engine off, waiting for the off; gaudy sponsors stickers down the side proclaiming automotive fuels, oils, and components, except for the one which simply said, "Ranjeet's Emporium." Such was the dichotomy of life on the fringe of civilization.

As Pero and Mbuno emerged, Amogh grinned, "Cool, eh Mr. Baltazar?"

"I'd heard about the Rally, Amogh, congratulations. Any room in there for the two of us and these two bags? Or should we take a taxi?" Pero indicated Mbuno's wrapped bundle and his soft-sided case.

"Sure, there's room," he leaned in and popped the front trunk hood, "I took the spare out to make room already." They threw their stuff in. Amogh pulled a lever and the passenger-racing seat tipped forward, Mbuno climbed into the back. "There you go, Mr. Mbuno, Sir, and you too, Mr. Baltazar," and then mimicking the singsong voice of his father perfectly said, "I'll get you there in very great haste." Pero sat in a bucket seat and set the shoulder straps. *Kids can make mistakes*, he thought.

Amogh started the car with an explosion of noise. They must have woken half the guests as they pulled away.

"Lord, Amogh, doesn't this thing have an exhaust muffler?"

"Sure, but I have it on bypass, want to give you the real thing." He dropped his lead foot and they careened around the traffic circle, rear end drifting out, doing sixty. In rally cars, you brake to steer, and use the steering wheel to brake. The brakes are useful to stop or get the tail to hang out. Momentum is key to winning. Amogh knew this car well.

Unlike his father, Western ways had rubbed off on him, and he patted Pero's knee with words of thanks for all the years of help. "I found out, on graduation, that it was your family trust that paid my school fees . . . I can never thank you enough." Pero assured him it was unnecessary—that's what the trust was for. "Yes, I have come to study these tax shelters," they were passing Government House, the old colonial ruling building, "they are very rich. Some of them need good managers. The Gates Family Trust people were recruiting last year at LSE. But I'll do some banking first, to help the family." Asians were always loyal to family first; it's what kept their culture together, no matter what land they were in at the time. Pero knew he was chitchatting, wondering about what he could say, or shouldn't, glancing at Mbuno in the back—so Pero told him Mbuno was always to be trusted, even with his life.

They made the road leading to Wilson Airport averaging sixty and then speeded up, over potholes big enough to swallow most cars' suspensions, this one just bottomed out. "Steel bottom plate, no problem." He piled on more speed. Pero leaned over to read the speedo, they were doing well over 100—miles per hour that is. "Don't worry. No one is going to follow you this morning, Mr. Baltazar." Pero, too, had seen the Toyota taxi pull away from the back of the taxi queue as they moved off from the InterConti.

"What did you find out Amogh?"

"Two guys, reporting to someone at the Holiday Inn. My dad found out from their Giriama cleaning lady, the one who also cleans Mr. Mustafa's, the shop next door, a stupid Pakistani. One is an Arab, not Saudi, maybe Yemeni, called Salim and has been in Nairobi for years, hates Americans, likes to order locals around, she remembered he smiled when Beirut happened." Everyone in Kenya had watched it, over and over again, on TVs in every shop all the next day. "The other guy was very dirty, you know, like he came from safari . . . and we checked, he's Afghani like I thought, speaks bad Arabic, no Swahili, less than you . . ." he paused to smile softening the jibe, "name of Nadir—she heard them talking at the back of the shop—he's staying in a trucker's hotel half-way out of town to the north. My cousin, a trucker, stopped in last night and asked if there were rooms available and found out that this Nadir fellow is checking out today, paid in advance. He came by truck, hitched a ride from Wajir up north. Mean anything to you?"

"Yeah, thanks Amogh." Pero glanced back at Mbuno on the rear bench seat, sitting sideways. His face said nothing except, with a nod, indicating that he had heard. After a few moments, "Amogh, let's get this straight. You are to do nothing, understand, nothing. Stop checking, stop getting cousins to help, tell your father to never check on Salim or Nadir, or this Mr. Mustafa again. These people are, I think, very dangerous."

From the back seat came three words that caused Amogh to swerve and almost hit a stray dog "Arab Mau Mau." Mau Mau still conjured up scenes of horror and carnage for all Kenyan families. Before the word terrorist existed, these people defined the term—they meant acts of violence to be unforgivable, it's the true definition of terrorism.

In Kenya, everyone had lost someone to their machetes and house fires and torture in the dead of night, no matter what race or skin color or status. The rioting that ensued took most of the Ranjeet family fortune and forced them to start again. Mau Mau was a term you never used in jest—they were still a quasi-religious fanatical sect, much feared. To have these words come from Mbuno must have struck fear in Amogh's heart only more than it had in Pero's the day before.

In a way, the latest western version of terror was certainly more media friendly, more sanitized on TV screens, less immediately savage than the Mau Mau uprising. And somehow, the new terrorists everyone was whispering about had a less threatening name: al-Qaida or al-Shabaab in this region. The gentleness of those names belied the ruthless, driven, hatred and violence all these people were capable of. They were Mau Mau indeed, Arab or otherwise.

Amogh said nothing for a few moments and then asked as they approached the beginning of the Wilson Airport road, almost as if nothing had been said, "Where can I drop you, Mr. Baltazar?"

"You can drop us at Bluebird Charters. And Amogh, thanks for the great, fast, ride, it made my day." Pero also meant Amogh might have given the duo a clear space of time to meet with Tom.

As he disgorged them and handed Mbuno and Pero their luggage, "Okay, take care, really Mr. Baltazar be careful. I'll see everyone does as you ask, but only if you promise to call, no matter what the risk, if you need us. Agreed?" He extended his hand more to seal the bargain than to say goodbye.

Pero felt Amogh struck a hard bargain—he would make a fine banker. Pero nodded as they shook. "Okay. And good luck next year on the rally, she's fast." Amogh smiled, waved a gloved hand, and roared off.

Tom Baylor had arrived ahead of them, early. He frowned when he saw Pero approaching with Mbuno.

Pero had made a decision during the night. Pero was now in the game, whatever the game was, inescapable, whether he liked it or not because he and the crew were being tracked first up north and now in Nairobi. He might need to fight back in some way and phrases like "offense is the best defense," kept popping into his head all night. So, he figured what better person to have by your side than a field expert, someone who knew hunting and hunting evasion better than any. Mbuno was that proven expert in the field. He had known Simon was shot before Pero did, he had seen the encampment (it was his original intel Pero had passed along, not Pero's, come to think of it), he recognized (before Pero had fleshed the thoughts out) that Pero needed to bury the satellite phone, and it was his cross-country driving skills that had saved them all. All in all, he was the field expert, Pero was simply the patsy for the State. Pero wanted to change that. Being a patsy made him angry.

So Pero had decided it was Mbuno and Pero to meet Tom or nothing. If Tom wouldn't talk, Mbuno and Pero would go and take their chances. Pero introduced them.

Tom looked at Pero in silence and must have sensed determination and came to a decision. "Okay Pero, have it your way. I do trust you, you know. As long as he knows what's at stake."

"And exactly what is at stake Tom? I've never been compromised by your lot before, never been thrown to the dogs either. Or am I wrong here?"

"No, Pero, you're right. After you were spotted and that fellow Simon got killed—it wasn't an accident, I assume from your panicky transmission—and the target on your back has been allowed to glow a little." He paused. "Well, perhaps more than a little."

Pero, for all his nighttime resolve to take control, felt the bile of fear escape, "A little, a little?" His eye's flared and he clenched, shook his fists at Tom. "Look, there's a guy called Salim, resident in Nairobi, al-Qaida or al-Shabaab probably, reporting to someone, mysterious, in the Holiday Inn. He's also got a fellow from up by where we all were, near Ramu, name of Nadir, assisting him in tailing me, so far just me." He shook his head, slowly calming down, "They had me coming out of the embassy yesterday and tailed me all through Nairobi. This morning, it was only Amogh Ranjeet's driving . . ."

"Yeah, very subtle, I heard that car five minutes before you arrived. Pretty fast, but too noisy."

"It's a rally racing car, no one could keep up . . . but that . . ."

Tom interrupted, "Okay, okay Pero, but my guess is we have a limited time before they follow you to the airport. Everyone here will know where that car dropped people off." He was right and Pero was fairly sure they would have found out by now they were booked to fly out this morning with Mara Airways.

Now, feeling the need to hurry, Tom asked Pero to launch into a debrief. He didn't ask questions, no recorder needed, Tom was trained to remember, "Just spill everything, go."

Pero gave him the whole story as he knew it. Pero handed him the flattened .22 bullet. "There was never an approach to the encampment, no scouting recce, nothing. We filmed, I observed, but it was Mbuno who spotted them and almost by accident, Simon might have as well. I did later from the air, next morning. There was no one at Ramu, when we got there or when I asked, no one knew anything. When I spent tea time with Chief Methenge, it was clear he knew of no one was in the region, let alone twenty or more people from whom he could get Park-use fees or call up the troops from down south. He wouldn't have passed that up, you can be sure, he loves the attention, sees it as his ticket out of the desolate north." Then Pero made a recap of the crew's Nairobi stay and his plans for diversion to Arusha for Dr. Mary Lever and that was all.

Tom had to ask, Pero just guessed he had to ask, "And what do you think about all this Pero?"

Pero's anger came back, full force. "Think Tom? Bloody think? Wasn't it you who told me never, ever to think? To cut and run? Jesus bloody Christ Tom, first you and State paint a bulls eye on my, no our, backs and then you tell me to think, to break your rules?"

"Okay, calm down Pero, you're getting too old for these histrionics. I didn't paint the bull's eye. What you need to realize is that you are no longer the Outside Asset here—you are the hunted. The bull's eye, which bad luck painted on your back, has been enhanced, a little, maybe by the embassy snafu, to allow them to track you and thereby allow us to sneak a peek at their structure in Nairobi and encampment north of Ramu. Satellites have spotted the camp from your description, plenty of hardware, mostly mobile living equipment. There's no plane, landing strip or helicopter, so it's not a large cell. There are two truck cabs, but no sight of the trailers, but these could be underground. There is a bulldozer."

Pero had seen a German news special on TV once that showed that, when in the desert, the IRA or al-Qaida always bought a bulldozer first. You could, literally, bury anything with a bulldozer. Buy an old forty-foot freight container, drop it on the sand, bulldoze up the sand and, voila, one sub-soil home or headquarters. No construction, plenty of speed, plenty of invisibility.

"Tom, there were six . . ." Pero looked at Mbuno, he nodded, "Six mounds, six containers?"

"Yes, they think so. Now you're thinking. And there's one other thing, they have no trace of any importation of explosive, weapons, or high-tech gear. Whatever they have, they brought with them from Ethiopia."

"I think you are wrong bwana." Mbuno spoke softly.

Tom turned to face Mbuno, "Could you explain?"

"The lugger, north of their camp, is not possible for trucks, even if you make a road with a bulldozer. These men must have come from Somalia." Pero had seen the lugger, a dry river bed, thirty feet deep carved on one side from rock, not sand.

"But that's sixty-five miles or more . . ."

Mbuno was determined, his voice flat and calm, "It is the only way."

"All right, I'll take your word on that, but our guys in DC will not be pleased." Mbuno avoided asking him who these "guys in DC" were. There was no need, Mbuno was already in bush mode, speaking only essential things, refining his thought process to the hunt, the now and the next step. Pero got the feeling Mbuno didn't like being the prey and would, if it went that way, turn into the hunter, his natural instinct kicking in.

Tom went on, "I'll double check it, this lugger. I'm headed up there with a group of UK Bristol Bird Watchers—it's a hunt for the desert flycatcher, very rare, arranged two years ago. I've got orders to scout around, and I've taken some bird watcher's place."

"Be careful. Very, very careful bwana."

Mbuno's stern face worried Tom, "You think there is danger?"

Pero didn't wait for a reply, but gave Tom the capsule version of Mbuno's Kenya Troubles history, the Mau Mau, and the killing fields he witnessed or prevented. Pero told Tom that Mbuno called the people who chased them Arab Mau Mau.

"Well, well . . . mzee Mbuno, mimi nataka . . ." and Tom launched into fluent Swahili, to Pero's surprise. Tom was always doing that, keeping one ahead of Pero, ever since they were at school. Superiority was his game, not Pero's.

For the next few minutes, Mbuno answered in short clipped sentences. It wasn't Mbuno's way to steer a conversation, just respond, or tell Tom he was wrong. The language skills were partly beyond Pero, but Pero could tell, when they squatted down and drew in the dust of the hangar floor, that they were sketching out the mesa and the placement of the encampment. As Pero said, Mbuno was the real scout, his information accurate and fresh, yesterday fresh.

Tom was looking up at Pero, "Pero, Mbuno here . . ." Tom had that upper crust way of referring to someone, even when standing next to them, in the third person. He meant no disrespect, but it still irritated Pero. Pero was still on edge this morning, for good reason, and he looked away in disdain. "Pero, are you with me?" Pero looked back as Tom continued, "Mbuno here has a perfect memory for details, and it'll make my job easier. You were right to include him. Is his family safe?" Pero told him about Giraffe Manor. Pero was desperately hoping Mbuno would not have to go through the loss that he had had, years ago, the pain still always fresh.

* * *

Lockerbie was the turning point of his life. His wife of just too few years was on the Pam Am plane returning to their home in Manhattan after seeing her folks in Wales. She had a lilting voice, looked slightly gypsy or Italian depending on her mood or playfulness. *Addiena*, which meant beautiful in Welsh, was exactly that. The tattoo of her name on his right forearm was there to place over his heart when he slept.

Addiena could have been a model or a pin-up. She was, instead, a determined woman with one desire, to belong to a partnership with her man. She had chosen Pero. They were "joined at the hip" as Pero's mother always said. His job sometimes got in the way, so Pero was thinking of giving it up, especially when she got pregnant. Then Lockerbie, the Pan Am they all trusted falling from the sky. It was after that when Tom approached him with the additional risk, ever so slight at first, to help State with little errands. Pero, alone without his Addiena to complete his life, simply agreed and used the excuse for extra work to avoid missing her too much.

* * *

Tom was still speaking about Mbuno's family—Pero hadn't been listening. "Okay, Pero, you get this? We can drop a hint that extra police, up there at Giraffe Manor for the next week, would be a good idea. Meanwhile, you go about your filming business. My guess is that you'll be in the clear in Tanzania, out of the line of fire, so to speak. Whatever they are doing, it's here in Kenya, of that our guys are sure, they've tracked tons of communications that indicate it's Kenya, nowhere else, they are focusing on. And it's soon. Make your way to Pangani and make a report if anything unusual happens or you spot something. But as I said, Pero, I think you'll rid yourself of them when you go south. They have nothing going on down there we know of, for the moment."

Pero rounded on him, determined to make a dent in his unflappable demeanor. "Okay, Tom, but get this and get it clear. You guys changed the rules, don't expect us to play by them. If it comes to your goals and mine, I'll choose us over you from now on." He took a breath and added, "And I didn't like Arnold Phillips being openly selected in that sieve of an embassy . . ."

Tom interrupted, "What do you think, we're nuts?" He laughed. "Phillips only thought it had gone around, that's all, it's what they wanted him to think, to keep him in the dark. They asked him in front of his secretary as if it was all down to him finally. They know she has a brother who's connected with the Red Star, local al-Qaida sympathizers. Your Mr. Mustafa is their leader by the way and Salim is her brother. They needed you to run, as you are supposed to do." Tom was getting up a full head of steam now, "But did you run, you idiot, as you were told to do? Oh, no, you went shopping and, now we find out, had Mustafa and his minion Salim spotted and this guy from up north watched and spied on. You made your bull's eye glow even more. And you put the Ranjeets all at risk."

"Your point is? I was supposed to be the only one at risk, right Tom? You provoked me into action, or dropped us, the whole crew, deep in it, more likely."

"Yes, that's right, DC are opportunists, and your point is? You were spotted up north, we didn't paint the bull's eye. And, Pero, you didn't follow training."

But now Pero had him. "Bullshit Tom, you knew I wouldn't, or else you wouldn't be at this meeting. Your flight was already arranged—yesterday." Pero had him and he knew it. The time line of Tom's departure at least fifteen hours earlier sealed the truth. Tom looked slightly sheepish.

Mbuno had been standing patiently while they bantered, listening. Suddenly, he moved Pero aside behind the pillar they were standing next to and kicked off, launching himself at Tom. Tom and he went down, but Mbuno had his hand over Tom's mouth and was pointing with his free hand. Pero peeked around to see a boy, with a broom, open a closet door, extract a bucket, and go back out a door at the far end of the hangar one fifty feet and six planes away. The sound was faint and, with all the angled surfaces of the parked planes in here, Pero would never have known where it came from.

Tom and Mbuno got up, Tom looking down at the slight man with clear respect. "Okay Pero, good decision." He was referring to the decision to include Mbuno. "Care to lend him to me?

"Mbuno goes where he wants. This time I need him, the crew may need him to keep us safe." He paused and smiled at Mbuno, Besides, he's saved me before."

Mbuno looked at Pero and said, "And you've saved me before bwana." If Pero said it, Mbuno always said it, to even the score. It was part of their friendship, that exchange.

It was many years since their first safari together. Back then, Pero was new to East African filming and they were setting up a water shoot with hippos near Tsavo West Park. Hippos are notoriously dangerous on land and, if you disturb them, also in water. That big mouth kills more Africans every year than crocodiles or any other creature, except maybe snakes. Pero was setting up the cameras on a raft, to float out into a herd, over clear water, one camera on top of the water, one in a plastic bag below, when a female on land spotted Pero and made a charge. Mbuno, showing no fear ran straight at her yelling at the top of his lungs and never flinched, never wavered. At the last second she veered off and brushed him and Pero— sending them reeling like leaves in the wind—as she dived, exploded, into the water. If Mbuno hadn't taken action, quick action, Pero would have been run over by a one-ton cow and eaten. Hippos have big teeth. They eat meat as well as greens. One bite, you're dead, end of story.

Three days later, Mbuno was surprised by a puff adder as he was finishing his business in the bush. Puff adders are deadly creatures, spitting venom six feet or more. The venom was meant to blind, but with his quick reactions, it hit his hand and arm only. Pero killed the snake. The pain was excruciating, the necrosis of the skin and tissue immediate, almost as if nerve acid had been poured on him. He would have died except for the Flying Doctor service that Pero radioed to come and rescue him, money no object. The hospital in Nairobi (the better one with an Italian surgeon flown in specially) became Mbuno's home for a three-week recovery, skin grafts and all. The nurses loved him. His wife made his favorite chai with goat's milk on a Campingaz stove until the fire alarms went off. Nobody complained—he was that popular.

He still had the scars, but he lived, that was the main thing. It made a bond between them that they were both shy and yet proud about.

"Okay, it's probably better Mbuno here, stays with you. He can be your eyes and ears while you do that filming you've planned. With Mary Lever in tow, you'll have your hands full. Is she showing up with that husband of hers?"

"Not that I know of. She said one seat for the plane pointedly. Rumor has it that relationship is over anyway."

"Good thing too. That ass was too well connected and arrogant." Tom was probably referring to the media stories last month when Lever's husband got an elderly couple thrown off a plane. They had "mileage tickets" and he was first class, all cash. The media ate it up. He couldn't have cared less. It was Lever's money and his social position. If Mary Lever was rid of him, so much the better. "So, Pero, get your crew to the beach in sunny Tanzania and do your filming. I'm off north to see what you found. Anything happens, radio in, there's a sensible fellow. Don't take the embassy thing too hard, it was necessary and the damage is past now."

Pero had calmed down. "Okay, Tom, going away to film suits us fine. You shouldn't be doing fieldwork either; you're no damn field agent, so keep your damn head down. They have already killed, quickly and very expertly. Two shots, moving—no flying—target, range over a half mile, .22-250 or no .22-250, that's expert shooting. So, as I said, keep your bloody head down." Pero stuck out his hand. They shook. Then he nodded and walked out the side door.

Mbuno and Pero carried their bags and walked down the flight apron to Mara Airways and found their plane from the day before sitting there, door open, a customs inspector guarding the steps. Pero asked Mbuno to wait and walked to the office to talk to Sheryl. Past the loading doors, Pero had to squeeze past people, every inch of the hall and waiting room was full, the place was jam-packed.

Over their heads Pero called, "Sheryl, Sheryl, what the hell is going on?"

"Mr. Baltazar, she's here, with **him!**" And she turned around in a flourish and, voila, her arm movement said. There they sat, on Sheryl's red plastic couch (reserved for dignitaries— who later always stood with a wet bottom from perspiration) talking as if they were in Hyde Park on a bench by the Round Pond: the holy man, Jimmy Threte and his niece, Mary Lever. They looked up and smiled. His smile filled the room with the charm, the sincerity, the oneness with everything he preached so often. It was either very, very good or very, very bad. Pero hadn't made up his mind yet. He was a big man with the slick media hair of his TV evangelical vocation, going gray at the temples just like Pero's plus a broad forehead and broader shoulders to carry the responsibility. With over 100 million followers, that burden was awesome indeed.

Her smile was as Pero remembered, assured, confident, and open, nothing was hidden there. There didn't need to be. Her frame was slight, trim and a bit tomboy, yet without any hint of anything except womanliness. At forty, her face, with the bright green half-moon spectacles that serve as her trademark, is still that American every-girl next door classic, even down to the freckles on her nose. Heep's camera would love her, of that Pero was certain. Problem was, would she love the new TV cable company proposition?

CHAPTER 8

Arusha

Pero looked at each of them in turn, "Reverend Threte, Mary, glad to see Sheryl is looking after you." Sheryl giggled again. She was totally star-struck—it was almost embarrassing—almost, but not quite.

JT spoke first as he got up. "Good to meet you finally, Mr. Baltazar, I've met your folks, good people, good people." The parents' stamp of approval, the Reverend Threte believed in evolution and genetics, but he qualified his approval with, "They should find time to pray a bit more, but then survivors of that terrible war," he meant the second world war, "often feel God has forsaken them. They spoke about it and they told me their faith rests with you." He raised his eyebrow, "Curious notion, but good people. And my Mary here," he gestured to her, "speaks highly of you," he paused for effect, locked eyes with Pero's, "So, I trust you are going to *look* after my niece?" It was clear he meant protect her or, God forbid, he'd come after Pero.

"Oh, and here I was assuming she'd look after me."

Mary laughed, JT chuckled, but poor Sheryl looked aghast. Her face said: *how dare you correct JT?* Then Pero stuck out his hand, JT took it in a sixty-year-old bear claw and squashed Pero's knuckles. Pero struggled to maintain composure.

Mary moved to intervene. "Now boys, let's take it easy. Leave him some fingers JT, will you?" JT's iron grip released, Pero shook out the fingers to show that, yes, he had hurt him. "And you Pero, act your age, we've been friends for too long to start playing with my relatives."

Pero smiled, "Sorry Mary, it's been a tough few days."

Suddenly, everything got serious. "I heard. Poor Simon, wasn't it? He was a good researcher so the people in Parks & Wildlife say. Did he have family?"

"Just a solid girlfriend, Margarie, and an elderly mother who kept house for him over the other side of Ongata Rongai, on the Maasai plain."

Mary rested a hand on JT's massive forearm, "JT, could you include them, give the two ladies your blessing next week and a send-off for Simon?" JT called funerals "send-offs to meet your maker."

Halleluiah usually followed, Pero, being cynical, thought. *But he does good, mostly. At least he isn't into politics or meddling with the issues of the day.*

"Was Simon a local?" JT asked Pero.

"Yes, Sir, he was, twenty years studying eagles and such. Lived poor, contributed large." It was the slogan JT used on his TV show.

"Fair 'nuf. Thomas!" he bellowed. A small man with a baseball cap entered. "Include this Simon fellow . . . what's his name?" Pero gave it to him and the office contact. Thomas was scribbling away on an electronic device. "Put this fellow on the service, memorial portion, full works, good of nature, good of man, invite the relatives, on stage, I'll bless them for their loss." The aide nodded and withdrew; he knew when he was dismissed.

JT lightened the mood again as he turned to Mary and spoke with an exaggerated southern drawl, "I've got to go now, sugar, so you take care, y'hear? Don't let them nasty critters bite—nor him neither!" said with a laugh as he pointed at Pero. Like an emotional conjurer, JT became serious again looking at Mary, "And remember, I expect to see you next week on stage with me."

"Don't worry JT, I'm the expert, they have to do as I say around the animals. And it's only one show segment, I'll be back here in time."

"Well," Pero hesitated, "yes you will, of course, I promise, but there is the possibility that after the *Meeting* you could extend your shooting schedule a bit . . ."

"How much is a bit? How many segments?"

"Thirteen . . . a year?"

"That's doable . . . wait a minute. Segments or shows?"

"Ah, shows. Look, the company has asked me to make you an offer they hope you won't refuse."

"No way, never, forget it."

JT had other ideas. "Now, don't be hasty, hon. Let's hear what the man has to say. You do have something to add to this, don't you, son?"

"Ninety-nine thousand, nine hundred and ninety-nine dollars."

Mary stared. "A season?"

Pero paused for effect, "Per show."

JT was ahead of Pero again. "And that means it's all he was authorized to say. *Under six*, was it, son?" Pero nodded. "I like you, son, that's honest. Hon, let my people handle it, if you're interested that is. After all, with that—what did you call him?—that *twerp* out of the way, there's nothing better than a bit of globe-trotting, doing what you like best, to refresh the spirit. The Lord does work in mysterious ways." And he turned towards Pero. "I like a man who knows when the time is right, even if you used my presence here for leverage. It's okay son, but you owe me." Pero nodded agreement.

"Pastor Threte, we really need to be going." A redheaded, slight, young man said from the doorway.

"Coming, Jimmy Little. Take care hon and watch them critters." And with that he walked out of the room, touching Sheryl's head on the way, "Bless you, child, see you next week." He never saw her faint, dead away, from the contact of his hand. But she did.

In the pandemonium that ensued—JT's departure, the thinning of the crowd who suddenly remembered that they actually had something else to do other than stand around getting a glimpse of JT and, not least, the job reviving Sheryl—Pero never noticed that their crew had arrived. They were, of course, loaded with questions that Pero would have to explain on the way down.

Once revived, Sheryl became her usual efficient self, handed Pero the manifest and regained the rest of her composure and smoothing her dress while Pero read it through. Pero checked for the night arrival cargo. It was there, one airway bill, contents count two. Sheryl was not about to let JT's daughter out of her sight, so Pero was not surprised when she decided to close the front office and escort them onto the flight apron to the waiting plane, next to which stood Mbuno and the customs officer beginning to bake in the morning sun.

The crew and Pero followed the large, self-assured Sheryl leading Mary by the arm as if she were a china doll. The custom's officer stood aside and the film crew piled in single file filing the rear seats of the ten-seater, leaving the forward VIP seats for Mary and Pero. Sheryl waved another pilot aside, turned to the flight pilot and handed him the manifest, and sent the custom's officer running. Pero started to board, planning on leaving Mary and Sheryl to say their goodbyes.

Sheryl put a palm on Pero's chest, smiling as if she had a secret. "Oh, no, Mr. Baltazar, I have arranged a special flight for Miss Lever." She pointed. Behind their Cessna was a twin-engine Beech Baron, a pressurized four-seater. The pilot, a young blond South African, and two mechanics were standing to attention. "See? I have prepared this special flight to Arusha for Miss Lever, and then on to Pangani, later in the day. It is with the compliments of Mara Air!" The power of JT was at work, Sheryl, at least taking JT's instructions to keep Mary safe seriously. "There are no customs problems, just passports, as you have no luggage."

Pero thanked her profusely and not without relief, walked back to the Cessna and briefed the crew, asking Ruis to stay with the Cessna until all the equipment was off and cleared Pangani, as Pero would have.

"No problemmo, oh great escort of the high and mighty!" Even Heep was enjoying this, smiling away. Priit crouched feigning military attention, saluting. They knew how much Pero hated all pomp and fuss, so the ribbing was especially fun. Still, with the problem of customs in Arusha with the Cessna and his special cargo, just arrived, neatly solved, it was hard for Pero not to smile back. He knew Mary would get to Arusha and the crimes' trial on time, and they could leave for Pangani immediately she was done. Before he stepped back down the steps, he looked at Mbuno seated in the tail of the plane and gave him the thumbs up sign, tilting his head. Mbuno merely nodded, silent as always.

Pero was sure he and Mary would get to rejoin the film crew by nightfall. Shooting would not begin until the late morning the next day, so he'd have early morning to check everything. Pero knew they would have to wait until at least

11:00 a.m. as crocs, especially big ones, are unpredictable in the early morning. That's feeding time.

Pero walked over to the Baron, gave Sheryl standing by the starboard wing a hug, which made her all bashful. He helped Mary step up on the wing-step and then followed, in through the co-pilot's door, and settled into his seat: co-pilot's, on the right. Mary and Pero buckled in, Mary seated right behind. She was waving through the window at Sheryl, mouthing, "see you next week" as the first prop started to rotate. They taxied briefly before the Cessna warmed engines and then the Baron careened down the runway, straight and true. The boy was young, but good. He hit the landing gear lever as the wheels left the ground. At 5,500 feet, it is a requirement or the wheels cause too much drag and you can't climb.

The sky over Wilson Airport was ice blue, the 5,500 foot rarefied air punctuated only by massive columns of strato-cumulus clouds starting to form and gather over the endless African plains. Their tops were gray, and their bottoms wisped over the land, casting shadows and the promise of sudden, violent thunderstorms as the heat in the day climbed. These are what the locals call thunder heads or thunder bumpers, so the pilot gave his usual warning to keep wearing the seat belt at all times and please excuse the occasionally bumpy ride. Plane rides in Kenya are always choppy. It's the thermals, if not the imminent rain.

Like delicate-looking sentinels of the tropics, the clouds never touched, always moved at a pace unrelated to the wind on your face, and had hidden, internal, winds of tremendous force.

Local pilots know to avoid the thunder-bumpers—always. Once the top went from gray to black, hail grows in strong thunderstorm updrafts. Inside these equatorial, white, monster clouds, a speck of ice can grow to an inch in diameter in under ten seconds. Cruising, wings level at a slow 120 miles per hour, encountering hail traveling at sixty miles per hour on an updraft inside the cloud, a plane will get dented by thousands of ice balls in seconds. In under twenty seconds, the airfoils (wings, tail, and propellers) and any vertical surface (the windscreen and nose) will be ruined, un-flyable.

There was a Cessna one fifty at Wilson (now internally stripped for parts) standing out in the open for all to see. She was brand new when she was flown, accidentally, into a hail cloud for ten seconds. After, she looked like a gang of blacksmiths had worked her over with ball-peen hammers. There wasn't a flat surface left. How the pilot ever landed her, no one knows. He doesn't fly anymore, he has a phobia, with good reason. Kenya's like that, you learn by dramatic experience or you die from it. He lived to learn.

For Mary, on the way down to Arusha, Pero asked the pilot to do a flyover of Lake Magadi. Lake Magadi is a mirror lake, half crowded with flamingoes. It's beautiful and, from the middle of the lake, the view to the west creates a mirror lake set against the rising hills. Suddenly, it is impossible to know where you are in the universe, it all blends together, it's magic.

Mary had never seen Magadi, and she was thrilled. Halfway down the length of the lake, Pero watched the altimeter descending, the pilot flying using visual cues. Pero leaned over and tapped the altimeter in front of his line of sight. He glanced down and pulled the yoke back, affording Pero a little sheepish nod as they gained back the fifty feet he had lost, unobserved. The prop wash on the lake surface had been getting a little unnerving. Over mirror lakes, and mirages, you rely on instruments only; there are no reliable visual clues. Mary never knew, she was too thrilled with the view.

As they approached the end of the lake, the million or so flamingos were hastening into the air, their plane bearing down on them. The pilot knew what to do, gave Mary a last look at the fluttering pink sea passing under the wings, and gained altitude quickly, back to 12,000 feet and avoided any bird strikes.

The approach to Arusha was simple and the landing went without incident. They followed the little "Follow Me" car with the flashing yellow light to the UN apron. As the props stopped turning, a car pulled up to the starboard wing and a huge, bulky, uniformed, white-gloved soldier, Nigerian by uniform, got out of the front and walked over to the passenger side of the plane. He reached up and flat-palm smacked on the window. Pero looked at the pilot, who nodded his approval.

Pero opened the door and got out onto the wing, reaching back in and pushing the seat forward for Mary to emerge. There was no safe footfall on the wing for Mary and Pero together, so Pero indicated for the giant to move back and made to jump down. The soldier didn't move, just reached up, grabbed Pero's shirt, tugged, and swung him to the side, off the wing. Pero landed on the concrete, hard, reminding him of the painful thorn wounds in his rear from the day before. Pero could feel one oozing. Mary quickly stepped back into the plane and sat in his seat, closing and locking the door.

The soldier didn't know what to do. A gray-haired man, Malaysian Pero thought, emerged from the back of the car and approached Pero on the ground. "I am most sorry. This is really unfortunate. He had orders to secure the witness and, I am afraid, he took that literally. We've had many security problems here. Witnesses haven't made it to court. I am most humbly sorry."

Looking up from his sitting position Pero said, "And you, Sir, are?"

"Consul Jikuru, special prosecutor, third UN Trials for Crimes Against Humanity. And I really am most sorry."

Pero stayed down and dusted himself off. "Well, I've promised her uncle, Jimmy Threte," the Consul blanched, "that I would protect her. So far it is only my, uh, derriere that's insulted." He smiled, "So, if your fellow would step back, I'll ask her if she intends to disembark, or leave. It's her call."

Mary opened the door. "Thank you Pero, I know this gentleman. How are you Jiki-Jik?"

"Very well, Missy Mary." It was an inside joke between friends. They both laughed. The soldier stepped forward, put his hands on her waist, and lifted her, light as a feather, to the ground. It was the second time Pero thought of her as a china doll that day. The big fellow then turned on Pero, offered a hand and a big grin (no threatening teeth showing), and whisked Pero to his feet, and a bit beyond. Pero had to do a little skip. It really was embarrassing. Mary laughed, then "Jiki" laughed, then the bloody pilot laughed, then the soldier laughed and Pero felt compelled to join it, even at his own expense.

Pero knew he couldn't accompany Mary to the trials. It was forbidden, *in camera*, a closed court proceeding. Besides, Pero didn't want to. Pero turned to the soldier. Being Nigerian, Pero knew French would be the soldier's second mother tongue. "Si vous étes très gentil, je vous confirai ma charge, mais vous devez la protéger avec votre vie, si c'est nécessaire, d'accord?" Pero had offered to pass his protection duties to him, but only if he valued her life more than his.

The giant man grinned and gave a little salute. "D'ac, captain" ('kay, captain). And Pero knew from his simple intensity he would not let her out of his sight.

"A good compromise I think, don't you Mary?" Consul Jikuru asked.

Mary gave Pero a quizzical look, nodded to the consul, and placed her hand on the soldier's extended left arm, leaving his firearm hand free. They walked to the car, got in, and drove off. As they passed the wire fence security post, a Land Rover roared up with three officials, eager to establish their authority, "We are customs and immigration, you do not have the proper permit to be stationing your airplane here. It is irregular."

Pero showed them passport and visa entry (which were, of course, in order, complete with a twenty-five shilling immigration stamp receipt for duty paid). The pilot showed them his plane manifest and routing paperwork, also in order.

Nevertheless, the customs boys spent the next two hours examining everything, including his spare socks in his flight bag. Either the fracas, with Pero ending up on the concrete apron, didn't impress them that Pero was trustworthy, or security around the criminal trials for genocide required these extra measures, or someone had made a phone call with a hoax call. They weren't saying and didn't care. The pilot just sat in the shade of the customs' Land Rover and smiled as they asked Pero questions about everything from who, what, where, and why Pero was on this planet.

The pilot's expression said it all: *Oh, yes, I am enjoying this at seventy-five dollars an hour.*

By the time Mary returned, in the late afternoon, Pero was fit to be tied. It was hot, very hot, and he had not been allowed to get a drink and, worst of all, they had taken his passport away for an hour of nervousness. When they returned it, just as Mary's car pulled up, they had added another twenty-five shilling stamp and put their hand out for a refund. Pero paid, furious, but it was only seeing Mary's face that made Pero keep his miseries to himself. "You okay Mary?"

"Later Pero, later." She climbed into the plane, stifling as it was, and closed her eyes, wanting to be left alone. Pero looked at the Nigerian guard, he looked concerned and told Pero she was in shock and that there had been "des événements difficiles" (difficulties). Consul Jikuru was nowhere to be seen. Pero asked after him. The Nigerian shook his head.

The pilot knew his fun and games were over. He talked to the tower, got permission to continue their flight plan, and they were soon back in the air en route to Pangani. Radio traffic was busy, Pero listened in on the spare headset, luxury all the way in this Beech Baron.

Because of the distances involved, much of the radio traffic in East Africa is UHF instead of the usual air to ground communication via VHF, which is only good for line of sight. The pilot was busy, juggling between frequencies, and even more concerned because their flight path was from Arusha to the much smaller town of Pangani on the coast, and they were skirting along the border between Kenya and Tanzania, just in Tanzanian air space. Tanzanian air traffic control was sloppy, remnants of the communist era, and everyone knew it. And the coast of Tanzania has commercial flights, at low altitude (as they were, at 12,000 feet) between Dar-es-Salaam to the south and the major port of Tanga, thirty-five miles north of Pangani. They were keeping a watchful eye on the open sky indulging in the pilot's usual betting game: Last one to spot another airplane has to buy a coke for the winner.

Simultaneously, the pilot was trying to keep up with his course corrections, frequency changes, and sudden, incoming, change of route plans from air traffic control. Something big was going on up ahead, there has been a plane crash, maybe in Dar-es-Salaam or Tanga, they couldn't tell. Whatever it was, they were vectoring them this way and that, up and down, to avoid being in anyone's way. Such is the power of tourism in East Africa that no one ever thought of telling them to go away, little plane. They were on a pre-approved flight path, from a rich charter company, and, except for emergency stuff, they tried to keep them on track.

About half an hour before their scheduled landing, the traffic controllers confirmed their permission to vector on to Pangani and permission to land. Pero asked the pilot what the hell all this fuss was about. He had no idea. They waited it out. Mary seemed asleep in the back—no need to worry her. The setting sun was behind them now and the landscape was well, if obliquely, lit. At wheels down, the last of the sunset was turning everything a golden red, and they switched on the landing lights to taxi to the apron. That's when they saw it.

CHAPTER 9

Pangani

The Cessna 414's tail was still proud, the charter airline name, "Mara," and the prancing gazelle still visible, if a little scorched. Its angle gave the story away. As their landing lights pulled around, they could see there was no midsection to the plane and the pilot's seats were hanging from what was left of the forward fuselage. Whatever had happened, had been sudden and violent—there was debris everywhere. A couple of mechanics with flashlights waved them to a bay off to the left of the carnage and signaled a shut down. The pilot was reaching for the twin prop levers and throttles when Pero stopped him. Mary woke and asked, "Are we there?"

"Yes, Mary, but stay put for a moment." Pero turned to the pilot "Pretend you're doing a post-flight check on the left engine. Cut the right, I'm getting out, but if I raise my arm, even re-adjust my cap, rev the engine, use it to taxi, start the right and fly home immediately with Mary. Leave me, got it? Don't take no," Pero indicated the flashlight mechanics approaching the plane, "for an answer from them or anybody." The Pilot nodded approval, sensing possible danger.

As soon as the right prop came to a halt, Pero opened his door and stepped out. The burnt plane had a distinctive smell. Aluminum burns at a very high temperature, and plastic always reeks. It wasn't either of those that bothered Pero. Pero smelled explosive. Pero went over to one of the mechanics and borrowed his flashlight and examined the wreckage. No bodies, Pero was pretty sure. Their equipment wasn't there. The burn scene had not been disturbed either.

"Any idea what happened? Are the people safe?" he asked the mechanic who wanted his flashlight back.

"Yes, bwana, everyone safe, and the police are here, they want to talk to you. The passengers are already at Pangani Camp."

"And the pilot?"

"Here mate." Out of the early night left over sunset glow, the Australian they had used for the trip down from Ramu emerged into view. "Not pretty is she?"

"Christ, what happened, a fire?"

"Nah, someone blew the ruddy thing up, about three hours after we landed, ka-boom, broke the canteen windows," he indicated the little thatched hut fifty yards away, "and made me drop my Coke." He was talking calmly, but Pero could see his hands were still shaking.

"Glad you're all right. My people know about this?"

"They ruddy well should do, the cops are all over, talking to everyone. A half hour before you arrived, a Commissioner Madar Singh, brother of the Minister for Tourism no ruddy less, he arrived from Dar with six heavies, even commandeered the only two taxis when he landed. That's his plane over there." He indicated the Britain Islander with "Toyota" painted on the side. Pero knew the plane, and had been a guest on a trip to Zanzibar fishing waters a few years before with his brother, Virgi Singh, who had the Toyota concession for Tanzania. The third brother was the minister. All in all, a powerful family. But Virgi had, back then, told Pero not to trust "his policeman brother."

"He's up at the Pangani Camp talking to your crew right now, and I'll bet he's waiting for you mate."

Pero went back and explained everything to Mary and the pilot. The port engine still rotated. Pero suggested Mary leave immediately with the Beech Baron for Nairobi. The pilot needed to get wheels up before someone here thought to ground him. He got on the radio and filed a quick return flight plan with Dar control and got all the right permissions. The little airport of Pangani was hardly likely to know what to do in a case like this. Pero told him that when he got into the town of Tanga's airspace, they might ask him to land. Don't run, just ask for police protection, he needed to keep Mary safe. He nodded, he knew how important she was, Sheryl would have lectured him, Pero was sure.

That's when Mary spoke up.

"Just who the bloody hell do you think you are telling me to cut and run. I didn't today and I'm not now. Whoever did this missed *your* crew, it wasn't meant for me, my plane is fine." Pero looked at the pilot, his eyes widened at the sudden thought. Pero raised his eyebrows in question.

Everything went still. The pilot thought for a moment. "Nah, I prepped the plane myself for a flight to Magadi. It was a last-minute decision by Sheryl to send us to Arusha, as a VIP carrier. That little baby over there," he indicated the wreck, "she was in the customs' bay all night, all alone, but guarded. It must have been set to go off here or maybe here after just after landing, I'm sure. But I'm equally sure it is not safe to stay here. Better that we leave, miss."

"I'm staying." And with that, she pushed past Pero, onto the wing and stepped down. She was in no mood to listen to reason.

The Australian Cessna pilot interrupted, edged closer. "Look mate, mind if I hitch a ride out of here? They didn't say they needed me and, frankly, these ruddy Tanzanian ex-commies give me the willies."

"It's up to you. They could pull your ticket, but if they have a statement and witnesses . . ."

"Oh, they do, ten minutes to write one, signed a statement, told to go away, I was, ordered to rest and sleep . . ."

"Well, then good luck, climb up." Pero looked at Mary, beseeching her with his eyes. She shook her head emphatically. Pero shrugged his shoulders.

As soon as the door shut, the pilot revved the port engine, started taxiing, and on the way to the end of the runway, they heard the other engine come to life. They were clearly in a hurry, following Pero's instructions. Within a minute the Baron was airborne, leaving Mary and Pero standing on the apron, wondering what was next. They watched the Baron waggle its wings in a farewell gesture set against a rising partially full moon.

The two of them didn't have to wait long. Ruis leaned out of the left window yelling, "Hello guys!" The fat-tired Land Rover was clearly a rental Pero surmised, with Mbuno at the wheel. Ruis was glad to see Pero and Mary—he had been tuned into traffic control and knew they had landed. The police commissioner was getting difficult. And Heep was losing his cool. An angry Heep could spell real trouble. In Indonesia last year, he'd poured his water bottle on an officious customs officer and Pero had had to bribe their way out.

The Pangani Camp is a riverside tourist, thatch, and tented camp, the real African Queen experience (so the brochure says), lush tropical jungle, drifting hippos and crocs past the river bank, exotic fishing birds, wooden dugout canoes. Other than the Mkonge Tanga Hotel thirty miles to the north, it's the only reliable base camp for a film crew with electricity. And, besides, why be in the sweaty, bustling, harbor town of

Tanga of a million and a half people, with German nightclubs, great fish restaurants, and all-night bars when you can be in the sweaty, humid, malarial swamps of the Pangani River delta with insect-laden food and warm Tusker beer?

Why? Because it is the real thing. And the beaches were some of the best in the world. Besides, Pangani was, for them, the only choice. It was home to the world's second-largest crocodile, a dinosaur indeed.

They piled into the Land Rover and Mbuno rolled them off gently into the bush down a sandy path. He always instinctively seemed to know the way. He had admitted to Pero that he had never been to Pangani before, yet his command of the right pathway to take was as Pero expected, Mbuno perfect. The night and moon had taken control of shadows and glistening vegetation. There were no signs for reference Pero could recognize and yet after about twenty minutes, Mbuno made a sharp right into what seemed to be jungle without end and they soon ground to a halt inches from two taxi minivans and another Land Rover matching the one they were in, as well as six zebra-painted minivans with Dar-es-Salaam license plates. Tourist vans. The camp would be full, as Pero had been warned.

"Careful Mr. Pero, Miss Mary . . . plenty of hippo and crocs are out tonight."

Ruis agreed, "Yeah, Mbuno's right, we had to duck behind the fencing around the tent when we were coming to get you. Big fat cow just tip-toed through the middle of camp for heaven's sake."

They did as they were told, and made their way, watching carefully, staying under the suspended twenty-five watt bulbs, daisy-chained from palm tree to palm tree. The hyraxes were croak-screaming, left and right. It was going to be a noisy night. Pero squashed his first big mosquito on his arm, always a forceful reminder to take the malaria pills. The area was rife with the disease.

In the round main dining hall, with giant log beams radiating like an umbrella from the center, walls spit-spot with new whitewash, the thatch freshly repaired, and mahogany gleaming everything, dinner service was just being laid by the six or so waiters on one side of the room. At the other end, everyone was standing around the bar, drinking beer or something softer or weaker, as they wanted. The Pangani Camp has an open bar and drinks policy. You paid your fee and all meals and drink were included. You could tell the tourists from his crew, the tourists were whispering and gesturing at the men seated at the center table in the cocktail lounge portion of the big room, two burly cops in uniform either side, and Priit sitting opposite, answering questions posed by the Commissioner.

The Commissioner saw Pero enter and waved one of the cops over toward Pero, crooked his finger and gestured Pero over. As Pero moved around a chair, the Commissioner caught sight of Mary standing just behind. The speed with which he moved was amazing. He bobbed up, like a jack-in-the-box, wavered, stumbled over a chair that was in his line of approach, and mumbled profuse nonsensical greetings, seemingly to no one in particular on the way over. When he reached Mary and Pero, he stuck out a hand, to her, but Pero took it instead. "So nice to see you Commissioner. How's your brother, either of them, in fact? May I introduce Mary Lever?"

The official stared, boggle-eyed at Pero, then her, then Pero, not sure who or what to answer first. He chose Mary. "Miss. Lever, Tanzania," he was speaking for the whole country suddenly, "is so very, very happy you have come here. It is a great honor indeed, we are all very proud to have you." And then as an afterthought, "I mean, have you here visiting our country, that is."

"Thank you Commissioner, Singh isn't it?" The sugar was dripping from her lips—it was quite a performance. "I will make sure my uncle makes Tanzania a stop on his next trip to Africa. I am sure I will be able to take him home tales of your great hospitality."

Immediately, the Lever magic had its full effect. The Commissioner, in some haste, words tumbling out, asked her if she was thirsty, hungry, tired, needed to sit, needed anything, had a difficult flight, had ever been to Tanzania, and, so sorry for the tragic accident at the airport, isn't it wonderful no one was hurt, and what is she filming, could he stay and watch? Mary turned to Pero and said, "I leave those details to Mr. Baltazar, but for now I would enjoy a cup of good strong hot *chai*, please." The Commissioner pretended he was a head-waiter, snapping his fingers and settling Mary in a chair. The summoned waiter literally ran for the kitchen yelling, "Chai, magi moto!" (tea, hot water).

Pero could see the second mental light bulb go off as he released her chair back. He looked at Pero: "Mr. Baltazar? Mr. Baltazar? Not the Baltazar who was with brother Virgi when he caught the record Marlin three years ago?"

"One and the same, your brother was most kind to invite me out for some fishing. I think you were also supposed to come, but had last minute official business, as I remember."

"Yes, yes, that is most true. It was a great day for him, a great day, the trophy is in his office above the garage." The "garage" the Commissioner referred to was at least half an acre of spotless, gleaming glass showrooms for Toyota trucks of every kind, above which Virgi kept a five-bedroom penthouse and all the amenities, as well as his office and a swimming pool. Every bedroom had a harbor front view. It was spectacular and slightly colonial, certainly imperious. "Garage" was a term of reverse snobbery he used to highlight how rich the

Singhs really were. Tanzania moved mostly on Toyota. Every Toyota came through the Singhs. All in all, they were hard working, honest, and had the very best interests of Tanzania at heart, especially if there was a profit. Communism or not, the Singhs were the backbone of the country before and now.

Commissioner Munidar Singh held out a chair for Pero who saw the crew visibly relax. The danger of lengthy stays and endless questions—not to mention an absence of rights— was abated. Not over, but, surely, under control. And for Pero? He was happy enough to keep the Commissioner happy and planned to tell him the truth in private later, at least the truth as he knew it. Which was almost nothing.

What Pero *guessed* might be the truth was something he wasn't prepared to share: Pero had worked out the bomb was planted in Nairobi. Probably hastily this morning, probably by the fueling truck ground crew. When in bond, no one was allowed near the plane's contents. Refueling was not considered getting into the plane. Once his Nairobi tail lost sight of Pero and Mbuno thanks to Amogh and his Porsche, the only place they would be sure Pero was going to be was at Mara airways, getting on that damn plane. They wanted Pero, or maybe the whole crew, in the worst way. Having been spotted up there at Gurreh on the plateau, they must have assumed the worst—that their clandestine operations were exposed. They must have also calculated the crew knew about Simon's real cause of death as well. Either way, it didn't matter, bombing of the plane proved that the crew was now definitely a target.

They didn't know about Mary because she wasn't visually with them until this morning. The plane was the only target, a timer set to coincide with the flight plan logged with the tower by Sheryl the night before: to Arusha, then Pangani. The only people who would have had access to that were the fuelers, they needed to know how many pounds of fuel to pump into her. Pero wished he had thought to ask the Australian if the plane was fully gassed, it would have proved the fueler had still thought they were going to Arusha and then on to Pangani.

Bless your little obsession and kindness Sheryl; your decision to treat with a special flight to Arusha saved many lives, Pero thought. He would tell JT, he'd think of something appropriate—after JT maybe killed Pero, that is, for having placed Mary in harm's way. *Hmm,* Pero thought, *perhaps it's better not to talk about this to Mary just yet either.*

So, Pero sat there and answered every question truthfully and completely as far as Pero knew it to be true. Supposition never came into it. And to be fair, what was the point of worrying this nice Commissioner with a problem that was, after all, not a Tanzanian problem? On the other hand, Pero needed to keep Mary safe while they were here in Pangani. He saw the young woman night manager hovering with Mary's and his room keys.

Pero beckoned her over while he addressed Singh, "Commissioner, we have a long day tomorrow and the crew, Miss Lever, and I need to go over the schedule and prepare. We will be leaving for the mouth of the Pangani to a croc farm— Rudolf's, you know it?" The Commissioner nodded, Rudolf's was famous, half the handbags in Paris got their hides from Rudolf's. Rudolf was long since dead, but the croc hides were still the same quality. "Well, may I suggest, if it is not inconveniencing you and your men too much, that as we're only here for three days, that you stay as our guests—I'm sure the management can find you a room, and for your men in khaki as well." Pero looked at the night manager and she nodded vigorously—she had expected the Commissioner was going to get a free room anyway since it was already too late to fly out, but now Pero was going to pay, and she was only too happy to agree. "That way, Commissioner, you can watch Miss Lever being filmed with her *dinosaurs* and your men can, how should

I put this, ensure the pleasurable, non-interrupted, stay of Miss Lever in your country."

"If you think that was possible . . ."

"My dear Commissioner, not only possible, a pleasure." Pero put the final sweetener in. "And I am sure your brothers will approve, as I am sure they will agree with your extra generous help in protecting Miss Lever, personally."

"That is most kind, most kind. It is an honor." He bowed to them all. "Please enjoy your dinner and rest, we can speak tomorrow, when there are other matters of a police business, we need to discuss." He added to remind Pero who was the real boss in Pangani. Pero didn't mind. Whilst Pero felt police presence here was a good idea, the police presence was still, nevertheless, a threat in the event the Commissioner decided he had to blame someone, anyone, for the Cessna's fire and destruction. Pero was pretty certain the TV company insurance would not cover an act of terrorism.

The Commissioner turned towards the manageress, "Now, if you will excuse me, I will secure the grounds and discuss accommodations." He snapped his fingers at the night manager, and she followed him close behind.

The crew filled the vacuum around the low table as the police left. Mbuno remained standing behind Pero's chair. Mary was first: "I'm impressed. But he'll be hanging around all day tomorrow, getting in the way. Still, better safe than sorry." Mary seemed better, over whatever had happened in Arusha, tired but less morose. Maybe it was the sight of what could have been and much worse as well. Pero assumed she was glad to be alive, that sort of thing.

Priit chimed in, "Pero, you got here just in time, Heep was about to let him have both barrels."

Heep waved away the suggestion, "No, I wasn't, Priit . . . well, maybe, but honestly, wanting to take apart tour camera equipment to check for more bombs? It's ridiculous."

Was it, Pero wondered? But again, it didn't fit the timing, all that had happened pointed to a last minute crude attempt. They had a bomb with a timer and simply set it according to the flight plan, boom somewhere between Arusha and Pangani. Instead, the plane was on the ground a good two hours before. It didn't take much to destroy a plane; a half-pound of explosive would do it.

"Priit, is that new battery pack of mine in your tent?"

"Yeah. Mind telling me, Pero? What the hell it's for?"

"It's a surprise. Let me have one surprise, won't you?"

"We've had enough surprises today, boss. But let's drop it and get some food." And with that, everyone nodded on Priit's advice. As they moved to a dining table where all the other guests were already seated, Mbuno sat next to Mary and they talked intently about giant crocs he had seen at Lake Rudolf and no one ever discussed one more single unpleasant thing that evening. Dinner was broiled croc (what else?) and mashed poi, the cornmeal side dish of Africa. Fruit and more fruit were for dessert, with German cookies, slightly limp in the humid night air. The pineapple and apple mangoes were perfect. The tourists grumbled. The crewmembers ate like it was the last supper. Pero was determined to see to that it was not.

Two hours later, everyone was seen safely to their tented rooms. Mbuno had swapped his for the communal room with the drivers and the cops. The Commissioner took Mbuno's tent. Pero didn't ask why. One, Pero knew Mbuno would be less self-conscious there; two, he could gather intel and hear rumors, and three . . . Pero was beginning to sound like his father making a list. But the best reason that he was there and not in a tourist tent is that he was next to the Land Rovers if they needed one in a hurry. Unlike some other drivers, he was always trusted with the keys.

Before they turned in, Priit and Ruis welcomed Pero into their tent and gave Pero the battery pack. Pero told them that if they could keep a secret, he'd show them what it was. Pero needed a secret key, so he took it back to his tent. There Pero pushed the hidden latch on his computer, took out the plastic key hidden below the CD drawer. With the key Pero opened the box and took out the mini satellite radio, same model as before. It only weighed four ounces; the empty fake battery pack was four pounds, steel and lead lined, unbreakable. Pero took it back to them, leaving the radio under the towel on his washstand.

Pero showed them how to insert the plastic key and, presto, the lid slid open, leaving an empty box for hiding stuff in. The cavity was roughly the size of a Beta tape. Ruis knew immediately what it was for. "Damn Pero, where did you have this made? It's damn useful, I could have used this in Kosovo. I lost lots of tapes to the military guys. With this I could have stashed a few of the riskier ones."

Priit said he had seen one before, but not opened, when he was the cameraman on a shoot they did in the Maldives. "Never knew what equipment the damn thing was for. Tried to open it. It was sealed." He examined it closely, "Look at this. It looks sealed. Amazing."

"Okay guys, keep this secret, we may need it yet when we leave Nairobi with Heep's footage of Simon." They knew what Pero meant. The Kenya tourist people would not like it if the government minder had now gone back and told them Heep had videotaped the dead Simon. That was bad for tourism.

They promised to keep it secret and safeguard it for Pero. Pero kept the flat plastic key to make the point the risk was his, not theirs. They nodded. They spent the next hour going over the videotaping equipment and plans for the morrow.

Priit especially liked the new underwater camera. "Where'd you find that? It's small. Has fore and aft impellers. A bladder for buoyancy. And the book says it's rated to 100 feet. Guidance is magnetic-signal through water. No wires. Amazing. We'll need at least a few hours practice. What's the power for this thing? It says just plug it in. And recharge the batteries. Two hours for full charge. But if I can't replace the batteries when they fade . . . and Pero, we have no extras."

"The battery charge will last two days full-time use. They only power the computer, magnetic signal and camera zoom and focus, not the impellers." They looked amazed. Pero explained. Like kids opening a Christmas Eve package, they were dying to try it out, so they sat there, glued to his every description, turning the sled over in their hands to check it out.

The principle of the design was based on the thermodynamic properties of water related to depth. Not a new concept, this was the first production model of a Navy underwater rover camera platform—that worked.

Submarines have, for some time, been relying on a neutral impact buoyancy point somewhere amidships. What was above wanted to rise, what was below wanted to sink. Down was always greater because of gravity, but if you balanced them out, then simply venting, say, the conning tower periscope tubes could make the ship go up or down, depending on where you took the incoming water from. It was a temperature thing. They noticed, by 1975, that if you took the water from the keel, the effect was faster not because of gravity but because of pressure and temperature. If you ran that venting though a motor inducer, you had power for the impellers. The batteries were for the computer that controlled it all—and the camera lens of course. It took the Navy forty years to perfect this. Sony bought the rights to use the patents, and they were about to test out the first commercial model.

The camera mechanism would store the energy of the temperature of salt water at one atmosphere (the surface) and then use the differential at, say ten feet, to run the impellers. All it took was a pick-up flexible tube and small weight that dangled from the bottom of the SeaSled, as it was called, ten feet down.

Priit was thrilled, really thrilled. "Hey, I could stay here. In bed. And watch the monitor. And pilot the thing out in the river. It says the magnetic signal is good for five hundred yards through water. And two hundred yards through rock. Fan-tastic."

Pero jokingly pointed out that Priit was angling to get more sack time, again, and that he was pushing it as they had work to do.

Pero was saying good-night when Ruis stopped him and whispered. "Oy Pero, what's with Mary, she all right?" Pero told him he didn't know, she had gotten back on board in Arusha very down and never said a word until Pangani. "Well, Heep and Mary had a thing a few years back . . ." Pero looked surprised, as he didn't know that . . . "Yeah, so she's in there with him tonight—Heep said he'd hold her—she was shaking. Aftereffect I expect, shock from the plane, right? You'd better tell Mbuno and, maybe post a guard? Think there will be more trouble? Have they got revolutionaries going on down here now?" Pero knew Ruis wasn't afraid, he'd covered virtually every war zone for the past twenty years, he just wanted to know the score.

"I think it was a one-off, so does Commissioner Singh, a mistaken identity thing, who knows? The Commissioner and his men should keep us clear of danger here and, when we're done, we'll decoy flights and destinations, confuse any followers—I'll fix that, don't worry. But in any event, we'll beeline back to Nairobi and take the earliest plane out, okay? No risks, agreed?"

"Agreed, unless we have to. Like in Venezuela on the Rio Negro, remember?" That time they had to fight their way out between two tribes engaged in civil war, themselves caught in the middle. They never learned what started it, but they got the hell out of there, with a few wounds along the way. Ruis and Pero both hoped this wasn't a repeat.

Pero patted him on the shoulder, said goodnight, and went back towards his tent, time to make a call to State. Along the way, Pero listened at Heep's tent flap and heard low voices and, he thought, crying. Pero found the Commissioner and got him to post two guards, one at each end. Pero went off to tell Mbuno. Pero suspected he'd be restless tonight, perhaps even doing an anti-insurgency patrol. God help intruders if Mbuno thought they were up to no good.

In his quarters, Pero ran the shower in the back part of the two-room canvas safari tent. The water ran brown for a while, clearing the mud from the pipes until the Pangani River water came through, splashing on the duckboard making a masking sound. Pero dialed Tom Baylor's office number and heard a signal, a double click. So he simply talked, hoping it was being reported, recorded, "Baltazar, Pero here, south of Tanga, on coast at Pangani Camp in Tanzania. Our Cessna 414 aircraft destroyed by bomb, timer set to coincide with our flight from Wilson Airport, Nairobi. Flight plan change resulted in plane being early at airport Pangani when explosion occurred. No one hurt, no work equipment lost. Recommend investigate fueling services Wilson Airport. Dar-es-Salaam Police Commissioner Singh *in situ*, so we have secured his security services for Mary Lever, possible for three days. Lever is now part of my television crew. Pilots, one a witness to the explosion at Pangani Airport, are arriving Wilson Airport immediate. Recommend advise this message to Tom Baylor asap. Over and out." Pero heard the double click and was clear. Message delivered, he hoped.

CHAPTER 10

Pangani Beach

Eden could not have been better. With the rising sun, the tropical sounds reaching into the primordial brain that Mary called the reptilian brain. Along with the balmy breeze of the briny delta, the paradise beckoned them all and lifted spirits. Pero exited his tent only to bump into the back of a guard. "Good morning."

"Morning Sir, Commissioner Singh said he would be pleased to join you for breakfast at seven." It was 6:30. Pero nodded and went next door to check on Ruis and Priit. No way Pero was going to disturb Mary and Heep.

The crew's tent of Priit and Ruis was empty. Pero checked the case and found the SeaSled was missing. Pero didn't need three guesses to know where they were. It had gone early light an hour ago, so they were obviously in the water. *Boys with their toy*, Pero thought as he exited the tent, *Time for tea*.

Mbuno was having the same thought, besides which his internal radar had told him Pero was up and about. Appearing at Pero's side, he smiled and said softly, "Gani bosi?" (How are you boss?). Pero simply shrugged. "Ndiyo. *Mimi nataka chai*," (Yeah. I want tea) and the two men walked together towards the dining hut. Their spirits were matched, time to get the day underway.

In the dining room, Pero surprisingly found Heep and Mary already half-way through breakfast. On safari, crews eat together, always, this was unusual. Pero didn't want to probe too much, yesterday was tough on everyone. So he simply pulled up a chair and said in a casual way, "Feeling better Mary? Morning Heep."

"Yes, Pero, I think so, still a bit raw, but better thank you. A good night's rest and Heep to console my ragged nerves seemed to do the trick." Her eyes were challenging Pero to ask more. After a moment of silence, but not avoidance of eye contact, she understood Pero had no reservations. What happens on safari stays on safari and, anyway, who was Pero to judge? Pero knew them both, Heep better than her, and they were both his good friends. Pero hoped it worked out. Heep was between marriages (always looking, hated to be alone) and, well, "that twerp" husband of hers was clearly history.

"I'm glad Mary. Yesterday was a stressful day for you. Let us know if there is something we can do to help. Arusha creates problems that people just don't understand until they go through it."

"Heep told me. I didn't know you both had been called before as well. It's awful, just awful." And with that, her face got so sad that Pero wanted to reach over the table and hug her. Heep looked at Pero with sympathy also putting his arm around her shoulder. He mouthed, "I told you so." Pero nodded. He was right, of course, Arusha is the pits, Pero remembered all too vividly.

Almost ten years ago, Heep and Pero had been filming on the shores of Lake Victoria. It was a segment for the new cable channel *Discovery*. The budget was small, the crew smaller. It was just Heep, Pero, and one scout, Kamau, subbing for

Mbuno who was with other clients. Kamau was a useless, lanky, lazy racist. Their location filming fitted in between other work schedules. Heep was getting footage of the "smoking lake" that the early explorers first spotted and so nicknamed Lake Victoria. It was for an explorers' special—Livingstone, Stanley, Burton, that sort of thing.

The smoke rising off the lake is actually flies, millions and millions of flies. From a distance it looks like a series of campfires in the marshy reeds, up close it's a small tornado of flies. The tribeswomen from the region have woven intricate baskets they swirl around their heads acting like butterfly nets, catching the flies. They make patties out of the flies and fry them in hippo grease or sometimes Warthog grease. It's a delicacy and an alternative protein source from the fish of the lake. It tastes like slabs of pig fat, uncooked, tepid.

Lake Victoria is big enough to be slightly tidal and have deep currents. Every day, at noon, when the wind shifts, things move about. There they were filming as the tide changed, thigh deep in the marshes, leeches already attached to calves, when a log bobbed up, then another and another. But they were not logs, they were bodies that had drifted down the Kagera river in a recent slaughter between tribes. Two of the bodies had been partially eaten. The crocs and hippos thereabouts were well fed. The third body had identification—it was a UN inspector from the Chad delegation of peacekeepers. His throat had been cut.

As witnesses, they were called on to testify. They hadn't seen the killing of the UN peacekeeper, someone else had, they had only found the body. Their testimony was needed to firm the link between the crime, the location, and the autopsy. They were assured it would be over in a day. They spent three being grilled and all but accused of the murder by defense council. They were shown weapons, how to hold them to hack and mutilate people, asked if they had ever done so, were made to pretend they were slitting throats, to check if it could have been them, left and right hand, that sort of thing. It made no difference that they had witnesses to the suddenly bobbing bodies. The women they were filming were also there, but they were intimidated to silence by defense council—even though the Tutsi defense lawyer was rebuked, often, by the magistrates. It was a farce. A dangerous, potentially lethal farce. They received death threats, and one stray bullet pierced his shower in the Arusha Arms Hotel after the first day of testimony. After they were done, the death threats recurred and Heep had one narrow escape on Arusha's main street the next day with a truck that didn't stop. His left arm was badly broken, but otherwise he was okay.

In that courtroom, the stench of base human hatred for their own kind filled every waking moment of their three days. Now, if ever someone tells Pero humans are civilized, Pero tells them to go to one of those trials and watch the worst of humanity expose itself.

Mary, yesterday, had obviously had a full dose of Arusha's humanity as well.

"Jikuru, he stayed behind to argue that you didn't need to go back, didn't he?" It was the only explanation of how she could have given so short a testimony.

"Yes, he said he would resign if I was called again. He was protecting me, I know that now."

Pero and Mbuno sat, visibly concerned, for they sensed there was something else, "What happened, Mary?" Pero asked it quietly.

"Someone stabbed him in chambers when he was disrobing. He was dead before he was found. The killer was running in his direction, had the blade in his hand. As he ran at me, the Nigerian killed him with one blow." Pero nodded, Mary began to weep. Heep looked down at her hands folded on the table's edge, tightened his arm over her shoulder, and consoled her with kind words.

Mary suddenly seemed to make up her mind. "I have got to stop crying, this just won't do. Jiki knew the dangers and my testimony will put at least one bastard behind bars forever. The other killer is dead and good riddance." Pero was still marveling that the police hadn't detained her. And at her strength through it all.

"How'd you get clear?"

"It was your doing. You told him to protect me with his life. He did, not just stopping the killer, but he got me away before I could be questioned, exposed to more danger. His army career will be over, or worse. Is there anything they can do for him? Heep says there probably isn't, but Pero, do you know someone, something that can help him? If not for him Pero, I might never have left there." She paused. "Ever."

Pero promised he would, right after breakfast. "But now," Pero told them, "I need food to make the brain cells work." Pero made light of it, but made sure Mary saw the answer she was looking for in his eyes. Pero remembered the Nigerian's name, even if she didn't. It was stitched on his uniform pocket: Kweno Usman. Pero remembered it because Kweno is the Nigerian word for hope. And Usman is a mnemonic: us man. Easy. Pero would get State on to it immediately after breakfast, mark it urgent, link it to the great US hero, the Reverend JT. Pero was pretty sure it was the most effective method of protecting that big Nigerian with the white gloves. Of course, it meant JT would find out that Mary had been at risk under his watch, but, still, Pero had come through, hadn't he? Or rather, Kweno had. Pero resolved to never underestimate the word of a soldier, Nigerian or otherwise.

Like most of the crew, Pero ordered up, eggs and more eggs, loads of sausages (here in German-influenced Tanzania, the sausages were Nurenburgers, not the British style bangers of Kenya), toast, jam and fruit. Breakfast is a hearty meal when you are filming. Lunch may be a while off—and sometimes became dinner, if you were lucky. The Pangani people would make them packed lunches, but they were, mostly, inedible. Pero was sure the shore crabs would be fed scraps from lunch, *Swap Trafalgar Square's or St. Mark's pigeons for Pangani crabs, the feeding frenzy is the same.*

Ruis and Priit showed up, bathing trunks, tees, and sandals, gone native, with sand in their hair. They were grinning. Priit couldn't wait, before he even sat down, he started in, "Heep . . . man you gotta see this thing. It hangs. I mean hangs at thirty feet. Stable as a steady cam. No operator. Instant response to pan and zoom. It's great! And, what's really cool? It . . ."

Ruis interrupted, they were speaking over each other, totally excited, "And it can move laterally, Heep, laterally for God's sake. No noise, silent as a bunny, a few bubbles, that's all. It has an external mike, Heep, an external mike!"

"And when we moved into the reef to check the macro? It adjusted automatically. The coral anemones stayed out. The machine isn't alive, so they didn't sense it, they didn't duck in . . ."

"And then suddenly, I'm standing in three feet of water with the remote control panel . . ."

"Which is totally waterproof. Even to a hundred feet. So you can swim with the thing. If you want to."

"Yeah, anyway, I'm zoomed in on a clownfish doing his anemone dance when the camera, which I had set to auto, suddenly zooms out and refocuses on a passing nurse shark, and as soon as she went by, it pulled zoom and went back to the clownfish. It was perfect, Heep, perfect."

"And the best part? Heep, the damn thing picked up the swish. The actual noise of the nurse shark's tale. And never moved. Stable as a rock. Wanna see?"

Heep sat there, aware of the contrast of moods: the remnants of the tale of Arusha compared to these two professionals with their new toy and made a decision. Although a serious person, always the professional, but still Heep had a deep-rooted sense of fun, so he used a professional tone, shaking his head as if disappointed, "What do you think Pero, should we confiscate their toy now, or later?"

Pero joined in on the game, all serious, springing to their defense. "Oh, I don't know Heep, come on, they've been a pretty reliable crew up to now, maybe we should indulge them . . ."

Ruis raised his hands in surrender, "Ah. Come on, Heep and Pero. Don't be old farts. Come 'n see." He was so desperate, like a child. They all started laughing.

Heep smiled, "We will, we will. Let's finish breakfast and get our trunks on."

Priit's excitement wouldn't die down either, "But you got to see this thing work."

Pero and Heep told them they would, just to try and relax, as they just wanted to finish breakfast. But Heep wasn't completely through joking, yet. "Okay Priit, I will be right there, but, really, don't you think Mary should have a little more time to eat? After all, she's the one on camera, and those croc scenes in the nude take stamina."

With that, Mary spat a fresh mouthful of coffee across the table that landed on Pero's shirt and eggs. Everyone laughed, even Mary. Pero liked the smell of coffee in the morning, although preferably not on his food. The waitress hurried over with fresh napkins just as the Commissioner entered the hut. And, indeed, even the Commissioner couldn't dampen spirits and so he simply joined in. By the time they were loading up the Land Rovers, he seemed more like his roly-poly brother Virgi than the officious cop of the day before. Of course, Mary was still having a warming effect on him.

Leaving the dining room, Pero asked Mbuno, who was making a honey sandwich to go, if he had any problems with his accommodation. Mbuno guessed Pero meant if he had privacy, away from the extra guards the Commissioner had brought. So he explained he was sharing a hut with the other driver who kept pretty much to himself. Turning to face Pero, he put his hand on Pero's sleeve and asked, "Bwana, did you get another special box? One that also may need burying?"

Damn, does he know everything? Pero shot him a glance and caught him smiling slyly, so he smiled back and nodded, then added. "But remember, Mbuno, I know you have a weakness for that honey and I'll make sure there's none for breakfast or tea if you are not a whole lot more respectful."

With forced subservience, Mbuno dropped his chin, "Ah, bwana, Mr. Pero, Sir, I will do as you say, yes mzee, bwana, Sir."

"Oh, get lost." It should be one of those carefree days— Pero could sense it.

Back at his tent, Pero dialed Tom's office number on the satellite phone and sent another message: "Pero Baltazar, Pangani Camp. Yesterday Arusha attempt on Mary Lever, niece of Reverend Jimmy Threte, known as JT. Knife wielder was killed by Nigerian soldier, UN detail, name of Kweno Usman. The same assassin killed Jikuru, a Judge. I recommend Jimmy Threte be advised soonest that Mary Lever requests presence of Kweno Usman urgent. Also recommend your protection Kweno Usman soonest and most urgent." Here Pero needed a little white lie to make sure they did something this morning. "I think maybe that Kweno Usman knows information on

Gurreh encampment. End." As Pero heard the double click, for message received, he thought his message should be sufficiently cryptic and yet make them grab and protect, *well, okay* he thought, *arrest*, Kweno without delay.

Pero suited up in beach attire, shorts, sandals with socks and a T-shirt, grabbed walkie-talkies, and made his way to the Land Rovers. The crew was waiting anxiously to hit the beach, the mood still upbeat.

Tropical Africa, especially there, just south of the equator, on the shore of the Indian Ocean evokes all that is primordial, serene, and vital in the evolution of man. The sands of Pangani beach, south of the delta, are clean, wide, fringed with palm trees and as close to movie paradise as you'll ever find. Pero loved it there and, were it not for the pressures of work, would live here, year round. There are just three things that mar this Eden. One is the insects, which attack, without remorse, both newcomers and locals with equal ferocity. The second is the remoteness should anything go wrong, and medical attention becomes vital—you are at the mercy of the Flying Doctors, which, in Tanzania has not got quite the same access as in Kenya. But the last is a truly frightening bit of Nature that will, if you make a mistake, bring an end to your idyll in a hurry.

The Pangani delta sub-species of Nile crocodile.

Mary started to explain it all to them as they sat out in the open under palm trees at the edge of the beach. They were all admiring the morning sun glistening off the water. Pero nodded to Priit and he gently rotated the camera he was cleaning on the hood of one Land Rover towards her. He put his hand over the red telltale light and pressed record. The framing was Mary, stripped to her swimsuit, sexy but not provocative, palm tree over her right shoulder, early mid-morning sun illuminating her face, the gentle breeze whipping her hair.

The other safari Land Rover, very much Africana, was behind her, and the seemingly endless coast and blue water completed the scene.

"A hundred and fifty million years ago when great dinosaurs roamed the earth, the vegetation was more plentiful from the greenhouse effect of all the burgeoning life above and below the water as well as from the still-cooling planet and global volcanic activity. The dinosaurs, as we have been taught to call them, were the peak of evolution, perfectly adapted to their surroundings. There were herbivores, carnivores, and omnivores. They raised their young, they also laid eggs and deserted them to fend for themselves, and—we're not sure about this yet—even carried some eggs and hatched them internally, much like marsupials today.

"Nothing that is alive on the planet, then and now, is unrelated. To say something is extinct is a misnomer, for everything has evolved, passed on traits, shares traits with what once was and what will be. Our human brains have, at their core, a reptilian brain center that is a clear and present extension of who we once were, where we came from. And remember that dinosaurs came from amoeba, so there are traces there too.

"Back to one hundred fifty million years ago . . . how did these behemoths get around? The mass of their muscle, which we measure based on mud imprint as well as bone structure and density, was simply too heavy to allow for anything more than sluggish movement. And, indeed for years everyone has assumed that's how mammals (who have blood cooling and heating physiology) won the day, they could move faster and simply ran circles around the slower lizards. Then someone found out that dinosaurs had elaborate cooling techniques. The perfect example of this is the Stegosaurus with those huge plates sticking up. Amour? Yes they were, but they also had blood channels all through them, which bone doesn't need, to act as cooling radiators. Now they had a cooling system, why would nature evolve muscles too large to move?"

While she watched to see if any of them could possibly answer her question, she fingered strands of hair behind her ear and smiled at their silence.

"There could only be one answer: chemistry. Their baseline for chemical analysis was wrong. There had to be more oxygen. They excavated amber from the late Jurassic period—one hundred fifty million years ago approximately. Amber is the perfect canning process. The sap oozed from trees, much as sap oozes from fir tree wounds today. It caught water, insects, debris, and if they are lucky, air bubbles before it set. One hundred fifty million years later, they analyzed those air bubbles and found there was sixteen percent more oxygen in the air.

"So much oxygen would burn our lungs, kill us quickly. But, add that sixteen percent more oxygen to the chemical formula for those massive dinosaur muscles and you have a different animal indeed: a reptile, three times the bulk of today's elephant moving at thirty to forty miles per hour. Add in teeth and you can see why T. Rex was so formidable.

"Right here, where they're standing, they know of four important species unique to this area, and remember the whole world was full of unique areas—there was no population movement back then to homogenize species: The Barosaurus at eighty-eight feet long—all neck and tail, capable of eating a ton of vegetation a day. Then there's the Ceratosaurus who chased Barosaurus—Ceratosaurus walked on two legs, and looked like a smaller T. Rex, but he was still only twenty feet tall!"

She paused for effect. No one was moving. They were getting a free lecture from the world's expert.

"And there was Dicraeosaurus, forty-five feet long, on all fours, a plant eater with a split tail that could lash out to defend itself. And, not least, Dryosaurus, a tree dwelling lizard, the size of the Komodo dragon today, who was fast and an insect eater. Remember, the dragonfly had already been around for two hundred million years, dinosaurs were only newcomers.

"But let's not forget the ocean, it's what we're here to look at. Out there," she pointed out to sea. Pero glanced at Priit and he nodded imperceptibly, still filming . . . "was the king of the sea, the Cryptoclidus, all forty-five feet of him. He was an impressive predator, with grabbing teeth at the end of an eel-like neck. He was an excellent swimmer, maybe as fast as today's tuna—which was already around back then—literally flying through the water like a huge sea lion, but with bigger, much bigger, fins, powered by all that oxygen, see?"

The wind wisped her hair forward again and she shook it back in place, the way models do. Pero looked at Heep. This was excellent television. Mary's voice suddenly became dramatic, the way camp counselors do around a campfire deep in the woods.

"And there was another, an older dinosaur who had evolved during the period preceding the Jurassic. He was cunning, large enough to tackle anything he could catch, including Cryptocleidus and very large sea turtles. He's still with us, even if he is a bit smaller and slower without all that oxygen: the Marine Crocodile. The only difference between the Marine Crocodile dinosaur and today's Nile crocodile is flippers and a thousand pounds or so. The Nile crocodile has evolved claws, all the better to get on land and feed there as well. It isn't extinction, it's evolution, and a better, more capable beast—still eating mammals.

"The largest marine crocodiles today are off Darwin, on the north coast of Australia. They regularly get to thirty feet, a dinosaur indeed. These here, at Pangani, have never been filmed in the sea and never filmed under water. It's just too damn dangerous. They see you? They eat you. Oh, and although the Pangani crocs are four feet shorter than the Darwin crocs, they are not smaller, they weigh five hundred pounds more. The Pangani Nile croc is a fat, deadly, powerful dinosaur." Mary looked around, perhaps waiting for questions. Pero nodded to Priit and he flipped the camera to off.

Heep jumped up. "Let's see that Priit." Waiting until Priit rewound, he grabbed the earphones and held one to one ear.

"Set," said Priit and rolled the tape and Heep lowered his eye to the viewer.

"Perfect, just perfect, this is perfect." Heep was happy. Mary was looking puzzled. Heep stood and told Priit to unload the take, log it, and bag it, waterproof. "Mary, that's the hard part of the show segment. The intro, the voice-over, the talking head, everything. Well done!"

Pero laughed, Mary had no idea, just kept saying, "You're kidding, oh no, come on, you have got to be kidding, you weren't . . ." They were. They knew good dialogue when they heard it. And Mary had looked perfect—relaxed, professional and, above all, totally passionate about . . . what else? Dinosaurs.

"What do you say, Ruis, Priit, should we try out your new toy before we go over to Rudolf's?" The eager duo jumped, pulled the sled off the rear seat of Mbuno's Land Rover, and ran, scampered, towards the water, calling over their shoulders "Come on!"

Heep, Mary, and Pero looked at each other smiling and started across the sand, trailing in their wake. Pero called for the Commissioner to follow. Why not? He might as well enjoy the show. He wasn't dressed for the beach, but at least he had his shoes off, had rolled up his suit trousers, and unbuttoned his collar. The jacket he carried over his arm. Pero could see the weight in the pocket, probably a small automatic.

As they neared the water's edge, they could see Ruis standing in about three feet of water and Priit about ten feet in front of him, water lapping his chin, releasing the SeaSled, playing out the umbilical that would hang below. He turned back and shouted to them, "You have to initiate the bladder manually, pump it up, charge it, and then it's automatic, controlled by the onboard computer." He was pumping something with his thumb on the wing that jutted out either side. As he released the SeaSled, Ruis said, "I have got it," and Priit did that high stepping run in deep water, trying to get some speed, back to Ruis. They were just like kids, ecstatic with their new marvel.

"Hey, Ruis, why are you standing in the water, I thought Priit said you could be back in bed."

"Okay Pero, ha-ha, but I'm just not used to the capabilities of this thing, I don't want to lose signal. Magnetic transmission, it's really cool, but it's new for me. Anyway, what's the baud rate?"

Pero shook his head, "Who knows? It works, right? You can enjoy and read the manual, the one Sony sends to the purchaser, not the simple manual you have. It's like a phone book—I'll send it to you, after."

"Cool." Ruis was a geek at heart. It's why Heep always hired him on locations, he knew how every piece of equipment worked, and often could fix them in the field.

They all crowded around Ruis, Heep on his right, Pero over his shoulder. The LCD was difficult to read in the bright sun, but Pero could see enough to be amazed. The SeaSled was already down to thirty feet, according to the readout, and beneath the surf. The reef was just a hundred feet offshore, and the SeaSled was heading that way. Ruis asked Heep he wanted "a go-see on the reef."

Heep, the shoot's director, took charge and nodded. "It's not very fast, but it is stable. Can you pan left for me?" It panned the lens thirty degrees. "That only the lens panning?" Ruis nodded. "Okay, how about a yaw then?" The Sea Sled yawed, no movement, up or down, no judder, solid as a rock. "Damn, that's better than I can shoot underwater."

Pero needed to explain something to them. "Guys, remember that this thing works that way because it is part of the water, in synch with the ocean. If it gets into a current, it will go with the current, you can only make it break up or down. If you get it on the surface, you can retrieve it. You must be careful not to get into currents or something compromising . . ."

"Like?"

"Well, I don't know, a cenote in the Yucatan. The weird thermals there and changes in buoyancy due to changes in salination may defeat its mechanism. And, see that meter there?" Pero pointed to the top left corner of the screen showing eighty-five percent capacity left.

Ruis answered, "Yeah, below thirty percent and we surface. It's the bladder capability. Got it?"

Heep was all business, "Okay, guys, I want to see it with a swimmer. Mary, feel like getting wet? I need a shot of you entering the water and then plunging beneath." She nodded and went back for her flippers, snorkel, and mask. "Ruis, can it come in close enough?"

"No problemmo boss, watch this . . ." He yawed until the lens was pointing at the beach, small surf showing as a water dust cloud. A school of sardines swam by. He zoomed in as they all waited.

Flippers on, "Ready?" Mary asked.

Heep waved her on and told Ruis "Action."

Mary walked into the surf and, on the screen, her feet and then legs appeared, Heep ordered "zoom out" and as her torso entered the water, a silver shoal of sardines made a return pass, thousands of them, all around her legs and waist, as she dropped below the water and they scattered, frightened away. "Keep rolling, Ruis." Ruis nodded. Mary swam straight at the SeaSled. It was magic on screen, perfect framing, absolutely stable, Pero knew Heep would edit this as his opening shot for the segment. "Cut! Log that, Priit. Man, what a wonderful machine. Pero, it's Emmy time!" Pero knew he was right. Now all they had to do was capture the big brute on camera, preferably with Mary in the shot, but in no danger. Time to get over to Rudolf's.

But where was Mary? "Hey, Heep, she's still swimming. How can we tell her to stop?"

Priit had the answer "Yaw the sled. Back and forth. See if she sees that." She did, they saw her turn around. "We'll have to work out signals Heep. Or she could be in trouble. And not know it." Heep nodded, looking very worried. "It's okay, Heep. Ruis and I will work it out with Mary. On the way to Rudolf's." And they did. Yaw side to side was cut. Up and down was surface. Both together were danger.

As they piled into the Land Rovers, the Commissioner asked if he could see what they had been shooting. Heep asked Ruis to playback for him. The Commissioner was amazed, "It would be very useful for my brother to have a copy of this! It is so beautiful, the beach, the water . . ."

"Yeah, and the girl," said Heep smiling.

"Well, yes, but I mean, I didn't mean . . ." Singh was floundering.

Pero laughed and clapped him on the shoulder, "That's okay, I will give you a copy, and I do know what you meant. It is a powerful scene for attracting tourists. We may be able to work something out, but I warn you, Mary is a difficult negotiator, she won't come cheap."

"Ah, yes, copyright, artists' releases . . . . That is all still new for us here. How should I ask her?"

"Make it straight, no diversion. She's an up-front person." The Commissioner nodded and climbed aboard the second Land Rover, front passenger seat, of course. Ruis sat behind him, the SeaSled on his lap, Priit on the other side. They finished loading and Mbuno drove them off, leading, of course.

CHAPTER 11

Rudolf's Croc Farm

Herr Rudolf was a German "left behind" in the time of Tanganyika's heyday, after the Great War, 1918. A wounded corporal, of no family money, he was mustered out, left to live or die in a strange land. In any event, he couldn't afford to make the trip back to Düsseldorf. So, instead of dying, he lived, largely thanks to a local tribal family whose son had been press-ganged and had died in the service of the Kaiser they never knew existed. These coastal people of Pangani were cousins to the Giriama, the famous honey hunters of Kenya.

Rudolf gave the Giriama cousins of Pangani a new industry. Having recovered, but always with a limp (he would later claim it was a croc bite instead of the Lee Enfield bullet that had shattered his tibia), he wanted to settle down and contribute. His loyalty was to these people who had saved him and had shared their homeland. Their loyalty was to the replacement son. It seemed like a fair exchange. This new son could read, write and was a master tanner. It was his trade before he was drafted. At first he tanned hides, but cattle in Africa are not slaughtered with much regularity.

Then, for a while, the White Hunters used him to tan the hides of beasts that had been shot. Several of Hemmingway and Holden's floor and wall rugs were expertly tanned by Rudolf or by people he trained. He was generous that way, teaching anyone who wanted to know, all his secrets. "If I don't share, what will become of my craft?"

One day a White Hunter presented him with a croc skin to tan. Rudolf knew it was an easy skin to tan, but realized that the secret was shaving it thin, so it would become pliable in addition to its natural strength. He had a tool, his long, Essen steel army bayonet. It hung in pride of place for generations to come: in the main shaving shop above what used to be his roll top desk. He tanned that first croc hide so thin and so perfectly that, ever since, that has been a Rudolf's specialty, even after Rudolf himself passed away and sons inherited the business.

Great socialites would send for these hides and have Hermes, Vuitton and others make them into luggage, such was their reputation for quality. Delta crocs have very small scales, very supple skin (due to the briny water) and very large skins. They are a leather master's joy. So, eventually, it made sense that Rudolf's would start to raise their own little giant snappers. When wild Nile crocs were eventually put on the endangered list, their croc farm was exempt—Rudolf's crocs were not wild.

Rudolf's business improved, especially as they were now the sole legal supplier of croc skins from Tanzania.

Months before Pero had contacted them and asked if they could borrow Grosse Heidi, a sixty-five-year-old breeder, herself a third generation at Rudolf's. Heidi was about as smart as a dog. And trained. If you gave her a little medicine to calm her down, she could be walked, off the leash, to the sea to go for a swim. The way to get her back was to ring her feeding bell. She was trained to only feed in one spot, so she would whisk her tail, emerge from the surf, and waddle back to her pen and dinner. Pero had seen still images in National Geographic before but had never seen it filmed.

Pero wasn't sure Mary would agree to accompany Heidi. Even though Pero had showed her the rough video Pero had made on the scouting recce, and she seemed game, seeing Heidi up close was a different matter. Grosse Heidi was twenty-six feet long, four and a half feet wide and weighed almost two thousand five hundred pounds. She was, in fact, Mary's dinosaur for the segment. When Mary saw her, she just kept shaking her head, saying nothing and shaking her head. Finally, she spoke up, "This ol' girl makes that alligator at Gator World look like her toothpick. Cripes, but she's big. Someday, remind me to keep my big mouth shut."

"Mary, you don't have to do this, you know." It was Heep, to the rescue.

Pero told her, as an expert, she should, but really, really carefully. She glared at Pero. Pero waited silently. She knew Pero meant she did have to go through with the filming, but only on her terms. Nothing Pero would or could say—or want to—would place her in danger, or any danger she didn't evaluate and accept. She was the expert here, that was his point. A few seconds ticked by and she nodded. "Okay, let's do this." It was what she had come for, this dinosaur lady, "to see the largest approachable croc—up close and personal," was how she had put it when Pero offered her the job. Now, was her chance.

Heidi had already dozed away for thirty minutes since her chicken snack laced with drugs had gone down the gullet. Crocs stomachs can dissolve almost anything organic, but it is a slow process. They would have to wait another thirty minutes until Heidi was safe enough to handle. Mary gave a shiver, and Pero looked around to see where Mbuno was, to ask for the blanket they always packed in the Land Rovers. He was nowhere to be seen.

Kivoi Rudolf, the grandson of Corporal Rudolf, assured Mary everything would be fine. "We took her out just last week, it's her weekly bath in the ocean, she's looking forward to it. See, she's smiling." Mary shrugged her shoulders, frowning.

His mouth agape, Heep just stared at Kivoi. It was the Commissioner who just had to ask: "How can you tell she's smiling?"

"If a croc is not hissing, mouth wide open, you assume it's smiling. Either it has eaten or is looking forward to dinner." He paused for effect. "Which one is it? If it looks you in the eye, it's dinner." It was an old croc joke. Pero had heard it before. Tourists always laughed, as long as the croc was the other side of a fence. This fence was made of chicken wire, which would slow down Heidi "not a bit" as Kivoi had warned Pero on the previous visit. It's funny how visual barriers give security when there is, sometimes, absolutely none.

Mary stood up straight and asked Heep to help her get ready. They walked off to discuss what Heep wanted on tape— down the beach, the entry to the water, what would be filmed underwater, and then the return. All this would have to be one take, there was no "action" or "cut" call needed, Heidi would set the pace. Ruis and Priit would operate the underwater camera, Priit, their official camera operator, on the controls this time. Ruis was the technician, for the Betacam and the SeaSled. Ruis was prepping the Betacam. The four of them huddled and sorted out possibilities. Pero watched from a distance, next to the Commissioner, as arms moved in air, hands flew simulated croc and Mary movement in an underwater ballet of planning. It looked like pilots recapping a dogfight. Pero wondered who won.

It was Heidi who decided the time had come. Kivoi barked out a warning, as she lumbered forward to the gate and Mary, seeing Heidi moving, stripped off her shorts and tee, grabbed her flippers and snorkel-mask, and ran back to Heidi's cage. The Commissioner and Pero got out of shot.

Heep, the fastest camera operator Pero knew, was already rolling tape. Ruis and Priit were running the 100 yards down the beach to the SeaSled, hurrying to launch it, get it off shore, for the water entry shot.

Heidi lumbered past the now open gate, seemed to look right and left, and aimed at the water, taking the shortest distance to the surf. Mary walked by her right side. In her red one-piece, her shoulders were squared and—damn, but she's good—she never looked down. It was almost as if she was taking her dog for a walk. Pero watched in sudden horror as Heidi flipped her head to the right, gaped her mouth, and hissed. Mary never missed a beat; she bent down and patted Heidi's back and said, "Okay, I understand. Good girl, you can lead."

Pero knew they would have to re-dub her voice in to match, later. Her understanding of that beast was too good to miss.

They proceeded, sedately (thankfully giving the SeaSled time to get stable), until Heidi slid smoothly into the water. Mary had to wait to put on her flippers. Then she entered the surf, sat in waist-deep water, and spat into her mask. All old divers do this, you coat the inside of the mask with spit and it prevents fogging (young divers have artificial spit solution in a bottle). Once her mask was on, Mary flopped over in the surf and began sliding over and through the eighteen-inch sand-filled waves towards clear water. Suddenly, Mary stopped. Pero saw the swish of the tail as it brushed her. Heidi had been waiting in the murky brine.

The Commissioner and Pero ran down the beach to Priit, standing in deep shade under palm trees, operating the controls.

Ruis had returned from the launch of the SeaSled. They anxiously glanced over their shoulders at the scene unfolding below. Heep, Pero noticed, was still filming the above-water action. If something went wrong, Mary would surface quickly and with the telephoto, he would see it first.

On the screen they watched Mary swimming next to Heidi. It was incredible footage. Clear blue waters, shoals of fish flashing out of the way, woman and dinosaur heading out into deep water. "Bring her around Mary. See if she'll turn," Priit said to the mute screen as if Mary could hear, as they got smaller and smaller. It was clearly what they had planned, to play to the camera.

They were off the screen now, the distance too great even for the SeaSled zoom. Pero looked over at Heep. His camera, with a more powerful zoom, was pointed at the reef. My God, they were all the way out there, Pero could just see the water disturbance of the crocs massive tail and Mary's snorkel breaking the surface. She must have been really swimming as fast as she could. As Heep's angle changed, Pero guessed they were coming back. Suddenly the surface water went still.

Looking down at the SeaSled screen again, Pero could see the beginnings of a dot appearing. Pero tapped the corner of the screen to make sure Priit had seen it. "Got it Pero. I think I will cross, from bottom left to top right. Good shot. Ata-girl Mary," he said to the screen.

And then they saw it, Mary had her hands hooked on to Heidi's shoulders. Heidi's huge tail was powering them through the water. Two creatures, evolutions apart, in harmony. It was one of the most beautiful things Pero had ever seen. Pero imagined Heep seeing this and shouting "Emmy," while he thought how extraordinary and wonderful these two women were. There was no use pretending Heidi wasn't a woman, she was gentle, powerful, and protective. Mary wasn't bad either.

Then Heep started yelling.

"Pero, there's an intruder!" He was pointing the camera, still filming no doubt, to the left of the scene. There was no way to tell what he was seeing, nor to warn Mary.

"Heep, what is it?" Pero yelled.

"A croc, a big one, coming in fast. I saw it launch, left eye, off the beach after they got turned back towards the surf." Heep always kept both eyes open when filming.

"Priit, as soon as you think Mary can see the SeaSled, give the danger signal and then resume filming."

Priit switched to technical mode. "Roger that Pero."

As Mary's face became visible, that wonderful shot still unfolding, they saw a shadow pass in front of the camera lens, it pulled focus, and the scales of the intruder were visible.

Mary had seen it too, no need for the danger signal, but Priit did it anyway—but quickly—and came back on shot within five seconds. It was the longest five seconds.

When the scene cleared again, Mary was still with Heidi, but no longer on top, Heidi was moving too quickly. Would another croc provoke Heidi into a feeding frenzy? Would Heidi be threatened by this croc and run off, leaving Mary as a meal for the intruder? The water churned, the SeaSled stayed stable. Priit lost some altitude to be able to shoot upward a bit, continuity with Heep, who would capture the surface churning now taking place as two large reptiles thrashed about, posturing, Mary in the middle.

There was nothing they could do to help. Mary was the expert, she was the only one who would know what to do. They hadn't thought of this, an intruder. Pero was angry at himself, it was his job to think ahead, *and why hadn't Kivoi warned us?*

Heidi turned, ran over the slightly smaller intruder, and headed straight for Mary. Mary assumed the standard posture for humans trying to ward off the inevitable—she put her arms forward to fend off the impact that was coming. Heidi stopped her tail and sank below Mary's feet, momentum still carrying her forward. Mary got the idea, took a last snorkel breath, and dropped on to Heidi's shoulders again. Heidi headed for the beach. In shallow surf, Heidi paused and turned. The other croc was following, twenty yards behind. Mary slipped off and flippered towards shore as fast as she could.

Watching the screen, the Commissioner had had enough. He pulled his revolver from his pocket, dropped the jacket, and started running down the beach. Pero ran on his heels. Pero heard Priit call after him "Pero. No. It's okay. Stay out of shot." Pero stopped, but the Commissioner continued running towards Mary's surf exit point, she was half way out of the water by then, flippers in her hand, running. Heep was filming as the Commissioner reached her and dragged her from the surf, gun extended backwards in case anything came after her.

The surf was thrashing, the two crocs were entwined, rolling over and over. Suddenly the water went still and Pero looked back at Priit, who gave Pero a big grin.

What? Pero wondered, *Heidi won? What was happening?*

Mary and the Commissioner were walking up the beach, talking animatedly, Mary wanting to hang back, the Commissioner urging her away from the water. Then, at the surf's edge, a head appeared, followed by Heidi's eyes, neck and shoulders, which hung there, neither advancing nor retreating. The Commissioner raised his gun. Mary, lowered his arm, patted him on the shoulder. She walked towards Heidi. Heidi gaped her mouth. Mary stopped and turned to the Commissioner. Pero heard her yell, "Will you please retreat Commissioner? She's frightened."

The Commissioner had to shout to make sure she heard him over the waves "Are you sure?" Mary nodded. The

Commissioner walked backwards up the beach until he reached Pero. "Extraordinary woman. Fearless." His wavering voice said he was captivated. They all were.

The beach and her retreat towards home clear, Heidi emerged from the surf. Pero looked for wounds caused by the intruder. Pero could see none. Pero called over to Priit "See any blood in the water?"

Laughing, Priit and Ruis said, together, "No way, man."

What gives here? Two behemoths tangle and there's no blood? The light bulb went off. "Oh my God." The penny dropped for Pero. The intruder wasn't after Mary. It wasn't aggressive. It was after Heidi.

Heidi and Mary walked up the beach, side by side, all the way into Heidi's pen, Kivoi opening the latches. Heep was right behind, walking and keeping the camera as steady as possible, when Mary said, "There you go, ol' girl, raise them well. Good ol' girl."

Heep yelled, "Cut," and let out a whoop of joy.

Mary ran to Heep and hugged him and then, much to his surprise, hugged the Commissioner. "You really are the bravest man."

Bashful was never an adjective Pero would have thought he could apply to the officious cop who Pero first met yesterday. But there he was, looking at his toes, muttering, "I had a gun, it really wasn't so very brave."

"She would not have even felt those bullets and I doubt they could have penetrated her skull either." You could see the Commissioner knew it as well. The whole Singh family were hunters and fishers, there was no way he thought a .22 pistol was going to stop a croc that size. It was a brave thing he did, very brave. If unnecessary.

Heep had other worries. "Commissioner, now that you are officially part of the television show," the Commissioner's face lit up again. "I need to interview you on camera to hear your reasoning and what went through your head. Agreed?" And with that Priit, Heep, and the Commissioner went off to conduct the interview, still fresh, while the adrenaline was pumping. Visceral entertainment, that was their reputation. It never got any better than that.

Heep by taking the Commissioner aside also gave Pero time alone with Mary, if he could get Ruis to leave. Seeing his expression, Ruis volunteered: "I'll put the SeaSled to bed. It's longer to put away than set up. Hey, Pero?" Pero faced him. "How much was that thing? It's really amazing."

"It's a rental only, Sony is not allowed to sell them, yet. Fifteen hundred dollars a day." Ruis knew that fee was charged for travel days as well, one-week minimum.

"Wow. Still, it's worth it. Best underwater footage I ever shot or saw. Mary, you were great, really great. Wait 'til you see the footage tonight, it'll blow you away." Mary was all smiles.

Alone, Pero made the excuse to walk her back to her shorts and tee. Along the way they talked about the shoot, Heidi, and the experience. It was, even for her, the crowning achievement of a lifetime spent studying the reptiles, their evolutionary ancestors. Pero was thrilled for her, and yet concerned about something else. "Mary, where's Mbuno?" The only other person here Mbuno would have taken an order from was Mary. He was a sucker for a pretty woman. Their tête-à-tête about crocs the other night showed friendliness that Pero knew she could capitalize on. She probably could get anyone to do anything.

"Mbuno? Why do you think I know where Mbuno is?"

"Come on Mary, spit it out."

"He was the only one I could trust. I asked him to find out what happened to that soldier in Arusha."

"Oh Mary, you didn't. Damn."

"What, Pero, what? I couldn't leave that man to face the consequences alone."

"No, but what you've done Mary is make Mbuno maybe reveal where you, we all, are. Let's get back to the camp. He's there on the phone I take it?" Mary nodded, looking worried. The fun of the day had just evaporated.

Heep and the Commissioner had finished their session and Priit was reloading the camera so that they could shoot some feeding shots of the crocs at suppertime. "It'll build the audience anticipation of what could happen to Mary when we edit it in. Lots of teeth, lots of blood, carcasses being torn apart. The usual stuff. And Pero, I have asked Kivoi to do an interview on crocs, not that I think I will use it, Mary's stuff was better. Priit can shoot this without me and then he and Ruis can follow us up."

The Commissioner left a police officer with the driver, Ruis and Priit and the rest of them all piled into a Land Rover, Pero driving. "Where's Mbuno?" Heep asked. Pero explained he'd gone back to start making arrangements. What arrangements Pero didn't say. Heep had the good sense not to ask with the Commissioner next to him. Mary stayed quiet.

At Pangani camp, the mosquitoes were out in force and the baking smell of tonight's dinner rolls filled the air. There is very little more welcoming that the smell of baking yeasty bread in the bush. Pero went into the "office" as the sign proclaimed on a whitewashed, thatched, twelve-foot square hut, electric wires attached to one corner and telephone wires to the other. Heep, Mary and the Commissioner went to shower and, no doubt, change for cocktail hour. In luxury safari accommodation, sundowners are taken seriously, even if you only drink fruit juice. It is a time to recap the day's events, savoring the experience.

Pero found the manageress standing outside her doorway. There was no door, of course. Inside, there was a crude wooden desk with a phone, an outdated computer (with no mouse), and a printer/fax that had seen better days. The electro-static grime was prodigious. Talking on the phone, sat Mbuno.

Some older Kenyans never learn how to use a phone, nor do they want to. Mbuno was always different. It is not that he is modern, but recently the telephone enabled him to "keep in touch with his people" when he was away. He learned to use it while in the hospital, where they wheel in a public call box for "your convenience." You had to have a stack of shillings to make it work. Since then, it was the one perk he always asked of Pero, to be able to use the camp phone, cell phone, radiophone, ham radio, whatever, every few nights. Pero often accidentally listened in, simply because it was in a public place. The conversation was almost always the same (how are you, that sort of thing) at the same time, mostly 7:00 p.m. Pero learned eventually that Mbuno's wife always went to Giraffe Manor at 7:00 p.m. sharp, every night, in case he called. They had been together for decades. Indeed, they seemed unified, the way they sat whenever Pero visited them, side by side, touching, on a second-hand, faded velvet, moth-holed, Victorian, two-seater settee that the Manor had given them as an anniversary present. The anniversary wasn't their wedding anniversary—it was the anniversary of his surviving the puff adder bite, made into an annual family feast of thanksgiving, when dozens of relatives would, simply, turn up, from who knows where.

Mbuno, on the phone, was struggling to hear. In Swahili Pero heard him ask the other person to repeat the answer, twice. Then he said, "Ndiyo, jambo" and rang off.

"Mbuno, who were you talking to?" Pero was not looking pleased.

"I was talking to my people." That usually meant his wife. It was too early for that, Pero knew. "Mr. Pero, I have news, can we go out there?" he gestured out the door. He rose and Pero followed, saying something banal, but pleasant to the manageress as they walked past her.

Out of earshot, walking towards the drivers' quarters back of the car park, he explained: "Miss Mary asked me to help with the young soldier who saved her in Arusha. I know you have your special handy. I would not be thinking you would need me to call any person. It is right?" Pero agreed, nodding. "Something happened and I needed to talk to the lady manager, to question her, so I pretended that I needed to use the phone, so I called the duka, a nice man there, who supplies my village with sacks of corn. While I was waiting for the call, we talked." He meant he talked with the Manageress. In the remote parts of Tanzania, you booked a call and waited, ten to twenty minutes for a country-to-country call. "The call I also made was to my nephew, the one who works at Bluebird to warn him you could be needing a plane for tomorrow. He says they don't have any big planes for six people. And the word is that Mara doesn't want to send anything to you either, those pilots who got home safely scared everyone away."

It was good, innocent cover, and informative. "Okay, sounds like that took you five minutes, each call, good thinking." Most producers would never entrust such matters to scouts, but Mbuno was different, he had, over the years, often been the one to make many travel arrangements for them. It was a good idea to contact Bluebird, a rival firm to Mara, who had flown them down to Pangani. He had heard Pero say he would need to make a decoy flight back, to safeguard the crew, and had taken care of the rest. "And what else did you get up to? Care to start at the beginning?"

"Ah, yes, Mr. Pero. I am most sorry, but I had to kill a man."

CHAPTER 12

Mashangalikwa

"What do you mean kill a man? Who?"

"An Afghani, I think the man young master Amogh told you about. I walked back from the Rudolf farm as Miss Mary asked, it is only three miles, and found him just there," he pointed into the lush jungle cover between the car park and the river. "He was watching the camp, I watched one half hour, there was another man with him. The other man went into the camp, spoke to one of the waiters coming out of the first tent," he pointed to where one of the tourists slept, not their crew "and then he walked to the office of the manager. So later, when we talked, I asked her who he is. She knows him, he is from Zanzibar. He is the local union organizer, in charge of workers at the camp."

Tanzania still had remnants from communist days. The union organizers had been, until recently, local communist bosses. Anyone from Zanzibar, the lush island off the coast of Tanzania, was more Arab than African.

"Where is he now?" Pero meant the Zanzibari.

"He has gone down to the ferry to take the boat back to Tanga. He did not go back to the bush," he pointed to the place beyond the car park, "or I would have seen him pass me."

"Where's the Afghani?"

"Feeding the hippos. Come, I show you." They walked to the riverbank and Pero could see where something, or someone, had slid into the water next to the unmistakable footprints of a large hippo. Pero didn't bother asking Mbuno how or why or if he had killed him. If he had needed to, he would have found the means. Here in his element, Pero was sure Mbuno would have been swift and noiseless. "The cow surprised me searching the jacket pockets, the man was quite asleep, I took the jacket and let the hippo have the body, there was no choice. Come." Mbuno lead Pero over to the patch in the jungle. Under some leaves carefully arranged, flattened grass made to look like a waterbuck nesting place, was the jacket, a cell phone and a map case. Pero looked in the map case. Mbuno stopped his hand. "Be careful bwana, it is a trap." He had already checked it out and showed Pero the thin wire attached to the zipper. Open it and the wire breaks, recedes and, probably, a small explosion or fire would occur.

"Thank you Mbuno, I owe you, again."

"Ndiyo." Yes, it was a simple statement, not of account but recognition. This was his field, his expertise, he knew it, Pero knew it.

"And don't admit to anyone you killed the Afghani. Just say he attacked you and the hippo got him, okay?"

"Ndiyo. I do not think he was quite dead when the hippo took him, he cried out but no one heard. I waited, no one came."

"Okay, then stick to that. He attacked you." Pero looked at the map case, turning it over, carefully this time.

"Mr. Ruis? Could we not get him to open it?" It was a possibility, Ruis was the technical expert. Pero wondered if he should involve Ruis. Mbuno was thinking the same, "I think he is already part of the trouble, bwana, the plane was blown up for him as well. He is also in danger."

"Yes, maybe it's time he knows what has been going on. Maybe it's time everyone knows what is going on."

"Even your special phone and Mr. Tom?"

"No, not that Mbuno, that must be our secret, for now. They just need to know they are in danger. Someone knows we're here, most likely those Arab Mau Mau. And that Zanzibari will be back, maybe with reinforcements."

"I think, bwana, it is time to leave. Very fast."

Pero agreed. "Mbuno, if something happens . . . well, I want to tell you what I know and where I think this is going." There, standing in that small clearing, in the waterbuck false nest Mbuno had made, Pero explained and recapped all that he knew, all that had happened, the Embassy, the Ranjeets and all. Mbuno listened and asked no questions. "Mbuno, my friend, I have gotten you into this *Trouble*," Pero deliberately chose that Mau Mau association word as the time of revolt was known, "and I apologize. I really didn't mean to. It was a simple thing, to see if we could see anyone out there in a camp. Someone else would investigate, not us . . ."

"Mr. Tom?"

"No, perhaps not him, that's unusual. He's like a Park Ranger chief; he never leaves the office. There is something going on that is desperately urgent. First, we were attacked, Simon was killed even though no one knew if we had seen anything; they killed Simon because they thought he had seen something. In the air like that, maybe he did, or maybe he glinted in the sun and they thought it was a spy plane, I don't know. What I do know is that it made them act with no hesitation at all, they acted with violence, immediately."

"Yes, I can see. They are like a leopard mother, kill first, find out later."

"Yes, pretty much, predators. Dangerous, frightened creatures, eating—or in this case, killing—machines. I don't know why though Mbuno. Tom has gone to find out more, but I'm pretty sure he will find nothing. If they are desperate enough to kill so quickly, they will not stay there, will they?"

"It is right, they may be gone. Do you need to find them?"

"Not me Mbuno, I only need to protect our friends here, others will deal with them I hope."

"If they have left the Gurreh, bwana, you may have the only way to find them." He looked at the map case.

Pero nodded. As they made their way to his tent Pero quickly told him of the progress of Mary, Heidi, Heep, and the Commissioner. He told Mbuno to bring Ruis here, no one else, as soon as he came in, back from the beach.

"Are you going to tell the Commissioner, bwana?"

"Oh yes, Mbuno my old friend. And don't look so worried. I have a card to play there which will ensure he helps us out of this mess." Mbuno left, looking for Ruis to return. Also, Pero knew he would, he had no doubt, make sure the Land Rovers were full, the extra jerry cans as well. They would be ready to leave, plane or no plane.

Pero always left the satellite phone, his secret one, in an obvious place, a different place each time. This morning Pero chose his safari boots, phone keys towards laces, sock on the inside of the shoe, between the phone and the inside wall only. The phone was upside down, but with the antenna pointed down the shoe towards the toes. Then he laced the boot. If someone had moved it, he would know. It was unmoved. They hadn't had time to search his tent, yet. Maybe it was the two police officers left behind that had kept them away. Whatever, it didn't matter. Pero assumed it was still clean.

He raised the antenna, pointing it at the tent roof. "Baltazar, P. here, Pangani Camp. Probably it is the Afghani, name of Nadir, dead, hippo food, no trace. His booby-trapped map case and other items recovered. Will attempt to open and transmit case contents. Zanzibari, local union chief, contact of Afghani. Recommend surveillance Zanzibari, name to follow. Urgent you inform and advise Tom Baylor. Planning immediate decamp Pangani and possible to drive Nairobi to safeguard Mary Lever and crew here. End." The two clicks followed.

Mbuno came back and reported that Mary and Heep were showering or dressing. The Commissioner was sitting in the bar. It was time for Pero to get the difficult one out of the way. They emptied the Afghani's jacket pockets and laid them out on the small trunk at the foot of the bed. Nothing much there, except an air ticket Dar to Tanga that morning. No keys, no wallet, no matches with a motel name like in the movies. Pero placed the Afghani's cell phone next to the pocket items and asked Mbuno to fetch the Commissioner. Pero hid the map case.

Pero had to give the Commissioner credit. Today he had showed good humor, a great deal of bravery and, now, no surprise, just consideration for facts which had escalated beyond anything he thought he would be dealing with on this day. As Pero showed him the jacket, contents of the pockets, and the cell phone of the dead Afghani, Pero gave him an encapsulated version of their trip to Kenya: Simon's accidental death, the car chase to Ramu, the tails in Nairobi that the Ranjeets had spotted. Pero knew he would know them, at least by name, one merchant Asian family to another in a small region of the continent. He included details, as much as he had, about the truck stop identification of an Afghani, Mbuno's description of Arab Mau Mau, the switcheroo with the planes to Arusha, leaving him to figure out the bomb placement, and, not least, the death of an Afghani here by a hippo.

The Commissioner looked hard at Mbuno who remained calm and unreadable, almost innocent.

Lastly, Pero explained the problem they had with the Zanzibari who might come back.

"Purim, his name is Mustafa Purim and he is al-Qaida."
The Commissioner shocked Pero. "If I had seen him here, or
anywhere near the airport, I would have suspected and arrested
him. His usual beat is Tanga, the port there, smuggling weapons, out mostly. Weapons left over from Darfur, Congo and
Uganda's civil war, RPGs, SAMs, that sort of thing, channeled
through to Pakistan and then to the cells. We have been working on this with Interpol."

The fact that he revealed all this, told Pero something
else as well. "Your brother Virgi has informed you well." The
Commissioner must have known, then, that Pero was on their
side.

He smiled, "Yesterday, after I saw you," he pulled out a new
Navistar satellite phone, showed it to Pero. It had a green code
button. It could be scrambled, secure.

On that fishing trip years ago with his brother Virgi, out in
the deep blue Indian Ocean waters, there had been a Donzi
racer, a cigarette boat, approaching at sixty knots, straight at
them. Suddenly, automatic fire raked the Singh boat. Virgi, the
captain, and Pero had ducked behind the diesel engines, but
two of the crew were killed. Sure they had killed all on board,
the shooters had stepped aboard to make sure. But behind the
engines, the survivors had been waiting.

Pero used a 9mm Beretta that Virgi pressed into his hand
in the dark of the engine room. Virgi and the captain used
grenades, two of them each. His boat and the attackers' were
a mess. The attackers died, they didn't. Singh's brother, the
government minister, came out secretly in a forty foot fishing
boat, fourteen miles to sea, to rescue them and sink the attackers' speedboat. He towed them into a private harbor well south
of Dar. Pero learned that the Virgi yacht returned later to Dar,
fully repaired and with no tales to tell, except for the "caught"
Marlin, which Virgi had actually bought off a fisherman in

Mkwaja. Having it stuffed on his wall was another sort of trophy, an insider joke. Virgi was like that.

Pero also learned that the Minister had, even though he was
only the Minister for Tourism, forced through anti-terrorist
legislation, and had linked the country to anti-terrorist services in Lyon (Interpol) and the UN. Now Pero knew who
had the usual suspects connected with the boat attack arrested,
questioned, tried, jailed for life and, rumor had it, shot: the
Commissioner standing in front of Pero in the tent. Pero
should have guessed Virgi had been joking when he told Pero
to never trust his brother the police officer. Family reverse
pride. Good people the Singhs. Strange, but good.

The Commissioner picked up the contents of the dead
man's pockets, one at a time and pocketed them in his side
pockets. The cell phone was active, so he scrolled down to
the recent numbers, ten showing, wrote them in a little notebook common to police officers the world over, and called for
the cop standing outside the tent. He quickly told him to take
Mbuno to the site in the bush and then bring him back. Then
he extended his phone's antenna, pressed a series of buttons,
pressed the green code button, and waited. When it answered,
he simply read the cell phone numbers in an obscure dialect,
Hindi or Urdu, Pero thought, off his pad. Code on code, try
and decipher that, anyone listening. On hanging up, he asked,
"What are you planning to do, Mr. Baltazar?"

"Get my crew packing. Leave, as soon as possible. I have
checked, there are no aircraft available, unless you want to
loan us yours?"

"That is not wise." He paused. "Anyway, I think you should
not tell any of your people, yet. You are safe enough here, I
will see to that. If Purim comes back I will arrest him—or
shoot him—on suspicion of the bombing at the airport.
He will know that if I'm here by now, it is what I would be

expected to do, a simple police officer. But I doubt he will come back."

"Okay, but these people are clearly desperate; I cannot risk my crew's lives—Mary's life . . ."

"This I know Mr. Baltazar. You will try once more to confirm your plane with . . . Mara, isn't it?" Pero nodded, "Good, for tomorrow afternoon, I will put in a good word. Then, instead, you will leave when I give you the all clear in the middle of the night, this night, but by Land Rover. Do not go to Mombasa." He meant, do not follow the coast road, it went through Tanga. The only other way was through Mkomazi and Arusha, back into Kenya, the border town of Namanga, and on to Nairobi. The Arusha-Namanga border between Tanzania and Kenya was worrisome because of Mary. He seemed to sense his hesitation. "The border patrol based in Arusha will not be a problem. I have already made sure that Miss Lever is not wanted as a witness for the unfortunate death of Consul Jikuru."

Pero was relieved to hear it. But the Commissioner still had another shoe to drop.

"But a curious thing I just heard. The soldier charged with guarding Consul Jikuru will be moved by the UN security people to their office in Nairobi for questioning tomorrow. It is most irregular, all the more so because neither the Nigerian commander nor the Nigerian Ambassador made an objection to them holding him or the UN for taking him. Would you happen to know why?" And at this, he looked at Mbuno who had just come back through the flap of the tent.

Pero spoke up, convinced that a bit of the truth would defuse the danger, "Mary asked Mbuno to make a call to see if her word was good enough to safeguard the fellow. It seems that the Nigerian killed the man who stabbed Jikuru just as he was also threatening Mary. She feels he saved her life."

"Ah, the power of her uncle then? I see. And who did you call Mbuno from here to make such an arrangement?"

Mbuno didn't hesitate. "My nephew, David Bariti, at Blue-bird Charters at Wilson Airport. He *believes*."

"Most convenient. Mr. Threte, then, is his pastor?" Pero nodded, but Mbuno said nothing. "I should have so good an information service and contacts." He turned towards Pero: "I will do all this because I want these people for other crimes, and they want Miss Lever dead which is inexcusable," he still thought she was the target because of Arusha. He was perhaps assuming they were only in danger by accident, "I cannot allow that on Tanzanian soil. And I would suggest you make sure it does not happen on Kenyan soil." That frightened Pero. *And the implication is? Is he guessing?* Pero had to play it out.

"And how am I supposed to do that?"

"Call your embassy, arrange protection, how else?" He never explained why the same solution would not work in Tanzania. He didn't have to. They were being told to take their problem elsewhere and, if in the meantime they acted as bait for people he wanted for other crimes, so much the better. In the end, Pero didn't care, an escape out was being provided. And Pero quickly formed a different escape route in his mind.

"I suggest we all have a party Mr. Baltazar, your expense I am afraid, in an hour to celebrate Miss Lever's brilliant swim with two, how does she call them? Living dinosaurs!" And he stood and walked out before Pero could agree. He didn't have to have his agreement. It was an order.

"Mbuno, get Ruis the moment he gets back. Tafadali."

An hour later, they were hunkered down in his tent, Ruis, Mbuno, and Pero peering at the map case. Ruis was turning it over in his hands, carefully. "Tricky boss, it is a booby trap, but I'm not sure what kind. I can't defuse something if I don't know what it's set to do."

"Okay, Ruis forget I asked. And I mean forget."

As it turned over one more time, Ruis exclaimed, "No, wait Pero, look, see? It's not a latch, and it's very delicate, I mean really delicate. Touch that zipper and it would break, I'm sure of it. So that means it's never meant to open." He turned the case over, and looked at every side. "Ah, here it is boss, just like that special box of yours, it's a molded plastic seam that is not quite a seam, see, I can slip my nail in it . . ."

"No, Ruis don't . . ."

"And voila, it's open, leaves the zipper intact. Pero can now take things out and put things in. Hello, what's this?' Pero and Mbuno leaned in, "Pero, Mbuno, get back, it's a jelly device, soft molded blue burning jelly, probably ethanol in hydroxide propane concentrate. Just like camping stoves, only really condensed, very hot flash, not meant to explode just burn. I have got to defuse it if we're going to examine this thing. I think if I put it back together wrong the case will go up anyway. So I might as well try . . . but you guys can go, please."

Mbuno shook his head so Pero said, "We're staying."

"Okay, but first, Mbuno, take a peek outside the tent, someone coming in might startle me and poof." Mbuno peered out the screen door through the flap. Ruis was concentrating, "Ah, I see it, it's simple, no special tools, but four hands are needed. Pero, hold the strap, yes, that one, see the thread inside? Okay, now pinch it, so that it cannot slide, it must not move, okay? And with the other hand, I want you to support the whole case, palm up." Pero did as he was told. "Now, I follow the thread to this little safety pin here—see it's open?—and, if it were to pull, the fulminate of mercury switch would go off. Hold it there a little while longer, I just need to fasten that pin so it can't slide out, ah, there . . ." he grabbed the case, and threw it into his lap, "safe as houses, well tents."

Pero took a breath. "Is it really safe?"

"Yeah, mostly, but take out what you need and get rid of the damn thing, I wouldn't want to bet on it. In this humidity, fulminate of mercury becomes unstable. Heat's no problem, it's the humidity."

Afghanistan is dry, was all Pero could think of. "Thanks Ruis. Now off the record and don't tell Heep or Mary . . . get ready to bug out."

"When?

"Tonight, but no-one must know."

"More trouble?

"Nothing Mbuno and the Commissioner haven't handled or won't, but we need to be cool, but ready. Meanwhile, we're having a party."

"Okay boss." He got up to leave. "But really, get rid of that thing boss." Pero planned to as soon as possible. Mbuno followed Ruis out to get everyone to the dining room. He knew Pero needed time alone. Map case contents were not his expertise. Pero doubted they were his own either, so he took macro photos with the small Olympus digital.

With Mbuno keeping watch, moments later Pero raised the satellite phone antenna again. "Urgent report from Baltazar here, Pangani Camp. Afghani, name of Nadir, now dead, contents of his map case with booby-trap, now defused. Well, I'm going to plug in the camera playback USB wire and hit slide show. Hope you can get this . . . the handset hissed, without a double click, so Pero plugged in the mini-USB wire and pressed the slide show button on the Olympus digital camera now connected to the phone. As Pero watched the small viewing screen replay the images he had just taken, all fourteen of them, Pero still saw nothing that caused concern: The case itself; the detonation zipper device; the safety pin and thread (in macro); a copy of their Park permit, the one from the Chief's office; a copy of their filming permit from the film office files in Nairobi House; a print of their itinerary marking Arusha Airport and Pangani Airport with final destination Pangani Camp; the name of the Land Rover hire company in Ramu and Debbie Rose; a torn Tusker Special beer label; a sheet with the call sign of the Cessna aircraft and company Mara Charters; some Wrigley gum and used wrappers; a Kit-Kat bar, uneaten; a number on a plain small scrap of paper that Pero took for the Zanzibari's in pencil (Tanga 6430) with his name, Mustafa Purim and address; one free, tear-off tourist map from Hertz Rent-a-car at Tanga airport; and one Pakistani passport in the name of Saleh al-Nadir, resident of Islamabad, born twenty-three years ago in Khartoum. He hoped they would get all this at State. And he seriously hoped they could make heads or tails out of it. When the slide show had repeated twice, Pero unplugged the wire and continued his call:

"I will destroy the map case because it is still dangerous. I'll leave the contents for Commissioner Singh after departure. Urgent you inform and advise Tom Baylor. Also, we are planning decamp Pangani with a night drive to Mashangalikwa, there's an airstrip alongside the railroad there. Urgent evacuation requested. A Cessna Caravan will do. Repeat urgent evac requested. I feel a drive all the way to Nairobi will be unsafe for Mary Lever. But we will wait at Mashangalikwa strip only until of-four hundred Zulu. Over and out. " The two clicks followed.

Zulu is Greenwich Mean Time. oh-four-hundred Zulu was six am local. If they failed to make it, they were on their own, all the way to Nairobi. He didn't like the odds, with the al-Shabaab terrorists or the local bandits, not to mention the border guards for Mary nor what would be, by then, an angry Commissioner Singh, who might come after them when he found out they skipped.

Pero took the map case with him, nonchalantly walking past the open office doorway, said good evening to the manageress and, in a dark patch a few feet into the overgrowth, threw the empty case into the dark, as far as it would go, over some dense Wait-a-minute thorn bushes alongside the Pangani River. The fuse followed two steps later. He had had Ruis separate the mercury fuse from the jelly, so when it went off, someone could only think it was a gunshot by the river, not uncommon in these parts. Pero had also filled the case with rocks, in case it made it to the water.

Mbuno had retrieved Pero's secret battery case from Ruis and together they put the map case items in there. Pero planned to leave the key and the battery safe for the Commissioner as they left. He would figure out the rest.

There was a heck of a good celebration going on. Heep and Mary had seen the footage, and they were showing some of it to the tourists on the laptop computer, a digital download for security, copied and put on DVD just in case. Everyone, tourists included, was gathered around wowing or whooping depending on nationality with a few "merdes" thrown in from a Canadian French couple. It was spectacular footage. The copulation scene with the two crocs was an open water first. "Emmy time" was heard again and again. Heep was in his element. Mary was radiant, proud and, Pero thought, a little in awe of her good fortune. Pero was glad it had all turned out okay. The job of a producer is never to take the credit at the end; it is always limited to the responsibility of the shoot, the achieving of a standard. When that standard is reached or exceeded, as was the case that day, the credit rightly always goes to that which the producer did not plan for: fate, luck, and artistic talent. It is the nature of the job. Pero was happy. Well, as happy as he could be. At least half his life was in order.

Pero watched the Commissioner, who was as good as his word. Drinking fruit juice, he was toasting their heroes and the

SeaSled over and over. When the footage was shown, again, of his heroics, he was the toast of the whole crowd of tourists, crew, cops, and waiters alike. He reveled in it. Pero took his picture "For your brothers, to see you at your moment of glory!" The Commissioner laughed, genuinely pleased.

"To Grosse Heidi" someone yelled and Pero knew the old girl would be an international celebrity before long.

The party went on like that for about three hours and then people started to drift away. Pero went to get some sleep. He was going to need it. Mbuno left when Pero did.

Pero checked that the police were standing guard and walked Mbuno safely back to the driver's hut. Along the way Mbuno confirmed the Land Rovers were ready, but reminded Pero that he would have to drive one, they couldn't take the driver that came with them, after all they were stealing them. He put it this way "You cannot ask the driver, Joigi, to help steal a Land Rover he is supposed to keep from harm." Pero agreed, reluctantly. Pero talked with him about the balloon tires, now on the Land Rovers for the sand of Pangani beach, not the rough road, nor ever intended for pavement, towards Mkomazi. Pero thought they could handle the road, but at a slower speed.

Mbuno agreed, "At night, bwana, it is better to drive slow with lights, many lights." He was right, of course, animal collision was the worst they had to fear. They both hoped.

Pero told Mbuno about the hoped-for flight out of Mashangalikwa. "Will you tell the others?" Mbuno asked. Instead, Pero explained they would deal with telling them when they got away from here, and there was always the question of "if" the plane would arrive.

Back in his tent Pero went through his sleeping ritual. Lying on his front, right arm crossed under Pero, *Addiena*'s name, her tattoo, against his chest. "God, I miss her," he said softly and began to look for refuge in sleep.

Two-thirty in the morning. Pero was instantly awake. He heard someone unzipping his tent flap and the first reaction Pero had was that they were too late, the Mau Mau were already here. It was just the Commissioner. "Time to get your people up and out. We will help." Within twenty minutes. they were packed and loaded, almost without a sound. The manageress was sitting at her desk, his payment papers ready, a police officer sitting next to her. Pero signed the chit she would present to Flamingo and added a generous tip. She smiled. Singh explained the cop next to her: "He's going to keep her company until lunch, that should provide plenty of time." The woman looked scared. Pero was sorry for her, but only if she were innocent. But knowing Purim from Tanga was hardly a good omen for her future.

Mary and Heep asked no questions, yet. Pero knew those would come, once they were away. Ruis, good as his word, hadn't told Priit, but Priit had guessed when everything was packed for shipment—extra padding is a dead giveaway that they're moving, not filming the next day. The Commissioner had little to say. He assured Pero that, so far, there was no sign of Purim and, that probably, Pangani Airport would be their plan of attack, if indeed there was one. "That was why I could not let you have the Toyota plan." He was right, of course, Mbuno and Pero recognized that, even if it did seem churlish at the time.

The Commissioner explained he was staging an ambush for later in the morning when the Mara plane arrived, just in case. "Mara were quite helpful, when it was explained to them." Pero wondered who explained exactly what . . .

The Commissioner promised to wire or fax Pero the results of the ambush to Pero at the InterConti, Nairobi the next day. Pero had given that as his next address at the desk. Mbuno, Ruis, and Priit were in the lead Land Rover, Mary, Heep, and

Pero, driving, in the next. Just before Singh waved them off Pero handed him the plastic card. "It's for the battery pack I left under your mattress." The Commissioner raised his eyebrows. Pero didn't give him time to ask questions. They turned fast left out of camp as planned, as they were told. Mbuno set a quickening pace.

Within ten miles the road turned nasty and Pero felt, more than saw, Mbuno slow the pace. Thirty miles per hour over these rough roads was fast enough. The good news was that it had rained a few hours ago and the soft ground was better for the tires.

Mary and Heep, understandably, started pestering Pero for answers. "Hang on guys, let's get Ruis and Priit in on this, no need to explain everything twice." Pero keyed one walkie-talkie and gave Mary the mike to hold between them, Mary in the back leaning over the seat back, Heep next to Pero.

Heep picked up another walkie-talkie, checked which channel the first one was on and changed the second one, one channel up, to channel two. The one in his hand sprang to life "Priit here. Do you copy? Over?"

"Yes, they copy, let's skip the *over* and just speak freely, we have a two-way system going here." Heep had taught Pero this years ago. One mike, always on, channel, say one. The other radio set to channel two. In the other Land Rover, they set the receiver to channel one and on the other walkie-talkie to channel two, they keyed the mike always on. Worked like a hands-free desk phone. You get some feedback, but it's easy to handle by the one holding the mike—just turn it away for a few seconds.

To offset some of their anger—Heep especially hates being woken up, but with Mary beside him, he was doubly angry from the adrenaline rush of protection. Pero explained matters as best he could whilst keeping them on the road at the constant pace of Mbuno up front. The balloon tires and no power steering were a bitch to steer at this speed over deep ruts in the road.

Pero did not tell them everything. He avoided the meeting with Tom Baylor and his satellite phone, but he did tell them about Simon's death and that the Arab Mau Mau were an al-Qaida offshoot, al-Shabaab, and on their trail.

Ruis's voice came across clearly, "Sodding al-Qaida killed Simon? You have got to be kidding."

Heep answered for Pero "No, I saw the bullet and Pero's video of the feeding. When the jacket was ripped out, the wound was clearly visible. Probably a sniper rifle. Now go on, Pero."

So Pero told them about Mbuno's encounter with al-Shabaab's point man. The death of the Afghani shocked them.

Mary was shocked. "You mean the man is dead? Just like that, dead? You killed him?"

"Yes, Mary, Mbuno was attacked, defended himself, and a hippo finished the job and took the spoils. Mbuno thinks the man was still alive when he slipped under the river water. We recovered his map case, but it was booby-trapped. Ruis, who had no idea what was inside, defused the damn thing and I took pictures. Heep, in the flap of my Northface, it's the Olympus. Ruis, I downloaded a copy on the PDA in Priit's case."

"Got it, tell me what these please are?" It was Priit, his Dutch singsong voice, and swap in verb placement.

Heep pulled the pocket camera out and started scanning through the pictures. "I'll tell you what they are, it's a spy kit. Son of a bitch, he had their names, everything, from the permits. I don't see Mary's name, so they weren't after her anyway, it was just us." Pero was amazed how quick Heep was and shot him a sideways glance.

Priit called out, "Mbuno wants you to know. We're coming to a fork in the road. And not to take the right fork—that's right, isn't it? Yes. Take the left fork. It looks smaller. But he says it's the safest way. To Mashangalikwa. But coming round from the west. Hey. Why Mashangalikwa? Aren't we supposed to be pushing through? To Arusha?"

"Later Priit, I'll get to that. What is worrying me here is that Commissioner Singh knew al-Shabaab or al-Qaida, anyway they had all the dope on us and yet he wanted us to flee. He never offered to take us into protective custody. Also, thanks in large part to Mary here, he was miffed that the Nigerian was being taken into UN custody and out of Tanzania."

"Is that true? Oh, thank you Mbuno."

"Priit here for Mbuno. He says to thank Pero. He should explain."

"Not now, let's get back to Singh. Singh wanted us to drive out, across the border at Arusha, tightest security in East Africa. Going this way, left out of camp, there is no way, no road, across the border except at Arusha."

Heep asked, "Well, what's wrong with that? You said he wanted us to avoid Tanga . . ."

"Yeah, so why didn't he simply offer the Britton Islander he has sitting at Pangani Airport? It seats twenty-five. He explained that away by saying he thought an attack would be at the airport, but knowing that, why not flood it with troops?"

Heep put his hand on Pero's shoulder, "Pero, you don't think he's in on this, do you?"

"No, honestly, I don't, but I think he's content to have us as a baited hook for the people he really, really, wants to catch. This road is a one-way trap, any way you look at it."

Ruis chimed in, "Christ, he's willing to have Mary on that hook as well?"

And Heep was getting angry now, not just frightened. "Christ, what bastards."

Mary said, "Heep, Ruis, don't take the lord's name in vain."

Pero went on, "There's another part of this I can't explain fully . . .

Mbuno chimed in, "Just one bwana?"

"Yeah, okay Mbuno, but still, I mean I really can't explain how, but you've known me for years, all of you, and you must know I would not put you in that danger. If I can avoid it."

"Sorry Mary about the lord's name." Ruis' voice echoed as Heep added: "Me too Mary. Pero, what have you got in mind?"

"I need your trust, all of you. I have called for an evacuation, by plane. At a dirt strip at Mashangalikwa about an hour away now. And I don't know yet if they are coming."

"Oh, gott verdammt . . ."

"Swearing in Dutch doesn't help Priit."

"Sorry Mary. Yet again. Pero? What evac? What sort?"

"I don't know exactly, let's just say it'll be friendly. The people I asked know the risks and are definitely on our side. And Heep, somewhere in there, in one of those images, there's a clue to what these bastards have in mind, why all this is happening so darned fast. My brain tells me I'm missing something. Will you guys, and you Mary, go through them slowly, again. How about reading them aloud? Maybe something will trigger. Ruis you first, okay?"

Over the airwaves, his voice came through haltingly, but clear enough. "Okay Pero, here goes. I see the case, good shot of the fingernail catch dressed up as a welded seam. There's the detonator and then the zipper trigger, the booby trap. Next is the safety pin and thread. So far I know these. Here's a copy of our Park permit. Now here's a strange thing Pero, this must be from yesterday, see the first film location has been crossed out, they do that as you complete laps, or locations, in the office of Parks in Nairobi. Then there's a copy of Chief Methenge's office license with the shilling stamp duty, three days ago. Hey, Pero, this is in color. A color copier? Big office. Or a print off a digital camera?"

"No Ruis, the paper was copier standard, laser, not inkjet, not a photo print. So, you're right, it took a big office machine, well spotted."

"Okay, then there's our filming permit, no biggie; then a printout of our itinerary off someone's computer . . ."

"Wait Ruis, why do you say off a computer?"

"The font, Pero, look at the font . . ."

Heep chimed in, "He's right and this is a special font. Someone was working on a desktop who wrote this. An office or agency would use Courier, Arial, or Tahoma . . . this looks like, what?"

Priit chimed in: "Looks snobby. Like Garamond."

"I agree." It was Ruis again, "Let's go on. Then there's Debbie's name and details, no biggie again. Some beer label, some gum, and a candy bar. Then there's that font again with the Mara name and that dead Cessna and her tail number; so they *were* targeting her, bastards." He paused for effect, "Okay, then there's handwriting of a name—the guy you said Singh identified for you, right? Obviously his contact. There's a Hertz map. The bastards don't even spring for their own map. And then the mother lode, a passport of the bastard himself. Hey, did you photograph the visa entries Pero?"

Pero hadn't. Pero had known there was something he was forgetting. "Nope, forgot, sorry. Now Singh has the passport anyway. Let's hope he puts it to good use."

"Anyone else want to take a crack at this, did I miss anything?" One by one everyone commented. The consensus was that Ruis had found out more than they would. He took credit because he has a "technical mind for detail." Whatever, they were at a loss. The miles dragged on in the dark, punctuated by the hiss of the walkie-talkie.

Then Heep spoke up. "Pero, there's something very wrong here. Everything in this case is right, authentic, do we all agree? Copies yes, but none are forgeries. Right?" Everyone answered yes, even Mbuno's voice could be heard. "Okay then, why would there be one falsehood in there as well, why have a fake at all?"

Mary blurted out, "What, for heaven's sake, Heep, what?"

"Heaven has nothing to do with it. This Tusker label is a forgery. There is no such thing as Tusker Special Beer. There's Tusker Special Ale and Tusker Beer, but no Tusker Special Beer. It's a forgery. Now we have to ask: why?"

No one spoke. It wasn't funny or they would have teased the one guy who drinks a Tusker a day . . . no, this was serious. Why would the label be the only item in the bag that's a forgery? Priit got there first. "What's the sell by date?"

Heep was peering at the small glowing image. "Next month I think. It's almost out of date. Is that right, Mary?"

She peered closer. "Yes, it's next month, next week." And then Mary panicked, she suddenly thought of a connection and the woman who swam with a monster crocodile burst out in tears "It's JT, it's JT. The *Meeting* is being sponsored by Tusker beer in two days, no, wait it's already tomorrow. Hundreds of thousands will be there, they are giving away one bottle to each adult. You know JT says beer, in moderation, is okay, well, Tusker asked to sponsor the whole thing and he agreed. This label must be some kind of calling card, or reminder. Maybe a password. They must be going to kill JT."

Heep was suddenly very serious, shaking his shoulder as Pero wrestled with the wheel. "Pero, remember? Ruis, you too, remember when they covered the war in Iraq? Remember the bottling plant and the special brewing truck they filmed?

Remember what that army Captain told them it was stock-piled for?"

"My god, you don't think?" Pero was shocked.

Ruis yelled through the static, "No fucking way, man . . ."

"What, what is it Pero, Heep, tell me." Mary pleaded.

"You can hear while I tell somebody. Stop the car, Mbuno, I have to make a call."

"It is right here, *bwana*, we are here. Mashangalikwa." No GPS and he had gotten them here, the backwoods way as Pero's dad would have said. And with that they pulled out of the bush, looking over the railroad tracks, front tires on the sleepers, and stared, lights off, at a moonlit empty landing strip. They all exited. No plane.

The time for secrets and games was past.

CHAPTER 13

Moshi

They watched Pero as he pulled out the mini satellite phone and pressed buttons. Heep was the first to speak. "Pero, that's not one of ours, what the hell?"

"Later, Heep, sorry, but for now, please just listen." The signal connected. Heep's face was stern, demanding. "Please, Heep," Pero added. Heep nodded as the connection went through.

"Urgent update for Tom Baylor, I think I'm saying Priority One. Yes, that's it, Priority One."

Priority One was for a world emergency. As explained to Pero by Tom Baylor, it had better be "a guaranteed, gold-plated, atom bomb or else . . . ."

"Baltazar here at Mashangalikwa airstrip, waiting incoming evacuation as requested. Contents of Nadir map case analyzed by me, Mary Lever, Bill Heeper, Ruis Selby, Priit Vesilind, and Mbuno of the Liangulu, scout. Urgent you advise everyone there and Tom Baylor as follows: Tusker Special Beer label is counterfeit. Expiry date next month, next week. Jimmy Threte *Meeting on the Hill*, Nairobi, in two days, correction thirty-two hours, sponsored by Tusker beer. Tusker is giving away hundreds of thousands of bottles of beer as a sponsor. Draw correlation to Iraq portable breweries and bottling plants as seen at al-Hadr. Anthrax agent possible in Tusker handouts. Free handouts are always nearly expired product. Urgent action requested. Other map case details: color copies indicate large office printer or laser color copier. Also, the font used on printed matter is computer specific, suggest Garamond. Also, copies were made yesterday, date of alteration to permits as evidence. We are here at Mashangalikwa airstrip, evacuation still urgently requested, two hours to deadline as agreed. Over and out." It was 4:00 a.m. locally. Pero waited.

Nothing. No clicks. As Pero was taught, he repeated the message as closely as he could, that's what the two clicks are for, to tell him that they got it all or else he should repeat the message. The crew, all of them, were watching Pero, still aghast. Even Heep, who had seen the correlation, could hardly face it. *This couldn't be true*, his face said and then (for Pero had known Heep for so long) his look changed to wonder with hints of respect tinged still with gross distrust. Or maybe he was seeing how Pero felt: a charlatan finally exposed to friends.

And at the end of the repeat, Pero concluded with ". . . two hours to deadline at Mashangalikwa airstrip. End of message . . . get it?" And nothing, silence.

Then a voice, monotone. "Standby." Pero had never heard anything before on this phone, or any other call to State, ever, never.

Again "Standby" and the hiss of static. Pero wasn't used to responding. So he guessed and tried. He gave them two presses of the star key, hoping they would read that as two clicks. No, wait two clicks means sign off, Pero didn't mean that . . .

They responded, "Voice commands."

"Ah, roger, I acknowledge. Standing by."

"Affirmative."

With the phone glued to his ear, Pero started to explain to his friends, aware that State would hear everything. He didn't care. "Many years ago I was asked to help with little things. Sometimes I would carry a letter. Sometimes, on film work, I would carry some small gadget. This was the first time I was asked to gather information, that's all, gather information for the State Department, keep an eye out, see if I spot anything suspicious on the border up in the Gurreh region. I never spy, really, certainly no violence. All this is with an old school friend, Tom Baylor. He asked for help, national pride, that sort of thing. This time all I was to do is phone it in—that's what you heard just now. Usually I never communicate at all, just go about normal life. But when my production job coincides with the needs of Tom's requests or needs, well I get a simple request and if possible, I help them out. Sometimes it's a simple as a confirmation, yes, so-and-so is checked in at the Hilton, where I am, no there were no bodyguards protecting another group of Mid-Easterners on a beach in Australia, that sort of thing. A courier, or another pair of eyes. Noting special and if necessary I phone it in," Pero indicated the phone by tilting it slightly off his ear.

"What are you waiting for Pero?" It was Heep. He was, Pero could see, calculating all those distant lands, all those shooting assignments and trying to regain control of his life, a life he suddenly felt had been misused by his friend. Pero was not enjoying that. Until that moment Pero hadn't realized how vital his friendship.

"Heep, it's only that I have never, ever, been asked to wait on this thing. I was taught to deliver a short burst of whatever and they sign off with two clicks. No response from them ever. And don't go imagining things. When you and I have been out, there have only been three times I have done anything. The most serious one was at Dubai Airport, remember last year?"

"You went AWOL, blamed it on your gut and bad shrimp, we missed our flight."

"Yeah, well, I was actually across the other side of the airport, in a freight hangar, seeing if a box was waiting freight collection. That's it. It was, I telephoned," again the tilt of the phone, "and they rang off. Job over. That's how dangerous this sideline is, well, was. Then Simon happened."

"Just what have you got planned out here, Pero?" Heep raised his arms to take in the landscape. He was speaking for the team now, Ruis and Priit standing with him facing Pero, Mary with Mbuno between them, eyes glued on Pero. They were all standing in the middle of the train tracks. The moonlight glistened off the rails, to the right leading back to Dar, the left towards Arusha. The airstrip was just that, a dirt strip, no lights, no tower, just dirt and, thankfully, no goats or cattle presently. If there had been any, it would mean there were native cattlemen about. About 200 yards left up the line, there was a small railroad hut, tin roof, no signs of movement. It wouldn't be an equipment shed, more likely just a hut in case the train had a passenger waiting to flag it down in the rain or, more likely, to avoid the noonday sun.

Even at night, the heat there was oppressive. Pero knew it would make tempers flare. He needed to keep Heep and the others from infighting. If they were going to prevail here, they needed each other's strengths.

"Heep, I ask you to listen and then, if you want, leave me to my own devices. I won't drag you into anything, but I fear without you, there may be a tragedy here of epic proportions. I am sorry I have been deceiving you, Heep," Pero looked at the others, "And you all."

Heep literally shouted at Pero, it had been years since Pero had seen him so fiery. "Pero, is that how little you think of any of us? Who was it that has saved my ass time after time? Perot

Island, Tasmania, Grand Seychelles, New Orleans, Bangkok, Kamchatka . . . do I have to make a list for heaven's sake? You think I don't owe you? You don't think I trust you? What I need you to do is tell them what is happening, or going to happen and," he paused and leaned forward, raising his voice even more "and produce them, you idiot, it's what you do!" Then he smiled. Pero was speechless.

"Yeah, come on man, who was it who took my wife to the emergency room when I was away?" Ruis looked teary eyed.

Priit chimed in, words overlapping Ruis', "Yes. And who has shown me? Time and again? The honor of trust? Who's always writing letters? To other producers on my behalf? You think I don't know? I owe you like a brother. After rehab? A rehab I *damnt* know well you paid for? With the Family trust? Or no family trust?" Priit's singsong seemed, somehow, to blend in with the jungle sounds. For Pero, it was getting embarrassing.

Mary stepped in front of Pero, her nose shining in the moonlight, the freckles little dark spots. She was, even Pero could see, squaring her shoulders and about to let Pero have it, both barrels. "And Pero, it's my uncle we're talking about here. I am ready, willing and, with these his new friends," she looked at Mbuno, Priit and Ruis, holding contact for a second or two, "and I thank you all no matter what the outcome . . . to help you with your plans Pero. And since everyone is reminding you . . ."

"*Standby.*"

Pero jumped to the voice, and everyone froze. "Standby okay."

"As I was saying, since everyone is reminding you, who was it who pulled me from the Zambezi two years ago? Who was it who dived in those class-four rapids to rescue me when the raft went over? Was it the professional rafter? Was it the

Olympic swimmer who was the ratings celebrity for that stupid network Sports Special? Oh, no, it was you, you, you idiot, who saved me—and never hesitated. And you think any of us are going to hesitate now to help you, or hesitate to help you defeat these evil people who are going to attack my uncle and his followers? You aren't that stupid. In fact, you're one of the smartest people I know, you just don't seem to have any personal commitment, to anything, except the momentary needs of others, for which we," she looked at Heep, Ruis, and Priit, all nodding away, "will thank you, with our lives if necessary. Get it?" She moved aside giving Mbuno room.

"And one more thing, bwana. You saved my life."

"And you saved mine." Pero's response was automatic.

"No, bwana, you saved me as a man. You gave me my honor back as a tracker, the Liangulu honor modern Kenya that doesn't want anymore. You are my friend, Mr. Pero, it is my honor," he paused and put a hand on Pero's shoulder, "even if you are a crazy *mzungu*." And he smiled, the European way, teeth shining in the moonlight. It was so un-Mbuno, they all started to laugh. With the hissing, demanding phone glued to his ear, Pero could only marvel that they were laughing. *What must they be thinking back at State?*

The laughter diminished the tension in all of them and yet only served to make Pero feel more vulnerable. The distance between him and them was gone, if it really ever existed. He suddenly felt, and the word popped into his head, "family." He was shaken by their faith and had nothing to offer as thanks and yet, somewhere from deep within, came the most private thing Pero could share with them "I miss *Addiena*."

"Oh Pero . . ." Mary immediately started to weep and hugged Pero. The others gathered around, patted his shoulders and back. They all spoke at once, Heep first: "Now I know why you're doing this!" then Ruis and Priit almost as one, "That's normal man . . . yeah, we get it," Mbuno's, "Ndiyo bwana, ndiyo" reconfirmed his compassion and finally Heep again, who had so liked Addiena all those years ago, "Yeah, so do I Pero, so does everyone who loved her."

The phone started talking; Pero forced himself to listen as his friends peeled off, now waiting, keeping quiet.

"Message incoming, acknowledge ready to receive."

Pero responded, "Acknowledged," and pushed the speaker button so they could all hear, the volume out in the open was low, but he knew State would hear them speaking better than perhaps they could hear State.

"Mission status analyzed. Evac not possible until sixteen hundred Zulu." That was six that evening, fourteen hours away. "Acknowledge if you want to reschedule."

Pero wanted to make sure everyone understood, "They cannot evac us at this time, they want to know if we can wait until six tonight. We can't. By then Singh may be after us, the bad guys too, maybe Purim's lot, he may have tracked us. It's a no go. Mbuno, can we get across by Moshi around the eastern flank of Kilimanjaro, into Amboseli and through to Kimana and then Nairobi?"

The phone asked, "Acknowledge."

"Hold on State, you have to wait." Now his crew knew whom they were talking to. Mbuno knew it was Baylor's bosses, that much was sufficient. Pero lowered the phone but didn't cover the mouthpiece. "Well, that'll piss them off. Mbuno? Answer?"

"Yes, bwana, interesting way. We can make it, but the tires, it has been raining, they will help in the lowland, with the red mud, but on the slopes, there is no track, the thorn bushes will shred them. If we make it to Moshi, we could borrow a Land Rover truck, could we not?" Pero suddenly knew whom he was thinking of. Pero nodded.

"Ah, not a Land Rover, Mbuno, Alistair's tourist truck, the Unimog. Right?" Mbuno nodded.

Pero raised the phone. "State, cancel the evac, we're making for Nairobi on our own. Answer, now, real time the following: One, has Tom Baylor been appraised of our thoughts? Two, have you discovered identity and connection of man in Holiday Inn, Nairobi who Salim and Nadir were reporting to? Three, have bottling plant and printing press been located? Four, has Reverend JT been appraised? Five, has *Meeting on the Hill* been canceled? Six, will need armed help and equipment and full diplomatic support Nairobi, status priority one, repeat priority one, can you confirm?"

"Standby."

"No standby State, get someone higher up to talk to me and talk to me now."

"Standby, Director coming online."

A little surprised, Pero explained, "The director is coming online. Maybe we can get some answers. Heep, come closer and listen with me, I don't want to miss anything."

Mbuno kneeled down and placed his fingers on the rail, "Bwana, hurry, there will be a train coming in ten minutes, maybe more."

Heep and Pero stood there, their heads together, listening. "Thanks Heep."

"You are welcome friend."

"Standby. Director coming online."

"Acknowledged, standing by, but hurry, rail traffic incoming within ten minutes."

"Acknowledged, Director Lewis here. Interesting open mike there Baltazar. Your situation seems, at best, perilous. Your logic sound, perhaps. You need to forfeit anything and everything to keep Mary Lever safe, can you comply?"

Heep nodded, Pero said, "Yes, they all agree."

"This isn't a committee decision—you are now a field agent. I need to classify you as such to provide you the items on your list. Do you agree with State Department Articles thirty-four and thirty-five, confirm." There was a pause, then he added, "You can read them later."

"Okay, I confirm, but it's temporary, I may resign when this is over."

"When this is over, as you put it, you can either have a medal or you will be forced to retire in disgrace for having failed. Your timetable has accelerated everything to the point where we have no effective agents in the region until tomorrow a.m. Eastern standard time, sorry evening your time. Do you agree?"

"Well, what option do I have? Yes, proceed."

"None, of course. Okay, item one, your question: Has Tom Baylor been appraised of your thoughts? No. Tom Baylor is unconfirmed dead, sorry, yesterday your time, about the time your Mbuno, wasn't it, killed Nadir. Congratulations on that, one less to worry about. Baylor made no transmission after arrival Ramu. He went down," meaning his whereabouts went unknown shortly after arrival. "Bus of birdwatchers was blown up. He's known to have survived that, but one Chief Methenge, your acquaintance, claims to have his body for collection, found at Park HQ, dumped. We've sent Phillip Arnold with Kenya soldiers, for an official reclamation of a US tourist, simple police matter. The place is now crawling with police and soldiers. No sign of any encampment. Bulldozer has been identified by synthetic aperture radar, buried, and covered—approx location you gave. When they have a confirmation about Baylor, we will pass it along to you, when you call. Don't raise your hopes. Expect Methenge is accurate about Baylor, the description fits. Sorry."

Pero repeated the news, "My old friend Tom Baylor may be dead." Mbuno looked at Pero and shook his head, and touched his left hand to his head and raised it up towards the sky, "*Kuaga*" (farewell). It was a gesture of parting.

"Item two. Have they discovered identity and connection of the man in the Holiday Inn, Nairobi who Salim and Nadir were reporting to? Answer: Yes, he's in custody of Kenyan authorities and is in Trade House for interrogation."

Trade House is a well-known interrogation center for Kenyan police. It is also known to be a torture center. Heep and Pero had once interviewed a man who escaped, for PrimeTime Live, ABC TV. His tales were chilling.

"Salim was found dead, in the Nairobi market, a single stabbing. Suspect Ranjeet family. Ranjeet family are agents for the Indian government and a sideline with Mossad. We have no contact directly with them, you do. We have intercepted traffic from them indicating they have identified you talking to Baylor at Wilson Airport. Mossad is being asked to secure Ranjeet support for you on this. Awaiting that decision any moment. Will advise. But I suspect they would do it for you anyway.

"Item three. Have bottling plant and printing press been located? No. This is so far a blank. Man from Holiday Inn was commercial agent for Canon office products but was renting multiple rooms. Don't know the occupants of the other rooms. Canon products Kenya owned by Pakistani firm. They're investigating and getting cooperation from Kenyan authorities. They will stop distribution all Tusker products, all Kenya, and analyze batches. Their sources say the anthrax notion is probably not method. Tusker delivery van with bomb maybe. Also the concept of bomb with anthrax being looked into. They're stockpiling antibiotics in case you are right. I don't mind telling you, you've scared the shit out of everyone here. Oh, and that site in Iraq? It was one of six, German mini-brewery truck trailers, all unused, thank God. No such mini-brewery tractor-trailer was imported legally into Kenya, Uganda, Sudan, Somalia, or Ethiopia that we can trace. One was sold to Yemen last year, which has been diverted to Zimbabwe. Mugabe deals with al-Qaida operatives, it's a possibility. But how would it get from there to Kenya and where is it, if it did? There may not be enough time to find out before tomorrow.

"Item four. Has Reverend JT been appraised? Negative. We cannot reach him, he's in seclusion, prayer seclusion. We need Mary Lever to contact him. Believability is critical, his profile suggests. His number is—get ready to copy—zero two five four sixer sixer one two three two two. Get that?"

Pero held up the phone, Heep took out his pencil and notebook, "Say it again." The Director did so, more slowly.

"Yes, I repeat zero two five four—Kenya—sixer sixer one two three two two, Mary to call Reverend JT ASAP."

"Good. They suggest Mary calls him now, when we hang up."

Mary interrupted and spoke loudly, loud enough for Director Lewis to hear, Pero was sure: "No Pero, I don't have to call him. They can. Tell him to call the number and use the following sequence of words: *'Trust in the Lord,'* then say *'Mary says Proverbs are the center'* and repeat the words *Trust in The Lord*. He will immediately talk with you. Tell him everything."

"You get that Director?"

"Got it, repeating: 'Trust in the Lord, Mary says Proverbs are the center, Trust in the Lord. Will call when we hang up. Suggest Mary also call when possible."

"Roger that."

"Now, item five. Has *Meeting on the Hill* been canceled? No. They cannot cancel that. The Kenyan authorities say they do not have the political or public support to cancel the service. It's not practicable, seventy-five thousand are already there, camped out. Seventy-five thousand are en route and perhaps as many as one hundred thousand more from Nairobi area tomorrow. No security, no screening, it's a logistical nightmare.

"Item six. You will need arms and equipment and full diplomatic support in Nairobi, status priority one. Well, this is a dangerous situation for you and your team there. Arms are useful if you know how to use them. Our files indicate that Ruis and Mbuno are the only ones qualified other than you, and your armory scores are low, short range you're okay, but be careful where you aim. "

Heep gave a little laugh. Pero wondered how they knew his private shooting club scores for that's the only place he ever fired a gun, except for hunting with a rifle, of course. He shook his head to clear his thoughts as the Director was still speaking, "When you get to Nairobi, call us here and I will have contact for you. Side arms for three and thin Kevlar vests for six, I think. Maybe seven if Reverend JT doesn't cancel. Diplomatic support is being worked on, you can count on the Embassy, but stay clear, it may be watched, the embassy will contact you, this line if they need you. Suggest you stay at the Karen *Duka*, it's a safe house, our man downstairs, when you arrive in Nairobi. We can have delivery of the equipment there. An anthrax sniffer is incoming this morning off the aircraft carrier Kennedy, via Kuwait on a commercial flight."

"Yes, that's fine, I've shopped at the duka, oh and by the way, a niece of the Ranjeets is employed at the cleaners next door."

"Interesting. I'm always fighting for outside assets to send in more information, however useless, to build a better picture for moments like this. But now you are on your own, you need to calculate everything, and Pero, I mean everything. It's the only chance you—and they—have." He paused. "Anything else? Oh yes, we have no idea what you are going to try and achieve, but given the situation, even if it's not the Tusker, all here feel that the death of Simon, death of Baylor, and especially the swift movement of al-Qaida or al-Shabaab operatives to dog your location, there is definitely an urgent, speedy, schedule here and it does, our analysis shows, point at Reverend JT, if not also the *Meeting on the Hill*." He paused and said, "Turn off the speaker, comply."

Pero looked at Heep, who nodded. He pushed the button and motioned to Heep to listen in.

"We further suggest there may be a Reichstag motive here, which may involve elements of JT's staff. I will not tell him that if I speak to him. You must analyze that on site—and we will continue to ramp up all, repeat all, agency resources on this mission. Agreed?"

"Agreed." Pero said and Heep nodded. "Heeper agrees and I'm sure the team will do their best. Will you personally stand by?"

"So you let Mr. Heeper listen in? Your call." He meant Pero's responsibility and the enormity of the task facing them came into clear focus, not helped by the Director who was perhaps a little angry, "Oh yes, I'm only Lewis here, Mr. Baltazar, at your service." He was being a bit sardonic. Heep and Pero heard the Director's sigh, even across a crackling phone line. "Oh well, it's going to be a long night, well, day coming up, for you. Anything else?"

"Yes. What about Commissioner Singh? Is he a threat?"

"Our analysis says yes and no. Yes, he wants you as bait to sweep the al-Qaida operatives from Tanzania, that's clear. But he's rabid anti-al-Qaida. They're leaning on him to cease and desist using you, but Singh may not be reachable quickly."

"Oh, yes, he is . . . wait a moment." Pero reached into his pocket and extracted a slip of paper, Pangani Camp notepad from beside his bedside. "His satellite phone, Navistar, green button model, is zero sixer sixer four three five sixer eight niner two. Only he answers. If you can't get him, call his brother, Virgi, the Toyota man in Dar."

"A car dealer, you want me to call a car dealer?"

"Yes. But first, try the Navistar."

"Okay, computer here says it's an Interpol number. Got an Interpol scramble phone huh? I will make the call immediately—see if we can give you a clear shot out of the country. Okay?"

"Yes, thanks. And ask Singh about the passport pages—the visa entries—I stupidly didn't photograph those. Can you call and ask him?"

"Sure, will do. And I'll call when there's something to report. If you hear static, push two one one and it'll connect the cryptology program. Good luck, end." And it signed off with the two clicks.

A light appeared, coming from the northwest. In the morning mist, the light settled down into three beams, an international sign of a train headlight triangle. The tinny sound of the rumble cadence of the diesel began to bounce at them along the tracks.

"It is coming, slowly, bwana. We have to move. They have a radio."

"Okay, everybody in the Land Rovers, Heep go with Ruis, Priit ride with me, and review everything we heard, I'll do the same with Mary and Priit. Agreed?" Heep yelled yes over his shoulder as they scrambled to get in and away before the train spotted them.

For fifteen minutes the train diesel lumbered past. They watched from the bush, lights out, with a few snaps of small trees, hiding their shapes. Pero was about to pull out when the engine was already a quarter mile away when Pero remembered there was a caboose, American style, on these Tanzanian freight trains. The guard in there was usually in radio contact with the driver.

They waited. Priit counted, like a child, "Forty-one, forty-two, forty-three, forty-four, and the brakeman's car." Priit spoke English, not the American "caboose."

"Let's wait a moment here till it rounds the bend." Pero opened the window. Mosquitoes, smelling their carbon dioxide, crowded in. "Mbuno, you lead, I'll follow, okay?" Swat, smack, steer with one hand. Keep the bugs at bay, it was going to be tropical Africa all the way.

"Ndiyo bwana, but it will get very rough after one hour. We have to cut over country to get to the road to Alistair's by Moshi. Maybe an hour. It is better to get off the road. I know a hunting camp trail that will make it not so hard. We will be all right there." He was leaning out the window, looking down at the fat tires.

"Okay, but when we do leave the road I will need to stop to have Mary call JT, get that Heep?" He heard, nodded. "And if I stop, you stop. This phone will ring, but I can't answer moving. Okay?" Everyone said they understood. Mbuno nodded. "Priit, get the walkie-talkies hooked up, receive only until needed, okay?"

They started off.

Priit got to work, made a test call and Ruis answered right away. There would be questions, and now was the time to drive, talk, think, and plan. Later on, things might get too busy.

In the early pre-morning light they drove quickly, Mbuno setting a constant, reliable pace. Pero talked and they reviewed what they had heard and what it meant—or what they thought it meant. After an hour they rounded a bend, Mbuno slowed and inched the Land Rover off the road. In driving off-road here, you let the vehicle in front get a lead of 100 yards. The track wasn't hard to follow, but if the lead car got in trouble you would be on firm ground to use the winch if needed. As Mbuno forged ahead Pero inched his way as well. Pero could see Mbuno was driving around everything that could possibly puncture the balloon tires—three feet forward, two sideways—it felt like. It was slow going. When they were 200 yards off road, Mbuno stopped and got out. Pero inched forward, wondering if he needed a tow. He walked back and said, simply, "Clear sky here, bwana." He was right, they were in a clearing, around which was dense, solid vegetation.

"Mary, time to make that call. Use Heep's satellite phone, we need to keep mine," Pero patted his breast pocket, "free in case they call."

While Mary made her call to JT, her voice imploring and desperate, they all ambled about—taking turns behind the Land Rover furthest from Mary, fertilizing the plants. When she was done all she would say was "I did what I could, he refuses to cancel but he's already agreed with Director Lewis to allow US Special Forces to give him protection. They arrive this afternoon off the Kennedy. He's sure that is enough. He was shocked at the Tusker idea, Pero, thinks you and Heep are way too dramatic, no way they would kill that many people just to get him. Doesn't see the point. He made me wonder as well."

"Okay, so let's load up and discuss it, we've a long way to go." But then Mary reminded Pero it was her turn to "disappear behind the bushes." They all turned away.

She sighed, mumbling, "Men."

When she was finished, they piled back into the Land Rovers and ambled off down the scrubland, inching around the thorn bushes and baobab trees in this land of the southernmost Maasai. The driving was slow, slow, quick, quick, slow, like a dance.

The early day grew brighter, hotter, and dryer as they left the lowland costal humidity behind. Now and again small antelope called the dik-dik appeared, all nine inches of them, and scurried out of their way. There were hyenas of course, and once they had to wait while a family of giraffe neck-walked across their path. They came to a complete stop on a short plain when a herd of some thousand wildebeest, zebra, and antelope trotted by, kicking up so much dust they couldn't see a thing. It took only moments to clear. This is Africa, Pero was thinking, a tourist's dream, and today they only wanted to hurry on, past, forwards. It was strange seeing beauty as an obstacle.

Some questions went back and forth. Nothing concrete, they were all busy thinking. Pero felt over-tired and besides, he was fighting the Land Rover to keep up with Mbuno and not shred a tire. The conclusion of JT's reluctance to believe the Tusker anthrax danger was that it didn't matter. Experts would soon be able to deal with that danger. If it was real, it would turn up soon enough. If it was false and the *Meeting on the Hill* went off without a hitch, it still didn't mean they were wrong to be worried. Although, as the Director said, Pero might be out of a job. Pero had used the priority one signal—there was no backing down from that.

Two hours hard driving later the cars popped up onto the highway again, this time a solid surface. They pressed on faster, and at least now in a straight line.

Twice there was a single engine small plane that flew directly overhead, following the road. It happens frequently in East Africa, visual flight rules for farm pilots often means the best map from farm to town is to follow the road, cut straight by bulldozers fifty years ago with foreign aid funding. The plane was the same, going in each direction. Nothing suspicious. When it appeared a third time just as they were approaching Moshi, Pero radioed Mbuno to keep driving straight past

Alistair's turn-off, until it was out of sight. As soon as it was, they doubled back to Alistair's turning, two miles back. It was eleven o'clock already; the sun was full force.

Alistair and his wife were home, sitting on the verandah, and as welcoming as ever.

CHAPTER 14

Kilimanjaro

British ex-pats, Alistair and Sue, were getting on in years. After WWII, they had settled in the German colony of Tanganyika to run a small farm holding, raising cattle. Since then, cattle had long been replaced by a tourist service of off-road, special permit, excursions. Day trips only, they would pick up tourists and truck them up the side of Africa's tallest mountain, not all the way to the top, but just into the snowfield. Standing very near the equator, with your feet in the snow, was a tourist shot not to be missed.

Kilimanjaro, or Kilima Njaro in Swahili, meaning the Great White Mountain, is to sub-Saharan Africa what the Statue of Liberty is to the USA.

Kilimanjaro is an extinct volcano, or three to be exact, that lies east of the Great Rift Valley. Her volcanoes were the result of that last cataclysmic upheaval that split Africa down the middle from Northern Kenya to South Africa. Two of her volcanoes have eroded to mounds of debris over the eons, but the one that remains, called Kibo, is almost a perfect cone. All three hold the snow the mountain is famed for all year long. From below, it looks like one peak. Mountains are always deceptive.

When the first Western explorers came upon the massive mountain, straddling the Equator, they could not possibly believe they were seeing snow. They sent porters to the top to retrieve the "silver and precious metals" glistening there. The guides returned with water. The first British reports of snow were dismissed as "lunacy" by the Royal Geographical Society, and the explorers were mocked in the press.

The years went by and, eventually, a German expedition climbed the mountain—the highest ever mountain ascent in 1889—climbed into the snow and documented her majesty. Now that majesty of Kilimanjaro is conquered weekly, in fairly easy six-day ascents, on foot, up the eastern slope to 19,330 feet above sea level. She's trampled on by tourists, adventurers, and hang gliders keen to launch off the top (and wear the T-shirt to prove it).

"Animals," Alistair was often heard to say, "Who gives a damn about animals? It's the humans that humans want to see, quite often watching their ownselves, that's why they take so many bloody photos. It's the human experience they want to have, not always kissing the bloody cuddlies. Animal safaris, hah!"

The trucks he operated were open-backed, ex-army vehicles "always bloody German, only people who make good vehicles, those Krauts." In truth, he chose them because the carburetors could be adjusted and ignition advanced from the cab as he climbed at altitude. Ordinary trucks stalled out every 8,000 feet. Now in semi-retirement, he had sold his business and his fleet of specialized trucks just before computerized fuel injection made them obsolete. He ran a smaller tourist business as an amusement now. He bought a Mercedes Unimog and claimed to be able to climb into the snow "higher than the has-beens" who had bought his business.

The two Land Rovers' passengers found them at home, Alistair nursing a broken leg, "fell off the bloody packhorse."

He meant the Unimog. He was known to always call his trucks packhorses because they could "go anywhere a horse can." Pero made the introductions to his film crew. And then he explained what was wanted: "I need to steal your Unimog . . . please."

Alistair frowned but did not hesitate, "Conditions. Mbuno here does the driving. Best damn safari driver in East Africa. And you pay twice the rental rate even if I'm not driving," he tapped the cast, "and you leave those Land Rovers somewhere else, say Arusha. I know who owns those, over by Pangani, and I want no trouble."

Pero had no time to drive around finding a place to leave them. He offered money. No deal, he tried pleading. No deal. He tried to win Alistair over with promises of endless supplies of whiskey, no deal. Heep and Mary took Alistair aside and somehow struck a deal. Alistair, mumbling "always a sucker for a pretty lass," pointed at an old decrepit looking barn with his crutch "Put 'em in there. Never go in there. If they're found, I'll say you really did steal the Unimog! Fair 'nuff?" Pero agreed it was.

Sue, his wife, was smiling and shaking her head. "Daft old git, he always was going to help you Pero, he just wanted the company—and the woman—to stay longer." Alistair nodded and beamed.

Sue walked them over as Mbuno drove one and then the other into the barn. They transferred the equipment, SeaSled and all, to the house. "It'll be safer in the house, dear, in case someone liberates those two," pointing at the barn "while we're not watching. Besides, we have more protection in the house." Pero knew what she was referring to—he had stayed here once before. Their living quarters and windows had cage doors with shooting slots in them, and their closet was one-quarter inch steel box as a last refuge. On the border with Kenya, they had it built during the Mau Mau period "only way we could stay here dear, needed to sleep well. Untouchable, we were. They left us alone."

As everything was unloaded, Pero made sure everyone kept essentials, passports, and medical papers, the top priority. Ruis kept his tool kit, Priit kept three little cameras ("Hey, you never know"), the cell phones and his PDA. Heep took all the videotapes. He and Mary threw some clothes in a duffel with toothbrushes. Mary wasn't worried. "All my clothes for tomorrow are at the Norfolk," she said, referring to the oldest hotel in Nairobi. JT had apparently rented the whole building.

Pero took nothing except the satellite phone and a pair of walkie-talkies. And extra batteries as Ruis insisted. Mbuno simply took his whole meager bag. No one said anything, it was the African way, you carry away what you own because you might not ever have a chance to get it back. Pero put Heep's extra DVDs of their filming to date in Mbuno's pack—for safekeeping.

Out back of their one-story ranch home, next to a chicken wire fenced in vegetable patch, Alistair was waiting by his packhorse. His Unimog was a German off-road monster truck, sitting on twenty-two and one-half inch wheels, over ten feet high, and weighing ten tons. With a 280 HP high performance diesel injection engine, her muffler stuck out the top with a forty-five degree angle to give her a rakish look. In place of the flatbed, Alistair had ordered a "carbon-fiber full cap, so that it seats ten, with an open skylight the tourists can shut, just like the bloody Land Rovers." He turned to Mbuno who had taken the driver's seat, "She has eight forward speeds selected with those paddles mounted for finger control on the back of the steering wheel just like them bloody Formula One racers."

Mbuno felt the paddles, one either side of the steering wheel. "It is like a motorcycle, is it not?" He fingered the right one, "This one up a gear, yes?" Alistair nodded. "And this one . . ." fingering the left one, "down a gear?"

"Right you are. Now, the suspension springs give you fifteen inches of travel so that virtually any terrain is crossable unless you hit a bloody bog, then the bitch will sink, so if that happens, quick as a flash, you must use the winch on a strong tree, right? It's strong enough."

"*Ndiyo, namaizi,*" (Yes, I understand). Mbuno knew there were no bogs on the side of the mountain escarpment, but Amboseli Park was known for them.

Alistair was clearly proud of his packhorse, happy enough to share it with an expert driver like Mbuno, "At over twenty feet long and seven feet wide, she's a bloody stable, powerful, and capable little beast. She's my pride and joy, treat her well Mbuno, all right?"

"*Ndiyo, mimi ahadi,*" (I promise). Although Mbuno was sufficiently familiar with the controls, he knew there were unexpected challenges coming up, and all his skill with the unfamiliar handling of the Unimog might require a second pair of eyes and hands. "I feel it would be better if one other man helped me to drive . . ." and here he perfectly mimicked Alistair's voice, "this bloody beast, Mr. Alistair."

They all laughed and Alistair assured him that Ruis—who had already been peering under the engine hood and checking out the controls—seemed "just like the man to help you matey." It was agreed. Ruis would sit right seat.

Alistair addressed the crew, standing around, ready to board, "Where are you going to leave her? Or are you bringing her back?"

Pero looked at Mbuno and said, "Amboseli Lodge?"

"Can we not take it to Nairobi?"

Pero looked doubtful, "It's not fast enough, what forty tops?" Alistair wiggled his right hand indicating maybe more, maybe less. "And I will change extra road transportation if you take 'er there."

Mbuno seemed to have decided, "So, Amboseli Lodge bwana?"

"Yes, okay, as you think best Mbuno," who nodded and thankfully left it at that. Pero had plans they could discuss later. No need to involve Alistair and Sue. Alistair merely said to Sue "Pack a bag dear, you can drive us to Amboseli as soon as they leave, I will take the main road in your Datsun." He still called those Japanese cars with that outdated name even though for twenty years they had been made by Nissan. "We can have a little naughty night at the Lodge. We'll pick up the packhorse and drive her back home before anyone knows she was gone." Alistair always had all the relevant official papers for the border—he crossed it several times a week. Pero looked down at the cast on Alistair's left leg. The auto shifting Unimog had no need of a clutch pedal. Alistair could have driven them but wisely chose not to.

They piled aboard, happy that the full cap was open forward to the driving cab. Alistair responded to a question no one had asked, "How else do you think I can talk to the paying buggers while I drive? Besides, they love the view of the dashboard." The dashboard has gauges, lights, and at least a dozen switches, each clearly marked. It looked complicated, like the inside of a plane, demanding an expert at the wheel. Pero was sure the look of the beast was all part of Alistair's show.

Alistair was busy telling Mbuno which trail to use to cut across the Kilimanjaro escarpment, "Start down this hill, see over there, that's the trail. Stay on that, but turn right at the triple fork, about ten miles further on over Kili's hump—for god's sake don't miss the fork or you'll be on a route to the top of Kili. Anyway, stay to the right at the fork and you'll drive through, skirting Chala. Avoid that, right?" Pero nodded,

Mbuno frowned and concentrated, "Already you'll be in Kenya, but they know my packhorse. And then right into Amboseli's back yard. Follow the elephant tracks in Amboseli, only the elephant tracks mind, but watch the marshes in case they lead you to water."

They said good-bye and drove off, Mbuno revving the engine a little higher before each shift. "No clutch bwana," he shouted back to Pero. But within ten minutes, he became perfectly smooth with gear changes, as if he had always driven the beast.

Bushes and rocks of a size that could incapacitate a Land Rover were no match for the Unimog. They plunged on, keeping a steady fifteen miles per hour in a straight line. Soon they were climbing the escarpment, the foot of Kilimanjaro, and the scenery changed—every increase in altitude, each giving a new ecology for wildlife. They took the right fork and after about two hours, they crested a hill and looked down on Kenya and the green of Amboseli National Park. There was still the unfenced border to cross, but by staying northeast from now on, they shouldn't encounter anyone or any patrol, just wild terrain. Pero knew there would be a border plane spotter, but how often and whose it was, Pero had no idea. Anyway, the Unimog should be a regular sight to authorities. The goal was to press on, await news from State, reach the safe house outside Nairobi at the Karen Duka (Karen district grocery store)—and take whatever action they could to prevent a catastrophe that State might have already solved anyway. *Hopefully*, was all Pero thought, *hopefully*.

The noise, jostling, and sea-sick-making movement of the tiptoeing Unimog didn't promote much conversation. Everyone was waiting, hoping to receive good news, happy to be doing something, even if it was fleeing. Ruis called back "Hey, in case a plane flies over, why don't you people stand and ooh and ahh like tourists, it might be good cover." And so they all did all the way downhill. The view down to Amboseli was, as always, the best of East Africa.

Amboseli is in Maasai land. The park itself is not under their control, but the park pays a fee to the Maasai elders as tribute for allowing this tourist site—not to mention the three concession lodges in the park—to exist. There was better animal viewing at Kimana Lodge, twenty miles outside of the park, but that lodge was not for sunburned tourists who want twenty-four-hour service. Amboseli had the big five—leopard, lion, cape buffalo, elephant, rhino—as well as giraffe, Thompson's Gazelles, Waterbuck, bushbuck, dik-dik, zebra, wildebeest, eland and a whole host of photogenic animals. The lined-up zebra vans on every path around the park proved the point. But Amboseli is especially a haven for elephant.

Elephants are smart. Outside of the park, they were killed for trampling crops, poached for ivory, and generally not wanted. Inside the park, they can do no wrong. Smart animals, avoiding slaughter, in Amboseli they cluster in herds—never found in the real wild Africa—herds of five hundred or more in some seasons, making a wonderful sight. All those cameras click away hardly disturbing them at all.

In the Unimog, they were following one such herd making for the Park haven, there's a trampled path as wide as a boulevard, earth stamped hard, the Unimog in her element. The crossing from Tanzania into Kenya had been no problem. The Unimog was a familiar site in the park, so no ranger waved them down.

The satellite phone in his pocket beeped. "Mbuno, find a place to stop right away." He simply wrenched the wheel and they left the path into the bush off to the right. When he was away from view, behind some tall Acacia trees, giraffe feeding on the other side of them, he turned off the engine.

Pero pushed the on button, heard static, and then pushed 211.

The voice at State was clear and strong, "Lewis here. How are you doing?"

"We're in Kenya, just in Amboseli Park. We can be at the Karen Duka in three hours."

"Roger, that will be six p.m. your time, ten a.m. our time, fourteen hundred Zulu. Right?"

"More or less, depends on traffic."

"Okay, here's what we have got. We and the Brits have been busy. Jimmy Threte was a no go. He has agreed to Special Forces protection for the *Meeting*, they've just arrived Nairobi and are en route to the Norfolk Hotel. He has agreed not to move from there without calling me here. I gave him this number."

"Yes, Mary told us pretty much the same. Go ahead."

"There was an ambush set for you just before the border crossing on the road between Arusha and Namanga. Commissioner Singh has arrested six, but still doesn't know where you got to. He swears he was protecting you, but the tracking device he put on your Land Rovers stopped moving. He has sent people to investigate. Just where are those Land Rovers?"

"In a barn, unharmed. We changed vehicles."

"Well done. I do think he would have protected you, but I do not think he would have let you speed on, on your mission. And speed is of the essence."

Pero thought that if the Land Rovers were found at Alistair's, he could get into trouble with Singh, "Look, it would help if you would put in the good word for the couple who loaned us their packhorse for the trip here . . ."

Lewis interrupted, somewhat surprised, "You are on a packhorse, all of you?"

"Sorry, that's his nickname, it's a Unimog, four wheeler, he calls it his packhorse." And Pero gave him Alistair and Sue's details in Moshi.

"Okay, will do so. The brother, Virgi, is powerful—our ambassador in Dar vouches for him, and the Commissioner and a Minister as well. Virgi is very much your personal ally. If Commissioner Singh gets difficult, I was told that Virgi would "sit on little brother." That make sense to you?"

Pero smiled, and chuckled as he responded, "Yes, Virgi weighs two hundred and twenty pounds and stands five feet six inches tall."

"Strange people you know. Now for the important stuff— There are no anthrax traces in any of the beer inspected. They're taking one bottle at random from every case, breaking it (in case it's in a separate capsule inside), and sampling the air. Marines lent them a mobile unit that arrived two hours ago, via helicopter crane from their ship off Mombasa. So far, nothing. And no traces of that label either. All the factory bottles are printed directly on glass now, not labeled. Tusker people are sure there's no security breach at their plant either. Kenyans have air samplers of their own, rudimentary, but they work, and they've gone over the bottling plant, using heavy manpower . . . so far nothing there either.

"We have no confirmation on the identity of the body by Phillip Arnold, too badly mutilated without forensics. How the Chief thought it as Baylor was backpack with Tom Baylor's name in it found next to the corpse. That, and the fact it's a tourist. It may turn out not to be Baylor. We're getting strange signals from his phone, we're analyzing. I'll keep you informed." Lewis was speeding on, making sure everything he knew was shared.

"The man in the Holiday Inn turns out to be the brother of the man your Mbuno killed, sorry, was attacked by. We still don't know who was in the other rooms he booked and paid for. The other occupants have left the hotel. We're investigating, it's slow going, the Kenyan police are not very fast.

"Ranjeets know of your arrival, Mossad negotiated a sharing of intel on this mission with us. Ranjeet will meet you at the Duka if you want. One word of caution, Prabir Ranjeet does not, repeat not, want his son Amogh to know. Can you comply?"

"Yes, that's okay, but who the hell do you think told him I met with Baylor?"

"Pero, I have no idea. But that's his wish, okay?"

"Fine."

"The Canon dealer, the guy the Kenyan cops inter-rogated," he stretched the word as if it were in inverted commas, meaning tortured, "he was setting up a full Canon office suite for an insurance company opening offices there next month. They found the Garamond fonts on every computer and other samples of the Tusker Special Beer label there, including artwork on a computer, Adobe something. The authorities have sealed the place but will allow incoming visitors who will be arrested and checked out."

"They're still checking Tusker, delivery vans, that sort of thing. In case one van may go missing and be used as a suicide bomb. Leave that one to them, we've now got two hundred field support personnel in place, they should be able to control this." *My God, they already had two hundred agents in place? No, couldn't be agents.* Pero suspected that most of them were American personnel on loan or orders from Navy ships doing R & R in Mombasa, a favorite port for US forces.

"The *Meeting on the Hill* is not only going forward, there are now one hundred fifty thousand people in Nairobi, camped out at the site, awaiting the great event with another one hundred thousand expected from locals. They're putting up bulletproof glass around the lectern and some security cameras, even under the stands, that sort of thing, but, honestly, it's a hard site to secure. The Captain of the USS Milwaukee is up from Mombasa to take command of his whole ship's company, to beef up security, he has a green light on all your names, priority one."

Pero knew it. Available personnel from a ship in Mombasa were the only way they'd get help fast enough, nothing else fit the timeline. So, they too were amateurs being forced into this situation.

"The equipment you requested is already at the Duka. The lock code is Lever, as if it was a telephone dial."

"Got it."

"We feel your best avenue of action is to by-pass the Kenyans and find out who was at the Holiday Inn or who planted the plane bomb, and follow that up. And, if it is still anthrax, and we all hope to heaven you are wrong, then keep Mary Lever away and safe, at the Duka, got it?"

"I can't promise that. She's insisting that we drop her off at the Norfolk on the way into Nairobi. She's determined. I plan to have Ruis, Priit, and Heep go with her to protect her. But first I will pick up the vests and gun, then get her dropped off with a team of support."

"There are Kenyan permits with the guns. They, you, must carry them at all times. They give you absolute authority, from the Presidents' offices, Kenya, and USA. Get that?"

"Roger that."

"Now, finally, we need to discuss the Reichstag gambit. Have you discussed this with your friends?"

"No. I will discuss this with Heep later."

An order: "Discuss it with them now."

"Now?"

"Now."

"Okay . . ." Pero pushed the speaker button, "People, the Director here, Lewis, wants me to discuss a remote possibility with you . . ."

The speaker voice interrupted, "Not so remote."

"Okay, not so remote as he says. The Reichstag Gambit or motive is the Nazi scenario when they burned down the Reichstag and blamed it on the Bolsheviks, the Communists of the era, to declare a state of emergency and create a Nazi police stranglehold. Every once in a while, the media trots this gambit out as a possible conspiracy theory. The Director thinks there may be a Reichstag motive at work here. Someone targeting JT and the *Meeting on the Hill* in order to, what . . .?"

Lewis spoke up, "Provoke a Christian jihad."

"Oh, provoke a Christian jihad . . . yipes. Bad choice of words, Sir, let's use the more traditional one, a crusade." He looked at his team, "Thoughts?"

Mary stood there, in the open Unimog hatch, her mouth open. It snapped shut, "I don't like your Director Lewis very much. No one on JT's staff could ever, ever—you get it? Ever be disloyal. End of story."

"I heard that. She's prejudiced and you may be wrong."

Mary was indignant, "Says you."

Ruis and Priit had nothing to offer, just shook their heads. Heep, on the other hand, was considering it, he was old enough to have felt the ripple consequences of that fateful fire. He came closer to make sure the Director could hear. "Pero, to pull off that gambit, there would have to be a clear threat beforehand, a motive expressed, that was then so-called "enacted" to have people believe it. A threat followed by a disaster has a consequence that is far reaching. Here they have no public threat, just our knowledge of a threat—a failed threat of the plane bombing is real enough, but not public enough. If something happens to Jimmy Threte, the media will react, people will react to a tragedy, not an attack for which there should be payback. Pearl Harbor had to be portrayed as a sneak attack for it to galvanize the nation. If the President had gone on the radio and said, "We were caught asleep at the switch," Congress probably would not have declared war the next day. Maybe eventually, after an inquest and discussion with the Japanese and further aggression, they would have, but not quickly enough to counteract Japanese aggression in the Pacific."

Heep knew this to be true. He was old enough to know for sure that the use of the words "sneak attack" from the most trusted man in America, the man who had seen the USA out of the Great Depression—Roosevelt made sure there was war in immediate sight. Heep continued, "With JT, and the *Meeting*, with no public threat, I just don't see the pattern."

"I heard all that Baltazar, tell Heep he has a good mind and I agree with him . . ."

"I have you on speaker, he can hear you, we all can."

Lewis continued, "But it's a possibility and certain facts fit the Reichstag profile. One, the Canon printer and computer were designing the Tusker label two days after Threte decided to go to Kenya, two weeks before the press announcement. Two, the assassin in Arusha was meant for Mary—provocation, for the threat to JT. Jikuru got in the way and tried to stop him. The dead assassin's an Afghani, known to authorities in Pakistan as Taliban, suspected al-Qaida. His shoes had earth that matched the Gurreh-Ajuran plateau region. Mary was the target. Repeat that to them now, make sure it is clear." Pero knew he didn't have to, Mary had gone white, and Heep looked deeply pensive.

"And let's follow this up with the third piece of information: NSA communications analysis has intercepted heavy phone traffic from the Norfolk Hotel to London re-routed to the Holiday Inn, which stopped when Kenyan authorities lifted the suspect Canon salesman." Mary was shaking her head and Heep had a grim look that told Pero he now agreed with Lewis.

"Okay, Director, we get your point. We will probe into that . . ."

"No, Pero," Mary looked determined, "Heep and I will, with Ruis and Priit to help," she looked at them, one at a time, "if you will?" They all nodded.

"Director, we've got agreement here. The team of four will depart Karen Duka with weapons and proceed to the Norfolk, where they will do their best to identify the Reichstag element, if he or she exists. Mary will, I am sure, have access to all of JT's advance team," she nodded, "all movements and bookings. Maybe they can turn something up quickly to finger the person for you. That okay?"

"Seems like a plan. And you and Mbuno?"

"Something else is bothering me. As Mbuno was driving, I was thinking things over. I realized that, for this to work, Reichstag gambit or just plain assassination, the definition of terrorist comes back to mind: commit that which is by its very nature is unforgivable."

"Explain."

"When Mohammed Atta flew that plane into the first of the Twin Towers, he used a street map that the FBI found on a computer, right?"

"Yes, go on, don't ask, explain, there's a time element here."

"Okay, that map was a direct route down Manhattan and slam into the North Tower. He flew much lower than he needed, screaming engines above buildings to attract attention. It wasn't vanity or lack of piloting skills—he needed people to watch. Why? He couldn't rely on television, capturing his moment of destruction, he needed people to call the media and alert them. It was a fluke that the Naudet brothers caught it on tape, just a talented fluke. It was the only recording in a city filled with tourists and cameras. But the public heard, they saw, they called the police, fire, and the media in the hundreds. Then, fifteen or so minutes later, at the interval Atta had arranged, the second tower was hit. Cameras were running, perfect media coverage worldwide, instant real live terrorism, instant unforgivable sorrow and suffering.

"In Washington there was no video, yet it happened after the Twin Towers, but there was no video. But after the Pentagon was hit every camera available was trained on the sky, in case, in case . . . . And where was the route and timing of the second jet on the computer files the FBI found? It was to pass over the Pentagon ten minutes later, grab the eye of the cameras, and slam into the Capitol. Would that second plane have been filmed, live, for the entire world? You bet.

"Here in Nairobi, we maybe have a massive crime about to be committed, an act of terrorism. But where is the instant media coverage? Is it enough to have a few million watching on closed circuit Christian cable channels—and then have the news media only reply highlights later? No, they will want the whole of the world's media to pick up the feed, live, tens of minutes of it." Pero paused, saw the shock on his crew's faces, "Impact Director Lewis, the power of television is impact, to be live and long, that's the producer's goal always. For that the terrorists need that one-two punch. Anthrax followed by . . .? Or a bomb followed by the anthrax? I don't know, but my guess is that it's a one-two media game plan."

"Impressive. Standby."

The team was looking at Pero. Heep broke the silence. "So, even if we or they," he pointed at the phone, "thwart one plan, the other could still succeed, even if it's not the one-two punch, right?"

"Yes, and it may be a one-two-three-four that Atta planned, who knows? We need to divide and conquer—look at all the angles. You need to protect JT and Mary . . ." Mary started to rev up to protest. Pero interrupted her, "Yes—Mary, protect you. Because you may be the "one" in this gambit."

The Director came back on "Baltazar, the team here thinks you are right. It's a plausible explanation. They may have multiple avenues for this display of terrorism and will play all of them or only one after another until there are two successful or maybe three or more. It is known that Atta wanted three planes for Washington because he thought the Air Force would scramble fighter jets. He never counted on those passengers fighting back. Cell phones did his Washington plan in. Good call Pero. We here feel you must pursue every lead and call us here with any developments. Acknowledge."

"Yes, confirmed. And Heeper has a satellite phone, no encryption, can he dial in?"

"Yes, let me speak to him." Pero punched the speaker button off and gave Heep the phone, who listened and took out his own satellite phone and read the number off the back to the Director.

Heep was pushing buttons on his phone. "Okay, I have done that, now a one, a star and then three three three, is that correct? And press send." He lifted it up to his ear. "Hello? Ah, got it. Okay, I'll memory that in. Thanks." He gave Pero back his phone and Pero pushed the speaker button back on.

"He can call in and we can call him when necessary. When you split up you call in and tell us, right?"

"Roger that."

"Are you near to leaving Amboseli National Park?"

"Yes, about thirty minutes, need time to swap vehicles."

"Okay, suggest you take the Kimana road and connect with the A one oh nine, past Kenyatta Airport, through the Nairobi National Park, into Langata, and by the back roads to Karen. The roads in Nairobi are solid, people are everywhere for this festival of JT's tomorrow. On the way back into Nairobi, wait until just dark and take the A-two extension to avoid Nairobi center, second exit on the Flame Tree roundabout to the Norfolk."

"Thanks for the driving instructions."

"We have a feed here for Nairobi traffic, fed back to the captain for his sailors. Oh, and at the Duka are ID tags for the *Meeting* as well as ID when you meet the captain's sailors—they will comply with your any wish, they have been briefed, there's a call sign on the reverse of the badge, if in doubt, get them to radio that in. You need help? Call on them or me, right?"

"Right, will do. We will do our best."

"You've already done more than you can . . . wait a moment, something coming in. Tactical command says that they are sure it's Baylor sending messages using Morse with on off switch on the satellite phone, the cycle time is so slow they didn't read it yet, I will replay the full tape and let you know. I'll sign off." They heard Lewis say off microphone, "What? Christ . . ." He came back to them, "Wait, don't disconnect . . . more coming in . . . a crate of Tusker Special Beer, paper labels, has been apprehended with driver while delivering to the Norfolk. Analysis follows within one hour. I will let you know. Anything else?"

"Yes, can you secure the release, to them, of the Nigerian Kweno Usman? He's being held by the UN security people, so Singh told us."

"Ha, they don't have him, we do. Where do you want him and why?"

"How about in a sailor's uniform waiting for Mary as her personal bodyguard at the Norfolk. He's proven himself before."

"Okay, the Navy Captain will not like that, but I'll get it done. For your information, it says here that this Usman guy says it was all your fault, you made him protect her. He's angry. Seems to think he's in trouble and wants your hide."

"Please send him a message: 'Votre charge Mademoiselle Lever arrivera ce soir, continuez votre protection, signé le capitaine.' He'll get it." The message told Usman that Mary would arrive this evening and she was in his care again.

"Will do, now get a move on. End." And the two clicks.

Mary was desperate for her uncle, but clearly happy Kweno, the hulk, would be there. Pero banged on the driver's cab roof, "Mbuno, *tafadali*, drive like the wind, we're needed at the Norfolk."

In under twenty minutes Pero called out, "There's the turning for the Lodge, Mbuno, take the second entrance to the car park, not the hotel entrance." It was time to steal a zebra van.

CHAPTER 15

Karen Duka

It was simple really. They appeared from the Unimog as five tourists, no luggage, following their guide, ambling, tired looking (and they were), towards the hotel. Three of them, with their driver, stopped to talk to the other drivers waiting by gleaming new Mitsubishi zebra-painted minivans with Abercrombie & Kent stenciled on the doors. Pero broke off from the group and went inside to have the tour guide for A & K paged to the front desk. Pero slipped a twenty dollar bill to the desk clerk, he took an imprint of his Amex card, and Pero gave him instructions.

When the A & K tour guide answered his page, the desk clerk informed him that he and his group were the lucky recipients of a free lunch, à la carte, not buffet, with one bottle of wine per van, and free steak dinners for their drivers. The man, a young local boy, ran out to tell the drivers who had, until then, treated him as the novice he was. He bestowed his gift on them, currying favor. They all literally sprinted for the restaurant. Beef was still a luxury for the Kikuyu drivers.

As Pero came back out, his wallet a little thinner, Pero asked Ruis "Got one picked out yet?"

"Yes, boss, this one had the spare set of keys where you said they would be, magnetic key holder, offside rear bumper. How'd you know?"

"Mr. Kent is a careful person; he wants to make sure his clients never get stranded, so he hides the keys in the same place on each van. Our driver needed them once. Once was all it took to know where they were probably hidden on every van."

They piled in and drove off. A mile later they paused, pretending to view some zebra; and Pero called State to tell them they were leaving the Park presently in a zebra-painted A & K van as tourists. Director Lewis refrained from comment. Two clicks and they were off the air.

The road out of the park was watched and they were approaching the main gate when an armed park ranger stepped into the road. Mbuno was driving, but Pero assumed command.

"Yes, officer?"

"I am not an officer, I am a sergeant." He pointed to his stripes.

"Sorry."

"It is all right. I am not angry. But you have to close the top down before you leave the Park."

"Oh, sorry. Thought we could keep it up until Kimana."

"No, it is the law, the vehicle must be safe before you drive on the main roads, your driver should know that." Pero apologized, said it was his doing, and lowered the canopy, which also formed the top of the observation hole, and sealed themselves in. "That's better. You may now proceed."

They waved as they drove away. A little while down the road, Mary started to laugh. She imitated his voice "Ooh Mr. officer, Sir, so sorry, Sir . . ." everyone started to laugh including Pero. The drive past Kimana and on to the A109 was uneventful. If the alarm had gone up for this stolen van, there seemed few police to do anything about it. Pero suspected that the police were converging on Nairobi from all over the country to help with crowd control tomorrow. Their van followed the route the director had given them, nipped through the Nairobi Park again, and missed the bulk of the traffic. They pulled up to the duka, the grocery shop, where Karen Blixen of "Out of Africa" fame used to shop along with half the colonial farmers of Kenya. They were on time, exactly 6:00 p.m. They had been on the road since three in the morning and they were, all of them, beat. Mbuno looked exhausted; he had done the most driving.

There was still no time for sleep.

At the side of the shop, there was a flight of stairs and the door to the safe house. Pero keyed in the code "Lever" on the number-only combination lock as if it was a US telephone dial and the metal core door buzzed open. They all piled in. There were items left out on a long table, which Pero asked the team to familiarize themselves with. Pero had seen the Duka downstairs was still open, just.

Downstairs, he talked to the manager, a nice fellow, probably one of State's employees and asked him if he had someone to drive the van back to A & K in Nairobi. He said he did and Pero gave him the key. The man gave Pero the keys to a small Nissan station wagon parked in front of the duka. He asked if Pero needed anything else who replied no. He said he had put bread, eggs, and milk in the fridge "and some cooked stew from my wife in the oven on low." Pero thanked him for his kindness.

Upstairs they had already raided the fridge and their resident cook, Priit, was making eggs, "How many, Pero?" Pero told him six "Oh, very funny, same as everybody. So, everyone's hungry then? You each can have two, only two. And like it." He went back to cooking.

"Check the oven, there's stew in there."

Ten minutes later they were all sitting up one end of the table eating heartily, the vests, guns, paperwork, at the other end. The stew was excellent, some sort of *nyama* (game) meat cooked in broth and wine and loads of potatoes. They were really hungry by this time.

"Okay, after we eat, you four go to the Norfolk in a taxi I will order. You have the paperwork over there and those super-thin Kevlar vests. Wear them, please. Take mine," they stopped eating and stared, "and don't look at me that way—I'm not in any danger here and anyway, I think I'll just probe a few friends on the phone and let them do the physical stuff. No, really. Look, I want Kweno to have a vest, so make him wear it, okay? Heep, you're in charge. Keep me informed through the director or call me on the regular cell phone—Ruis, they still each have one, right? Charged?"

"Yes, Pero, everyone has one, and I had already put the same label with the numbers on the back." As standard location filming equipment, cell phones were always handy. He passed them out. Pero put his beside his dish and continued to eat and talk, his mouth full, but nobody seemed to mind.

"Mary, listen, the evidence for the Reichstag gambit is pretty strong. Who is using whom, maybe al-Qaida or al-Shabaab is using some stooge inside JT's organization or the other way around, it doesn't matter here and now. We need to find out who this person is, finger them, and extract information." Mary looked despondent at the prospect. "Mary, don't take this personally, JT must not either. It's someone who's wrong, dead wrong, about what's important in this world. And their contact with others who think in the same way must be uncovered. When you get anything there, radio or cell phone, call it in to Lewis and me, okay?"

But Mary was still looking depressed, "Look Pero, I'm a scientist. I can deal with it that way. I want this bastard as much as you do, if he or she is really there . . . but don't ask me not to take this personally. Uncle will be devastated. Disloyalty, not to mention mass murder, is very personal to him."

"Agreed, and I'm sorry for saying otherwise. We'll nail the bastard, I'm sure. Seems to me the place to start is with the front people, the advance team. They had the most likely opportunity for contact with al-Qaida."

"And that's three of his most trusted people. There is no one new there."

"Okay, let's recap the three clues . . ."

"No need . . ." Being the scientist she was, she listed them quickly for them all: "Two days after Uncle decided to go to Kenya, the Tusker labels were being worked on. The assassin in Arusha was meant for me and he probably came from Gurreh-Ajuran where you stumbled upon them. Someone in the Norfolk, where Uncle had rented every room, was calling the man in the Holiday Inn until he, the Canon salesman, was arrested."

Pero's phone beeped, so he went to the window and extended the antenna. "Baltazar here. We're at the duka, had a meal and the team is setting out for the Norfolk."

"Negative. The Norfolk is cordoned off. The labeled beer was full of anthrax signal, dust all over the bottles. They've inoculated everyone, but evacuation was necessary. The delivery boy admitted under duress—your boy Usman has some power over him, according to the Master Chief who was on guard detail—that he was to drop a bottle in the water tank. There was one bottle missing. They're checking the water system, something called a roof tank."

"Where is everybody?"

"They've moved them, they've taken over the top two floors at the InterContinental, here's the address . . ."

"No need, we usually stay there. Good choice."

"Tell the crew." Pero did. Mary wanted to know if anyone was hurt or ill. In his ear Pero heard Lewis: "I heard that, tell her no." Pero did, she looked relieved, "but it's early days, they could get ill tomorrow or the day after. They're monitoring. And antibiotics are usually effective. The trick about normal strains of anthrax is that it is really only effective if you don't know you have been exposed. Anything they could have brewed would have been pretty tame. Make you sick and without medical attention, you could die, but if you knew and have drugs, you should be no more sick than a bad cold. Tell them." Pero did as he was told. Lewis was right, keep them informed while it was fresh, not as a précis later.

"And Tom, Tom Baylor?"

"Here's what we have got so far. It's rough because the on off switch, oh hell, just know it's a rough transcription. It reads: "Bugged out . . . nothing left . . . L L P B . . . booby trap . . . phone damaged, blast . . . burn pile . . ." and that's all we have for now. The Brits have sent a SeaKing helicopter off the destroyer HMS Cardiff visiting Malindi to evac and assist. We will find him."

"The P B must mean his name and L L must be Lat Long— his lat long, tell them to start their search there."

The strain in State was showing in his voice, "Yeah, we figured that, you know. Baltazar, you cannot run the whole show from there. You can try, but allow our team here some credit. Now, get your crew moving. Out." And the two clicks.

"Okay people, we and JT's team are back at the InterConti. Get your gear and I'll get a taxi; there's always one hereabouts."

Pero went back downstairs, the manager had locked up so Pero walked around the other side of the building and knocked at his door. Pero asked for a taxi, and he was told the man himself was on taxi duty, ready in two minutes.

The crew came downstairs, the vest for Usman stuffed in a pillowcase, and Ruis handed Pero the cell phone again. "Keep it on you Pero, for damn sure." Pero apologized, he had forgotten and pocketed the phone. The four piled in and drove off. Pero didn't even have time to wish them luck.

He sprinted back upstairs to find Mbuno finishing his stew, eating slowly, as usual. Pero grabbed the safe room phone and dialed the InterConti, "Mr. Janardan, please."

"Under-Manager Janardan here."

"Keeping it together, I hear, Mr. Janardan. My people, who will arrive shortly, will be glad to be home."

"Mr. Baltazar, how very, very good to hear from you again." It was their standard patter, but he sounded distressed. "But, Sir, we have no rooms, Sir."

"Not to worry, Mr. Janardan, we don't need any; the crew are the guests of Jimmy Threte and have security passes."

"Ah, that is most good. So what is it I can be doing for you?"

"Make sure the guards out front know that four disreputable looking people, three mtenen and one woman—Mary Lever, Mr. Threte's niece—will be pulling up in about twenty minutes."

"Very good, very good. She will be made most welcome, of course. I had no idea; of course, we will find them all rooms . . ."

"No, Mr. Janardan, let Mr. Threte accommodate them, they have business. They are not really your concern . . . no, what I need is a favor from you . . ."

"Anything, Mr. Baltazar, anything, it is most definitely an honor." And Pero laid it out to him and gave him the phone number. Mr. Janardan promised to call Pero back, within ten minutes. It seemed the night manager of the Holiday Inn was trained at the InterConti, under his tutelage.

As Pero waited for the phone to ring, he looked out the window, through the laminated safety glass, rippled to look old disguising the true nature of this safe house. Pero focused far off, towards to Ngong Hills, as the sun set and cast them all into the night. Time to think. And time to try and keep emotions from getting the better of him. He had to admit that sending them to the InterConti felt a bit cowardly. They were going to where the action was. But him? *I'm sitting here in a safe house.* He was feeling guilty.

Shuddering, he was trying to shift tired mental and emotional gears. Events were spinning, they had had some gains, but without knowing what the one-two punch was, and it was no use pretending anthrax in the water at the Norfolk was an effective media hook, there were no real media visuals for the evening news, let alone live coverage. So, Pero calculated they still had at least two acts of visible violence to uncover. Pero still felt a bomb was the most plausible. Something at the *Meeting*, where the cameras were. That way, if the two punch failed, at least they had something "in the can."

Now Pero was thinking like a producer, and he was more convinced than ever that television production is a higher priority for them than bomb-making or collateral damage. It goes with the old saying, if a tree falls in the woods and no one sees it, does it make any noise? TV was like that, you had to have the eyeballs glued to be effective.

Mbuno now stood beside Pero, quietly sucking the last remnants of stew from his molars. They said nothing. The sun set. The phone rang very loudly, the non-electronic bells jarring the silence. His nerves jumped. Pero took a breath, "Hello?"

It was Mr. Janardan. He gave Pero the number of his trainee, now the night manager, and wished Pero good luck. Pero hung up and dialed the number. A woman answered, called out to "Balaji Mahavir," and the man came to the phone. He was prepared for the call as Mr. Janardan had told him that Pero was to be given "every assistance." It is not just a phrase to an Indian Kenyan, it is plain code for "refuse him nothing."

"The man they arrested? Yes, Sir, he had three rooms rented. One was a man who police have arrested this evening. I confirmed for them that the passport I saw on check-in matched the photo they showed me of that same man posing as a van driver at the Norfolk." He paused. "The Canon man was arrested; I have not seen him since." *Nor will you ever again, friend*, Pero thought. "And the third is not at the hotel. He even left some laundry."

"The police took everything else?" He said they did, he helped search the room, so Pero asked him what, if he could remember what "everything else" was. As he rattled off what he knew had been taken as evidence, nothing struck Pero as significant. Some toiletries, a pair of shoes, very dirty, a few books and some local street maps. Pero clutched at straws, "And the laundry?"

"The police did not seem interested; I will inquire and call you back, perhaps?" Pero said that was fine, asking him to use the cell phone number, reading the label on the back. They rang off.

Pero called Prabir Ranjeet. He answered on the first ring. "Ah, my friend, you are well?" Pero answered yes, asking how his wife was. They went through the pleasantries, even though, by now, they both knew they were other than they had previously thought, somehow their relationship was still equal. And Pero was sure they were still friends, even if they had secret sidelines. The friendship forged by decades of honest trade should come first in his evaluation and, funnily enough, in Pero's as well. To avoid an awkward silence Pero felt was brewing, he rudely got to the point.

Pero flatly told him that he needed his help, again. He explained that a man whom they both knew was probably dangerous was still at large: the third man from the Holiday Inn. If Ranjeet were to get a copy of the man's passport photo from his friends in the police, could he get it to Pero? He said he could. Pero told him to send it to Bluebird Charters by fax, Pero would use their offices since Mbuno had a cousin who worked there, David Bariti. "I'm going to stick my nose into Mara's schedule for the morning of our departure to Arusha and Pangani. Maybe I can find out who planted the bomb."

"There was a bomb? We had heard there was a mishap with your plane in Pangani. Are you sure it was a bomb?" Pero explained what had happened.

Ranjeet's reaction was typically Indian: "Oh, dear, oh dear, oh dear, most frightening, most frightening." Then he agreed that Wilson Airport was a good place to start a probe. "Maybe if you find out who planted this bomb, it will lead to other evil people."

"That's the idea, but I'm not sure how quickly I can find out anything useful."

"Then perhaps finding out is not what my friend should do. Perhaps more violent measures are called for?"

"Yes, perhaps, but except for Mbuno and me, we're a little thin on the ground."

"Ah, yes, well there are several armed forces, sailors I understand, who have been placed at your disposal; some are at Wilson, perhaps you could use their, ah, talents. I understand sailors can be quite physical. Of course, if there is anything I can do to assist, you have only to let me know."

Time to get moving. Pero said his thanks and rang off. Ranjeet was right, of course, Pero had to use any measure necessary.

"Come on Mbuno, we can't sit around here waiting for the phone to ring, let's see if we can track down that tanker driver, the one I think put the bomb on the plane." They both took their badges and clipped them on their shirts. They were police all-pass badges and, true to his word, on the back there was a security clearance for any US Navy personnel they would meet. Each pass had their photo. Pero looked at Mbuno's.

He was staring at it too. "I think it does not look like me." He was right; it was Mbuno twenty years ago, without the graying hair. They were both wondering where State had gotten it from at such short notice. Mbuno, as usual, had the answer, "It is my passport photograph, bwana, last time I renewed it."

"Okay. We will just have to tough it out together then, in case anyone refuses to accept the younger you." He nodded. "Could you call David and ask him to meet us at Bluebird?"

"*Ndiyo.*" And he picked up the duka phone and called. Pero tidied up the kitchen. After a brief conversation, Pero heard him say, "Kwa heri" (goodbye) and Mbuno hung up. "Pero, he will still be there for another hour. The airport is busy, very busy."

Pero put the revolver in his dust jacket pocket and Mbuno, not having a jacket or anything suitable for the Beretta 9mm, wrapped it into his bundle that, Pero had accurately predicted, was coming along. Mbuno put a hunk of cheese in there as well. "I was hungry today, bwana, this is good food."

They went downstairs and got into the Nissan and drove off back down the Karen Road towards town and Wilson Airport. The traffic was terrible. At the west entrance gate to the airport, they were stopped for a brief second, the flashlight showed their badges; and the Brinks Security man, a local Kikuyu Pero could see, snapped to attention and gave a perfectly British "Sah!" as he saluted them. Mbuno mumbled "*mtumishi mdogo*" meaning *small boy*, a slang expression for brat, and they drove through.

CHAPTER 16

Flightline

Bluebird Air was on the flightline, most charter companies were, so they parked at the side and made their way through the main hangar, past where they had met with Tom Baylor and into the offices in the back. David Bariti was sitting, alone, waiting.

"Jambo David, mimi nataka . . ." and Mbuno launched off into asking David's help to find out who the fuel truck supplier was, for Mara. David wanted to know why they didn't ask the Mara flightline people directly . . . so Mbuno filled him in. David's eyes got wider and wider. Pero understood the words for explosions, Afghani, and then a few moments later Jimmy Threte.

David switched to English, looking at Pero, "Jimmy Threte, they are going to try and kill Jimmy Threte? I do not agree with his kind of Christianity, but he is a minister, even the Pope says he is a good man, he says he is wrong, but is a good man." Ah, so David was a Roman Catholic? *Believer* indeed . . . Mbuno had told a white lie to Commissioner Singh. "What can I do to help you?"

Pero spoke up. "David, we need your help. How many petrol suppliers are there here at the airport and who is new—new staff—to any of them?"

"There are three fueling companies here. Agip, Mobil, and BP. Who works at which one, I do not know, but we can find out. Most office staff has gone home for the weekend. Maybe I can get the security people to show us around, would that help?" So they called security who promised to send someone over, with keys, as soon as possible.

The airport was still busy; Sunday was a busy charter time, people connecting with 2:00 a.m. airline flights back to Europe at night. Added to which, all sorts of private jets and planes were still arriving from all over Africa; and, in fact, looking out David's window, Pero spotted some tail numbers from as far away as Finland and Russia. The *Meeting on the Hill* was attracting devout followers—rich, powerful, followers. Pero saw them as a bigger media event for al-Qaida.

Awaiting the arrival of the security man, Pero stood at the open hangar doors watching crews working overtime, servicing planes, and the little yellow *Follow Me* truck plying its trade. Down the flightline of hangars, to the east, the lights of Mara Airways burned bright, so Sheryl might still be in; late arrivals from safari on Sunday were usual occurrences. From around the hangar, a security Toyota pulled up and two men got out. One was wearing a US Navy uniform. Pero walked over to him and showed him his badge. He snapped to attention. Then he saw Mbuno's badge, checked it, and saluted him as well. David, behind Pero, gave a chuckle. No doubt this would make a great story to tell the family, until, that was, Mbuno looked at him and he lowered his eyes. In the tribe, elders are respected, not the butt of gossip.

The security guard, with Wilson Airport and Securicor embroidered over his pocket, shot Pero a look and wondered what gave. The Navy man had SP—Shore Patrol—on his armband.

Pero asked, "First time you wore that band?" The sailor smiled and nodded. "Your Captain reachable?" Again the nod.

"Could you call him for me?" The sailor only nodded again, not a talkative fellow.

"Ensign Fellows calling Captain Burrows, come in please," he said into his hand radio.

"Burrows here, state your position and duty. Over."

"Wilson Airport, flightline security, duty roster of six, each with a local security officer, private service, Securicor by name. Over."

"Okay, go ahead."

"Two men here, one by the name of," he impressed Pero that he had memorized his name "Baltazar, Pero. Both those with special passes, we were briefed for. Baltazar wants to talk to you, over."

"Put him on, all assistance. Over."

"Captain, can we borrow your man here, Ensign Fellows, for some special duty?"

"You have the authority. What's wrong with the local security?" Pero looked at the Securicor man. Pero didn't answer; after a pause of silence, he got the point. "Make a good driver, d'ya think? Over."

"He'll do. So, can we have him? We're going to inspect the three fueling operations here, to see if they can find out which one put a bomb on board a plane two or three days ago. Over." Ensign Fellows, although a burly man, looked suddenly smaller, his shoulders lost their swagger. The Securicor man, on the other hand, reached for his nightstick, ready to draw, and looked about. Pero began to worry that either was hardly what he could rely on.

"Permission granted. Fellows is, as of this moment, under your command, this is considered a war zone for this operation. Get that, Fellows?" Pero handed him the mike and he replied that he did, aye aye captain and all that sort of thing. If he had thought this was going to be an easy operation, he now knew better. The Captain signed out, brusquely. He had his hands full, no doubt.

"What's your first name?"

"Jack, Sir."

"And your name?" Pero asked the Securicor man.

"Joshua Mdare, Sir." The Sir was a nice touch.

"Okay, here's what I want you to do Jack, Joshua. Go and arrest Sheryl at Mara Airways and bring her here. If she's not there, get the duty officer to bring the fueling records for the past four days, all Mara aircraft. You okay with that Jack, and you, Joshua?" They nodded, maybe they would work out better than Pero thought. They got in the light truck and sped off. The blinking light was turned on as soon as they started down the flightline. It is what Pero wanted, visible action.

Pero told Mbuno he needed to "arrest" Sheryl to get her away without argument or causing suspicion and that she was, really, going to help. Pero had known her for fifteen years or more. And besides, he knew she was JT's servant, first and last. They could count on her discretion and help. They needed to identify that fueling man, it was their only hope to backtrack to a cell and hopefully find out what they were planning.

In no time at all, Sheryl, looking very worried, was brought to David's office. They had commandeered it.

"Mr. Baltazar, what's going on? What have I done?"

"Nothing Sheryl, we need your help and I needed to get you here quickly and without argument."

"Sorry about that, ma'am." Fellows said.

"I thought Pero was in trouble. I am very frightened."

"Sorry, really, Sheryl, please don't be frightened, but we have an emergency and maybe only you can help. Here's the situation, JT is in trouble, Mary too. Maybe only we here can find out the people who are after them. That explosion the other day, your Cessna? That was meant for us and Mary."

"Oh God, no, Lord Jesus Christ no." She was visibly shocked. She knew the plane was blown up, how could she not?

"Sheryl, why are you so shocked? You knew it was blown up . . ."

"But the manager, Mr. Roberts," the owner of Mara, "told us it was a freak mechanical problem, not a bomb, that the pilot was wrong. The police don't seem very interested either. Who did this?"

Pero guessed why Roberts had lied, he had an airline to protect. But Pero needed Sheryl to get behind their probe, quickly, so he told her the truth. "Al-Qaida or al-Shabaab," names to strike fear in anyone so close to the Gulf. Everyone lost someone or knew someone who had died. Nairobi is, really, an overgrown town where everyone knows just about everyone else.

She repeated herself: "Oh God, no, Lord Jesus Christ no."

"Unfortunately, yes, Sheryl. Now listen, we need to know who fueled that Cessna, which service was the provider, and then we need to find out which fueling attendant actually had his hands on the plane. That's the only way a bomb got on board. No one else had access. Can you help?"

Sheryl straightened her spine, she became resolute, "Oh, yes, if it will save my pastor, I will help in any way I can. The fueling company, it was Agip, they have a contract with them. The fueling took place in the middle of the night because we weren't sure what time you would be turning up. The plane was, technically, still on charter to you because it held your camera equipment and was in bond by customs."

"And the man who fueled her?"

Sheryl was contrite, "I don't know, I didn't see anyone doing it at that early hour, I am sorry! I was off duty."

Fellows chimed in: "Excuse me, ain't there a security camera anywhere we could look at?" It was too simple. Sheryl explained she had a live camera so she knew what was happening on her hangar apron, but no recorder. "But the tower . . . maybe."

Pero stood and everyone started moving with him towards the door, "Ensign, you and Joshua go to the tower and check out if they have a recorder or a ground track recorder. I doubt it, but it's worth a try. Also check the voice logs for . . . What time, Sheryl?

"Between four and five, Thursday morning, there's a bill with a time chit."

"Okay, see if there's video, and also check the tower voice logs for that time in case someone radioed in for permission to cross the runway, see if there's a name." The fuel depots were on the other side of the airport, they all could see them way over there with their huge tanks and warning lights, "Agip" emblazoned and lit up as advertising. "Sheryl, you ride back to your office with them and pull the fueling log for the Cessna, see who signed the receipt or fueling slip and bring that sheet to me. Then we're going to go over to Agip and see if we can match it. Jack and Joshua can pick you up on their way back. Everybody get back here in twenty minutes, no more, okay?" All three nodded.

Pero decided it was time to call State. He needed more news of Tom Baylor. If Tom had found anything, now was the time to know it, while they had time, fourteen hours before "show time."

"Baltazar here. At Wilson Airport. Any further developments on Baylor and anthrax?"

"Lewis here, anthrax is lowest grade, mixed with talcum powder and sugar. Still, it was an effective scare, but may be a false trail meant to mislead us into complacency. They found the missing bottle. It was only dropped in the kitchen pantry. They're decontaminating. In case you are over-thinking again

Baltazar, it was not a trick only to get them to move. Original plan was the Hilton as replacement for Norfolk, but it was changed to the InterContinental by Threte himself since he had stayed there twenty years ago when he was a pilot," (for Pan Am). "And Special Ops, the Seals, searched the InterContinental top to bottom, no explosives there. It's clean."

The Director was in full briefing mode now. "Now, Baylor's full message decoded and SeaKing is landing that site as they speak. He Morse coded the whole message again and again. The lat long were your last location near an escarpment, and they've pinpointed him there. He's wounded, his thermal image is not walking, but they have hope, the Brits told me on the radiophone hookup that they saw him moving his arm, they think. The rest of his message, that you haven't heard, is this: "burn ashes, Jetson." That's all. Can you make heads or tails? We can't. I asked the Brits and our people here to repeat it to me two minutes ago, so that exact message is confirmed."

Pero stared at the ceiling, thinking, shook his head and said, "No, I can't figure it out yet, but I'll work on it. When will they know he's all right, when can they speak with him?"

"Depends; the SeaKing should have him any moment now. If he can speak, I will get his report and relay to you, and to Heep, affirmative?"

Pero was puzzled, *why is he asking me? Oh, damn, I'm a field agent now, I guess he has to.* Field agents called the shots, sometimes.

"Affirmative. End." And the two clicks. *What the hell are the Jetsons, a cartoon show from his youth, doing in this mixed bag of clues? Maybe it's someone's name. Maybe, well, maybe anything.*

Joshua and Jack returned with Sheryl. Mbuno and Pero were waiting for them impatiently in the office. They confirmed that Wilson had no ground radar or flightline video recorder, nothing other than a log entry that an Agip tanker had signaled that they were crossing the active runway. In the middle of the night, that must have been hardly even worth noting. Sheryl, on the other hand, had the expense and time chit, and the fuel delivery log. The times matched. It was without signature and she was despondent. "Sheryl, still, it's filled in by hand, the Agip people may know or recognize something. Let's go ask them."

They all piled into the truck, Jack and Joshua up front with Sheryl squeezed in between, her legs over to the left to allow for the stick shift. Mbuno and Pero sat in the open back. They sped across the runway, their blue light whirling away, just after a plane landed, its prop wash jostling the small truck. Agip was just ahead. Pero could see the fueling depot was busy, two trucks being crawled onto as top hatches were opened and replenished. Avgas is flammable stuff; it made sense to keep it over this side, away from the main airport. Unfortunately, it was also smack up against the Kibera slum, one of the areas of densest population on the overpopulated continent.

Kibera is where a majority of Nairobi's citizens live. As a slum, the tin roofs on mud houses are not the problem, nor are the people and their makeshift churches, nor the tattered clothing of the poor. A lack of running water, no garbage collection, and raw sewage running down shallow ditches at the side of dirt lanes between closely packed single room houses, where as many as sixteen people lived, was the problem. Cholera and typhus always reared their ugly heads. Poverty and starvation were slower killers. False baby adoption clinics, no medical facilities, and preying ministers who only gave aid in return for fealty to one god or another contributed to the horror. Hyenas dared not enter Kibera, it is said, since they would be eaten. The rats fared no better. AIDs claimed ten percent of Kibera's population every year and still Kibera's population grew as the nation's poor increased, forcing them to this area of lawlessness and human decay.

Up against the slum of Kibera, on a slight rise of a little more than fifty feet, sat the avgas and kerosene tanks (jet fuel) of the three suppliers. The lights that lit up their signs painted on the huge thirty-foot high tanks are, sometimes, the only illumination for Kibera's residents except for the thousands of charcoal fires preparing a simple maize dinner.

The Securicor truck pulled up at the Agip depot office, three piled out of the cramped interior, and two slid off the tailgate. Pero immediately asked Jack and Joshua to march in and arrest everybody, everyone working there, and line 'em up. Pero was sure if someone tried to run they might get a break.

No one did.

The manager, when questioned, said he knew the handwriting on the slip. It was a temporary employee who was moonlighting, for extra cash. They needed extra people this week because of the *Meeting* tomorrow, they were so busy. Pero quizzed him some more and it turned out that the moonlighting man, who worked at a car gas station in Ngong (an Agip gas station, of course), would be on duty tomorrow night, if they wanted to talk with him. One of the jump-suited fuelers, with his hands still up, started to babble. Pero turned to Mbuno "Could you tell him to lower his hands and speak slowly? Find out what he knows, take him outside."

Jack wanted to know if "the old man," meaning Mbuno, needed anyone to help him in case the man decided to run. Pero smiled and shook his head. No one would get away from Mbuno who would know before they did if they were even thinking of running. Pero told Jack it was all right.

"Okay, listen up, all of you. You are under arrest. This facility is closed down. Ensign, get some help from your other shipmates, and take these people to the Aero Club—which you will commandeer—and lock them up until the police can take them. And shut this operation down."

The Aero Club was a relic of post-colonial period when the power was still with the remnant colonialists of "better days." Pero knew the Aero Club had room to spare, and it was on the lead apron of the runway—very handy to access to the rest of the field.

Jack was unsure. "All of them?" When Pero frowned, sternly, he snapped to attention and said, "Aye aye, Sir." Then he got on the radio and called the captain to request backup, "seven detainees to be taken into custody to the Aero Club." Pero told Joshua to pull his nightstick and if anyone moved, to hit them, hard. Joshua grinned.

The Agip manager looked angry. "You cannot do this, who are you?" he lowered his hands and advanced towards Pero. Joshua's club whirled through the air and the manager took a blow on his forearm. It must have hurt. He stepped back sharply.

Pero was loud and clear, "Well done, Joshua. If they are more of a problem than that, have Jack shoot them. Dead would be fine, understand?" Joshua nodded and Jack, still on the radio, asked the captain if it was okay "to shoot someone on Mr. Balthazar's order."

Everyone heard the answer "If he says shoot, sailor, shoot. He can kill them all—he can order you to kill them all—he has that authority from the Presidents of the United States and Kenya. This is a state of emergency, get it? No more questions."

"Aye aye, Sir!" And Jack clicked off, "Sorry Mr. Baltazar, it's just that I have never shot anyone."

"And let's hope you don't have to. But we have a mass murdering group out here and we can't, for now, know who's with us or who's against us. We need to press on, inconvenience some folks, and stop the bastards." Pero turned to the Agip people. "If you behave, it will all be over soon and you'll be free to go, but Agip planted a bomb on an aircraft Thursday, so until we find out who, you are all arrested, get it?" Everyone, wide-eyed nodded and when the Navy reinforcements turned up, they walked meekly to a minibus to go to the "makeshift brig, in the Aero Club." Pero said thanks to his two deputies and went outside to see how Mbuno was getting on. Sheryl was helping him. The man nodded vigorously.

"Bwana, this man is, like Miss Sheryl, a follower of Pastor Threte. He is very unhappy that a man who worked here, a Maasai Muslim he knows, put a bomb on Miss Mary's plane. He is swearing revenge. Miss Sheryl has told him that it is not right to kill. I have asked him to take us to this other man's *boma*; he's Maasai from Ngong. This man has said he will. He will show us."

Pero left Joshua and Jack in charge, promising to be back within two or three hours, and told Sheryl to return to the Mara offices and say nothing. They took the petrol manager's jeep, with blinking light, back across the runway to switch to their Duka car, dropped off Sheryl at Mara, and, with Pero driving, sped off.

Crossing the Maasai Plain, where only fifteen years ago, there was only open pasture for wild animals, now fences and plantations, small and large, whisked by in the headlights. The main obstacles were the hyenas, scavenging at night. One particularly big male was dragging a dog, probably someone's pet. A few antelope scurried past, jumping from one fenced field to another, quickly followed by just a glimpse of a leopard skirting the edge of the road, its coat glowing with the sheen of a ghost blue moon as it leapt away.

Heep had reminded Pero, twice that day of his expertise, "Produce this thing . . ." he had said. Pero knew he was right.

It was what Pero did, and did well. The very same skills it took to take a bunch of talented strangers and mold them into an effective, efficient television crew were needed here. As a producer, Pero needed to keep hundreds of thoughts and details turning over in his mind, ready to bring any one of them to bear. Pero needed to understand power—both officialdom and personal ego—and balance that with appropriate action—Pero's and theirs. But more than anything Pero had to be single-minded. It is what attracts everyone to media production—the invigorating, mono-focus, passion—putting everything else out of mind. It was what kept actors waiting to work only two weeks a year and what kept his job interesting. It wasn't the travel to exotic places, it was the ability to manage problems quickly and produce something concrete from nothing. And Pero did that well, working over forty weeks a year. It was what Pero had to do here. Mono-focus, concentrate, produce this endgame. Heep was right.

The only difference was that the stakes were higher. Too high, if Pero thought about it too much.

CHAPTER 17

Ngong

Pero knew the road to Ngong well. He went past the Langata turn-off and took the next left towards Ngong. Tourists flock to Ngong to get to the Karen Blixen Museum set in the grounds of her old coffee plantation farmhouse. *Out Of Africa*, her seminal work, still attracted people to Africa, people captivated by the sheer romance of the landscape, people, and fauna that imbued her life so richly. Mbuno was translating driving instructions from the Agip man on the back seat. In less than forty minutes Pero was being gestured, palms down, by Mbuno, to slow their progress. The young Agip man, in the rear-view mirror, stared ahead, pointing. They drove past an Agip gas station, closed for the night, then two all-night open-fronted bars with blaring music and immediately turned left, off the main street, into an alleyway and then clear of the village, for about two miles on a dirt track. He gestured again to slow further and stop. Pero cut the engine and, as it was downhill, drifted, silently, closer until the passenger pointed to a circle of thorns, a *boma* enclosure, the typical Maasai camp barrier, off to the right of the dirt track.

Pero took a flashlight from the glove box that almost every car in Kenya keeps there for emergencies, but didn't turn it on. The moonlight was strong enough. Pero pulled the gun from his pocket. Mbuno retrieved his from his bundle hidden under the front seat and put it in his trouser waistband. Pero kept his in hand; he wanted to be ready, for what he wasn't sure. At the sight of the guns, the young man held out his hand as if asking for one. Pero shook his head. He reached into his coveralls, down his side, and pulled out a sixteen inch panga Pero never knew was there. He was clearly still thinking vengeance. Pero shook his head at him, trying to convey an order not to start anything. He nodded, but he still had that look in his eye.

A panga is called a machete in South and Central America. The blade is the same. The user is not. A sub-Saharan African with a panga will swing the blade, day and night, with an unceasing rhythm and strength. If he started to swing that thing, Pero pitied the bomber, but only a little.

They walked up to the thorn bushes surrounding the boma, the living compound of a Maasai homestead. The dried five feet high, sharp bushes, to prevent lion attack of the goats at night, were held in place by propped sticks and ground driven stakes. They kicked two sticks out of the way, pulled the thorn entrance apart, and walked into the compound. As Pero walked over a ring of prayer stones, the prayer oval facing Mecca told Pero this was a Muslim camp, Mbuno moved swiftly to the left and Pero heard an "oof" as someone hit the dust. Mbuno came back and whispered "young morani, not a worker, he's sleeping." He meant that the *morani* (warrior) was not someone who *worked* in a European man's business.

They soft-footed closer, the back of the blade of that panga sticking ahead in the moonlight, the sharp edge glinting. *Was it only this morning*, Pero wondered, *that I saw that same glint off the train rails at Mashangalikwa?*

In the near pitch dark, a man emerged from a manyatta; the dung covered, sapling framed mud hut traditional to the Maasai. Another came at his heels. The first was an elder Maasai, traditional clothing and arm amulet signifying rank as a village elder, but the second was much younger and had dirty overalls on. The moment the overall's man saw Pero and Mbuno he started to run, a faded Agip logo on his back clear in the moonlight. The unmoving Maasai elder saw him run and said, barely above normal volume, "*Kusimama.*" It was Swahili for stop. He had not spoken Maa, the language of the Maasai. The overall's man stopped. There had been nowhere for him to run. Pero and Mbuno were between him and the only *boma* entrance or exit.

Out of the night wafted two morani silently, spears held at the ready. The Maasai elder said, "*hatari*" to tell them there was danger, but added nothing, just stood there, waiting.

Pero looked at him, put the revolver back in his pocket, turned on the flashlight, and pointed it at the ground between them. Then he slowly pushed the Agip man's panga down until it was by his side, unthreatening. "*Mimi nataka, mzee, huyu mbaya mwanamume.*" Pero told the elder he wanted this bad man, in very poor Swahili. The elder responded and Pero had to wait for Mbuno to translate.

The elder wanted to know what the *kijana* (young man) had done that was bad. As Mbuno was explaining, their passenger Agip man leapt forward and with a shriek ran after the other, clearly trying to attack him with the panga. They raced around in the dust, part of their struggle appearing in his flashlight beam, some just glints of teeth or *panga* edge in the moonlight. The elder did not move. Their Agip man finally made contact, the unmistakable sound of blade on flesh, stopping at bone, painful to hear. The *kijana* in overalls staggered to the elder for protection. The wound was deep, and the swinging arm had been strong. The gash ran from collarbone across the chest. He felt the wound quizzically and then fell screaming in pain to the ground in the circle of Pero's flashlight, bleeding, clutching his chest, calling up to his father for help, "*Auni mimi baba!*"

At the same moment Pero was registering this scene of father and son, the Agip man who had come with them fell dead. The five-foot Maasai spear had moved so swiftly through his heart that Pero hadn't seen it fly. The *morani* who had thrown it was standing, at ease, now spearless as if nothing had happened.

The wounded suspect still writhed in the dirt, pleading to his "*Baba.*" A woman emerged and was told to go back. Pero faced the elder. "Mbuno, translate for me. Tell the chief that that man," Pero pointed, "that boy, is evil, he is not a true man of Allah, he is a coward, he is a jackal, he deserves to die." Mbuno translated. The elder took a half step forward, tightening his fists and answered that he was still his son. Pero continued, "This jackal tried to kill many people and put a bomb on a plane to kill, not with his hand as a brave, honorable *morani*, but as the jackal, waiting and sneaking, like a worthless virgin coward." Mbuno translated.

The elder stood listening. Now no emotion showed on his face, as he peered down at his son cowering in fear, knowing that this young man had brought dishonor and likely retribution to his whole family. "*Ninyi kuua ndani ya bomu? Ninyi mvulana?*" (Did you kill with a bomb? Did you, boy?). The boy's pleading grew stronger. The elder watched, pity filling his eyes.

Pero held the flashlight on the ground scene before them both. The elder raised his gaze to match Pero's and asked, in halting English, "What is it that you want?" His English was fine if slow.

Pero was in no mood to allow any pity to infect his need for information, he raised his gun and pointed it at the morani standing off to one side and then down at the boy, "I need answers from this cur, this dog, honest answers or I'll kill him and everyone here." Mbuno moved his sweater to show he was wearing a pistol as well.

Imperceptibly, Mbuno moved slightly sideways and caught the other morani's spear in mid flight. It was aimed at him and had flown faster than Pero could see. He stuck the tip into the soil and spat at the morani who had thrown it. As a display of native expertise, it was awe-inspiring. The elder wanted to know the mzee's name. "Mbuno Waliangulu" (Mbuno of the Liangulu tribe). And taking Pero's flashlight, Mbuno showed three distinct tattoos at his hairline indicating he was an elder chief in the Maasai. Honorary rank or not, he carried official status, and his manner impressed them all in equal measure.

Heads bowed. The morani who had thrown the spear sank to his knees. The elder made up his mind, ordered the whining, wounded young man to shut up. He simply said, "Ask. I will find out truth."

Within a few minutes the son had told the father who had given him the package, apologizing for being so worthless, a failure as a son, begging in the name of Allah to be saved. Mbuno translated as the confession was dragged out of the sniveling coward.

The box was in a bag, he said, sealed with gray plastic tape, he didn't know what was in it, but he was told to do it in the name of Allah, a strike for Allah to kill the infidels. The man who had given him the package was from Tanzania and he was coming back today, to the mosque, to pay him more money as he had promised. "When, and what is the man's name?" his father asked.

He whined the answer and Mbuno translated, "At evening prayers. He is called Mustafa." Mbuno looked quickly at Pero who nodded agreement. Tanzania and Mustafa were solid clues; it was likely it was Mustafa Purim from Tanga.

Pero asked the elder who relayed the question to his son, "Where did you meet him?"

"Our Imam father, Imam Kahal, introduced us at the Masjid." Masjid is a mosque for Koran study. Pero remembered the one in Nairobi; he had shot some footage of young English Asian boys on a religious exchange program there two years ago.

"What Mosque are you meeting Purim at? Again at the Masjid?"

"No, he said to meet at the Abubakar mosque in Eastleigh." Eastleigh was a suburb of Nairobi, across the city, on the east side.

The father asked Pero if he now had enough information. Pero said he did. The elder turned, said a few words to the morani who stepped back, and said to his son "Ninyi ndani ya hizi." The word "hizi" was said with a spit in the boy's direction. Then the father pulled the spear from the Agip passenger's chest, turned, and speared his son to death before Pero could stop him. Mbuno held Pero back.

Calmly, then the elder asked what to do with the other body, indicating the dead Agip man. Pero, shocked by a father's action, simply told him they would take it, to please have the body put in the back of their station wagon. They would explain it to the police that it was an accident. Pero thought a father killing a son was something he would never have to see, Mbuno sensed Pero's shock and held his arm, guiding him backwards, taking the flashlight.

The elder's parting words were, "I am most sorry." Pero said nothing, he could not find the words. Mbuno and Pero withdrew, the morani carrying the dead Agip boy's body, who loaded him, fetal position into the rear of the car. Then they bowed, looking at Mbuno and were gone into the night.

Pero started the car and engaged gears as they drove off.

"It was a matter of honor, bwana."

Pero asked Mbuno what the father's last words were to his son.

Mbuno explained that the elder had used the word *hizi* for disgrace, loss of honor. "Such a thing infects the whole family; it was his duty to stop the path of the dishonor, Pero."

Pero understood. He was shaken by the abruptness of the violence. East African was a place of sudden violence at times, animal and human. There was no room for the indulgent pageantry of the finality of death in this sometimes harsh land and cultures.

As they drove back along the same roads towards Wilson Airport, Pero told Mbuno what he knew about Mohammed Kahal of the Council of Imams of Kenya. A powerful man, the Imam had once, years ago, been linked to an explosion at the port in Mombasa. "He was, is really, a man to be feared and might have links to al-Qaida or al-Shabaab."

Mbuno was emphatic. "Not might, bwana, it is now most true."

As they rolled out of Ngong, on the open road, Pero stopped the car and called Director Lewis. Pero asked Mbuno to listen in, his ear pressed to one side of the phone, the other side pressed to Mbuno's ear, the speaker between them. Pero dared not hit the speaker button for fear someone could hear, the evening humidity possibly carrying sounds for hundreds of yards.

"Baltazar here, on Ngong road on way back to Wilson Airport. The man who planted the bomb on board the Cessna was a part-time worker at Agip and is now dead, speared by a Maasai, his father. The Agip employee we took with us to identify him is also dead, speared by *morani*, young warriors. Information gleaned is as follows: Mohammed Kahal of the Council of Imams of Kenya introduced this Muslim Agip worker to one Mustafa from Tanzania whom we suspect to be the same Mustafa Purim from Tanga. Tell Singh. Dying confession of bomb-planter indicated Purim is due back today to pay him an assassin's fee," Pero suddenly remembered the Daily Nation article on the opening, years ago, "at the Kuwaiti-built Abubakar mosque in Eastleigh . . ." Pero hesitated and Mbuno shot him a glance. "Right, so we have arrested all Agip workers at Wilson . . ." He hesitated again as the thought came more clearly into focus, "Damn, I just thought of something, we also need to also round up all Agip off-duty personnel and morning shift in case one of them set the schedule for the bomb-planting, no way Purim knew that. It cannot just be him or the dead bomb-planter; Purim must have another accomplice there at Agip to arrange the duty roster. Suggest you place a police or Navy stake out at Abubakar mosque in Eastleigh to arrest and detain Purim. That's about all."

"Understood. Will comply. Sorry you lost the witnesses." He wasn't blaming Pero, it was a statement of fact. "Things are advancing. SeaKing crew still has not revived Baylor. They collected him without examining his fist, which contained some partially burned ashes, which blew away out the helicopter door. He's alive but unconscious. Legs broken, arm broken, teeth missing, internal problems. He was beaten, booby-trapped with explosives, then left for dead. Medic says he suspects blood in the chest cavity with broken ribs. His satellite radio is broken, keyboard smashed. He was connecting and disconnecting power battery to send Morse. SeaKing will reach a medical facility on board ship in ten minutes. I will keep you advised."

"Any news from Heep and others?"

"Yes, but no news on the Reichstag gambit. All leads there turn up false. Otherwise, all is secure. The Nigerian is in Mary Lever's room and keeps her under close watch. Ruis and Priit have swept the hotel. Ruis has adapted a walkie-talkie to pick up open frequencies. Heep says JT is more determined than ever to go unprotected into the audience."

"Yeah, well he would. If Purim is coming back, can you get a likeness of him?"

"Commissioner Singh doesn't have a recent picture. Seems the passport they issued has a photo at least twenty years old. Slack security standards. Singh's sending it tonight, so at least we will have something. The Iman might be a safer bet for arrest and hold, he's on all tour watch lists, effective immediately."

"Yes, but do not arrest him tonight, just watch him, we don't want to miss catching Purim."

"Agree and will implement."

"Have you got any ideas yet on what they are planning? Other than tracking down who this missing Agip employee is and the missing man from the Holiday Inn, I have no other ideas other than the usual car, bus, truck bomb, or missile attack. There are plenty of SAMs around this region. Have you got that covered?" SAMs are surface to air missiles, much feared, because a single person can aim and fire on the run in remote terrain.

"We're doing our best. SAMs have a very ineffective surface-to-surface effectiveness, so I disagree that it is a weapon of choice. Maybe a rocket-propelled grenade, they're looking for those with the Kenya police and military, they've already started searching all the people gathering. And they are searching the whole hillside with dogs and explosives' experts. They say there's nowhere they can see to effect collateral damage—beyond the usual suicide bomber—as there are no buildings there."

Pero went silent. Something Lewis had said triggered another thought. *Explosives, collateral damage . . . surely it couldn't be . . .*

"Lewis, take a deep breath, this just occurred: Kibera, the slum, is mostly a Christian community, the missionaries in there control the food and bible readings. Muslim Imams are known to be hostile to their evangelizing. The Kibera slum spreads almost to where the *Meeting* will take place, tomorrow." Pero looked at his watch. "Sorry today. Kibera is certainly within camera range if they pivot one hundred and eighty degrees. These, those people there, are collateral damage targets, the largest ones you can imagine. If the Agip Avgas tanks at Wilson Airport, standing above Kibera on top of the hill, facing the place for the *Meeting*, if they should be wired to explode, no-one will stop a bomb or resultant fire until it's too late. It's a mile from where we're doing searches."

"What would happen if they blew?"

"The flaming gas would spill downhill and engulf a large part of Kibera, roasting people alive."

"How many?"

"Maybe two hundred thousand."

"There's a *huge* act of terrorism. Not sure al-Qaeda will want to alienate that much of sub-Saharan Africa. Check this out immediately. Need any additional support?"

"Wilson Agip fueling depot covers two to three acres of gas tanks, pipes, tanker refueling stations. To sweep that in the dark? The problem is, it's not just Agip, there are two other massive holding tanks there."

"Damn, okay. Proceed. One more thing: the analysts here say you are spot on with TV scenario. Years ago Lee Harvey Oswald had an easier shot vantage point on another part of the route, but he relocated to the book depository because he saw the TV cameras being erected for the drive-by. It's something they should have thought of and didn't."

"Director," Pero had to interrupt him, "wait, there's something else. I think their deadline is first camera live, as scheduled. Say eleven thirty local here for the USA Christian cable companies, that's three thirty in the morning your Eastern Time, but twelve thirty in the morning LA time, where JT's main audience is. Of course, if they follow the nine-eleven timing, all that they may be waiting for is the cameras to be set up and manned, ready to roll. So assume their deadline for any camera activity is earlier, say eleven in the morning local, three in the morning Eastern, midnight LA—and it will continue until JT is through, right?"

"We agree, will check it out our end, and call you if our team thinks you need to advance that timing. Anything else?"

"Yeah, what do I do with the body I now have in the truck?"

"I will call the local cops to come get him, no questions asked. Where will you leave him?" Mbuno suggested the broom closet in the Blue Bird hangar. Pero agreed. Lewis said a crack, something about how the stiff would "have to come out sooner or later," and rang off. Two clicks.

Pero didn't get the closet joke until they were driving on and thought, *gallows humor.*

When they got back to Blue Bird, they put the now blood-soaked body in the closet, shut the doors with a broom handle, and told David the cops would come for him and to keep quiet. David then sat, head in hands, at his desk. He didn't look like he wanted to talk to anybody anyway.

They had two people to trace . . . and the fax for the first one had ground out of David's ancient fax machine. The likeness wasn't very good. Pero called Balaji Mahavir at the Holiday Inn and thanked him for the fax. "Oh, I am very pleased you have called. We have his laundry back. Would you like me to itemize the articles of clothing for you?" Pero told him "yes please" and to send the list in another fax, as soon as he could. Pero didn't see the relevance, but who knows? Mr. Mahavir added one tidbit that Pero did find interesting, the hotel floor's rubbish had been collected by the police, probably from the Canon man's room—"a maid said there were black boxes with red writing in the wastebaskets, red letters spelling Schneider and the number four hundred."

Pero knew what those were for; he'd bought some on location in France years before. The garbage had turned up Schneider lens' boxes, telephoto boxes, 400mm stuff. Pero suddenly thought of a use.

Back on the satellite phone: "Baltazar here, police turned up four hundred millimeter Schneider telephoto boxes from Canon man's room at the Holiday Inn, from the garbage thrown out. Someone needs to check every cable or other news camera setting up here. Okay?"

"Roger that. We're on to it ASAP. Message from Heeper, we have been keeping him and JT up to date on your progress. He wants you to know he thinks that Baylor may have been sending you the message, you're the only one, other than Mbuno, who he knows was up there. Also to quote Heeper: "Produce this thing all the way through, Pero." Heeper message ends." And the double clicks. Lewis was gone.

Pero pondered another reminder from Heep. Heep was like that when they were filming—anything that he thought was moving too slow made him impatient. He prodded, he pushed, he asked for your best. It had served them well as a team.

"Come on, Mbuno, we need to get over to Agip. And let's find Jack and Joshua."

Jack and Joshua were drinking Cokes from the machine in the Agip office. They seemed glad the two were back, but the blood on the two men's trousers didn't please them overmuch. Pero explained that someone got hurt and they left him for the police to deal with. Well, it was a half-truth, and there was no point in causing too much alarm.

The Agip people had been removed to the temporary holding area in the Aero Club. Jack wanted to know what was next. "How many sailors can you round up, Jack?" He started to call the captain on his radio. Pero told him to slow down. "How many are here at Wilson, that you can rely on?"

"Well, they are six, but three are busy, patrols and guard duty for your prisoners. I did tell them they could shoot anyone who got out of line. That still right?"

"Yes, marshal law prevails." Pero faced Joshua, "Joshua, how many Securicor guardsmen do you have here now at Wilson?"

"Well, *Sah*, I have called the company and they told me they called the Nairobi police and the police told them to do anything you said, but they were too busy to be coming over shortly. So they will be calling Langata Police Station for help. So, I told my company boss to send six more men. Just now we have six to equal his." He pointed to Jack. "They will be at the tower just now."

"Good, get them over here, fast, with big flashlights." The Securicor man picked up his little hand radio and started speaking.

Pero turned and said, "Jack, tell your boys to come running with flashlights, plenty of light."

"What are we looking for?" Smart man, Jack, flashlights could only equal a search.

"A bloody big bomb, as the Brits would say."

"Oh, great. Easy duty, they said . . ." and he walked out to make the call across the base for reinforcements. Pero went over to the vending machine and saw that it was unlocked, well, broken was more accurate. Pero swung open the door and removed two Fantas, orange flavor. Kivoi and Pero popped open the cans and they drank. From inside his trouser pocket Kivoi extracted a piece of cheese. One look told him Pero was amused. He shrugged and kept eating.

CHAPTER 18

Gas Depots

The search of the kerosene and avgas depot would take a while. But with help on the way, Pero was hoping it could be completed in four or five hours. Now, what he had to consider was whether, if they found anything, it would be a time bomb or remote detonator. In either case, they would need a bomb squad. Pero was sure the captain would have one. And yet, if it were radio controlled, how would he discover who had the detonator? The more he thought about it, Pero knew it had to be a radio detonator because the *Meeting* might be late and if the enemy were planning this catastrophe for maximum media effect, the enemy would need to control the timing of any explosion and almost holocaust fire as a live event.

Pero looked at Mbuno and said, "Mbuno, I have begun to think of these people we're after as the enemy not merely murderers. Do you feel the same?"

"*Ndiyo bwana*. A murderer is someone you must catch or stop. An enemy you must oppose while you are alive. These Arab Mau Mau will not be stopped, they must be killed like an enemy." Pero simply nodded. His face at the boma had shown

Mbuno that he did not relish seeing anyone killed, let alone killing anyone. So Mbuno added, "It is not easy taking a life, even a bad life, except when taking that life saves so many others." Pero nodded. "So let us see if we can find this bomb of yours and save those people down there." He pointed to the twinkling fire lights stretching for miles down the hill in Kibera.

So, where would they locate the transmitter? It was a large airport. And, there was always the sky that would be filled with aircraft in the late morning, early afternoon. The country would not be allowed to grind to a halt simply because there was a possible threat. If that were the case, the present threat would have halted everything. No, Pero and Mbuno needed to find the bomb, if there was one, and render it safe.

Awaiting the extra help, Pero and Mbuno studied the picture Balaji Mahavir had faxed over from the Holiday Inn. The man's name was Altair Smythe. Altair Smythe . . . the name was very British, but the picture was in a passport from Morocco. If the police had this, they would be checking it out. Time to call State.

"Baltazar here. The fax from the night manager at the Holiday Inn is the Moroccan passport copy for registration, number seven eight four seven three niner zero one, called one Altair Abdul Smythe, age thirty-five, born in Casablanca. One meter, seventy-five centimeters high, blonde hair, brown eyes. Originally given to the Nairobi police yesterday. Also, the man's laundry list will be faxed over later. I will advise on that. Any idea who and what this Smythe is?"

"We had his name and image two hours ago. No matches and the Moroccans, who are very keen to help, assure us it is a forgery. No such name exists. They've tried combinations, no luck. I will keep trying. Keep a look out."

"Will do, anything else?"

Nothing, just two clicks.

"Mbuno, I'm going to leave you to start the search for the bomb, if there is a bomb. Anything that looks disturbed, anything that looks like it shouldn't be there, don't touch it, just call me—use one of the sailor's walkie-talkies, okay?"

"Ndiyo, Pero," he was fine with that. No point in discussing tracking prey with Mbuno, he knew what to look for, even if he might not know a bomb from a carburetor. The unusual, the out-of-place, the track left by prey—that was his expertise.

The Securicor crew showed up, followed by the Navy personnel. Joshua told Pero the police were going over to the makeshift Brig at the Aero Club. They did not seem happy when they learned Pero, a civilian, had arrested people. Jack and Joshua got their teams sorted out. Some of the Securicor men didn't like Jack taking charge. Jack pulled his pistol, Joshua explained who's who, and they calmed down. Jack turned to Pero and said, "Ready when you are, Sir."

"Thank you, Jack. Okay men, Mbuno will explain what we're looking for and how to look. You will not go anywhere without Mbuno, is that clear? He's the best tracker in Kenya, so don't think you can do better. I want you, Jack and Joshua, with two men each to come with me. The rest of you do exactly what Mbuno says, exactly when he says to do it." Pero shined his flashlight on Mbuno's badge and a few of the Navy boys said "wow" and "gee." They were that young. But Pero didn't need experience, he needed fresh eyes, so they should do well.

"But what are we really looking for, Sir?" It was a young, tussled-haired kid, with freckles.

"See these tanks?" Pero pointed up the largest forty-foot side of the curved steel next to them. "There's a bomb on one of these, a bloody great big bomb." They all took an involuntary step back.

Jack and the two men he pointed to walked away with Pero. Joshua took a few seconds to decide and then chose two and followed, quickly. They all piled into two trucks, one a little more beat up than the other. *Securicor must be short of trucks tonight*, Pero thought. They started at the BP station. Pero posted a Navy man there with a Securicor helper, both shook hands and sorted out who stood where. The manager of the BP fueling depot took offense and Pero told him, well showed him, that Pero had authority. The guns and the small army convinced him. Pero told him he could continue to supply avgas and kerosene, but each driver must be an old hand, no one under two months of employment. If there was a new one, that person was to go to the brig. Anyone else could continue as normal, but each load, each tanker, had to be checked by their boys. Anybody takes a runner or attempts to leave without authority, signed on each clipboard, for each load, would get shot, that simple. He blanched but got the idea. They weren't shutting him down, something they clearly had done to Agip, so he was, in a way, relieved.

The tussled-haired boy took Pero aside, outside, "Sir, shoot? You want us to shoot someone if they simply make a mistake?"

"Use your judgment, sailor, but get this, there's a chance that these tanks," Pero pointed to the brightly lit BP on the side of the tank next to them "will be used to kill two hundred thousand people down there." Pero pointed down the hill to the slum of Kibera, faintly shimmering in the moonlight. "What's your opinion? One accidental shooting of somebody who doesn't do what he's told in a situation like this? Is it a fair trade?"

"Aye, aye, Sir. Got it." He looked down the hill at the human anthill. "Grew up in one like that in Mississippi. Smells the same too." It made Pero wonder. But Pero knew the sailor would protect those below as best he could.

The Mobil station was next and went pretty much the same way. By the time they were done, Jack, Joshua, and Pero had been gone about forty-five minutes. Daylight would be coming in a few hours. They checked on the search.

Mbuno reported that there were tracks everywhere. The avgas men had been using the backside of the tanks as a latrine. One side looked modern, the other side looked like "a water closet, not very good." Still, Mbuno said that the tracks were one way back and one way forward. There are no tracks all the way around. It should make the search easier. He had completed the first tank, the avgas one, and was starting on the kerosene (jet fuel). One of the sailors was a mountain climber and volunteered to climb the tall ladders to check the top. He had reported there was nothing there, not even a bump. Pero didn't expect anything there, but it was safer to check. To flood Kibera, you need to break the tank down low. Mbuno said that; so far, all was clear.

But at almost an hour per tank, this was going to take longer than they had. The problem was that Mbuno did the searching; the men just followed him. "Mbuno, is there danger if they search, with you, not after you?"

"Bwana, I was just about to say, I will go round each tank and make sure, very fast. No traps, no pits, nothing I can see that they will not. Then they can search the ground all round." And he gave instructions for the second tank and started his famous low, fast, reconnoiter. Pero was watching when the cell phone in his pocket buzzed and rang.

"Pero?" She sounded breathless, frantic.

"Yes, go ahead, Mary."

"Priit has been stabbed, in the thigh, it is serious. He found a man loading a cart with JT's mid-show refreshments, you know something to keep his throat wet, and Priit started to question him. Ruis says the man panicked and took out a knife and lunged at him. Priit did this dance thing to get away into the kitchens, but the man stabbed him in the leg as he was running. Ruis called for help and two Special Forces caught the man who suddenly stopped struggling, went limp, and died. He killed himself Pero, they don't know how, but he's dead, all blue. I came down to help Priit after I heard it all on their sailor's walkie-talkie, in my room. The call came out "Man down, kitchens." Pero, he was bleeding badly." She was almost hyperventilating on the phone; the words were coming tumbling out.

"Will he be okay, has a doctor seen him?"

"No, no, not yet. But Ruis saved him, Pero. The sailors had applied a pressure dressing and a tourniquet, but Ruis saved him. He pushed them aside. He said he knew the femoral artery had been cut, he's seen it in a bullfight gouging. Ruis grabbed his tool kit and pulled out these little tweezer-plier things and a Swiss Army knife, a little one. He made a cut down Priit's leg and opened him up, stuck in the little plier thing and squeezed. Then he asked a sailor for a rubber band. They took one off an ammo clip and he doubled it around the pliers handles. The bleeding stopped, Pero, it really stopped, except just a little from the large cut Ruis had made. The sailor dusted it with a white powder, antiseptic I think." Priit just looked down and said, "What do you think I am? A camera you get to fix?" and then he passed out. They're waiting for the ambulance now . . . oh, Pero can hear it . . . I'll take him to the hospital." "No Mary, it may be what they wanted. It could be a trap. Give the phone to a sailor."

"No, Pero it's . . ."

"Mary, do as you are told, I beg you."

"Oh, all right . . . here . . ."

"Who's this?" A male voice, monotone.

"Baltazar, State Department. Do not, repeat, do not allow Mary Lever to accompany Priit to the hospital, nor Ruis, that's an order. Lever stays in the hotel under your care. Oh, and thank you for saving my friend."

"I'll check. One moment." Pero heard a muffled part of an exchange, military clipped phrases, acronyms and a clear "Aye aye, Captain." He picked up the phone again. "Seems you have the authority. I will comply. Actually, I was already arguing the same, glad to have the right to restrain the lady if necessary." Pero hadn't given him that right, Mary would be furious with Pero. She came back on.

"You have no right . . ."

"Yes, Mary I do. Priit saved JT and you, but I need your mind working there Mary. We're not out of danger yet. Two men died here at Wilson this evening. There's a whole army of the enemy working against us here tonight. Be on your guard. Now, take control there and order the sailors to have the whole, and I mean whole refreshments' tray—tray, wheels, glasses and all—impounded—the whole tray understand?"

"Oh, fine Pero. Oh, I know you're right. Time for poor Priit later. They are tending to him now. His eyes are open and blinking. He's in shock, I think, but looks better. They are putting in a drip feed . . ."

"Mary, where's Heep and why isn't the Nigerian with you?"

"Kweno is right here. He is staying with me. He even comes into the bathroom; he turns his back like a little boy. He's marvelous, that's why I felt it was safe to go with Priit." Pero started to interrupt . . . "No, no, I won't. I agree. I'll go back upstairs. Oh, and Heep? Heep's with JT, they are like mad scientists, analyzing clues. That man Lewis has called every time you've called him—Heep says Lewis refers to him and JT as his "Nairobi think tank." He's hoping they can see something everyone else has missed—something you've missed."

"I wish they'd tell me! What I have missed I mean. We're clutching at straws here. Still, that's two attempts they've foiled. Like the eleven Madrid bombings, they are not counting on a one-two Nine-Eleven punch anymore Mary, they have a whole line up to hit us with. I do wish JT would delay, just for a day, give us more time."

"Pero, have you seen the *Hill*, have you seen all the people already there? There are over two hundred thousand and they are still coming. You cannot let the word of God be thwarted." Pero knew that came from JT and so he told her to take care and call if there was anything, anything at all, no matter how small, to report. Pero pushed the red off button and sighed. Time to call Lewis.

"Baltazar here. There's been a stabbing . . ." and Pero gave him the whole story. "Will you coordinate the examination of the tray, cart, and contents?"

"Affirmative."

"Nothing else, avgas tanks being inspected, will report more later."

Two clicks.

Mbuno returned from his search, shook his head, and they watched as the men fanned out to conduct the rest of the search. Pero explained what had happened to Priit and Ruis' quick surgical action. Mbuno told Pero he had seen a man bleed to death from a rhino horn in the thigh that way. "Mr. Ruis is a very good doctor, *bwana*. It is what my wife Niamba has learned, it is called First Aid." Pero agreed.

The night ground on. Pero kept the police waiting. Pero wanted something concrete to show them. Kenyan police are a bullyboy lot, asking questions later, after they've made up their minds. It's a power thing left over from the reign of President Moi. Pero's mind analyzed the typical Kenyan power play, *Give them power and they corrupt easily. And the judges are not much better. Only good Nairobi judge anyone has ever heard about is a woman. It figures.*

Hours later, Mbuno found the bomb in a pile of trash up against the largest Mobil tank, stinking of urine and feces, wrapped in plastic—a small wire antenna played out, running up the tank about two feet, held with plumber's epoxy putty. It wasn't the wire that told him, it was the feces: "It was put there, not made there *bwana*, it is a fake." The stench wasn't.

In the early morning sun, Pero arrested the Mobil crew. On the Navy radio Pero reported to the captain and asked to obtain a bomb squad. He also asked to have them save the radio detonator if possible or at least get the frequency. Pero asked the captain to attach a radio detonator, one with an identical frequency or the original al-Qaida one, to a large gas can of avgas with just a little C-4 explosive. "Captain, I think we can set off a Hollywood special effect, doing no damage, say at the end of the runway, and these guys will think they have succeeded. It may help us to catch them later on." The Captain agreed. "And Captain, that's four attempts down, but who knows how many more to go?"

CHAPTER 19

Aero Club

It was time to brief Lewis again. "Baltazar here. The Navy is over defusing the bomb Mbuno found up against the largest avgas Mobil tank. I will know soon how they fare." Pero explained his conversation with the captain and the idea of the false bomb. Lewis agreed, it may mean nothing or it may make the enemy show their hand at a critical moment. Pero told him it would, at least, give them the al-Qaida kick-off time.

Pero went on, "I have cleared away personnel, but one sailor is standing guard as they defuse the thing, uphill of the bomb, to report anything he sees. There's nothing I can do if it goes off early, the gas will roll downhill, there's not enough time to evacuate Kibera. Sorry."

"Well done, it's the best we can do under the circumstances. That's three . . ."

"No four. The Cessna, the beer bottles, the refreshment cart and the bomb. No wait, five if the attack on Mary in Arusha was them as well. Any report on the cart, what was the weapon there?"

"Bottles of fizzy water had cyanide in them, as a gas. Once open, anyone within two feet could suffer a heart attack."

"Would they turn blue?"

"Yes, and that's what killed the guy planting it. He must have had a glass capsule. They found glass in his mouth."

"Have you checked the camera crews?" Pero knew from experience they would be down there facing the *Hill*, and had been setting up all night. Now, with morning and the *Meeting* only hours away, they would be fully staffed.

"Checked, yes, but there is no one using Schneider lenses. All the cameras check out as clean. To a man. We've stationed sailors and Kenyan soldiers with every camera crew, weapons drawn."

"Any news on Baylor?"

"Not really, I have passed this to Heep and JT. There's just one word he's repeated every so often, that "Jetson" thing. They have no idea what it means."

"Okay, well keep at it, I'm sure Tom has something to tell us, otherwise he wouldn't be saying that strange word. Can you try other variations? If he's been beaten, maybe he's saying something close, but different."

"Baltazar, what do you think, we're just sitting here? There are over thirty analysts working on just that alone, cross refer- encing with maps of Kenya . . ."

"Wait, what did you say?"

"Cross referencing with maps of Kenya . . ."

"Not Kenya map, airport professional maps. It's not Jetson, it's Jeppesen, jay ee pee pee ess ess ee en."

"Oh Christ . . . okay, I will get on that right away. I'll tell Heeper and JT. Why a map for an airport?"

"Jeppesen are aviators' maps. There isn't a decent map of an airport you can buy unless it's an aviation map, I know I have used them when we have filmed the arrival of Air Force one or some other big wig. The information on those Jeppesen maps gives you radio frequencies, runway layouts, fuel depots, the whole works. It's like a schematic of an airport, everything a pilot, or in their case a bomber, would need to know. It would show the Mobil tank clearly."

"So that's that then? No other purpose?"

"Not that I can think of. Aren't two hundred thousand dead enough? If you lock down flight paths during the *Meeting on the Hill*, say for the first two hours, even if they were going to try and hijack an airliner, you would thwart them."

"I will do better than that, I will ground everything large enough for the first two hours and check and recheck every plane, passengers and pilot. Well done."

"Well done to Tom." And Pero hung up. Now, more than ever, Pero needed to find out who the real Agip stooge was—only he had ordered the dead Maasai, only he had known who was behind all this, he had been getting his orders from someone. By then the day shift had arrived and had been put in the makeshift brig. Pero grabbed Mbuno, Jack, and Joshua and headed over to the Aero Club. By now Pero knew the police had arrived. Their three cars were parked outside, engines off, but blue lights twinkling.

The police arrested Pero. Well, they tried to. Jack, with Joshua looking like a puppy dog by his side, pulled his sidearm and told them to stand back. The police sergeant was angry, very angry. He had twenty men there, and it was clear the sailors and Securicor men had been having a tough time for well over an hour preventing him from releasing the detainees.

The police sergeant raised his voice, "You, you, are under arrest. They say you have killed a man. You have killed a Kenyan, an employee of this company A-jeep, they are not criminals, you are a criminal. You will be under arrest!"

"No, sergeant, I will not. Listen and listen carefully." Pero extended his cell phone towards him. "Use this phone, right now, to call your police Commissioner . . ."

"I cannot call him, I do not know him."

"Okay then can you call the captain in your station, Langata Station, I assume?"

"Yes, it is right, he is at home. I have the number."

"Okay then call him and have him call the Commissioner. They will tell you I am in control here, you will do as I say." The sergeant looked like he was about to burst. His men were pushing forward, angry that Pero would talk to their leader this way. He felt the pressure, the loss of face coming. A *mzungu* telling him, a policeman, a junior potentate, ruler of this Langata to Wilson stretch of ex-bush? No way. The Agip and Mobil employees were egging him on, several calling him by unkind, cowardly, names. He raised his hand, about to order a charge and, Pero had to admit, it was brave, stupid, but brave. So, Pero shot him. In the leg. At this close range, there was no chance of missing, but he was lucky, Pero just grazed his inside thigh, so the sergeant fell down.

Pero pointed the gun at the others. "Sit." They sat. "Hands on head." They put their hands on their head. The prisoners went very silent. "Now, let's get this sorted out. You," he pointed to a police officer, "yes, you, help the sergeant, put a dressing on that minor wound. Stop crying you big baby. Give me the number of your Captain." He did, one digit at a time, slowly. The phone rang and was answered by a man. "Police captain? Captain of the Langata Police Station?" Pero heard a yes. "Good. Listen, and listen well. You will call the Commissioner of police in Nairobi. If you cannot get him, call the President's office. Give them my name, Baltazar, listen to what they tell you, and then call me back at this number." Pero read it out to him, one digit at a time slowly.

It was under three minutes when he called back. "Mr. Baltazar, Sir, how can we help you, Sir?"

"Talk to your idiot of a Sergeant, who I just shot in the leg, and tell him who's boss. I need his help, not stupidity." Pero handed the phone to the man on the floor, the sergeant's other hand holding a pressure bandage on the lightly bleeding flesh wound that he had received from a sailor. The dialogue started with Swahili for "he shot me" and quickly changed to "yes, Sir," repeated several times. He looked even more glum. He handed Pero back the phone. Pero listened.

"Mr. Baltazar, it is most unfortunate, I see why you needed to shoot him, I give you my word, you will not have to do so again. He—and we—are most cooperative, now we all understand. I hope you can forgive our men?"

"Absolutely, Captain. Thank you. Do you think you can hop over here and take charge? We have suspected al-Qaida or al-Shabaab terrorists under arrest . . ." the prisoners started saying all the usual shocked remonstrations.

Joshua shouted, "*La neno*," and they all shut up.

"As I was saying we have prisoners here, which I am sure should be under your care, especially if they are indeed al-Qaida and one or more of them are, I am sure. I think it is only right that any real arrests should be made by your station, not the Nairobi police who will probably be here shortly, I am sure." Actually, if they weren't here by now, Pero figured they weren't coming. *They also must have their hands full.*

The police captain on the phone seized saw the carrot of al-Qaida arrests to his credit and replied most eagerly, "I shall be right there. May I speak to my sergeant, one more time?"

Pero handed the Sergeant the phone. There were a lot of "*naam*," this and "*naam*" that (yes), and presently the sergeant got up, and the sailor strapped the bandage to his thigh like a big band-aid. The sergeant bowed to Pero and handed back the phone. Pero checked, the captain had hung up.

"I am to go to the infirmary. The captain will take control here. I am," he paused, looked at his leg, "sorry."

"No sergeant, it is I who am sorry. What is your name?"

"Gibson Nabana."

"I will see to it that you are mentioned for your bravery and," Pero looked at his leg, "that you are recognized for the wound you sustained in this difficult al-Qaida case." Suddenly the big man beamed, he really beamed. He gave Pero his hand and his men gave a little cheer. Pero told them to take him to the infirmary and bring him right back, as the police captain was sure, Pero stressed *sure*, to need him. In truth, it was Pero who needed him. He would do fine now as his loyalty was all sorted out.

Several of the police stayed behind to help and readily took orders from Jack and Joshua. Joshua was rising to the occasion. Pero took Jack aside.

"Jack, we need to figure out who the Agip bad guy is in this lot. I think all the Mobil people are in the clear, but I will hold them until the day is over. But we need to fool the Agip guy into thinking they've won. Here's what I have in mind . . ." And Pero laid out his plan.

Jack listened, went outside, and called the sailor on guard at Agip on the walkie-talkie. Pero heard the automatic response and Jack said, "tack two" and the radio went silent. They had changed frequencies. A moment later he came back in and said into Pero's ear only "They've isolated it, it is now safe. Your special device will take about another twenty minutes. They will radio when it's ready."

So, together, they started interviewing the Agip employees, Jack one side, Mbuno and Pero in the middle and Joshua the other side. They stood in front of the old mahogany bar, deserted at this hour, and grilled one suspect. The others really looked frightened. Even though one, in the process of being taken aside for interrogation, had gotten angry, had deserved a thwack from Joshua's nightstick, that suspect hadn't been aggressive, he was just testing authority. Since then he had been very silent and very compliant, infecting the others with calm obedience.

They pressed on. They needed answers.

One man at a time, in the little room next to the bar separated by clear glass walls, Mbuno or Pero told the story of the Maasai killings that night. Some were sad at the loss of the Agip man, others not so much shocked as worried that they would get the blame. In a situation like this, Pero thought, they would be looking for the man who wants to look shocked and sorry. If it's a surprise the shock comes first and then the sorrow. If the emotions came together, it could be fake. The night manager passed the test. It was the clerk, the day fuel manager who Mbuno thought was the most likely candidate and he winked at Pero. Pero did not react, but inwardly agreed. The daytime clerk, the paper pusher who balanced the accounts and handled billing, gave himself away, expressing sorrow and then shock as an afterthought. Pero was sure he was their man.

Pero said nothing. Mbuno, catching Pero's signal of crossed fingers behind his back, asked the question they had prepared in Swahili, "Why did you take over the duty schedule and assign the Maasai to the Cessna?"

"It wasn't me!"

"The night manager says it was you. Why did you do it?"

The man showed fear, sweat breaking out on his upper lip, "I had to, I had to. It is my duty, I was told."

"Who told you?" And he went quiet. Nothing would budge him. Mbuno went to find Jack, as arranged.

Jack came back and told Pero openly that the search had revealed nothing. No bomb, no arms, nothing. Everyone heard. Pero watched the clerk's face. There was a flicker of recognition there.

Pero's Wilson team needed to get the word out that they hadn't found anything, and now everyone knew. They wanted this clerk to think the terrorist plan was operational. If the clerk knew they had not found anything, he would be smug. Pero had a way to change that. The plan for a dummy Hollywood type explosion had given Pero another idea, one he knew was not morally right, but they really needed to stop these people. Any group willing to incinerate two hundred thousand innocent lives, really needed to be stopped, no matter what the means or, in this case, personal morality. The truth was, Pero and Mbuno, along with Jack and Joshua, has conceived a torture.

Leaving Mbuno to carry on the questioning, Pero told Jack to bring the clerk and explained that they were going over "to the avgas." Jack frog marched the man to the truck. Joshua drove, Jack and Pero held on to him in back. They headed, as planned, towards Agip. The man said, "See, you haven't got anything to hold me for." As they neared Agip, they quickly veered left and headed towards the Mobil tanks and the clerk's eyes darted this way and that. The truck stopped in front of the Mobil tank. As they disembarked, none of the three talked with the man. He wanted to know what they were doing here. They said nothing.

Suddenly Joshua and Jack grabbed him, his mouth especially, and body cavity searched him. Jack found the little glass cylinder and held it up for Pero to see, "super-glued to his gums, nasty." He held it at arm's length. Pero told Jack to throw it far away and he did. They dragged the guy around the tank to the garbage pile. The wire was still epoxied to the tank, the feces and rubbish put back, but only they knew the bomb was now gone. The clerk didn't know and, in his sudden panic, couldn't guess.

Pero refused to look at the clerk, instead addressing Jack, "Did you know that Muslims believe that if you die soiled, especially if you soil yourself and people see, you may not make it into heaven? No? Well, it's true. All the al-Qaida Nine-Eleven terrorists and suicide bombers wore several pairs of underpants to make sure they didn't give themselves away. See? Look, see how his urine stains the front of his trousers? You have those handcuffs, Jack?" Jack passed the four pairs to Pero. "Hey, Joshua, what do you think, shall we spread-eagle him on the rungs of the ladder, off the ground or standing comfortably?"

Smiling, Joshua replied in a casual tone, "I think, bwana, he won't care when the gasoline bursts into flame and roasts him alive like a warthog on a spit." Even though it was all staged, Joshua, Pero could see, was hoping they'd leave him there to die in a real fire. They fastened the leg cuffs first. Pero remembered reading that prisoners were always more frightened having their legs tied down, even more than your hands, because, somehow, if you can't run away, you are trapped, doomed.

Seeing his complete failure and certain horrible death, the clerk started shouting words, all in a jumble, "He said I should obey him if I wanted to go to heaven. It was Imam Kahal, Imam Kahal, oh Allah, please, it was Imam Kahal . . ."

Pero grabbed his hair and put his face close up, "Where, when, who, make this good or I leave you here."

"The Imam, he brought Bwana Purim to meet with me on Wednesday. Please, I don't want to burn. Allah, please, I don't want to burn, please."

Pero finished clicking the other two handcuffs in place. "What about the glass pill?"

"He promised. He promised. I would only go to heaven if I bit that little glass pill. I would sleep and awake in heaven."

"With the usual virgins, no doubt . . . Did you know the avgas would floor Kibera and kill thousands?"

"They are infidels, my Imam said so, fire will cleanse them and Allah will allow them into heaven."

Pero was sick to his stomach, turned to Jack and Joshua, and said, "Leave him here. He's not going anywhere. We won't waste any manpower guarding him."

As they walked away towards the truck, the clerk was shouting, begging, pleading. There was no bravado, no threats, just raw, animal fear, and the stench of urine. Pero pretended not to hear, but his cruelty only went so far, "Joshua, in about twenty minutes bring the police Sergeant, the Sergeant mind you, out here to arrest him and take a full, signed confession. Then make sure the Sergeant understands it is my order that he prevent any harm, any harm, coming to his prisoner. Got it? *His prisoner.*" Joshua smiled and nodded his head vigorously. Like Pero, he was sure the confession would be clear and accurate and the prisoner would remain unharmed, useful to parade in court against the Imam.

They drove back to the Aero Club in silence. Jack and Pero were in the back, looking at each other. They should have been happy. Neither of them was. As they stopped, he grumbled "a sailor's duty, hah" and spat. He jumped out of the truck and walked into the foyer with Joshua. Pero wasn't too proud of himself either, sitting there, feeling dirty. He called in just to have something less shameful to do, "Baltazar here. We've identified the Agip contact for al-Qaida or al-Shabaab, the company clerk" and Pero passed the clerk's name, "arrest about to be made by Langata Sergeant Gibson Nabana. The clerk's contact was Imam Kahal, introduction to Purim who gave orders. We took away his glass pill."

"Lewis here, you say about to be arrested, is he in custody?"

"Yes, handcuffed to the Mobil tank where the bomb is—was. The bomb's defused and the site is secure."

"But he doesn't know that right?" There was an edge to his question.

Pero wasn't rising to his bait. "Right. Bye for now." Pero went to find Mbuno, something else was beginning to bother him. Would this day never end?

CHAPTER 20

Ndugu

Pero found Mbuno sitting on the road-side railing at the side of the car park. He was eating, again. "Mbuno, how in the hell has Purim been here on Wednesday and in Pangani the next morning. Over the past days, probably weeks even, he's been up and down to Tanga like a yo-yo. For someone Commissioner Singh is watching, he sure moves around a lot." Mbuno said nothing. "And another thing . . ." Pero pulled out the fax from the Holiday Inn and showed it to him, "just who in the hell is this Smythe?"

"Purim bwana."

Pero was dumbfounded, "What?"

"That is the man I saw in the bush outside Pangani camp."

Waving the flimsy fax in the air, "This is beginning to make no sense whatsoever. This man was still at the hotel in Nairobi three days ago when we were at the InterConti . . ." He stopped, lowered his hands, "Wait a moment, there is someone who might know. Let me make a call."

Pero dialed Prabir Ranjeet, who answered quickly. "Ah, Mr. Baltazar, how good of you to call. Are you still at Wilson Airport? Seems you've had a busy time. The police are most impressed, you have a captain of the Langata station, how do you say it, eating out of your hand."

"Well, I had to shoot his sergeant to make the point."

"Most wise. They need a little lesson from time to time. Now, how can I help you?"

"The man in the Holiday Inn, the one who got away, when did Amogh see him in the past few days?"

"I will check, one moment . . ." He talked to someone. Amogh came on the line.

"Mr. Baltazar, good to hear you are well Sir. How can I help?"

"Ah, sorry, your father said not to involve you. Orders."

"I have convinced father it was time he considered me as a grown up. Besides, he needed to know what Mr. Baylor and you discussed."

"You could have asked me."

"Yes, I know, I am most sorry for my lack of trust."

"Doesn't matter. Look, give me your details on tailing the unknown man, name of Smythe, from the Holiday Inn."

"We tracked him every day, most of the day, until you arrived back in Nairobi—about the same time the Canon man was arrested. The police still haven't gotten anything much out of him. I think he was a stooge."

"Yes, there are others calling the shots, one Iman Kahal at a Nairobi mosque for starters and a trade organizer from Tanga called Purim. Look, here's our problem. Mbuno has identified the fax of Smythe's passport as Purim, one and the same."

"Ah, father just heard that, he says Mbuno doesn't make mistakes."

"I know, except Mbuno tracked this other Smythe, our Purim. He killed his accomplice . . . well a hippo did, the day before yesterday in Pangani. No way he could be there in Pangani and here at the same damn. What gives?"

"My father is still listening in, he says we will discuss it. Can we call you on the number Director Lewis gave us?"

"Yes, but Amogh, if you're free, and if your father agrees, I could use you here in case I need transport, fast transport."

"Father's nodding. One Porsche run to Wilson coming up. Twenty minutes tops." They hung up.

"Mbuno, they were tracking this same guy," Pero tapped the fax, "in Nairobi while you were seeing him in the bush. I cannot figure it out. Can you?"

"It is not the same man. He looks the same, so they are *ndugu*." It was as simple as that, relatives; the Swahili word was, exactly, brothers. Pero realized with a start that they now had two Purims. Pero dialed up Lewis again.

"Baltazar here." He waved Mbuno over, "Come here, listen in . . ." they put their ears together again either side of the satellite phone, "Mbuno and Amogh Ranjeet confirm they saw Purim in two places at the same time. Mbuno's never mistaken on likeness and the Holiday Inn had a passport photo of Smythe, Smythe is Purim, Purim is therefore Smythe. Mbuno is sure. Mbuno's conclusion is that they are brothers, maybe cousins. Please evaluate, and please tell Heep what to be on the lookout for—oh, and I have told Ranjeet."

"Frightening possibility. Okay, stay on that. There's news this end. We have only forty-five minutes before deadline. The Mosque has had no visitors; it's clean. What we did was access the Imam's bank records with Interpol's help. They show transfers of money to buy tickets and pay the credit card bill of the Canon man at the Holiday Inn, three rooms and all room service altogether. We currently think Canon man is small fry, but they're not through with him yet in Nairobi. So the Imam is the moneyman, some of it going to an account in Tanga, you know who. Some cash withdrawals there in Nairobi, probable payoffs, nothing too large. And there's one other thing, some of the incoming money is from Swiss accounts that the Swiss have given us access to under their new anti-terrorism change in banking laws. Here's the bombshell—the Christian America Group, a charity, has been funding that Swiss account. There's the link, the Reichstag link . . ."

"But who?"

"Jane Seeland, the sister of JT's secretary, one James Small. James Small's sister is the founding chairwoman of the Christian America Group, very right wing. They've been calling for a crusade against the Islamic Jihad for years."

"What does James Small look like?"

"Slight, red hair, five feet ten inches . . ."

"Kind of like a handler for JT? About thirty-five?"

"That's the one, his nickname is Jimmy Little." He had been at Mara's offices, three days ago and would, surely, still be with JT. Pero had to warn Mary and Heep.

"Have you told Mary?"

"No . . ."

Pero hung up. Pero picked up the cell phone and dialed Heep's number, reading it off the label on the back again where Ruis has thankfully listed them all.

"Heep, that you?"

"Yes."

"Listen, don't repeat. The Reichstag Gambit is real. The man is Jimmy Little, or real name James Small. Get him away from JT. They've arrested a guy here who had a super-glued glass cyanide capsule stuck to his cheek. Maybe Jimmy Little won't have one, but take no chances, grab his mouth and do a search and then arrest the bastard. Lewis can explain."

"He's calling on the other phone . . . thanks, Pero, and keep your head down." Pero could hear Heep's satellite phone ringing. He hung up.

Mbuno and Pero were still outside the Aero Club, Mbuno balancing on the top rail, Pero leaning on a stanchion. Mbuno

looked at Pero and Pero looked back at him. They didn't
know what to do next. The sun was getting hot, the airport
busy, people who couldn't get gas were getting angrier and
angrier with the police, Securicor and the sailors. The men
would hang tough—Pero knew that. They had so little time
before the deadline. Pero was sure they still had something
planned, but what?

Where was this Purim, either one? If Purim from Tanga
were in town—if at all—and the *ndugu*, where would they be?
Doing what? Pero really had nothing else to do and he needed
quiet to think. The quiet needed to be in his head.

"I wish it were four in the morning and we were still waiting for the day to start. I'm having trouble getting my thoughts
in order, planning what's next."

"*Ndiyo*, we need to start over . . ."

"Mbuno, what do you say we go over to Mara and get a
nice cup of tea?"

"And some biscuits, Miss Sheryl's tea biscuits?" Pero nodded. "I missed breakfast, we could start with breakfast." So
they walked down the flightline. Just thinking of tea seemed to
calm his thoughts. Something would come, Pero was sure of it.

Amogh pulled up behind, coasting, no noise, and honked,
scaring Pero. Mbuno just frowned like he would at a small boy.

"Come on Amogh, we're off for a cup of tea at Sheryl's
office."

Amogh looked frantic. "No time for that, I just saw Purim
getting out of a taxi by the west gate. It's road-blocked
by the police, on foot entry only, so I took the east gate."
His hand waved towards the far distance. "He's over there
somewhere."

"Over there" was a mile away, anywhere in one of twenty
huts, hangers, and customs' buildings.

Mbuno opened the car door and started to climb in, "I will
have tea later, *bwana*."

Once piled in the racing car, they sped down the runway, Amogh determined, pushing the revs beyond the red line. Pero told him to slow down. "Let's start at Bluebird, see if David knows anything."

When they stopped, Pero quickly called Lewis and told him they had a positive ID on Purim arriving Wilson Airport. Pero asked him to radio Jack and Joshua at the Aero Club and get them to sit in wait at Agip as Pero thought Purim, well either Purim, might go there to meet his contact, to pay people off. Pero knew the police had Mobil covered, he could see them milling about over there. No doubt, Sergeant Gibson was busy arresting someone.

Director Lewis also had an urgent message for Pero: "The sniffer teams, dogs, they found more bombs, hidden in the scaffolding, every pipe was stuffed with C-4. The wiring for the sound systems caused them to miss them in the visual inspection last night, but the dogs smelled it and so they looked again and found the leads. The switch was radio controlled. They still don't know who. Copy that?"

"I did."

"Also, we told JT not to react about James Small on the phone, but he did, called him a Judas. James Small kept telling JT he didn't understand, it was necessary, it was the will of God and then Mary slapped him so hard he went down like a ton of bricks. Stayed down."

"Don't tell me, he had a capsule . . ."

"Nah, she just clocked him good, they checked. The Navy Captain has him under arrest. They're going to fly him home pronto. They're rounding up the three thousand members of their so-called charity back in Virginia. A couple of whacko celebrities will be caught in the net. Tough. The Kenyans have now lifted the Imam and a few of his followers as well. Maybe we're seeing the end of this thing."

"Not yet, Purim is on the loose." Pero rang off.

Inside they found David, still at his desk, trying to conquer a mountain of backlogged paperwork. He looked a little less worried. Pero guessed the body was gone from the closet and since David hadn't been personally arrested, things weren't all that bad. Pero feared they were about to be and showed him the photo and asked if he had ever seen the man, Purim. No, he was sure he hadn't. Then he remembered the second fax had come in and handed it to Pero as the cell phone rang. Pero went outside, past the steel girders of the hangar, to get a clear signal for the cell phone, stuffing the fax in his pocket as he walked.

Mary sounded frantic, "Pero, JT is very low. Jimmy Little's treason has hit him hard. He's still going on, but with the bomb in the scaffolding tubes, the bomb you found on the oil tank, the deaths, the cyanide water . . . oh, Pero, I don't know how much more of this he can take."

"Mary, will he cancel?" Pero sounded hopeful, even he could tell. He knew he was beginning to sound desperate.

"No way, Heep says not and I agree. It's in God's hands. What we're going to do is this. We're going to go down and stay with him, backstage, in five minutes, as the gospel singers are warming up the crowd. Maybe their wonderful voices will warm up his heart. This is a bad blow Pero, a bad blow"

"I know Mary; make sure, though, that Kweno goes with you. He must be there to protect you."

"He will be, Pero, he's a Christian, he's been reading Psalms with JT, French and English, in unison. They are very . . . well . . . simple together in a powerful sort of way. Anyway, I just wanted to tell you we're heading down to the stage now. Thanks for everything, no matter what happens Pero, you really did save us again and again. God bless. Bye." And she rang off, leaving Pero with a sense of deep sadness. Her faith in God overwhelmed his by a mile.

Pero leaned in, turned on the car AM radio, spun the dial, and listened to the singers, already belting out their rhythm versions of traditional hymns. If anything could help JT, maybe it was those happy voices.

The satellite phone rang again. It was Lewis: "Baylor's saying something in the sick bay on the HMS Cardiff, off Malindi. Sounds like—déjà vu? Wait . . ." Off the satellite phone Pero heard him ask for a repeat from the HMS Cardiff, and Pero could hear the radio voices as he turned up the gain: "Director Lewis, he's repeating this," pause, "Pero déjà vu, Pero déjà vu, over and over again."

Lewis came back on, "Did you get that? It makes no sense to any of us."

On the contrary, it suddenly made perfect sense to Pero.

Then the voice of the HMS Cardiff floated over the airwaves again: "He's fading, we've got to stabilize him and prep him for surgery, we will do what we can, over."

"You get that, Baltazar?" Pero told Lewis he did. "What's he mean?"

"He means my wife died in a plane crash, Lockerbie. Déjà vu, for me, can only mean one thing—it has to be an aerial attack." Pero signed off.

At that moment, as Pero pushed the off button he heard the gunfire on the public radio. Pero looked at his thumb on the off button. A crazy thought . . . Did he cause that? There were screams, yelling and pandemonium, even on the radio the effect of automatic, quick burst gunfire, was unmistakable. There was nothing Pero could do for them there. Mbuno had his head cocked to the side, listening. "Over a hundred bullets Pero, many will have been hit."

"We can't help them, Mbuno, we need to concentrate here, on Purim." They knew he was somewhere near and Pero needed to find him—the one punch was underway, cameras definitely rolling now, live satellite feeds were opened up across the world. Sets would be going on in every country as the word spread—A live terrorist event to catch, live, on TV!

As Pero was listening to the carnage on the AM radio, he was also thinking about the clumsy Langata Police at Mobil who would frighten off Purim at the Agip depot.

That's fuzzy thinking Pero, get a grip. The sounds of chaos continued from the radio. "People have been shot, there are many wounded." The one punch . . . the only two punch left to them was Purim, Pero was now damn sure of it. But which plane?

Pero looked out across the tarmac and saw at least thirty planes taxiing, fueling, loading tourists, being inspected, rolling on or off the apron or the runway. With the advent of gunfire and the airport state of emergency, Pero could see many small planes lined up for the runway suddenly turn and start to head back towards the hangars. No one was allowed to take off now, but there were others still being prepared, readied, moved, fueled, loaded for safari. In short, the airport was busy as usual, yet one of these was Purim, or a plane for Purim. But which one?

Pero lowered his head, stuck his hands in his pocket to think, and brushed the fax. Absent-mindedly, with the radio still blaring the terrible news—*I wonder if my friends are alive or dead*—Pero looked absently at the fax. It was a simple laundry list. His eyes drifted down the list. One line snapped into focus and threw cold water on his fatigue: *One, shirt, heavy starch, careful with the Gazelle logo and epaulets . . . twenty-five shillings.*

Nairobi Purim-Smythe was a pilot. Jeppesen, déjà vu Lockerbie, Gazelle Charters, it all made sense. As fast as possible, Pero hit the buttons and told Lewis, "It's Gazelle Charters, a piloted plane, small but big enough—if loaded with explosive— to kill JT and everyone around him." Pero grabbed Mbuno and Amogh and raced to the Porsche. Mbuno and Pero jumped in the cramped single seat and they raced down the flightline to Gazelle. "Drive straight into the hangar Amogh, if they try and stop you, run them over."

He was as good a driver as Pero knew; he side-slipped the car, drifting into the hangar doing forty just as a startled Purim took two quick shots at their arrival. The bullets entered the car's back quarter panel and lodged in the back, low by the gearbox. Mbuno and Pero parachute-rolled out of the car and Pero got off a quick shot at a pair of running legs, running away that is. "That's not Purim, he's too old," Amogh said.

Mbuno's whole physique looked focused, eyes locked on target, "No, he is my Purim. My prey. I will get him." And with that Mbuno went into his crouching run and started tracking "his" Purim, the one from Tanga. Pero was sure Purim didn't stand a chance of escape.

"Where's the other one?" They looked around—he hangar was empty. Pero ran into the office and found a very scared woman crouching behind the desk probably because of the gun shots fired. With the blood on his trousers, Pero must have been an additional fright because she fainted dead away. Pero looked at the log entries recorded in her open ledger. Ah, there it was. Pero keyed the desk VHF radio microphone and called, "Wilson Tower, Wilson Tower, Gazelle Ops here, this is an emergency, a Cessna Caravan," he studied the numbers in the ledger, "seven, seven, three, two, Kilo has been hijacked. Advise whereabouts."

"Roger Gazelle Ops. Caravan seven, seven, three, two, Kilo is on unapproved final on take-off. On ascent leaving ground vectoring two three zero true. V two now, advise request. Are you declaring an emergency?"

"Affirmative, Wilson Tower, this is an emergency. Caravan is being used as a flying bomb to attack *Meeting on the Hill*, repeat a flying bomb."

"Roger Gazelle, we will advise ATC." ATC is air traffic control. *Fat lot of good they could do*, Pero thought. He knew he needed to do something, and something immediately. He ran out into the sun. There was no one with a pilot's uniform near the Gazelle operation base. Amogh was talking into his radio.

"Amogh, forget that, do you fly as well as you drive?" He nodded. "Solo?"

"Flying Doctor service, volunteer. I fly small singles, normally one fifty or one seventy series Cessnas, a Piper Aztec a few times and only twice a Beech Baron."

"Okay, let's steal a plane, hurry." They ran towards the Porsche. They got in and roared off down the line. The closest plane that matched Amogh's needs was a Beech Baron being fueled. They pulled up as the tank caps were being closed and flashed the gun and badge at the fueler who ran off to his truck cab. "Get in, Amogh, prep, do the checklist, I'll call home."

Amogh left the Porsche running, climbed up the right wing, and entered through the only door of the Baron, stepping carefully over the co-pilot's seat and settling in. Taking a moment to familiarize himself with the controls, he started the engine start-up sequence.

"Baltazar here. We've found the Purim brothers. Mbuno is chasing one on foot, the Tanga one, he'll get him. The other is in a Caravan cargo plane—the plane is probably stacked with explosives. It's smaller than a commercial jet, but it will look big enough on camera. Also, if he crashes the plane into the stage the explosives in the struts could still go off too unless you've removed them. We will intercept him and try and prevent it. I found his name, Smythe, entered into the Gazelle daily rental log, he's listed as a pilot. Al-Jazeera is his listed TV feed. I suspect the woman at Gazelle may also need detaining, but Mbuno can arrange that. Right now, I need a Navy intercept, priority one."

Amogh waved Pero into the cockpit, as the engines caught. Pero climbed the starboard wing—all Beech Barons have the entry over the right wing—worried over the spinning prop only feet away and quickly sat in the co-pilot's seat, leaving the door open for the antenna to work. They started taxiing. A man ran out waving, Pero took out the gun and pointed it at him as well, telling him he would shoot him dead. He retreated, running.

"Sorry Director, it's a little busy here . . ."

"I can hear. Al-Jazeera went live throughout the Arab world seconds before, repeat, before the shooting. James Small had the radio detonators in his watch, so he could detonate them from nearer the stage, better timing. We're jamming those signals in case there's a backup. And you were right about the media angle."

Amogh got them moving faster. Pero had to ask, "The Navy intercept? And who was hurt? The shooting . . ."

He went silent, Pero didn't know if he lost the signal, moving that fast, sometimes you do lose satellite lock, or Lewis cut off. Either way, it was time to help Amogh. Pero clicked off. They were starting down the main runway, full throttle, and Pero was still fussing to shut and lock his door.

CHAPTER 21

Mungu La-Ubawa

The lumbering single turboprop Cessna was up here somewhere. A Beech Baron can cruise at two hundred and sixty miles per hour, Amogh had her at full throttle, full prop pitch left full from takeoff, doing two hundred and eighty. The Caravan, a workhorse, is much bigger, stronger but slower, doing only one hundred and sixty miles per hour, one hundred and seventy five tops. Pero knew they could catch her if they could just see her.

The wheels came up. "There, over there is the *Meeting* stage, but it's too soon Amogh, he must be loitering around up here somewhere, waiting until all the media cameras are on, watching." Pero scanned the skies hard, "Maybe hiding behind these clouds. I just know it. He's here somewhere."

Pero was right, the Caravan could be using the clouds as cover, it made sense. Solid, dense white, these thunder-bumpers were massive sentinels over the land, twenty or thirty of them dotted the land below, casting shadows. With a mile or so between each, each one twenty thousand feet high, they were beautiful, if deadly, cells of tremendous forces. More importantly, Pero could not see the other side of any of them. You could hide a Jumbo up here until it was too late.

Pero got on the radio: "Wilson Tower, this is an emergency, Baltazar here in a Beech Baron six, one, three, two, Foxtrot" Pero read the call sign off the dash where all pilots put it, in case they forget. "Clear all airspace, no excuses, over Wilson, Langata, Kibera, and western Nairobi, including the *Hill.* Confirm please. Over."

"Six, one, three, two, Foxtrot, we copy. You have authority, there is a sailor here with a gun says so. Squawk four, three, three, five, six. Confirm. Over."

"Squawking four, three, three, five, six" as Pero rolled the numbers on the transponder, "Urgent you clear airspace all other aircraft, we are in pursuit of Caravan seven, seven, three, two, Kilo, terrorists on board, suspect suicide attack into the *Meeting on the Hill.* Am expecting USA Navy fighter intercept, vector him to our target once identified. Over."

"Roger Beech six, one, three, two, Foxtrot, airspace is now being cleared of even emergency cases. One aircraft transponder just turned off, suspect it's your objective, we still have him on radar. Turn right to a heading of two seven zero, he's above your position, plus three zero feet. Navy planes not on radar yet. Will advise. Over." Amogh banked the plane and the compass came around totwo seven zero true.

Suddenly they spotted him, three thousand feet higher, coming around from the southwest, circling a cloud fringe. Something about the way Pero could see him flying told Pero he was qualified, competent, but not local. He was fighting the currents, the updrafts, as one would in, say, Europe where you needed to maintain strict flight level. Here, in the bush, flight levels were, at best, a recommendation. The currents and turbulence were in real control over the equator for smaller planes. Your plane lasted longer that way.

Over the years, flying at these latitudes, there were many times that his pilot had to suddenly veer off when aircraft converged, off their assigned flight levels. Without on-board radar, clear visibility was often the only asset pilots had sometimes, to avoid midair collisions.

And that's what Pero feared he needed to do, have a midair collision, if the Navy didn't get here in time. Putting the Baron between the Caravan and the *Meeting* like a blockade was too easy to get around. They couldn't block them. Defense was quickly becoming offence. As the faster plane, Pero hoped they would come off better. It was foolish to hope so, he knew. They were in a sports car compared to the Caravan, which was like a small truck, so the Baron probably wouldn't win any kind of contact. But what else could they do? Pero's mind was a blank to alternatives, so he concentrated on simply catching up, urging Amogh to make the little twin Beech climb and run faster.

As they came closer, climbing, the pit of his stomach protesting, cold sweat on his brow, the Cessna demonstrated a different option to the one Pero had thought of; from the open doorway, a fixed camera position, with telephoto camera lens protruding, a shooter was firing at them. One shot hit the nose and, after they peeled away, Amogh said, "killed the weather radar." He turned it off. The color radar screen in the middle of the display, now a jumble of colors, all mixed up, faded to dark.

Pero got on the radio: "Wilson Tower, Beech Baron six, one, three, two, Foxtrot. Closing on target. Air-to-air shots fired. Will attempt to force him to the south, keep him away from the *Meeting*. If that is impossible, will make air-to-air contact between our two aircraft. But awaiting Navy intercept, please advise soonest."

"Six, one, three, two, Foxtrot, we copy. No Navy planes on radar. Is contact the only option? If so, God be with you. Over."

"Amogh, let's stay behind him off to his left, port side, and slow down so they don't shoot past. Flaps?" Pero suggested flaps so they could keep the prop speed up, allowing a quick burst of speed simply by retracting the flaps when needed. In the game of cat and mouse, speed was their principle advantage. Only in this game, Jerry was chasing Tom.

"Fifteen," Amogh said. Pero put the flaps down to fifteen degrees and marveled that Amogh handled the Beech like his Porsche, with ease and firmness of command.

"You do realize that when he starts his descent, if the Navy isn't here, we're going to have to ram him."

"Now you tell me? Not just a little bump and run?" Amogh looked at Pero. "Yeah, I guessed. I wish there weres another way . . . How long will the Navy take to get here?"

"I don't know. Watch them Amogh, stay with them, I have an idea, maybe State can help." Pero opened the cell phone and called Amogh's father. Thousands of feet up, the line of sight to several cell towers was clean and clear.

Pero had to yell to be heard over the engine. "Mr. Ranjeet? Baltazar here. Sorry to trouble you, but Amogh is flying and we're chasing a Caravan with al-Qaida on board. We suspect a bomb-suicide thing. Meantime, they've fired at us, but we're okay. Look, the satellite phone won't work well here with the plane's aluminum skin. Could you relay this to Director Lewis so I can stay on the cell phone?"

"I can call him right away and connect." He went silent. "Here he is—can you hear each other?"

"Lewis here, this is unsecured. Go ahead."

"We're in the air chasing a Caravan with at least two operatives aboard. Their target is a suicide attack on *Hill*. Is the *Meeting* proceeding or canceled? Over."

"Proceeding. Four dead, several wounded. JT is starting a funeral service for the dead and your Simon. All the media cameras are live. Your one punch scenario was right, the *Meeting* is live everywhere, throughout the world. Are you in a position to stop the other plane?"

"I was hoping the Navy would get here in time."

"Answer! Can you interdict the Caravan to prevent the two punch on your own?"

"Yes, but maybe only by ramming, we have the speed, they have the mass."

"Survivability?"

"Poor. Do you have any suggestions? Like a Navy Tomcat or F-18 on afterburner?"

"None may be inbound in time. Sorry. They estimate twelve minutes. Can you stall the Caravan?"

"Not more sorry than Amogh and I. We'll try to stall them, but we can't block them. How about a SAM or something?"

"Sorry, nothing on hand. The Kenyans were preparing to defend against those, not use them." Lewis sounded paternal, "Sorry it has to end this way."

"Yeah. And sorry for Amogh, Mr. Ranjeet."

Mr. Ranjeet sounded paternal as well, "He makes me proud. He is a man. It is not your fault Mr. Baltazar."

"Thank you Mr. Ranjeet, I will still regret it, always." And Pero signed off. He wasn't really being maudlin. It was not time to say good-bye, yet. He was simply busy and just wanted thinking time.

"Amogh, your father says you are a man and you make him proud."

"Yeah, well, I would have liked to be a banker for a while, help rebuild the family fortune . . . never mind." He smiled. They continued their game of catch-me-up whilst dodging the shooting angle with the Caravan. They were gaining time, though, keeping them away from the Hill, maybe those Navy planes would get there in time.

Amogh was doing all the work. Pero crossed his arms and frowned. Why can't I think of something?

Through the cockpit glass, Pero mindlessly watched, as he often did during filming, for visual clues and interruptions. The sky was endless, punctuated by the white sentinel clouds drifting over a brown green landscape all the way to the Rift Valley 500 miles away. On location Pero had to be a jack-of-all-trades, an improviser, ready for things to go right and things to go wrong, and find a way through both. Permits, plane delays, lost reservations, canceled guests, and broken equipment always threatened shooting. Those clouds could spell rain for a shoot tomorrow; they indicated gathering humidity. Bad weather is usually the most common obstacle they faced in filming outdoors, clouds can also suddenly change the light and, in winter, obscure the horizon with haze. Rain, snow, ice, hail, they all . . . *hey, wait a minute*, Pero thought. He looked at the canceled weather radar and said, "Damn . . ."

Amogh, hands clenched on the yoke, looked over, "What's wrong now?"

Sitting straight up, Pero put a hand on Amogh's shoulder, "Amogh, my friend, I have an idea. If they make their move towards the Hill, we've got to take action, no waiting for the Navy, right?"

"Yes, I agree."

"Okay, so here's what we're going to try. First, the Navy needs us to stall for time, right? And at the same time, we have to be ready to take action. You with me?"

"Sort of, I am, Mr. Baltazar, but I don't quite see . . ."

"I'll explain, just remember I have a one-two punch of our own to give the bastards. First, we need to put ourselves between the Caravan and the *Hill*. Every time they come around a cloud, I want you to get so damn close they will have back off, a few feet, that's all, just pressure them."

"I'm not sure I can fly that well, Mr. Baltazar. Anyway, that won't stop them dropping faster than we can, it's a heavy bus that Caravan. And they will be homing in on the stage."

"Okay, so we'll always stay below them. And let's hope the Navy shows up before then. If not, let's hope this plan works before their suicide run. Let's be prepared to give it a try. If not, we will have to dive on them like a World War Two fighter on a bomber."

"Oh, great. What fun." He imitated a British accent, "Tally-ho and all that." He gave a small nervous laugh, "I'm more British every day . . . hardly. Or not, as you Americans say."

He edged the twin-engined Beech to their left, the Caravan's right and immediately the gun appeared and they saw puffs of smoke. They heard their airframe being hit, but Pero had no idea where they'd been hit. The air was much choppier now and the shooter didn't have much of a chance to aim accurately. It was a chance they had to take. "Okay, go under their wing, Amogh, but keep the pressure on—I want them to think we're trying to force them away. We are, but there's something else I have in mind too . . . I know this is a dangerous game, but I have a trick in store for them, which I don't think a pilot who's not local will know about."

Fighting the controls, using his feet on the pedals to yaw the plane, skirting the danger posed by their proximity, Amogh asked, "Care to explain it to me as well?"

"I want you to bump them . . ."

"You want me to do what?"

"I need you to make them think they have to get rid of us first or their mission is compromised. I need them to want to swat an angry wasp, us, wipe us off their chosen path. I need to force them to need to deal with us first."

Adjusting the throttle, concentrating on the difficult job of proximity flying, Amogh raised his voice, "Holy shit, you are nuts. You want me to fly up and touch wings? Look, Mr. Baltazar, you're talking Red Arrows' skills. There's no way I'm that good."

"I don't think you need to be. Look Amogh, if we don't try all we have left is ramming them now, and there's only one outcome of that . . ."

"Shit." He was quiet for two seconds, "Okay, okay, I will try it." He wiped his brow. "I will try, but crikey Mr. Baltazar, it could kill us just the same. If I bump them, we will probably lose control." Then he smiled. "Oh, sure I get it, we're dead anyway. Great options, can't you think of anything else? Couldn't we shoot at them?"

The Beech was a pressurized plane, no opening window except a tiny plexi flap, Amogh's left side, next to his shoulder. To fly, dodge their shots, and have Pero fire over Amogh's left shoulder at their right side—and their shooter—both men knew it didn't seem possible. Amogh looked, Pero looked, Pero held up the small pistol, and they both shook their heads.

Amogh rolled his shoulders to try and reduce tension. "Damn. Okay, I will try it with your bump and run. But don't you think touching them, wing to wing, will make them so damn mad they will run through the gap—any gap—when we open one up? After the bump, if we get away with it, we'll have to roll out of it, away from them. Then, they could aim right at the stage, you'll give them a direct line Mr. Baltazar. Why do all this to end up giving them a direct line?"

"Yeah, I know that's a possibility. It depends on how close we can stay and how familiar he is with a Caravan's controls. Look, this is a sports car, that's a truck, he may not be able to dodge us that quickly." Pero was feeling sorry for Amogh. The strain of flying close to a plane that was shooting at you and then some nut was telling you to bump . . . Pero knew in Amogh's shoes he probably would be even more frightened and stressed. "Look, if the Navy doesn't turn up—and Lewis said they may not in time—we *will* be giving them a gap, a gap of our choosing. We have to make sure they see the need to turn behind us, towards the stage, right, you get that?" Amogh nodded. "And then the only direct line they will have is through that baby there." Pero pointed to the strato cumulous, thunder bumper, with an ominous darkening cap, about eight miles off.

"If they do, they will . . ."

"Yeah, that's what I'm hoping. A serious ice hammering."

"They can't be that stupid, can they?"

"Look, at Gazelle Smythe's entry for his license said it was a French license. He's used to Europe. If I hadn't seen that Cessna one fifty at Wilson, you know the dented one by the end of the line?" Amogh again nodded "Well, I would have thought anyone can get through that there puffy cloud with that big, fat, solid Caravan, don't you think? In Europe you avoid them in case of lightening or rough winds. No one in Europe knows how damn dangerous those clouds are on the Equator. I didn't, 'til I saw that one fifty."

Amogh was still nodding, keeping the Baron on a tight trail of the Caravan, "Okay . . . Let's hope you are right. But I'll tell you one thing, the way that big thunder-bumper looks, if we can nudge them in there, or if they do turn into it trying to get away from us towards the *Hill*, the hail and the updraft will tear her apart. And we better not get sucked in either." Amogh repositioned his right hand on the throttles and his left on the yoke, his feet controlling the rudder. "Okay, here we go. You take care of flaps, cover me on the throttles, I need to keep engine revs and prop pitch fully up for a quick acceleration or deceleration, the flaps will control the airspeed, okay?"

"Okay Amogh," Pero rested his left hand atop Amogh's on the throttles, "I have got the flaps. Set at fifteen."

"Here we go . . . flaps ten." Pero dropped his left hand to the flap wheel alongside the center console and spun the wheel to read "10," then returned his hand to cover Amogh's.

Planes flying in formation are at extreme risk. A good, solid contact can alter the pitch of any wing, making the plane unflyable, one wing up, the other down. The plane will spin in—crash and burn. On the other hand, any contact with a spinning prop will be even quicker and more deadly to both planes—the twin Baron more so than their single engined Caravan. They had the one fat turboprop engine up front. The Baron had one piston engine either side. If one of the Baron's was disabled, they'd be flying like a crab, sideways, not to mention a broken prop, trying to rotate and rip the engine off the plane like a broken spin cycle of a dryer.

Aerial display teams practice for years to perfect flying in formation twenty feet apart. From the ground, it looks as if they are touching. They dare not. Any closer and you have the turbulence from one wing affecting the following wing's performance, jostling the planes in dangerous proximity.

Amogh eased their plane up closer under the Cessna. Above them, leaning forward and looking through the top of the windscreen, Pero could see the shooter trying to lean out and get a shot down at them. As they hid under the Caravan, they were out of his line of sight, just. Then Amogh called for no flaps, Pero rolled the flap wheel to zero. The plane sped up suddenly and Amogh pushed the right pedal to put the rudder over slightly to the right, causing the plane to yaw to the right and, one second later, he turned the yoke to the right and pulled back on the yoke.

It was crude, but it worked, almost. They popped out from under the Cessna's tail under her right wing, the shooter got off a burst of automatic fire, one bullet passing through the windscreen, the others hitting behind them somewhere. As they came dangerously close to the Caravan's right wing, Pero was sure they had over-shot and were going to make contact, their left prop with the Cessna's right wing. Pero watched in slow motion as Amogh pushed the yoke forward, trying to get the plane's nose down and away. The pilot, Smythe in that Gazelle uniform, must have seen the danger and he wheeled off to the left, lifting the wing from danger. From inside the Baron, they saw the Cessna shooter thrown off balance, his mouth open in what appeared to be a scream as the Cessna veered away from the Hill.

Quickly, Amogh followed back in chase by barrel rolling the Baron up and left, recovering chase below and a little right of centerline to the Caravan and called, "Flaps fifteen." As Pero complied, the shooter, recovering, squeezed off another short burst back at them, which missed. The Baron shifted left and reassumed position behind and directly below the Cessna.

"Mr. Baltazar, there's no way I want to do that again." Pero looked over. Amogh was sweating and had a slightly glazed look. Pero looked down at his hands. Like Amogh's his were also shaking. "A roll Amogh? Jesus . . ."

"He's banking right . . ."

The phone rang. "Mr. Baltazar?" Mr. Ranjeets voice sounded sketchy. "The live telecast has begun and all the news media have cut into the regular broadcast . . ." The phone went silent.

"They're making a move Mr. Baltazar; we don't have time for the Navy . . ."

"Okay, we have to calm down here Amogh. I mean me. Look, you were successful last time, that was amazing, well done. Think you can do it one more time?"

"I really don't know . . ."

"Look, we have to try it again, only this time let's make contact. He needs to think we're nuts—that we will risk contact and are too stupid to realize what that means. He'll be frightened of air-to-air contact, and it'll keep him from thinking of the danger in the cloud. Only then will he take the gap when offered."

"Think we're nuts? Think? Hell, I know we're nuts. . . ." Pero took his hand from the throttles and tossled Amogh's hair, like a father would do with a little boy. "Okay, okay, but I'll need a hand with the rudder now too, that last yaw was way too much, something back there must be damaged, it's sloppy and stiff." Pero turned and looked down the empty fuselage. There were wire bits hanging, frayed ends, and little pencil beams of light where bullet holes let the sunlight in.

"Something's been partially cut, some of the rudder control cables I expect. I'll give you a hand—just call instructions. This time, let's just go up above them and come down, wing to wing. And make just a little wing contact."

"How much wing contact?" Amogh's voice sounded incredulous.

"One teeny tiny little bump should do it."

"Do you know what you are asking? His wing is stronger than ours, I will take damage."

"Yes, I know. Then, next time . . ."

"If there is a next time . . ."

"Amogh, if you've got a better plan . . ."

"No, we'll go ahead, I'm just scared shitless really." He was following the caravan's right bank, staying below.

"Me too, but we've got to do this. They and we have no time, that TV going live is the signal they were waiting for, I'm sure of it. If we come down, one gentle touch of wings this time . . . Then next time, when he thinks we're going to touch wings from below, he'll turn into us trying to make solid contact—he knows he's bigger. And then you can dodge out of the way and he'll roll into the cloud. Agreed?"

"It's a plan. If the rudder stays on, if the first contact doesn't kill us . . . oh, hell, here goes."

They spent the next two nail-biting minutes in closer proximity to another fixed wing aircraft than Pero would ever want to be again. Amogh was pretty sure their port navigation light touched the Caravan's starboard light, because Baron's glass cover seemed to have vanished when the wings came clear. There was a jostling on impact, and the shooter again fell backwards and the headdress of a desert Arab flapped in the open doorway, caught on the door latch.

The Baron kept up the pressure—coming back, flying over, under, side to side, always keeping between the Caravan and the *Hill*. They were buying time, but each time the Caravan seemed to take a tighter angle for the *Hill*. The Caravan had a schedule to keep.

Amogh, although sweating and nervous, was flying the Beech Baron like his Porsche, way too close for comfort. Flying in this close proximity, both planes' occupants felt they each had at least one and a half feet in the grave already. The problem was, two of them wanted to die, only not a wasted death. The Caravan was avoiding them because they had a target, a suicide mission, and the Baron was a real threat to them and that mission.

It is what Pero wanted them to think, to concentrate on. As he hoped, the Caravan's pilot's fear was giving way to anger and offensive tactics. The last pass the Caravan had initiated contact and feigned towards the Baron.

Before taking a course correction towards the *Meeting*, Amogh said flatly, his emotions exhausted, "It is time." They were edging the Caravan nearer to a white death, a white death Pero hoped they wouldn't have previous knowledge of. Pilots not familiar with the energy in warm tropical clouds might make the frigid mistake Pero and Amogh hoped for.

"Okay, they're ready Amogh, this is it . . . can you do another barrel roll?" They were behind and below the Cessna again. The white monster loomed on the right front, about two hundred yards off to the right and a mile ahead. Pero and Amogh reviewed the plan again, to come up from below right, and, as soon as they saw the Cessna wing dip towards them, to roll up and over the Cessna and block their escape away from the cloud.

"Yeah, I can try. When I call flaps, take them off to zero, then when we emerge from under, put them to twenty and when I call flaps again, put them at zero again, and when we complete the roll put them immediately back to fifteen, no make that twenty, got it?"

"Okay, will do. Flaps zero, then twenty, then zero, then twenty."

"Roger that. And you have to tell me when he's pointing that gun so I can know when to start. This roll must make it look like the shooter scared us off, right?" Pero nodded, "Okay, so, when I get out from under them watch the shooter, your hand on the flap wheel."

"Will do, but watch the Cessna's wing on the left prop, he's getting aggressive."

"Bullets frighten me too." He said it with a smile. "Okay, ready? Now flaps." Pero set them to zero and they accelerated. He came out from under the Cessna's belly, both of them steadying the sloppy rudder, and Pero put the flaps back to twenty by touch and memory, never looking down. Pero was watching for the shooter. The two men spotted him at the same time, a little evil machine pistol nosing out of the Caravan's open hatch.

They were headed for contact with the front wing. Amogh was repeating, almost to himself, "Hold it, hold it . . ."

Pero looked at the cloud now at their position off the right, "Now he's aiming again . . ."

The Cessna wing started to dip—he was feigning at them . . . Amogh simply commanded himself, "Okay, roll her up. Flaps!"

Pero spun the flaps wheel to zero and the Beech, released again of her brakes, zoomed alarmingly up towards the Cessna's wing. Amogh executed a barrel roll over the Caravan and came neatly down on her other side slightly ahead of the Caravan's wing. Pero put the flaps back to twenty degrees, to slow them to match the Cessna's speed. Now they were blocking her escape away from the cloud. Pero looked to his left at the Caravan pilot. The older Purim, Smythe, looked grim.

Like an upside-down mushroom, the cloud filled the sky off to the right and below them completely.

The Baron edged nearer to the right, Amogh nudged and pushed the Caravan, threatening to bump twice on her left wing—very unnerving for the Baron as well as the Caravan. There was no open doorway on the left side for the shooter to use to aim from or fire. Pero could see Smythe's face, now stricken with horror at the Caravan's controls as they edged in closer.

He mouthed something and suddenly started to bank right, tightly, away from them to escape, turning into the only available airspace, the awaiting cloud.

"Mr. Baltazar, we're losing control of the rudder, I'm yawing all over the place." Pero had thought it was tactics. "If the rudder goes, I can't fly this plane safely."

"Wait, Amogh, hang in there," Pero helped with the pedals, which felt almost useless, "we're almost done, just keep ahead of him, cut off his escape." For the moment, Pero had other worries, watching Purim's Caravan, making sure it got into the cloud.

Smythe had decided, finally, to take the only chance of escape the Baron didn't cover, especially as the route for escape would put him back on target for the *Hill*. One moment the Caravan was tight off and just behind their right wing, the next she had executed a sixty-degree full sharp right turn into the heart of the cloud which quickly surrounded them. Pero raised flaps fully, Amogh checked full power, and they turned to gently follow the Caravan keeping the pressure on them to head into the cloud, making sure there was no escape. As a smattering of peripheral small hail hit their screen, they banked left, away from danger. It was all the rudder controls could take; they parted, and they were rudderless.

A Beech Baron is a very stable plane. The dihedral, up-angle of the wings, is sufficient that, if you let go of the controls, it will stabilize with a little trim setting. Amogh had the good sense to do exactly that, he set the trim flaps and let her fly straight and true, reducing throttle at the same time.

Pero got on the radio, "Mayday, mayday, Beech Baron six-one-two-three-Foxtrot . . ." Pero gave their call sign and status. Pero wasn't asking for help. It simply had occurred to him that perhaps it would be easier to find their wreck if he called it in.

Amogh had other ideas. "If we can do a gentle turn to the right, and she's got the fuel, we can head for the coast and ease her down into the ocean. What do you think?"

"Is it only the rudder that's gone?"

Amogh did a quick check, little yoke movements. "Yes. I think so."

Suddenly the radio blared out, "Six, one, three, two, Foxtrot, Navy Tomcat here, your six, do you copy?" Amogh and Pero instinctively looked backwards. There was nothing to see except the dangling wires and bullet holes.

"Navy Tomcat, Baltazar here. Could you pull up alongside and give us a visual?"

The giant gray shape of the F-14—airbrakes deployed, landing gear down, slid into view, Amogh's side. The radio intoned a friendly American, "Howdy."

Pero grinned, "And howdy to you. We shoved the Caravan, suicide bombers, into that strato-cumulous back there, two miles back. Can you see him on your radar?"

"Negative, I had something there as I approached you, two planes in formation. One lost altitude suddenly. Glad it wasn't you. Can you confirm threat eliminated?"

"We hope so, we don't know. Could you fly a look-see, over-fly the Stage where all the people are. If there's no damage, the threat is eliminated. I think. Also, could you relay all this to your carrier?"

As the air brakes and heels folded into the body, he literally zoomed off ahead of them, "Roger that, relaying message to the carrier as per instructions. Message coming in. Well done, Lewis. You copy?"

"Yes, thank you."

"Six, one, three, two, Foxtrot, this is Navy Tomcat Two, now flying formation your six to escort you home. State destination."

Amogh responded, "Well, as we have no rudder, that's really the main damage, so I am currently aiming to get as far as the coast and set the plane down in the water, gently."

"Roger that six, one, three, two, Foxtrot, but you still have two working engines, aileron and elevator control, right? Your rudder is oscillating as if disconnected."

Amogh sighed and gave a timid, "Yes . . ." Pero couldn't see what the Tomcat was getting at. Pero looked at Amogh. Amogh was nodding. He wasn't looking happy, but he was nodding.

"Navy Tomcat Two, could you please spell it out, we're," Pero looked at Amogh, "well, maybe it's only me, but I'm not sure what you're hinting at here."

"If an ex-Navy pilot can land a DC-10 without rudder control, using his engines, why can't you?"

Pero suddenly understood. "Oh! Okay, it's worth a try."

Pero looked over at Amogh who said, "Yeah, why not? Today's been full of firsts, now I'm going to pretend I'm a DC-10." In Iowa in '89, a DC-10 lost a cargo door and it took all the hydraulic rudder controls along with it. The pilot used differential throttle control to land the plane. Amogh explained his new worry to Pero, "I was worried that's what he was hinting at. I have never done that before, but okay, you have the flap control again and I'll take throttles, feet off the rudder pedals, okay?" Pero nodded. Amogh keyed the microphone, "Navy Tomcat Two, let's give it a try here at altitude. If it doesn't work, I will head straight on for the coast. Can you stand clear in case I get it all wrong?"

"Oh, roger that, I'm well clear. Good luck."

"Six, one, three, two, Foxtrot, Navy Tomcat One here, I hit the deck and proceeded to the Hill." With afterburners, it could have taken twenty seconds. "I can confirm other radar target not visible, not flying, repeat not flying, and not at Hill, nor any evidence of disruption or blast. The event seems to be proceeding normally. Will circle and maintain watch. Over."

Pero responded, "Thank you, Navy Tomcat One."

And so, in the clear air, going nowhere, Amogh and Pero practiced. It wasn't as hard as they thought it would be. With fifteen degrees of flaps and using the right and left throttles, the plane was perfectly easy to handle. Sure, it was slow to respond and Amogh had to use fine hand control on the yoke, but they could turn and control the aircraft.

"Neat, Mr. Baltazar, we can do this, let's go back to Wilson . . ."

The Navy clearly agreed, "Six, one, three, two, Foxtrot, Navy Tomcat Two here. You seem to have 'nuff control. I am leaving to rejoin Tomcat One. Confirm. Over."

Pero responded, "We confirm. Please tell your carrier. And thanks, fellows, for everything."

"Nothing to it—seems you did the work before we got here. Couldn't take a shot sixty miles out for fear of hitting you. Over and out."

Pero looked at Amogh, both with mouths agape. Each must have been thinking the same thing: How long would they have held back that shot with over-the-horizon missiles? On radar, they were one target until the Caravan broke away into the cloud.

"Enough already," Amogh said as he rolled his shoulders once more, "Wilson Airport Mr. Baltazar?" Amogh's deadpan face told Pero he'd had enough even if he were trying to be satirical.

"Okay Amogh, as long as you can fly this Baron okay." Pero radioed the Navy what they were doing and got permission. The Navy now controlled the airspace.

At two hundred miles per hour, it took them under two minutes to over fly to Wilson, passing over the *Meeting* on the way. As the Navy man had said, the Caravan was nowhere to be seen. What they saw were people, a sea of people, and there, as they buzzed over his head, stood JT, proud and tall, preaching to his converted. He looked up and his radiant face captured the afternoon sun. Amogh waggled their wings—a little bit—and Pero thought he saw Mary wave.

They did one slow turn over the crowd, following ATC directions, increasing the radius, and were straightening out for the approach into Wilson Airport, Pero spotted wreckage in Nairobi National Park. It was still burning, but the wreckage was contained in a ten by ten yard square of scorched earth. The vultures were already circling below them.

Pero could imagine the deadly realization, by the pilot, Purim-Smythe, when the updraft and hail started. The vacuum capacity of the turboprop, the motor sucking in ice, and breaking the internal fan blades. Maybe the engine seized or threw a rotor back into the cockpit, like shrapnel. It didn't matter by that time the outside of the plane was being pummeled. The windscreen would have shattered, and the pitot tube would have been ripped off. Flying blind, with no airspeed indicator, no working horizon, no power, and with dented, un-glide-able, wings, no pilot could bring such a heavy lump of useless metal to earth safely. They hadn't.

That old Cessna one fifty pilot at Wilson Airport never realized why he survived. His plane was slow, the motor was enclosed and, most important of all, his plane was light enough to be able to be captured by the hail updraft, not fight it and gravity. That little Cessna one fifty had been spat out of the top of the cloud.

No such luck for the lumbering Caravan with its huge turbojet intake. The cloud had killed her and then it cast her away to fall, like a *Mungu la-ubawa*, a wingless god, to kill her occupants.

"Home Amogh, safely, slowly, please. I too have had enough." Pero looked about them. Two little men in a big, big sky.

Amogh called up the tower. "Wilson Tower, Beech Baron six, one, three, two, Foxtrot. Scratch one rogue Cessna Caravan; it's a flaming wreck in Nairobi Park. Tell the authorities." And he started to laugh, "Oh, and again for good measure, Mayday, Mayday."

"Roger Beech Baron six, one, three, two, Foxtrot, we've been monitoring. State your emergency, over."

"No rudder, throttle control only, bullet holes all over the fuselage, coming in to land. Please prepare emergency crews."

"Beech Baron six-one-three-two-Foxtrot, that's affirmative. Good luck."

Past the outer beacon, they got the Baron sideways for a moment in a crosswind, Amogh and Pero, one hand over the other on the throttles again for safety, pulled the port engine throttle back—gently, gently—until they squared up, Amogh called for overall reduced speed and Pero overdid things with the flaps, setting them at thirty. They almost stalled, landing short, on the grass, one hard bounce, something groaned; the left wing was a little low. They rolled to a stop, watching the fire truck race towards them. "Sorry Amogh."

"That's okay Mr. Baltazar, we're down, and you know what they say . . ."

They said it together, finally laughing like kids, reciting the pilot's motto "Any landing you can walk away from is a good landing!" Pero was sure the poor Baron, shot up and bent, wouldn't agree.

CHAPTER 22

Aga Kahn Hospital

It is never wise to overlook a wound in Africa, no matter how small—or how embarrassing. Pero's was not much of a wound compared to his other friends' injuries, but it hurt all the same. Actually, it hurt his pride more than anything. There he was, lying in a hospital room, bottom sticking up in the air, with a nurse scheduled to come in every hour and change the dressing on his septic thorn punctures. When uncovered, his rear was a colorful shade of purple and yellow. The Gurreh bushes Pero landed on turned out to be toxic. Pero had a temperature the day they landed at Wilson and even rated a lecture from the doctor that night while being admitted. But Pero explained that his tetanus and other shots were up to date, so he was hardly likely to die, was he?

The Italian hospital resident wasn't amused: "You have huge blood vessels in your *posteriore*, *Signore* Baltazar, you get an infections there and it goes to your heart. Presto, you are dead."

Cheerful doomsayer, Pero thought. Actually, he was feeling great. The headlines of the Standard and Daily Nation said it all: "al-Shabaab Captured & Killed." Typical exaggeration, perhaps, but there was a great picture of Sergeant Gibson Nabana, "wounded in the course of his duty." He was shown with the three suspects in chains. Behind Sgt. Nabana were a grinning Joshua and Jack, who "aided the brave sergeant in his daring raid."

In the hospital, there were more of his friends, some patients, some constant visitors, none of whom featured in the papers, thankfully. Tom Baylor had been transferred from the HMS Cardiff. He was recovering, nurses reported. It was touch and go in the ICU for a while, but the staff finally reported he was out of danger. They were keeping him unconscious for a day or so more, allowing the head and chest wounds to heal.

Mary's faithful bodyguard, Kweno Usman, took four bullets from the shooter spraying bullets at the stage, but only one hit flesh, his leg. He was hospitalized but already on crutches, twenty minutes at a time. Kweno even hobbled by Pero's room that morning very early, just after they were woken by nurses at dawn. Even in his hospital gown, he was a vast hulk of a man. He wanted to thank *mon capitaine!* for saving his life. Pero explained a loan of a vest was hardly saving his life, that Kweno was the really brave one jumping in front of JT. Kweno's natural humility would not allow him to believe he did anything brave at all. He was learning English, so his simple explanation became a statement of fact Pero had to accept, "It was duty." Then he saluted, waving a crutch in the air and turned, ambling down the corridor.

Later on in the morning, Ruis stopped in and delivered the information Pero was longing for, mostly delivered in a technical way with little or no emotion. Ruis knew there were enough emotions flying around, everybody whispering their fears and gratefulness. The shooting at the *Meeting* resulted in three dead and four wounded. JT was taking personal charge of the families of the deceased who were, sadly, all local staff of the good Pastor's church. The official mourning period following the service extended his stay in Kenya. JT was, thankfully, completely unharmed, full of vitality and making converts. The failed al-Shabaab attempt, he assured the reporter from Time Magazine, "was resolved by the firm hand of God inside that thundercloud!"

Ruis was, however, a little disappointed with that conclusion, "Never mind the bump or two from your plane, Pero."

"Well, what else could he say?" he changed the subject, "Priit doing okay?"

"I'm off to see him again. They say he's fine today, the leg will heal no problemmo," said with justifiable pride.

"Well done Ruis, really. Impressive." Ruis turned as he heard Mary and Heep walking down the hospital corridor.

Pero could just hear Mary, "No, Heep, I will not allow him to be sent back; I want him with us, period." Heep, it seemed, was being bullied against his wishes, which Pero knew must signify a strong bond between them. Heep seldom gave in to anyone unless he cared more about them than his own opinion.

As they turned the corner of the open doorway, Mary first saw Ruis, "Ruis, is he here?" Ruis stepped aside allowing Mary to see Pero's behind sticking up. "Oh, for goodness sake, you look ridiculous!" and then she started laughing. Heep peeked around her and, eyes bulging, and joined in the laughter. Ruis joined in.

"Okay, guys, that's quite enough. You try lying in this position . . ." and then Pero laughed as well. "Yeah, even I think this is ridiculous."

Heep couldn't resist, "Shall I get the NY Times photographer in here to snap the aviation hero in all his glory?"

Ruis, still chuckling, turned to leave, "See you soon Pero. I'm staying until my patient is better, well enough to travel. I'll call in tomorrow." And with a wave, he left, no doubt to check on Priit down the hall.

Mary and Heep seemed happy together; she slipped her arm in his. After they stopped laughing at him, one after the other leaned down, Mary kissing his cheek and Heep holding Pero's hand and patting him on the back at the same time. Well done old friend, well done."

"Me?" Pero asked, "Who was it who jumped in front of Mary when that shooter opened up?"

Heep didn't answer. Pero had heard Heep took a bullet in the vest, for which he sustained a broken rib and loads of kisses from Mary.

JT had stopped in to tell Pero it was the unselfish gesture she needed to regain her faith in men—well, "This man Heep anyway. I like him son." *Praise and approval*, Pero thought.

There was little else to say among friends. Each of them was equally in the debt of the other and yet each of them felt they had not done enough. Both Heep and Pero knew it could be like that when you care about friends. Mary simply felt she could never repay the honor the two men had afforded her. Silence was, in a way, testimony to their mutual admiration.

So Pero turned the conversation to "the walking giant, he's just down the hall. He came in this morning; the leg is healing pretty well. JT told me he was going in there to read psalms with Mary's protector as he calls him. I guess Kweno will have to take English lessons."

"My uncle has already arranged for some, although psalms in French have interesting subtleties; JT is quite enjoying the mental exercise." She looked at Heep, "Anyway, Kweno is staying on with me, it is all arranged. We just haven't told him yet, something about his Nigerian military service. But we'll get that worked out . . ."

Heep held up both hands in surrender, "I give, if Kweno raises no objection, why should I? Anyway, you haven't asked him yet; he may so no."

"Want to bet?" Mary's eyes were flashing, and Pero hoped Heep would recognize the danger. He did, smiling; he bowed to her. Pero was certain Mary would be his future wife since he felt they were already bickering like an old married couple. Mary kissed Heep's cheek and said to Pero, "Keep him here, will you, I have a favor to ask down the hall . . ." and with that she left.

With Mary gone, Heep stopped smiling, took a chair and sat next to Pero's bed. He looked like he was about to cry, so Pero asked, "What's really up Heep? Spill it."

Heep had been bottling up emotions, keeping his sorrow from Mary, "Pero, they all could have died, and all those Kibera people roasted alive, will we ever get over that? I'm already having nightmares."

"I don't know. It is seriously depressing; their level of hatred to do the unforgivable. The drugs they've given me here have helped with sleep. But I know what's on your mind, it's as we've always known, the real world revealed, a world you and I may well know about, be closer to than most people, have seen before, always on the edges . . . Jakarta, remember the faces of those rioting bastards?" Heep nodded. There was no way he would forget the thugs that had robbed them. They had wanted violence; they rioted as an excuse, robbed for pleasure. "Look, just because we've seen—and you've filmed—more death and violence in the wild than most people, doesn't mean we're immune to the experience when we're the target. Our ability to truly see, *reality vision* I've been thinking it should be called. It is what makes us who we are. We are professionals who care about what we do, yes, and Heep, we only care about what we do because of what we've seen, what we know is out there. This experience is far more personal than anything I've ever experienced, for you too, I imagine." Heep nodded, and Pero dropped his voice, "Look, I know you Heep, you'll turn this experience into art, somehow, somewhere. One day, another Emmy, you'll know you found something here that needs to be shown to the public, someway, somehow."

"Maybe Pero, but it also taught me that I don't want to risk anyone's death, ever again."

Pero knew Heep secrets well, too well, "Still thinking about that diver?"

"Yeah, I sent him down there, the currents were . . ."

"Heep, for God's sake," Pero raised his voice on purpose, desperate to alleviate his friend's suffering, "He was the fucking expert, he was the professional diver, I know you, you deferred to him. It was his decision. It has nothing to do with you. Stop wearing that damn hair shirt, we're all bored with it."

Heep was silent for a moment. "Well, at least you're well enough to shout." Heep laughed, so did Pero. "I just don't want people I care about or who I am responsible for to be at risk because of me."

"Heep, I think you proved that by jumping in front of Mary. That was the craziest thing I have ever heard of."

Heep lowered his chin and focused on his hands, clenched in his lap. "Yeah, well, it just seemed the thing to do at the time, no crazier than Commissioner Singh with his pop gun going up against that croc . . ."

They both smiled at the memory. Pero changed the topic, sensing his friends need to arrive at a greater admission, "Love her?"

Heep's chin came up and his eyes focused on Pero's. "As the bullet hit. Yeah, Pero, I knew it then, *gott verdammt*."

"You're going to have to watch taking the Lord's name in vain when you ask her to marry you."

"Marry?" Heep stood, "Who the hell said marry . . ." He paused, sat, and nodded. "Yeah, I guess so. Trust you to push. Producing my engagement are you? Well then, you'd better get well enough to be the best man."

"Done." The two friends smiled at each other. "Now, go find out what all that racket is, sounds like Kweno is causing a ruckus."

They could hear the Nigerian raising his voice in his broken French and JT's booming voice responding with, "But son, you'll be with us, and we'll make sure your family can come as well."

"I better go translate, see you tomorrow Pero, feel better and, thanks."

Pero raised himself up a bit and turned his face towards Heep at the door, "Hey! Remember Mary needs you, she's feeling guilty over Jikuru and Kweno; those are her divers Heep, one died for her, the other was prepared to. But remember this: the one thing I'm sure about all this is that stopping these people was about life, not death, life to come, thousands of lives to come. Get out there and enjoy it." Heep looked at Pero, shook his head, and then nodded, turned and was gone. He didn't want Pero to see his tears.

In the mid afternoon, Mbuno arrived, trailed by three nurses whom all remembered the old *mzee* fondly. He had groupies! When they were alone Pero could finally ask him. "Did you catch your Purim?"

"Not as well as you caught your Purim, *bwana*. I locked mine away safely and used that special handy of yours to call the police. They arrested him, oh, many hours later." He had a twinkle in his eye.

"Oh, no," Pero was worried at Mbuno's newfound weird sense of humor, "Where did you lock him up?"

"In the broom closet Mr. Pero."

"Not that same bloody broom closet, surely?"

"Oh, yes, the very same. It was not very clean; it was very smelly in fact." And he laughed. "Then I went and had tea with Miss Sheryl. We had many, many cups of tea—and biscuits, with chocolate—as we waited to call the police, that handy of yours is most complicated, the man who answered kept asking me my name, I said I was you. I am afraid it caused more delay." He paused, for effect. Mbuno has long had a theatrical streak after so many years of telling stories around a safari campfire. Coupled with this new humor routine, Pero feared more teasing that was coming. "I watched your landing, bwana, it was not very good." He smiled.

"Ah, well, Amogh was happy enough. He was the pilot; blame him, not me. You missed with that teasing old friend."

"Perhaps. Yes, Mr. Amogh is becoming a fine man, bwana. His father told me to pass his regards on to you. It would seem his lady wife is making something to eat called samosas and sending them over this afternoon . . ." he looked out the window at the sun, "in about an hour I think, they said four o'clock."

Pero knew Mbuno was never in need of a watch, so what was he hinting at? "That'll be nice, she's a great cook." Pero thought he would probe a little, "Perhaps you should stay to try them, they're sweet and delicious."

"No thank you Mr. Pero, I am sure you want to rest, it looks very large and painful." He feigned sincerity.

"It's fine . . ." Pero loaded up the hook, "Mbuno, Mrs. Ranjeet's samosas are made with honey."

Mbuno nodded, economical as always with words, and immediately settled in the armchair, waiting for the samosas' arrival.

Somehow, Pero knew the honey samosas would be too good for Mbuno to refuse. But, feeling better, he thought he'd try teasing Mbuno for once. "Are you sure you can stay? I am sure you have other clients needing your skills, not to mention help eating all their food."

Mbuno fixed his eyes on Pero, "Ah, but not all clients can make some very, very foolish mistakes, and have big accidents, like you bwana . . ." he paused again for effect, "like causing an explosion that breaks all the windows at the police station in Langata. The police were not amused."

"The plane hitting in the Park did that?"

"Oh, yes, bwana, you made quite a big accident with that plane." Although he saw Pero smiling, Mbuno kept a straight face. "The captain of the police station was not smiling yesterday when he was interviewing people to know who caused this explosion. He badly wanted to know who was going to pay for the damage."

"You're kidding . . ."

"Ah, Mr. Pero, I wish I was. I was thinking that these samosas might be fair pay for my silence . . ."

"Oh, shut up, old friend, you win."

Mbuno chuckled, "Anyway, Mr. Pero, the captain received a call this morning from the President's office and it is my understanding that the captain is having to be buying the glass. And the captain is having Sergeant Nabana fix the windows in punishment for all the newspaper photographs he posed for."

Both men chuckled then. Mbuno carried on, "Also, I think I am not so old Mr. Pero. It is not me lying there with his *kinyume* looking so sad and wrinkled, like one of a baboon." He smiled. *Kinyume* is behind, in a rude way.

With that, Mbuno took a seat in the mock-leather armchair between the bed and the window, enjoying the afternoon sun streaming through the rippled glass windows, awaiting the honey samosas with Pero, both of them enjoying the silence. Pero lay, face down, in bed, rehashing the past few days, waiting for the next change in his life, the next show he would have to produce, the one life-fulfilling, life-changing moment that, somehow he knew would materialize out of the ashes of the past week.

Mbuno, ever aware of unspoken thoughts, summed life up—his and Pero's, "Sometimes, *bwana*, it is a blessing to be able to wait."

Murder on Safari is the second novel of the legendary guide in East Africa, Mbuno of the Liangulu. The first story is called "A Tribal Rumble: A Safari Campfire Tale" also by Peter Riva.